BOOK TWO

VILLEINS

VILLEINS

A TRILOGY

BRETHREN
VILLEINS
AUSBUND

JEREMIAH PEARSON

The characters and events portrayed in this book are fictitious. Any similarity to real persons, living or dead, is coincidental and not intended by the author.

ISBN-13: 978-0-9895467-1-3

Dedication

Dedicated with all my love, to my wife Velvalea, who inspired and urged and nurtured this book into being.

If the lion knew his own strength,
hard were it for any man to rule him.
...Thomas More

Cast Of Characters

The Mission Cell of Brethren Reformers

Kristina, orphaned at 12 when her parents and sister were burnt at the stake for heresy; raised in a convent by radical Sister Hannah who fled with her to Kunvald, where she is further educated to become a printer and teacher of literacy

Marguerite, known as Grit, 43, once a beautiful stage singer and absinth addict rescued by Brethren, now a devout reformer and papermaker and printer

Frieda, sheltered pretty daughter of Brethren Johannes and wife, Rita; trained to be a teacher

Dolf, converted ex-magistrate, now a teacher of literacy

Symon, escaped villein and Dolf's best friend; printer

Veterans of War

Lud, of Giebel, villein, disfigured and widowed by pox, illiterate yet of restless and penetrating mind

Waldo of Giebel, Dietrich's groom, mute, will not tolerate unkind treatment of horses, father of wild daughter, Kella

Mahmed, Ottoman Janissary cavalry commander, fourth son of physician, intellectual, chess master, taken hostage as war prize

Ulrich, mercenary, Landsknecht cavalry commander, professional duelist

Ambrosius, grandson of cobbler and harness maker villein

Ferde, dreams of learning to read

Frix , son of tiller parents

Little Golz, tall son of potters Deet and Berta
Steffan, tiller parents , oldest of young band of Giebel pikeman
Jakop, plowboy
Kaspar, miller Sig's son, loses a leg during the war
Linhoff, apprentice of blacksmith
Max, jester, thin son of cheese maker Brigita
Tomen, son of barley farmers

At Wurzburg, the City and the Fortress Marienberg, Southern Franconia, the Holy Roman Empire of Germany

Konrad von Thungen, prince, propagandist cousin to Dietrich and Lady Anna, godfather to their son, Florian, becomes bishop after death of Lorenz, and founds Veritas Press
Lorenz von Bibra, prince-bishop of Wurzburg, liberal reformer, enlightened patron of the arts
Tilman Riemenschneider, artist, city councilman
Brother Basil, monk in confidential service of Konrad
Martin Luther, priest, sensationalist reformer, best-selling author

At Giebel, the Geyer Estate South of Wurzburg, From 1519

At the Castle

Lady Anna von Seckendorff, beautiful wife of Dietrich, father of Florian Geyer, devout churchwoman, but illiterate
Lura, maidservant to Lady Anna
Leta, laundress
Vogler, aged castle guard

In the Village

Father Michael, estate priest
Arl, weaver, baby catcher, mother of Fridel, Hermo, Greta
Greta, villein, daughter of Arl, betrothed to Kaspar
Ruth, villein, mother of Matthes; candle maker
Merkel, villein, smithy who demands to be taught to read
Sig, villein, miller, father of Kaspar

Joch, villein, tiller, father of Linhoff
Ferde, villein, cobbler and harness maker, grandfather of Ambrosius
Deet, villein, potter father of Little Golz
Berta, villein, potter mother of Little Golz
Huber, first steward, driven out by Lud
Peter, infant born to Kristina at Geibel
Old Klaus, road pushcart peddler, distributes broadsheets
Steinmetz, impoverished knight; living in the woods, foraging with his followers

At Oxford, England, 1523

Erasmus, lecturer priest, philosopher, liberal who vies with conservative Luther to be best-selling author in Europe
Florian Geyer, student, heir of Dietrich and Anna
William Tyndale, reformist student, friend to Florian, dreams of publishing modern version of Wycliffe Bible
Radical reformist students

Konrad

For days, riding his majestic white horse, Seiger, in the soft rolling hills above the Marienberg, Konrad was hardly aware of his bodyguard riding behind him with wine and condiments to stimulate his meditations. Spring had ripened and the land was deep green with lambs everywhere, bleating in the pastures and presented fresh upon the banquet platters.

The steady rhythm of Sieger's massive gait gave such a sense of power. In his chapel alone, Konrad had prayed long and deeply upon his role in the life of this world. Again and again, God had sent an astringent river of thoughts churning into the prayers. Bishop Lorenz was too weak and too liberal in all ways. Konrad felt the will of God and knew he was chosen. But where were the answers?

He had not the funds to start his own press, but the presses of Werner Heck sat dormant since being seized. It was like a cannon unfired. Maddening.

One day Lorenz would be dead and he, Konrad, would become bishop. Until then it was important to set himself up as an authority over the people. Helping fund the military expedition had been ruinous. He wished to borrow no more, and perhaps his creditors would even refuse him.

To control opinion was to control knowledge. And truth? Ideas were like mercury in the palm. But how best to persuade, how best to convince?

With the new literacy, the people were adrift, increasingly unmoored by too many ideas. Konrad's hand would be the force that would steer it back. They could not be stopped from learning to read. But, for their own good and by the good of God, the people could be stopped from learning to think their own ideas. This, God had revealed to him. Knowledge itself was an illusion, for whatever people could be made to believe, that became knowledge. And when people were shaped into one mind, they were strong clay in the hand of their master.

Let them read. The printing press was the key. To fight fire with greater fire, cleverer fire. Irresistible stories for simple minds. Sensations topping sensations. Tales that outrage, that fuel fear and gather the people scrambling back into the fold of the church-state.

Surely even Lorenz would realize this. But Konrad needed the right bait.

Inspired, Konrad visited Mahmed in the Marienberg's west tower. The view of the river in summer was splendid from Mahmed's casements. Imprisoned nobles were kept in towers, not dungeons, the pits below the castle.

It was quite shocking, how comfortably Lorenz had chambered the Muslim, but Konrad reflected that were he taken in war, he would expect the same, or far better. That said, Konrad had long ago promised himself that he would never so expose himself, neither to pain nor capture in such an ugly affair as war. Such risks were for those of lower station who placed less value upon human life.

Konrad's spies had reported that the old guard soldier posted outside Mahmed's door was in truth more servant than guard. In fact, he was a messenger and lackey for Mahmed's pleasure.

"A member of my bodyguard shall relieve you. You are discharged from this duty."

"Sir, your grace?" said the guard, obviously astonished to be addressed directly. Konrad waved a hand, and his men took the door key and hustled the old soldier away.

Then Konrad entered the chamber.

For an hour, Konrad sat at a table with Mahmed in the sitting room, on fine chairs with velvet cushions, and they drank wine, which Mahmed seemed to dislike, taking it in politeness with that fake and faint permanent smile of his.

"The air is fine up here," said Konrad. "You can hardly smell the river at all."

"For all kindness I am grateful," said the Turk.

"Is the wine not to your taste?" said Konrad.

"I am acquiring the taste," Mahmed said, "for the sake of the dulling of my thoughts."

"You are very frank," said Konrad.

Mahmed just looked at him, and took another sip.

Konrad knew that Muhammadans drank no wine. Their faith forbid it. There was hope, then. Obviously, they were as easy to corrupt as most other men.

Here was the bait he needed to convince Lorenz to let him have Werner Heck's presses. Lorenz obviously was soft toward Mahmed. Konrad sought to exploit that advantage, if he could.

"Mahmed, I have a problem. Perhaps you can advise me. I plan to start my own printing press."

"An admirable endeavor. To enlighten the people?"

Konrad stared at Mahmed and sensed Mahmed was subtly mocking him, but could not be absolutely certain.

"You were taken during our campaign. Why were you there? What was your mission against us?"

"Our border villages were being sacked. We were sent to intercept your march and stop you."

"You were sent to kill Christians."

"If the invaders were Christians, that is certainly true."

"So you admit you were sent to kill Christians," Konrad said. "Our priests blessed our mission. There was resistance in those villages. Militants hid their grain and some even tried to fight our soldiers."

"Without grain they would starve. And fathers are often peculiarly fond of their wives and daughters."

"And their sons were attacking our merchant traders."

"If you already know everything, sir, why ask me?"

Konrad turned his back for a moment, so Mahmed would not see his sudden flare of anger. When he had recomposed his face into a smile, he turned back again. On Mahmed's face was the same glacial, almost imbecilic smile.

"I want to print the truth," said Konrad. "About everything."

"I see. Wonderful. The truth. Even about Islam?"

Now Konrad frowned and did not look away. "Beware. I feel you mock me, sir."

"If it seems so, forgive me, for calm agreement is a way of politeness in my country."

"We want your stay with us to be most pleasurable, but we do expect good will from you. Cooperation."

"Always, I am glad to cooperate with truth."

"You see, Mahmed, I need good stories. I want the bishop's blessing for my press, and for that I want the truth about Islam, about other things, too, like war, markets, trade, or heretics or Jews."

"To you, am I not a heretic?"

Mahmed's faint smile deepened, and Konrad wondered if Mahmed already knew the answer to any question he asked.

"No. To be a heretic you must first be Christian."

"Then praise Allah, I am safe. What of Jews? They were not first Christian, yet from time to time you roast them. Was not the prophet Christ a Jew?"

Konrad felt his face go hot.

"Wurzburg has a safe place for Jews to live, behind a strong wall. They prefer their own kind. We let them alone."

"That is good, to live and let live." Mahmed nodded, as if considering. "Unless you need their loans. How fortunate for those in need. And how unfortunate for the Jew who loans more than a Christian noble can repay, and is burned in lieu of repayment."

Konrad narrowed his sight on Mahmed. He wondered if Lorenz had confided in Mahmed that Konrad had several large loans out with Jewish bankers in the city. Konrad made an effort to conceal his anger.

"Now you take Jews," he said cordially, "I know you hate them, being a good Muslim, is that not so?"

Mahmed gave his meaningless smile. "It is my purpose in life to strive for the good."

"Very well. Bishop Lorenz is very, shall I say, tolerant, even to Jews. I know you are Muslim. Tell me, how do you rid your cities of such vermin?"

"With all respect, my prince, you are mistaken. Our sultan, the great Suleiman, has welcomed the Jews that Europe chases away. In fact, he praises and gives thanks to Allah for the oppressions of the infidel kings, who foolishly send away such valuable citizens, so that by providence some find their way eventually to live and prosper in Ottoman lands, and so help those lands to prosper."

"Enough," said Konrad, lifting a hand.

"Indeed, gun making is wholly a Jewish industry there, did you know? Suleiman's closest advisor is a Jew. In fact..."

"I said, enough!" Konrad said, sharply this time.

Mahmed merely smiled, but this time not so implacably. There was steeliness in his black eyes.

"Forgive me, for saying things unprintable."

Konrad saw that he could not break Mahmed's gentle insincere smile no matter what he asked or said.

"So you will not give me stories?"

"I will not lie, sir. When my ransom arrives I shall return to my home without lies on my heart."

He thought of Heck, under interrogation, and wondered how Mahmed would smile then, were he to be treated so harshly. That smile would vanish quickly, no doubt. But he also knew that Lorenz would have none of that. Mahmed was his prized houseguest, at least until confirmation of a ransom returned from the border states. And it further chagrined Konrad that Mahmed and Lorenz played chess daily; and that Lorenz seemed compelled to describe every brilliant move by Mahmed, and to convey every insightful statement the captive heathen might say.

The next day, at breakfast with Lorenz, Konrad worked his way back toward the subject of the press.

"Just yesterday," Konrad said, "Mahmed quite politely, but frankly, related to me, that the Ottoman intellectuals would consider us quite barbarous and backward. That would be of most interest to our people, if it were properly printed and told."

"You want me to give you Werner Heck's press, I know."

"It is there, for nothing. It should be put to use."

"Your use, your ideas, your press. Mahmed has told me of your ideas, your conversations."

Konrad felt his ears burn.

"A dose of our magistrates' medicine would bind that serpent tongue of his," he said.

"Why so impudent? You sound almost jealous, Konrad."

"How dare this captive look down upon your grace."

"Oh my dear, flattery, that is a cheap trick. You must not be fully awake yet. And he looks down upon you, not upon me," said Lorenz, with an impish smirk. "Or rather, he said that the intellectuals of Istanbul would."

"I am well educated." Konrad said.

"Educated, yes. But at Wurzburg? I suppose, in that regional fashion, you are. I myself studied at Vienna. And yet Mahmed traces his education back a thousand years earlier than yours. Or mine."

Konrad said, "At least we have the fifteen hundred years of our church scholarship to fall back upon, as our rock."

"Indeed," said Lorenz, "Indeed. The church card—your trump. You always play that card when trapped. And it is the truth. But there is much we can learn from Mahmed."

"Infamies."

"Perhaps. You know we have reports of the pox. The army brought it back from war, as it almost always does. Mahmed says that the Ottomans prevent the pox with a procedure called pricking."

"The trap of a devil. He would have us pox our own people. He too told me of this, some time ago. Besides, the reports of pox are always exaggerated."

"Let us hope so. I have sent couriers out to learn of areas that are affected and report back to us."

A few hours later, Konrad took up the subject of the printing press again. This time during the rub after a steam in the stone steam chamber.

Two novice monks—young, strong men both—dried Konrad and Bishop Lorenz with lush woven towels of linen. They each were laid out on two opposing tables, their heads at the same end, facing one another, as hands began to knead their bodies. Konrad found this deeply soothing, and clearing of the mind.

Konrad watched the bishop's face across from him, just a foot away. It was suffused with enjoyment, with heat and moisture, and the bishop looked like a skinned toad with blue eyes.

"What of our duty to the state?" Konrad said.

"Our duty? For you and for me, quite different."

"Indeed, your grace. For you are bishop. The people are given to your leadership. Your counsel can reach the most important of them, those who can read, and would be greatly facilitated with a printing press."

"Konrad, please, that again?"

"We speak of duty, your grace."

"Do not presume to lecture me on duty, please. You value your horse more than I value my duty. Buy your own press, if you will. You are free to express yourself. But remember, always promote our faith, our trust, and give the people breathing room to grow. Help the knights understand that we are all one. And do try to show that we are educated men, not the unschooled dolts that some take us for in other lands."

Now Konrad felt his spite surging. He worked to control it, wondering if indeed the bishop played him a fool for anger.

Rising on one elbow, Konrad said, "More than that, we must be believed. We must have the people think what we want them to think, when we need them to think it. At the top, I mean those who already can read, the merchants, the burghers, the artisans, the guilds. At the bottom, those soldiers who so recently were digging along the river. All the country folk on all the estates. Rather than cursing us, they should be singing our praises for letting them contribute to the greater glory."

"Is that your dream, Konrad? To be praised?"

"Rather praise than curses. Think on this, your grace. What if they all tired of paying their fair taxes, and simply rose up against our abbeys and village monks, and then even against us?"

The bishop closed his eyes now. "Impossible. They are not that ungrateful."

"They are dim. They are strong. There are sometimes mad priests to rile them up. It has happened and can happen."

Konrad watched the bishop's narrow face change to a deeper pensiveness, and he knew he had scored a hit. The bishop moaned and waved an arm, and both young novice monks went away silently. And then Konrad and Lorenz were alone.

Konrad could hear only their breathing and a drip of water somewhere. He heard Lorenz now decisively suck his teeth, and Lorenz suddenly said, "Would that we tear open their hearts and pour in love, and pry open their skulls and pour in goodness!"

Konrad felt heat in the moment and he sat up and chased the gain with more vigor. He reached across and dared to grip the bishop's hand in both of his. He made it a gesture of comradeship, of brotherly love, accelerated by urgency for the common good.

"That is exactly what we must do, if more and more of them are going to try to learn to read, we must stay ahead of the thing. We must shape minds, your grace."

"Yes, I see. The pawns must ever defend?

"They must. Yes."

The bishop swung his legs off the table, kicking distractedly like a child. His legs were like chicken bones, Konrad thought, his feet like two knobs. This weak man, with so much power.

"Konrad, listen to me. The truth is belief, it is faith. But faith is sacred, the Scriptures are clear, and truth is not whatever we humans might shape it to be."

A monk came and respectfully interrupted.

Konrad watched Lorenz confer with him in whispers. When the monk was gone, Lorenz hung his head and shook it slowly. It took great self-control for Konrad not to continue to press Lorenz, and to wait.

Finally, Lorenz looked up, and said, "The first courier did not return, but the second came back with word of pox in some of the estates to the south and some to the east."

"The names of the estates to the south?"

"Unknown. The courier to the south died of pox."

"A good press would tell the people of the pox, and report its progress daily, among all the other dangers a good press would report, for the common good."

"You speak truly, if your press would be truthful."

Now Konrad leaned toward the bishop, heart hammering, waiting, hoping he had not overplayed his hand. And he flashed his most comely beseeching and earnest smile. The smile that he knew the bishop could not resist.

"I need Heck's press, your grace. I cannot afford my own. Yet there sits the means for me to reach the people, if you will only give it to me."

Bishop Lorenz looked searchingly back into his eyes, and blinked and sucked his teeth; then, dropping his gaze, pensive and smiling softly, he lifted his hands.

"Buy your own press, for God's sake, but not with my monks and funds, nor my seal. You tortured a confession from poor Werner Heck, you and that shameful Basil creature. You already have the secular power."

"Poor Werner Heck was a heretic and enemy of the state. Heck's statements were all verified."

"By force of torment, not means of truth."

"You are too liberal," said Konrad. "I will try to help you feel the rightness. Heck was in violation of our laws, your grace. Let his lamentable death serve the bishopric. What better disposal of his property than to print the truth? You would compose sermons, if you wished, and we would serve them in the markets for all who can read."

"And you would also print your views."

Konrad knew that he must have Heck's press. The work had to be done. The people had to be reached. If the bishop gave him Heck's press, it would solve everything in an instant.

And then, Konrad felt himself crossing a line from which he knew he could never return.

"We are both princes. And you are more—a duke and a bishop. You above all know that we must be united."

"The recent military action was in great part due to your influence," said the bishop. "It did not serve us well."

"The trade routes must be widened and protected. The other cities do their part. As must we."

"Yet you relish war so, almost feeding upon it. Now you would stir up more flames, more passions, more anger, I fear, with this press you want so keenly to promote."

"To protect God I will do anything."

Lorenz sucked his teeth and laughed. "God hardly requires our poor efforts to protect."

"I only know this, that I feel compelled to serve. I have my own retainers and resources. If you refuse me Heck's press, you will have no control whatsoever upon anything I may print, should I resort to other sources for funding."

The bishop regarded him with a keener caution now than before, averting his eyes, as if he had never seen him before and did not know him.

"Enough," Lorenz said.

Lorenz got up slowly, indolently. He stretched his little body, turned his back and went to the door, lifted the iron ring and let it drop. Immediately his young novice monk appeared with new white linen towels.

Konrad waited, dripping, alert, still not moving. The bishop paused at the open door, turned, and looked at him, an appraising look now, then sucked his teeth.

"Take care, prince. You say you wish us to go forward into the light and not backward into the barbarism of intolerance, into darkness. Be very clear in your meaning. I advise this in all ways. For the good of all."

Konrad smiled emptily and bowed. He spoke very carefully and slowly: "Wherever they are found, your grace, whoever they may be, we must root out all enemies of our truth."

"Beware the word 'our'," said Lorenz, gently and firmly. "It is an imprecise term corrupt with assumptions. And if it means so much to you, that you would shame us both this way, take the press and be content. I would have no more of these exchanges, please. Let us be civil."

Konrad said, "If I have pressed too hard, it is only from ardor for our obligations to our people, to their future, under our guidance."

"Very well. I am tired of arguing. I give you Heck's press. Use it well."

Konrad felt an exultation race through him. He knew it was a pivotal moment in his life.

"You shall never regret it," he said.

"Only remember, my personal approval shall be required for whatever you print to distribute to our people."

"As I have promised, your grace." That much was easy to agree to, for once the press was rolling, the bishop could be shown anything to appease him, and the real work of public influence would be done down in the streets.

"We are dedicating the new Virgin Ascending tomorrow," said Lorenz. "I would have you at my side."

"Glorious, I would not miss it," said Konrad.

Then the bishop was gone.

Konrad stretched and felt contentment fill him inside.

Nearby, silent, Konrad saw the young monk who had rubbed him. The monk stood waiting for instruction, with his head hung low and his eyes averted. He had obviously witnessed Konrad's triumph in receiving Heck's press, but perhaps without understanding the enormity of what just passed. No matter. All the monks were tools, like Basil.

"Another rub," Konrad said, and reclined fully upon the table.

Heck's press was his.

It was wonderful to keep thinking of that, over and over. God had a hand in this, of that there could be no doubt.

The young monk came silently and commenced. There was mint in the aromatic olive oil. It was heated with fragrant sage. His hands moved upon Konrad's flesh without resistance, pressing deeply.

Konrad closed his eyes and savored the irony that a monk dedicated to denial of bodily cravings could so fully give pleasure in massage. And as he relished his body's comforting response to the massaging hands, he dreamed of coming glories. The massage deepened his serenity and he prayed for closeness to God, and promised in his prayer that he would bring the people back to the ancient truths of the Church; that he would destroy the heretics and Jews, and defy the defeatists and liberals who would make peace with Satan and evil and Muslims.

I pray only for this, only the power to do Thy will, to restore the old sacred values and reunite the people behind the might of Christ and the Church and the truth...

He had his own press now. It was the best press in Wurzburg. And it had cost him nothing.

It would be still another week before the last couriers returned and Konrad learned of outbreaks of pox on the Franconian estates and villages, including Giebel.

KRISTINA

From the balcony she looked down through the morning mists, and as the sun burned them off she had seen the digging of the graves, on the far side of the fields, in the little cemetery.

So many new graves, nine in all...

She saw some of the boys from the march digging down there. Someone wailed. It was Max, the jester, on his knees sobbing over a fresh grave, and Lura told her it was his mother, Brigita, the cheese maker.

Then farther yet, Kristina saw Lud digging, too.

He was digging a larger grave than the others and he was digging it alone, apart from the rest. She knew that had to be the grave being prepared for Dietrich. Lud was bare-chested, his shoulders and arms dirty and streaked with sweat. He stood inside the rectangle of earth, carefully shaving its sides with his shovel. He seemed intent upon making the grave as perfect as humanly possible. She watched him a long time and did not look away, not until he suddenly looked up, straight at her, as if sensing her eyes all this time. She ducked back inside the balcony.

So many had died since she had left Kunvald. And she bore her own anguish like a wound inside her chest.

Berthold, my poor Berthold...

Later that morning, in the courtyard below, the women brought the body of Dietrich, wrapped in white linen, and laid it in his plain oak casket. The knight looked smaller than in life, cocooned in the linen, arms folded upon his chest.

The sun was high when a wagon bore the casket out across the fields to a burial place with large stones, which had been set aside from the other graves. The church bell tolled.

"I shall attend from the balcony," said Lady Anna. "Prepare me, and prepare a seat for me there. I will not go out there to see my husband lowered into the common dirt, and to hear the priest who did not give him final rest."

Aside to Kristina, Lura said, "She calls for a black lace veil. Her spirit is like fire but her body yet remains weak. Take care if you speak to her. She is in a state."

On a blue velvet chair, Lady Anna sat on the balcony, under a heavy woolen shawl. Kristina could see the far-off crowd of villagers and the Mass ceremony for them, and then everyone moved to the other side of the cemetery where the large stones stood, and there they buried Dietrich. Kristina could vaguely hear the murmuring of the priest.

"Nine," said Lady Anna. "Nine dead. Every family is touched by death from war or pestilence. Such is the mysterious will of God. And I know the virulence of this pox has passed, for I can see Father Michael out there, come from hiding in his church. But perhaps better a meek coward rather than a belligerent saint."

That was when Lady Anna waved Lura away. Lura withdrew back inside the chamber. Now Lady Anna spoke to Kristina, without looking at her directly.

"Kristina, first, I thank you for your many pains and ministrations during our illnesses."

"You are welcome, more than you can know."

"Very nobly said. Lud has told me you were chased here like animals. You and the others that you call brothers and sisters."

"We were hunted, yes."

"Lud says he has seen to your husband's burial."

"Lud is a good man."

"I have heard Lud called many things, but never good. But yes, he is a man. More man than others here, and that is one reason I speak to you now. Dietrich has made Lud steward, and his word stands. Dietrich made other pronouncements as well. As his lady I shall endeavor to fulfill my lord's wishes. To the extent, that is, that those wishes do not violate my own salvation before God, nor those of the villagers and other souls in our power and care."

Kristina said nothing. She felt something coming, and in this place—stranger than any place in her life—she felt helpless and alone. There had been a sense of protection with Dietrich, and now that was gone. Lud was a man in whom she found no center, only a savage sense of survival. Her brethren were in a hut healing one another. Magistrates and bounty hunters were abroad and would certainly return when word of the pox had ceased. She felt ill in the mornings and did not know why. And then, the face under the black veil said the words that sounded like a sentence from a court.

"Kristina," said Lady Anna, "you shall serve me."

"Serve you? I?"

"Listen to me, girl, and listen well. I am in a quandary. You see, my loyalty to my husband compels me to keep you, but I do have one way out. If you will not obey me, I can get rid of you. I would no doubt hear of your burning, after I turned you away or had you bound over as a heretic."

Kristina shivered, though the morning was warming in the sun.

Said Lady Anna, "Two serving maids are dead and being buried over there. Lura only remains. I shall wear this veil now all my days. And I have the last words of my husband as my cross to bear. You shall serve me, for ten years, and you shall swear to it now."

"Ten years? But I cannot..."

"You shall tend my body, and serve as needed, and each day you, Kristina, shall teach me to read, and we shall read together. The priest can teach Lud to read. In turn, I shall turn any magistrate away, and tell them there are no heretics on my estate. My son, Florian, is heir and I his mother. My own cousin Konrad von Thungen is a prince, and my family's word is ancient bond. You see, I have sufficient power to save or condemn you."

Lady Anna paused, perhaps for emphasis, as if she expected Kristina to protest or attempt to bargain. But Kristina said nothing, hearing this all as if she were in a tribunal. Once she saw Lura listening at the edge of the alcove. In Lura's face was something beyond astonishment, more like disbelief. Perhaps Lura would avoid her now, or resent her, or worse.

Looking out beyond the fields, Kristina saw the villagers crossing themselves, on their knees, heads bowed. They were all under the power of all that ruled here, of their faith and the estate itself.

Lady Anna continued, "If you disobey me, however, I shall give you over, and also your so-called brothers and sisters, all. They who came with you must work in the fields and toil with whatever skills they may own, as anyone must for their bread, by the sweat of their brow."

"Teaching anyone to read would be my greatest pleasure. And hard work is good work. But you keep me like your prisoner this way. Like a slave."

Lady Anna blinked, as if she could not be hearing this.

"Slave? Foolish girl. You should be on your knees in gratitude. This is a reward, not a penalty. You are a heretic, and that will change, under my guidance. You are given this castle's protection for ten years, and all you have to do is serve inside safe and warm and fed."

"Forgive me for seeming ungrateful, but..."

Said Lady Anna, "You shall serve me ten years and I shall protect you. You will avoid want and troubles. That is when you shall be free to go if you wish. But mark me, should you spread any heresies among these ignorant folk of my estate, you and yours will be given over. On all this, good and ill, you have my sacred word."

"Ten years, that is over half my age."

"Yes, ten years, to trade for all your lives. And now I will have your answer and your promise."

"May I have one night's sleep to pray on this?"

"No. And you have your unborn child to think of."

"My unborn child?" Kristina looked at her sharply.

"My God, child, did you not even know that of your own self? Lura tells me you suffer the morning sickness."

Kristina felt so dizzy that she feared she might indeed sink to her knees. She felt anger and in the strength of the anger she gripped the cool stone of the balcony rampart and held herself still. Her hands went to her belly, in wonder. Her mind sought back to seek another strength, back to her poor strange Berthold.

Berthold coming to her in Wurzburg, that one time. Her husband had left in her his seed, without passion, without tenderness. Yet he had left life inside her. That was the strength he had left.

"Your answer," said Lady Anna. "Now."

Kristina swallowed and shut her eyes and fought to clear her head, and with her hands touching her belly she knew there was only one answer to give.

"I shall serve you ten years," she said. She felt one door close, and another open. The finality of the moment was like a seal wrapping tightly upon her.

Lady Anna said, "On your oath, to whomever you pray. So swear it."

"I shall not swear, nor lie, nor shall I make any oath on the name of God. But I give my word as one who loves."

"One who loves what?"

"My fellow man. The truth. My Saviour. All."

Lady Anna turned her face; her eyes, glittering inside the veil, regarded Kristina thoughtfully, perhaps with surprise.

"Girl, are you brave or merely foolish? Swearing an oath is no sin. I will have your word."

"You do have my word, lady. I am yours."

Now the church bell began tolling again. Out in the fields the mourners were returning from the cemetery, many with heads low, some weeping. Yet still others were pausing to inspect the crops, to look at the sky, to kneel and sample the soil, sifting it, tasting it.

"Very well, then, I accept your word," said Lady Anna. "It is agreed that I shall protect you and yours so long as you serve my will, and no heresies are performed here, nor any seductions of the simple villeins who make lives here."

Kristina, looking up, felt her belly with her hands, wondering if it could be true, that she was blessed with child. She stared out at the cemetery across the fields, where among the big stones Dietrich was being buried by Lud and the priest and the villagers, as if an ancient truth were being locked away forever; and she thought of Grit and Witter and Dolf and Symon.

Then, as surely as she knew she breathed, as surely as cold air was warmed in her body, she knew it was true. Berthold was not dead, for his blood had joined hers, his flesh had joined hers, and the union of their child lived within her. Her hands gently cherished her belly.

God has blessed me with a new life...

She felt a dizzying sense of all her world changing. Her sacred duty to life shifted and turned inward. She would be a mother.

"The ten years," said Lady Anna, "commences this day."

Witter

It had been months ago, in early summer, that he landed here in this rural farming village, with its small castle and its illiterate war-shaken villeins and its bygone pox, and now his dog bite wounds were healed.

Here, he was invisible more than ever before. All villeins were invisible. They were beasts of burden. You could not sink lower. It was a strange thing to realize such safety, but at such a hard price—unrelenting work.

At first, his soft artist's hands had been torn up by the shoveling. Blisters became bloody holes. He wrapped his cracked palms in rags and worked on, and Grit smeared lard in the raw broken skin each night for sleep. Then the palms hardened and he became hard all over from the work.

Before first light, out in the muddy fields, the villeins were ready, standing in the chain traces behind their mules and plows.

"When you can see your feet," said Lud, "you begin."

The villeins stood in the dark waiting. The first orange rim of the sun broke across the land, and the brutal day commenced. The mind gave in, dulled by default to the labor of the body. Routine took over, broken only by the killing of a snake dug from its hole, or an escaping rabbit. About him the plows broke and men cursed and mules groaned and the earth gave up, broken at last.

Sometimes he worked with a shovel. Sometimes he swung a hammer to break up clods turned by the plows. The salt of his own sweat ran into his mouth. His tongue dried out. Children brought water buckets from field to field. Well water had never tasted so good, better than wine. The sweating villeins stopped to pass their water and to laugh when children stoned snakes and rats and chased rabbits startled from plowed burrows.

Never had he labored so hard in his life, and never had he slept so deeply. For months, he dreamed a recurring dream—of an ark at sea and he had been on it and it had wrecked, and he was naked and marooned upon an island. It was a village, this island, and the seas around it were dangerous, untrustworthy in that way of emotion that only dreams can smother one with. He had escaped the predators, for now, and while he remained on this island he was protected.

Near waking, each time, he realized that the island was a rough little village estate called Giebel, with a small rural castle of no distinction. The sea was the great forest outside the estate of the Geyers, supported by its law-bound population of common villeins. The predators—the magistrates and bounty hunters—seemed to have lost interest in this rough meal, at least for now.

He bedded with Dolf and Symon on the hard-packed earth floor, on straw, in Ruth's little hut. Grit slept alone above them in the loft. Knees and elbows kept jabbing Witter in the back, and he would half wake from his deep sleep, gasping and in fear. He found himself on the straw floor of a hut, sometimes aroused, deeply disturbed by the dreams of Kristina, which lingered like a spell.

Kristina visited in the evenings after work often, but she did not sleep in the hut. She slept in the castle—nowhere even close. Perhaps that made it worse.

He did not want to think about her at all. But he knew he would have already been long gone from this place if it were not for Kristina being here. For, sometimes in half-sleep, there was the other feeling, stronger than all the rest, coming upon him like a thief, taking him unaware, the Song of Solomon, and erotic visions that he knew were of Kristina...

Your lips are like a crimson thread, and your mouth is lovely.... Your cheeks are like halves of a pomegranate.... Your two breasts are like two fawns, twins of a gazelle, that feed among the lilies....

He hated waking in the crude hut—opening his eyes to Dolf and Symon—still aroused from those delicious dreams. Sometimes, like a hangover, he thought of Kristina all day, and fought not to. It made him work harder.

Each dawn, he gathered his thoughts about him like a threadbare cloak that offered too little protection. It had been years since he had been so exposed during sleep, with no plan of escape. He had gone out once and tried to sleep inside a haycroft, dug a burrow into the one place where he could find privacy to say his true prayers, and to find a shameless place to weep in privacy. But, even half-buried in the musty hay it was too cold for sleep, and the night chill ached his healing wounds. And there was something else. Here, inside the hut with the others, like animals sleeping in a hive, there was a deep warmth more than heat—a warmth of brotherly kindness. He was accepted among those who had taken him as one of their own. This comfort was a discovery that greatly surprised him. He needed it as much as he feared to trust it. When he laid himself down to rest, his exhaustion crushed him to sleep, and dawn always came much too soon, an unwelcome surprise.

Working, he tried to use thoughts to distract his mind from the pain of his body. He had never realized how tough villeins were. How little they expected. How unceasingly they labored. Was it because they knew so little of the outside world? Perhaps that was best, for they were trapped here. Then surely it was best they could not read, could not know how other lives could be.

Witter thought it so typical of life in this world, that Symon, the only real farmer among them, was still healing, while Grit and Dolf and Witter himself went out to the fields every day. They dug and weeded and worked the estate fields with the villagers, who had little use for them and their clumsy ways. But Lud told them they were to work, so they tried to get along as best they could.

Ruth had them pick up their food, mostly bread and cheese, at her little stone house next door.

One night Ruth came to their hut and sat and ate with them, and Witter greedily devoured his share of bread and cheese she had brought. But she obviously had something on her mind.

"Do not always expect cheese," she said, when they thanked her. "I want your strength back for work."

"Is our work in the fields not done each day?" asked Grit.

"That is estate work. Then my fields must be worked."

"Your fields?" Witter was already exhausted each day. His back ached, his legs felt as though they were on fire, and he could hardly feel his hands from pushing the shovel into the clods and breaking them up behind the mule-drawn plows. How could he do more?

"How can we repay you?" said Grit.

"Why, help work my share fields," said Ruth without hesitation, as if this were understood. "Do you not know anything? You can work my little barley patch to earn your food and use of my house. It is the bearded barley and we must hull it after harvest, and you will help flail it with me as well. We shall sprout some in water for the chickens, and with the spoilage make ale. Nothing to waste. So when you work, think on the goodly bounty to come."

"But you are a candle maker," said Witter, feeling the first sinking urge of despair.

"Only in my own little free time," said Ruth.

Symon obviously understood. "Everyone in the village, unless they are skilled as miller or smithy, they must work their own food crop and the estate land no matter what else they do."

Said Ruth, "If not, they would not eat. First they herd the sheep of the lord, breed his cattle and his fowl, his goats or hogs, whatever, and then they may tend their own. We work the land of our lord, then ours last."

"We will do our share," said Grit, "with thanks."

Ruth said, "Candles I trade for hard goods. Food I barter and grow. It has always been so. We must pay back the estate for the use of the land we are loaned. And when milling time comes, we pay part for milling. And half of what we have left goes to the church."

"That's it," said Symon. "It will never change."

Said Ruth, "We agreed among ourselves not to obey Huber. And now we wait to see how long Lud will last, for he is not well respected—other than by Dietrich himself, and now he is gone—and we know Lud surely cannot ever learn to read. He goes to Father Michael each day for a lesson, and leaves angry. We see it."

"You consider Lud dim?" said Grit.

"Not dim, but impatient. Lud is sharp the way a wolf is sharp. But he is not patient as wolves are. He is quick and too restless. We all thought he would leave for the city and become a rogue or mercenary and never return. Yet Dietrich made him steward, of all people."

"But Lud," said Dolf, "is a man of his word. He can be trusted. He will do what he has been bonded to do."

Ruth thought on this, and sadness crossed her face. "Years ago my son, Matthes, had wished to learn to read, and he asked the old priest we had then to teach him. The priest was ugly to him. Said my Matthes was a dreamer and too slow to learn. That was not so. And Lud? Is Lud brighter than was my Matthes? Yet he must learn to read from the priest? I feel sorry for them both, I do."

Ruth got up to leave. "I brought four candles. Make them last. Use them only for mending and cooking when you must have light."

"Thanks to you for all these gifts," said Grit.

"We will do our best in your barley," said Symon.

"Good cheese and bread," said Dolf.

Witter said nothing.

"For villeins," said Ruth, "when there is daylight, there is work. And for those who do work inside at night, there are candles to buy."

Then Ruth was gone.

From that day on, when it was daylight, Witter worked.

During daily tasks among the people, Witter worked hard and kept his head down and his mouth mostly shut now. He did not need to fear silence or take back anything unsaid.

The work with the shovel in the barley field was backbreaking, brutal, and unrelenting. One of his tasks was to fill their own bucket from the well. Greens could be picked from the margins of the crop fields, and Grit and Dolf saw to that.

With the pox gone, now the surviving children, some scarred, were out in the open. They all had tasks and no time to play, yet they still found little ways to tease one another, to chase, to climb the linden tree, to throw things, and sometimes to fight. Witter loved to watch them, so full of life. So much the opposite of the pox, of everything adult.

When Witter came to the well, any adult there went away quickly, without speaking to him. Most would not make eye contact with him, and some even covered their eyes with a hand. But one or two of the children were always sneaking around the well, spying on Witter, and he began to wink or scowl or stick out his tongue, and they would squeal and run away laughing.

At night, in the little house, as they shared the gruel and greens from the pot, their eyes wincing from the smoke, Witter and the others discussed their situation.

"The villeins," Dolf said. "They may turn us over, or cut our throats. Like animals, they seem to me."

Witter said, "They fear because they do not know. They do not know because they cannot read."

"Is that not why we came?" said Grit.

"Teach them?" Dolf laughed.

"You were a common mule driver yourself," said Grit, "before you were taught to read and write."

"Brothers and Sister," said Symon, "better you fear hunger instead of country villeins. They have far more to worry about than the likes of us—whether they have enough to eat and enough wood to burn."

Witter was silently amused at Dolf, so much like a mule, thinking the villagers were like animals because they feared outsiders. He knew nothing of the outside world.

"Your leg should be healed enough to work," Dolf said.

Symon stretched his bad leg. "I do not shirk."

"No one said you shirk," said Dolf.

Symon said, "It still hurts when I stand too long."

Said Grit, "Ruth said the nights are cooler now, and we must lay by all the dried greens we can, and gather nuts and seeds all we can. And firewood. You can help with that, Symon."

"Ruth is right," said Symon. "The squirrels are more active this year and that means a hard winter and early frost. It is the second barley coming ripe. The barley moon hangs light till midnight and people work on till they cannot see their feet. All the villagers will be laying by winter stores."

Grit said, "We must not count on them sharing as we do. By their law, somehow we are protected, but it is a decision made in the castle, not in the village."

Kristina, thought Witter, *Kristina knows...*

As always, in the evening when Kristina came to pray with them, Witter tried not to stare at her.

She was a vision—clean and fresh with glistening hair, and his heart jumped a beat at the sight of her. She smelled like fresh air after a spring rain.

Kristina brought a bundle wrapped in woven wool and she wore the long, blue cloak of linen—the wash-worn cloak that service in the Geyer castle required and provided. Kristina's shoulders were too small for the cloak, and the hem of it hung over her feet, dragging, so that she had to pull it and hold it up to keep from tripping as she moved.

"A fine cloak," said Grit.

"Leta brought it to me. She washes all the linens for the Geyers and priest. Lady Anna and I have reached an...understanding."

Kristina told them the bargain she had made. She told all of it, how Lady Anna gave her word to protect them, if Kristina served her for ten years—teaching her to read, and comforting her with the harp.

"Ten years?" said Grit, shocked. "You will teach the lady to read, and teach Lud, too?"

"Not Lud. The priest is doing that."

"Thank God for that at least. But Kristina? Is this to be your fate? You have sold yourself for your brothers and sisters? Have you prayed upon all of this?"

"I did pray, every evening. And I found in the Scriptures what I sought."

Kristina looked around at all of them. Witter felt her gaze pass over his face like a soft feather.

"*By the waters of Babylon,*" Kristina said, "*there we sat down and wept, when we remembered Zion...on the willows there we hung up our harps.*"

Grit nodded and completed it: "*For there our captors required of us songs, and our tormentors, mirth, saying, sing us the songs of Zion.*"

Witter knew it well. It was one of his father's favorites, and Judah had used it many times, when Witter, as a boy, strayed or did not study well enough.

In this strange place—with these persecuted people who accepted him as one of their own—it seemed so fitting. So now he added to it:

"*Let our tongues cleave to the roofs of our mouths, if we shall not remember you.*"

Kristina said, "Is that not why we came out into the world? To teach reading? To open the Scriptures to all?"

Said Dolf, "Perhaps this is the will of God. There must be a reason for us to be here."

"I vote we stay here," Symon said, "at least for now. For where would we go? How would we survive?"

Grit said, "But we cannot share the word of God? We cannot do the work we have vowed to go forth and do? We have come all this way to be trapped here and to take an oath of silence, simply for fear for our lives? Is that righteous and just?"

"Be right with yourself," said Kristina. "For me, it is ten years. I have given my word."

Witter watched them for signs of dissent and fracture. His world now depended upon too many variables. Grave looks were exchanged, and a long time of thinking passed.

He finally broke the silence, saying, "Kristina? Do you trust that lady? Will you not want to go and do your work elsewhere?"

"Here is elsewhere," said Kristina.

Dolf said, "But we are in a trap."

"I cannot run farther," Kristina said. "I must not."

"Why?" Grit said, reaching to touch Kristina's arm.

"I am with child." Kristina touched her belly.

Kristina lifted her young face; she was rosy with the new life in her belly, and Witter felt a pang of regret that surprised him. He tracked it down; he realized that he wished that his baby was ripening inside her.

"You bow to her, to this lady?" said Grit.

"Lady is how she expects to be addressed," said Witter.

Kristina's deep blue eyes regarded him. She said, "She is not my lady, as no man is my lord, for I have only one lord, our Saviour. But Anna's word, I do trust, for she is bound by it as are the villagers."

"And yet anything can happen," said Grit.

Kristina said, "But I trust in God more. I believe Dolf is right. There must be a reason we have been sent here."

Grit said, "Sent? You mean chased here?"

Witter said, "For me, I will not leave. We know what is beyond this estate, and none of it is good. It is well to bide our time. But keep your eyes and ears open."

Said Grit, " Perhaps the lady of the estate has given you her word, but there is that Lud, and the villagers, and who knows what whim will move them next? And you are with child. Think of the life of your little one, of Berthold's life that blossoms up in you, like a fire from hearth ashes thought cold and dead."

Witter had never seen Kristina look so beautiful. Her eyes so clear and skin so soft. She glanced at him, seeming to sense his intensity, and he forced himself to stop looking at her. He looked down at his hands, at his nails, filthy and broken by hoeing weeds and chopping clods.

"Take heart in this," said Kristina.

He looked up at her. Kristina pulled her woolen bundle forward and unfolded it.

"A good blanket," Grit said. "Will you not be punished if they find it missing?"

"I was given it to share with you," said Kristina, "by Lura, the serving maid who tends such things. They are not hard-hearted.

They know we all can read. Many are curious about you, and about me. But they will not pry."

Dolf said, "They fear us, too. Some, anyway."

Witter had seen that at first but now it was less and less. The older superstitious folk were always fearing the evil eye or spells, but curiosity almost always won over, and the village all knew that Dietrich wished them to be here.

Grit ran her hard little hands over the wool. "I sleep up in the loft where the heat rises. But it is getting much colder in the night down here on the floor, and this warmth the men can share."

Said Symon, "With Dolf's big elbows and knees."

Said Dolf, recoiling, "And your foul breath and belly gas?"

There were chuckles and teasing.

"A fine blanket," said Witter, inspecting it gratefully.

Then Witter saw something hidden inside the blanket. Kristina's clean white hands brought it out. A leather-bound book gleamed in the candlelight.

"A Bible," she said. "In German language."

"A Bible?" said Grit.

Witter stared. The value of that volume was more than the house that sheltered them.

Symon spoke, his voice quavering and terrified, "They will have all our heads if they catch us with this. Did you steal it from the priest?"

"It is from the library of Dietrich. If anyone enters while you are reading it, tell them you are studying your lessons of reading."

"That would be a lie," said Grit.

"It is borrowed, not stolen," said Kristina.

"I vote you return it at once," said Dolf.

"I vote we keep it and study at night," said Grit.

"I vote it is returned quickly," said Symon.

"Witter," said Kristina, looking at him.

He realized his was the tie-breaking vote. And he surprised himself when, looking at Kristina, he could not reject her courage, her gift, her sweet eyes. Yet she was with child and locked away from him forever.

"I vote it stays," he heard himself say, amazed.

Kristina looked happily at Witter. "Take good care it is not soiled."

They argued where the Bible should be hidden. And it was decided that since it must be kept clean for return eventually, for it was only on loan and must not be soiled even slightly, that the precious blanket was the only thing clean enough in the house with which to protect the incredibly valuable book of scripture. Inside the folded blanket the Bible would fit perfectly under the roof thatching farthest from the fire pit. That was how they got a blanket and lost it the same night.

"I will try to bring another blanket if I can," Kristina said.

Said Dolf, "We are punished by life itself. My back is breaking from the work in those fields."

"The old women here work harder than you," said Grit.

"Unless it is food," said Symon. "Bring food."

"Your gifts are blessed," Grit said.

"Not gifts, sharings," Kristina said. She blinked her long lashes and was clearly embarrassed. "I dearly miss the comfort of my brothers and sisters. Before I go, please, let us join hands and pray and rejoice with song together. Let us raise a joyful noise as one together."

Witter watched Kristina and wanted badly to hold her hand but it was Dolf's thick hard hand that was closest and took his. Witter sang with them the words that praised God, and he did not sing thanks for the torture death of the prophet Jesus on the Roman cross, for that to him was an obscenity. To thank God for such cruelty was to fling insult into the face of all creation. Finally, Dolf's hand released his.

Let each praise God as they will if they praise truly, with all their heart, his father Judah said.

Witter understood Jesus as a goodly servant, an incredibly wise and kind man, a visionary even as his father Judah had been. Destroyed by church-states, both of them, beautiful souls who preached peace and love, now in heaven with God.

And Witter had only cold hope that those who had destroyed such gentle souls now writhed suffering in the garbage heaps of *Sheol*—unwanted, discarded, forgotten, lamenting eternally in the torment of a perfect awareness of sin.

No, God was not forgiving. He gave the precious gift of life. What you did with it was how you shaped your own fate.

So, Witter's lips silently prayed with them, but his own prayer went forth; and yet it was odd, for with these few this way, his prayer seemed much stronger, even though they did not share the same faith, and with them there seemed an energy, the whole stronger than the one, as if their disparate beliefs were minimized, made trivial by the sheer joining of their human spirits together.

Witter opened the Bible with great care. In the Old Testament, he turned the pages and they crackled as fine paper does. He saw how hardened and cracked from work his fingers looked against the soft, white paper.

The print was sharp and crisp, the ink lush. Witter thought of the dead knight Dietrich with wonder. What it must be to own such a thing. It was as good as the best he had ever seen. Witter's eyes luxuriated in the splendor of the blocks of print, and the hand-painted embellishments of color in the margins. To view such beauty was a comfort in this dreary house as they sat on straw in the golden light of flickering candles.

He carefully turned the fine pages and found the words he wished now to say.

"And Abraham stretched forth his hand, and took the knife to slay his son. And the angel of the Lord called unto him out of heaven, and said: 'Abraham, Abraham.' And he said: 'Here am I.' "

Witter waited and looked up at the others. His eyes moved to Kristina and she smiled at him, her smile warming him all over. Had she understood him?

Said Kristina, without looking at the Bible in Witter's lap: *"Lay not thy hand upon the lad, neither do thou any thing unto him; for now I know that thou art a God-fearing man, seeing thou hast not withheld thy son, thine only son, from Me."*

"And yet," said Grit, "they do as the church-state commands, and sacrifice their own sons to death in war."

"Because they cannot read," said Kristina.

Witter listened. They were right, of course. Yet they missed the point he had wished to make: the conflict of God sacrificing his own son.

Now Grit took the Bible and carefully went through the pages, going to the back, and her stubby fingers stopped.

"*You have heard that it was said, 'Love your neighbor and hate your enemy.' But I tell you, love your enemies and pray for those who persecute you, that you may be children of your Father in heaven.*"

Beautiful words, thought Witter. Words that removed all blame of cruelty for all eternity. Words that could not have come from a vengeful God.

"Look," said Grit.

"What?" said Dolf.

"The imprint, the little owl, on the Bible's last page."

Witter saw it. They all stared. It was the owl-head imprint of Werner Heck's press.

"Let us pray for our brothers and sisters," said Kristina.

She reached and took Witter's hand in one of hers, and Grit's hand in the other, and they prayed for all those destroyed by hatred and ignorance.

Witter wanted to think of beauty and light. He desperately wanted to feel the prayer with Kristina, to sense it rising from this crude reality into a higher plane, borne upon an energy of grace, the prayer reaching an all-encompassing mind. He wanted to be one who cared.

But his mind was vivid with the sight of Werner Heck, hanging from the bridge by the chain ring that had broken his neck, and the magistrate's lantern light and barking dogs.

Kristina's hand released his.

Father, what must I do? Father, where are you?

There came no answer. Not even an echo of himself. Perhaps there were no answers at all, and it was foolish self-seeking to search for one. Or perhaps the answer was there, he thought, right there before him. He watched Kristina pray with them, and then she sang with them.

Then, as each night, she was gone, vanishing like one of his dreams of her that lingered long after waking.

LUD

The air was more chill at dawn and dark, and harvest was coming soon. Every day brought new weight to Lud's indecision and new worries about his impossible role as steward.

First thing each day he went around to the village mill, where the great stones groaned, the bakery and its rich yeasty scents that made the mouth water, the wood shop where he often sneezed in the yellow saw dust, the pottery where the kick wheel turned and hands made magical shapes from mud, the cobbler shop and harness repair, the butchery with its battlefield blood stench, and the barns and the coops that always needed repair, to keep animals inside that would rather be outside.

Along the way, there were nods and tokens like a bread bun or a twist of beef to chew. But no backslapping or handshaking. Lud sensed that they waited for him to ask something, or demand something—a bribe or a "gift" or a favor. He knew that was done. And he knew he would never do it. He could not control whether they respected him or not, but he could control himself. He saved the smithy for last; it was always warm there.

Sig the miller and Big Merkel the blacksmith—the two most respected and wealthy villagers—were together at the smithy. Merkel was not big in height but his arms were huge and his way was big, his manner larger than life, somehow, as smithies are always expected to be, and perhaps he had adapted to that expectation over many years. Merkel was hammering at his anvil, the steel ringing, sparks flying, and Lud marveled at his skill in welding the iron straps on a grain wagon yoke. Linhoff was a helper at the forge now, pumping the bellows, glancing at Lud but saying nothing. Like Merkel, his white eyes blinked away ash in his soot-blackened face.

"Be damned!" Sig said.

Sig the miller stood back from the sparks flying up. He wore a white miller's apron and he slapped at sparks trying to land there. With pulsing sweat-gleaming muscles, Merkel laughed and rhythmically swung his big hammer.

Between each swing Merkel said, "Sig is greedy. Always overloading his grain wagon. And his big ox keeps breaking the straps."

Sig took the backward compliment with a grin, for it hinted of the miller's wealth. Lud knew that Sig hosted in his mill a drinking club of the most influential men in the village, by invitation, and Lud was not in that select group—never had been, likely never would be.

"Why do you not take the steward's house?" asked Merkel. He paused with his hammer, looking at Lud.

"It would smell too much of Huber," Lud said.

Sig said, "Why take the pains to be steward if not to enjoy the rewards of such worrisome problems?"

"To benefit the estate," said Lud.

"You?" Big Merkel frowned as if deeply perplexed. "How will you benefit us?"

"By trying my best," Lud said. "My best to do what Dietrich told me to do. I did not ask for it and I certainly did not wish it. But I will try my best."

Lud saw that Linhoff was watching and pretending not to listen. He pumped, and each bellows pump made a whooshing wheeze, and sparks rushed from the live coals, crackling on the crisp fall air. Anything said here would be repeated many times throughout the village. He considered that. Linhoff's father Joch was a tiller and the tillers would hear it first, over bread or ale.

But how Linhoff would say it—that was only a guess. If Linhoff hated him it would be: *Lud the braggart. Lud thinking he is a lord now, strutting about.* If Linhoff were a friend, it would be: *Lud refused to let those big mouths get his goat, calm and humble…*

"Fifty gold pieces," said Merkel. "So you are a wealthy young man. Is dueling your new profession, as well as acting steward?"

"I was challenged and had no choice," said Lud.

They know everything, he thought.

But they always did. Were there ever secrets in Giebel for long? Lura was there, she might have told her mother, and her mother told a sister, and so on…

"Fifty gold marks. My God," said Merkel, "you can go to the city and have yourself quite a fling."

"Or buy land," said Sig. "Or buy yourself a fine horse and armor and hire your skills out for what you are best suited to—for war."

"Is that what you think?"

"Is not war where villeins become heroes?"

He thought of what Dietrich once said, *"War is where faith goes to die…"*

But he would not share that with these men. Dietrich belonged to him, not to them.

Instead, Lud said, "Heroes are dreamed of by those never in war."

"A thinker, now," said Sig.

Said Merkel, "Yes, no longer a villein, now our Lud is a wise man."

Lud said, "Ask young Linhoff there, he knows war. Did you see any heroes, Linhoff?""

Linhoff looked down at the coals and said nothing. Merkel's good graces were Linhoff's lifeline, Lud knew.

Lud said, "A poor choice for any man, war. Filthy, vicious, ugly. One would think you want to see the last of me."

He saw Sig and Merkel trade a look and open smirks. Linhoff stopped pumping the bellows. The whooshing sound ceased and their voices were clear now. They did not respect him. Nor did he expect them to. His role was one that confused them all, and it was his to live out.

"I hear you are learning to read," said Sig, chewing on a twist of beef. Sig held it out for Lud to take a bite, which he did, gratefully, and chewed the coarse hardness, and the dark blood-juice filled his mouth with the life of the slain beast.

"I said I'd try," said Lud, chewing.

Then Merkel leaned close and whispered, "If you cannot learn, will another steward be chosen?"

"If Dietrich can come back to life and change his mind, then perhaps so," said Lud, and he went on his way, turning his back on them, behaving casually to hide his anger.

It was so strange, for all knew him from his childhood. He did not know how to pose or speak or even how to regard himself this way. Now Lud realized why they were so upset with him.

It was so clear suddenly.

The main men of the village were no doubt jealous. Men like Sig and Merkel had expected to be named steward. Once the bar was so low that the steward did not even know how to read.

Who will be first to try to murder me?

Then there were the boys he had taken to war and brought back. They were the most strained, having obeyed him as soldiers, and now they were under his eye again in a new way. Kaspar hated him now. Little Golz worshipped him. The mothers he had dreaded, the women who had lost their sons, did not seem to hate him at all. Getting food for the winter, making a last good harvest, was everything now. Those wretches who had survived the pox wore hats to shield their scarred faces from the fall sun, but that did not keep them from their fields as soon as they were strong enough to work.

As usual, life went on as if nothing could stop it. None of it made any sense. Or it all made sense. Food was life. The past was the past. Winter would come as sure as the sun moved and circled the earth—Dietrich had told him this, where the sun went at night, and at first he thought it impossible. But Dietrich had never lied.

Lud rode out with Waldo, for Waldo had signed to Lud to see several things that he had found on his patrols. It was good to get out of the village. The light was clear and the crisp scents of fall were on the air.

Waldo, who could hear and understand words, was mute, but his signs were easy to understand, and had been since Lud was a boy tagging after Waldo in the horse barn and the woods.

As soon as they entered the deeper shades of the forest he knew what it would be. People were hunting in the estate woods, where they could stalk and trap unseen. He had done it enough, himself.

Dutifully, without expression of disdain or anger, Waldo pointed out the loop-type traps on rabbit trails, and some netting in the trees where birds and squirrels nested, and the gut pile where a deer had been cleaned.

"They fear this coming winter," said Lud.

Waldo nodded, and Lud thought on what to do next. He saw Waldo watching his face carefully, as if trying to send a mental message.

Lud said, "Let them take what they can, for the good of the village."

Then Waldo smiled and nodded, and looked relieved.

It was an open secret that Dietrich had always allowed hunting in the estate woods when crops were poor and the signs of winter strong. So Lud could look the other way and not violate the role of steward.

While they were gone to war, Huber had severely punished anyone caught poaching, seizing foodstuffs for penalty and keeping them to himself, and whipping one youth and branding another. Huber had caught Waldo's daughter, Kella, this way, snaring birds, and had used her fear and a few trivial trinkets to bed her. Huber had cunningly saved himself from Waldo's wrath, but at a price.

"Huber has married me in a woods wedding, all proper," Kella had told them proudly.

A woods wedding was common for men wanting to seduce naïve young girls—no witnesses, no priest. In the old woods way of ancient times, the couple would just say some meaningless words so the man could lay the girl down and have her. But if the girl had a father like Waldo, the wedding would stick. So that was a problem that had solved itself. Kella was growing fat, both with child and with the rich foods Huber had stored for his gluttony. The spoiled girl now lived with Huber and made his life a hell. She could lie of abuse to her father Waldo anytime she did not get from Huber anything she demanded.

Finally, Huber had come begging to Lud and pleaded for help. Lud had expected that—Huber's hoard could not last forever at this rate.

"Please let me remain in the steward's house, Lud, for now I am wed, and need a good place for her to bear a child. She threatens me with Waldo."

"Keep the house, I do not want it."

"You are a good man. I always said so. When anyone would say Lud is no good, I would back them down."

"Who said I am no good, other than you?"

"Lud, listen, please. When you went off to war as a patriot, I thought emergency measures were needed. It was all on me, to control things. Yes, I made mistakes. But I love our village. Let me help you when time comes for the harvest tallies. You need not worry that you cannot read or count, let me be your mind, and give me a little share for mercy's sake."

"Beg Waldo, not me, you fat sack of dung. I would not ask anyone who works with shovel and hoe and plow to trust you. Why they did not put your head under the millstone is a mystery to me."

Later, riding the fields and nodding to this one or that, he felt their disdain and mistrust. Trying not to seem like a tyrant, but also not wanting to seem soft and placating, or easy yet firm, Lud went to the church for his daily lesson. By then he was almost paralyzed with frustration.

But the church was cool and dim and at least an escape from the duties that so compelled him outside.

"I am no pedagogue," Father Michael said over and over again, until, finally, Lud demanded to know what a pedagogue was.

"Do not throw such words like cuts at me."

"A teacher," said the priest, looking down his thin nose, then bowing meekly, and Lud knew the priest was also afraid of offending. It was ridiculous—both of them like this.

"You will teach, and I will learn."

"Please hear me, Lud, I give sermons, I am not trained to teach anyone to read. You must help me help you learn."

"I only must learn as much as Huber learned."

"Huber?" said the priest. "He cannot really read at all."

"But...how?"

"How did he account? For each crop and each share he marked tally sticks, and I acted for him as clerk of accounts and would add the marks and write down the tallies for him and the bishopric."

"Huber cannot read?"

"It is my fault. It is what comes of making a villein into a steward."

"Like me."

"We speak now of Huber, not you. I knew it and let the lie stand, for the stability of the estate. Dietrich said this was well to our purposes, so that we could increase the villeins' share, so that they would always have enough, no matter how hard the yearly increases by the bishopric."

"Dietrich deceived the bishopric in the tally?"

"He forced me to do it. Please do not expose me. I was forced to comply against my own Church."

Lud felt his mind bursting.

"Huber did never realize this?"

"Huber had not the brains to. But you do, so I tell you what you must now know. You would discover it anyway. And it is up to us whether we continue Dietrich's bounty for the villeins, at dire risk of punishments if we are ever discovered."

"We shall do as Dietrich did, in all things and ways."

"No, please. We should act by the law. If the bishopric ever discovered our falsities in the tally, I dread their wrath, Lud. I could not bear it."

"You heard what I said, priest."

"Lady Anna does not know. She must be told."

"No. And if you tell her, I will be your dread punishment, before the bishopric magistrates could ever reach you."

"You threaten me?"

"It is no threat. We shall tally shares as Dietrich did."

And so Father Michael said no more of this.

There was much to learn: much of reading, of counting; of life.

The book that Dietrich had given him was still his secret. It lived well hidden in a locked box up in the rafters of his house. He had not brought it out for Father Michael to read for him. He wanted to learn to read first, for it was something intimate between himself and Dietrich, and Dietrich had said, "*When you can read...your life will never be the same.*"

For many weeks, every day for an hour, timed by the priest's hourglass behind the sacristry, Lud sat as if on broken glass, and he fought his wandering mind, listening as Father Michael tried to teach him to read.

It was dullness beyond bearing. Every day, the priest brought out sheets of coarse paper and a quill and ink and told Lud to copy what he wrote on another sheet. Father Michael first copied these things from a little cloth book of only a few sheets, its covers worn thin and faded. Then Lud was expected to copy that as best he could. His fist was thick and work-clumsy and the task was beyond humiliating. He saw the grace of the priest against the crudity of himself, as measure of their lives, one against another.

"What does this all mean?" said Lud, feeling small.

"This is Latin, a primer I used when I taught other novices at the monastery."

"You? Taught? You told me you were no...what was the word?"

"Pedagogue. That was then, this is now." The priest stared at him, it seemed to Lud, oddly. It was a strange and lingering stare, part appraisal, part something else. Lud noted the stare, and perhaps the priest saw his discomfort, for he looked away.

Lud, feeling the need to throw off his unease at being stared at by the priest, said, "Why were you sent down here, out here to this village, if you were a professor there?"

The priest did not look at him now. He looked at his thin hands, and ignored the question. "They learned and you can learn."

"I do not wish to learn Latin. I wish to learn our language."

"But Latin is spoken throughout Europe. It is the universal language. Traders, diplomats, all men of all countries write in Latin."

"I wish to learn our language only."

"At least a little Latin first, then German. We must crawl before we can walk, and walk before we can run."

"Then let us begin."

The priest spent the next two hours showing him pages of ink scribbles like worm tracks in old wood.

"That is an A," said Father Michael. "First letter of the alphabet. There are twenty-six in all."

"It looks like a rooftop," said Lud. "But why does it not sound like a rooftop? And what is an alphabet? What learning do you have that so compels me to obey your teachings?"

The priest took a pause. "Lud, let me share with you the description of an ideal school curriculum. I know it by heart. It is very old and universal. Will you give an ear and be patient and listen?"

"I am listening."

Lud watched the priest hold forth, as if a dam had split its walls and a flood spewed forth. The priest spoke proudly in a meaningless jumble of names and words.

Said Father Michael, "The useful compendium of morality which the multitude supposes to be that of Cato, and let him pass from the *Eclogue of Theodulus* to the eclogues of the *Bucolics of Virgil.* Then let him read satirists and historians, so that he may learn about the vices to avoid in the age of minority, and let him look for the noble deeds of those to be imitated."

"Enough," Lud said, trying to interrupt.

"From the joyful *Thebaid* of Statius, let him pass to the divine *Aeneid,* nor let him neglect the poet Lucan whom Córdoba brought forth."

"Priest, stop," said Lud.

"Let him reserve the moral sayings of Juvenal in the secrecy of his breast, and study hard how to avoid the shame-fastness of nature. Let him read Horace's *Satires and Epistles and Art of Poetry* and Odes with the book of *Epodes.* Let him hear Ovid's *Elegies* and *Metamorphoses,* but especially let him be familiar with the little book, by Ovid, *The Remedy of Love.*"

Finally, the priest was done. Lud's mind had shut down midway, and he stared.

"Do you see?" said the priest. "Much to know."

"You spoke to brag and to try to daunt me."

"To instruct you."

"I should already know all of that? You know all that?"

"All quite basic. I knew it as a boy."

"Then teach me, priest."

"If you will let me. For now, the alphabet, please. We crawl before we walk, and we walk before we run."

Every day, Lud dipped the quill in ink and made scratches and ink blots and other ink marks on the paper, without the slightest meaning to him, other than being a waste of his time and proof that he could not learn.

And every day went this same argument, in one form or another. The priest said, "You are not trying very hard, you must look at the letter I write, and copy it exactly. Or else I must not waste my time."

"What else is more important? Wine?"

"Wine symbolizes the sacred blood of our Christ."

"Then you drink too much blood, priest."

Father Michael would get up from his stone bench and pace in circles, sometimes standing behind Lud, saying nothing. Lud could feel him watching, hear him breathe. And then suddenly the priest would stir as if from a dream, and move about waving his arms like a startled goose. His black cloak would drag the floor behind him, the loose sleeves slapping the air like crow's wings.

Lud let him rave.

"Do not blaspheme, Lud. Please. There are two widows from the pox, one widower, and three orphaned children, two blind, and I must pray for them."

"I know well enough, I buried them. The mothers were laid out with their arms around their dead babes. As for the living, bread will help them better than prayer."

"It is madness that you are supposed to be steward. So I must pray for you, too. Please do not leaden my prayers with harsh words and keep them from ascending on high. You are impossible to teach."

When the raving was done, Lud said, "You will do the will of Dietrich."

"But he did not name me, specifically, to do this thing, did he? Did he not say the heretic girl would teach you?"

"She is Kristina, not the heretic girl. We harbor no heretics at Giebel."

"Yes, that is our game, false or no."

"Just as Dietrich willed it so. Kristina is tasked with serving Lady Anna, and teaching. Just as you will teach me, as it has been decided."

Father Michael lowered his eyes. "I will try."

"You will not just try, you shall teach me, priest."

"We have come not very far in such time."

"However long it takes, it takes. But I must be able to read by the time the harvest is counted."

"That is too soon."

"Then let us stop wasting time in argument."

And so it commenced, day by painful day.

Lud knew that Father Michael was unnerved by the need to keep looking directly at Lud's face when Lud tried to form the letters he was memorizing, the sounds that made the words.

"As each stone is set upon another, in a structure they climb up atop one another, and soon you have a wall. You see how it all fits together now?" That was how the priest tried to describe reading.

Lud listened and tried to learn, but his mind was like the stones that the priest said were letters that made words. And he did not know what letters were in the first place nor how they could fit and be solid, and his mind kept straying out there on the fields of the estate.

"Again, Lud, you are not listening. You must repeat each letter after me, and then I shall say the word they make. You write each letter down as I say them and then you shall see the word. You shall feel the word."

"Feel the word?"

"Do you not feel the words as they come from me to you? Do you not feel them come from my spirit into yours? Do you not feel my thoughts touching your own?"

Sometimes, without understanding why, Lud was very uncomfortable alone with Father Michael.

"Begin again, priest, and make sense this time."

Father Michael paced and droned on, and Lud saw the averted eyes, and he thought of Kristina, and of the fields, and of Dietrich. His mind was like a fox slipping this way and then that. His life was all dig dig dig. A life spent close to the earth, on the end of a shovel or swinging a pick.

"Priest, stop. I want to know the words for tools, to be able to read the lists of shares of crops, and the names of the various grains and goods, and to tally and add the tally, and to be able to detect a cheat from the letters and the numbers."

Father Michael dropped his face into his hands and moaned. Lud stared at him.

All those words, he needed to know—for fighting the earth with a pick and shovel and harrow and hoe; for provoking food from dirt for life sustenance; and then digging deeper to hide in the earth the husks of the dead.

But here, this priest, was a man who never had understood any of those things. And how could such a pompous and weak man, a shallow yet learned man, teach him the words that a steward must use to guard the good?

How could he, Lud—born only with a strong back and weak mind—learn to do anything more than to hunt other men? How could he learn this secret way of speaking that was not in sounds but in ink?

Once a week, on Saturday at noon, he was to report to Lady Anna, for the steward's weekly meeting. It was brief and the lady was veiled. The worst was that he had to bathe and wear washed clothes and tie back his hair to present himself.

Lady Anna had reamed him out the first time: "Never, ever, present yourself here, this way you come—all boots and mud and smelling like a horse!"

In truth, Lady Anna was the only person whose wrath he feared. She had been such a beauty. And now he glimpsed, when the light was right, the ruin of her face under the fine lace veil.

The good part of it was that he would see the one person in the village who might be able to explain reading to him. The only one he could trust, whom he always looked so forward to seeing there.

"What of your reading lessons?" demanded the lady this week.

He stood with his arms behind his back, wearing his washed tunic, and he had bathed with ash soap in cold well water from a bucket.

Lady Anna sat in the receiving chamber on the ground floor where the hall widened and the long table stood with oaken benches. She sat in the big chair at the end. Dietrich's chair was the only one with rests for the forearms. Upon entering he had heard the harp playing, but did not see it now. Kristina stood back in the shadows as if mute, unmoving, waiting.

On a pedestal now, behind Lady Anna, in the alcove where armor and swords had been before, was a painted plaster statue of the Holy Virgin, haloed in gilt with her wounded eyes woefully skyward to heaven, as if blaming God for the death of her son and His.

It had always unnerved Lud, this immaculate conception, the way the priest said in sermons that God had visited a farm girl, probably while she slept, and had His way with her. The strangest part was that God had created everything, including Mary herself, and so that meant it was incest. Of course, he realized that it was his ignorance, to think such things that could never be openly shared with anyone. Perhaps when he could read well enough he would search for the answers in the Bible, even though that was an illegal act under bishopric law. Perhaps then life would make sense.

He realized that Lady Anna was speaking to him.

"Are you listening, Lud? I said, I hope you are learning more rapidly than I."

Kristina said nothing, but lowered her face. He now saw the ornate harp, Dietrich's harp, on it's little stool behind her, and realized she had been playing it for Lady Anna.

Lud had only seen this room a few times, when he had helped serve at banquets for visiting dignitaries, knights, and others far above his station. Now he sat on such a bench with the lady at the end, regarding him through her veil. Kristina stood beside her saying nothing.

"The priest insists upon Latin. I want our language. The priest does not teach me well."

"It begins with Latin. I am learning Latin. Letters are sent in Latin, accounts are made in Latin, and commerce and decrees and so on. Father Michael told me you do not learn well. And he warns me that if you learn to read you may not understand what you do read, and mistake one idea for another. But then, he is often a fool, and in fairness to you, I do not know how hard he tries, considering all else we had seen of him during our distress."

"He is much with wine, my lady. And he has troubles I think, of some kind."

"He is much with thinking himself above us in our small estate," said Lady Anna. "But he must teach you. You must learn before the tally, you know. He wants more time with you."

"More? Perhaps I can have another teacher?"

"Why another? Is there something you have not told?"

Lud looked at Kristina. She lowered her eyes, as she always did, when his gaze touched her and moved over her. She said nothing, as if it had not happened, that touching of eyes, like a fondling, brief and forbidden.

"The priest is impatient," he said. "Perhaps, Kristina...?"

"Kristina is mine. She is hard put to teach me as is."

There was a silence. Then Kristina spoke.

"There is Grit."

"Grit?" said Lady Anna.

"Marguerite. She is called Grit. She reads well."

"Where is this Grit to be found?"

"In the field of Ruth with my brothers Symon and Dolf. They also can read."

Lady Anna said, "You can read, all?"

"Yes," said Kristina.

"All can read?" Lady Anna was incensed or disbelieving, or both. Lud sensed that she was deeply insulted. A handful of homeless commoners could read, but not the lady of the estate.

Lud had known this since the line of march, when they had burned the carts and the books. It was now almost as an accusation by Lady Anna, and Lud wondered at the whole thing.

"All of my brothers and sisters can read," said Kristina, without pride. "It was expected of us."

"And who had taught them and why?"

Lud had wanted to know more of this himself and he stared at the floor, at his feet, and listened with intensity.

"We teach one another. He or she who knows teaches the others that they may know, and teach in turn. We do this in our belief that all must be able to decide what is truth, each for oneself, each with God."

"God and truth. Truth, as my beloved Dietrich said, that we must somehow find if we learn to read. But it seems that is not so simple. Do you declare you have found this perfect and absolute truth all by yourself?"

"I fear you mock me."

"I assure you I am in most deadly earnest."

Lud feared for Kristina now. He feared for himself, as well, should Lady Anna order him to seize Kristina and somehow punish her for insolence, or worse. The lady was never mild-tempered, he well knew, and recovering from the pox, anyone was more erratic, more emotional, more prone to release spite upon the nearest victim. He looked up at the Virgin. She had not changed. Still beseeching, her eyes like pearls, and he thought of the wooden Jesus in the church, with the eyes that followed him wherever he passed in the sanctuary.

"Answer me," said Lady Anna.

Kristina spoke in a clear voice that sounded of simple honesty. Hidden there also he heard fear.

"My truth, yes, for me. Yours will be yours to find. Lud's his to find. All to find, all to know."

"Indeed," said Lady Anna. "And how can you be so certain what this truth is when it is found? How can you know when you see it in books?"

Kristina did not speak for some time. She seemed to wrestle with her thoughts, and Lud felt it was the same as when he knew exactly what to say, exactly what he felt, yet feared the consequences of speaking his mind. She was a brave girl but foolish, he thought, just as she always was, risking everything on a gamble for her beliefs.

"Speak," said Lady Anna. "No one will punish you here. I must know the point of this reading we all must learn. My own father kept it from me, saying it was not important, that others should advise. My husband argued with me to learn but I resisted. I ask you, how can truth be found in books?"

Kristina said, "To know what is written for ourselves, not through the tongues of others, who may change or amend."

Lud saw Kristina's fear. She had answered without thinking first, and surely she realized that she now was condemned out of her own mouth. He saw her face quaver and sensed that her sense of righteousness had trapped her.

"I see," said Lady Anna. She said it strongly and her breath lifted the veil slightly.

There was a long pause. Kristina stood there, fixed.

Finally, Lady Anna said, "No doubt you mean the Bible. That is how the heresy spreads. It is clerical law not to read the Scriptures for oneself but only have them read by a priest, who is trained to interpret them wisely. Because you live here under our protection, you imagine you can say whatever you like?"

Lud saw that Kristina, though fearing this powerful lady, seemed unable to force herself to be silent, or to lie. He understood that well. But he wished she would not speak. And he knew she would.

Kristina said, "To seek the truth, your husband Dietrich said. Truth means to read many things, not only the Bible. History, philosophy, essays. Dietrich ordered it so, did he not?"

Lud realized Kristina had not answered the lady's question, and had made her own bold statement instead. The girl had more courage regarding lady Anna than he did. Or perhaps she did not fully comprehend the power of life and death that the lady possessed over all of them here.

"Be still, girl," said Lady Anna. "What Dietrich my dear blessed husband bound me to is my burden, right or wrong, and I will honor his word. Because I tolerate you, you take advantage. I may be a country woman, but I am lady of this estate and my son, Florian, is heir."

"I meant no offense. I have betrayed the baby inside myself. Nothing is the same as before. I have just risked not only the life of my baby's mother, my own self, but the new life itself. I am no longer free to say and do as my soul commands. I have given you my pledge to serve."

Tensely waiting, Lud saw Lady Anna's eyes glitter darkly, staring at Kristina through the ornate black lace of the veil. Lud steeled himself for whoever spoke the next words. If Lady Anna commanded him, as steward, to arrest Kristina, he would be faced with a brutal choice, and did not know how he would act.

But Lady Anna nodded, as if thinking out loud.

"Your honesty serves you well. You won over my departed husband, but I am not so easy. Tell me, Kristina, how do you know how to teach reading and writing?"

"We were taught to teach."

"We? You mean all of you?"

"Yes, in Kunvald, in Moravia, in our village. We were schooled to read and write, and then we were taught to teach it, so all could learn, and then they teach others too, giving reading as a gift of love wherever we might go."

"What has love to do with it?" Lady Anna's tone hardened. "There will be no reading of Scriptures here. Tallies, letters, decrees, law agreements, yes."

Said Kristina, "I am only trying to help the steward."

"The steward," said Lady Anna, not without irony, her distaste obviously meant to be detected.

Lud said nothing. He felt his blood rise and the heat sting his face and ears. Behind his back, his hands tightened into fists. He wanted to run away to the city and go wild and buy pleasures with his fifty gold marks, abandon this all, but he had given his word to Dietrich, the only man who ever loved him.

If words could make truth, hunger could make crime. Words did not fill bellies.

So he, too, was trapped. Still, if all else failed, he could bully the priest into the system Huber managed, with tally sticks, and Father Michael adding and writing the accounts. The priest would always protest, then soften, with that strange lingering stare of his, which so quickly pulled away. No doubt Michael was a lonesome man. But that should not be, when his charge was filled with the needy. Kristina and Grit did far more here to help the poor and feeble than any priest had ever done.

And it angered Lud, thinking he was still no smarter than fat Huber. Worse, it was wrong that he would give up learning to read when Dietrich had believed in him so.

Lady Anna said, rising, "Lud, I am tired. Go now. You must try harder. Learn from the priest. You must be ready for harvest tally and sharing out, or we will have everyone fighting for food and killing all winter."

Kristina

It was a frequent theme between them, the fear of Lady Anna for her soul, if she learned to read. They stayed with the most innocent of books for that reason.

To avoid the cutting social satire of Erasmus, in the library Kristina searched for something safer, and finally settled upon *The Vision of Piers Plowman*…

"In a summer season when soft was the sun,
I clothed myself in a cloak as I shepherd were,
Habit like a hermit's unholy in works,
And went wide in the world wonders to hear.
But on a May morning on Malvern hills,
A marvel befell me of fairy, methought.
I was weary with wandering and went me to rest
Under a broad bank by a brook's side,
And as I lay and leaned over
and looked into the waters
I fell into a sleep for it sounded so merry."

They fought their way through it, copying the letters endlessly, and Lady Anna began to learn from memory rather than by the process of analysis. The poem was sweetly dreamy and yet, like all good stories, powerfully seductive.

Lady Anna fretted upon the issues of hidden meanings, of allegory and sin, and she was wary of the temptations of ideas that she dreaded so.

With every thought and every belief she held, with every word she spoke, Kristina too was cautious. She carried a child, and the protection of that life was paramount now above all, and she walked a fine line between teaching and proselytizing.

Even the books she randomly chose to read with Lady Anna could prove a pitfall. Great caution must be taken.

Later, with the sun full up, they went out on the balcony with Lady Anna wrapped in furs, for the chill of first frost had come, and out in the fields the harvest was in full work.

The villagers and wagons and horses moved like locusts through the rows out beyond the orchards, and the trees beyond were colored gold and red and purple now.

Kristina felt life move in her belly and warmth suffused her wonderfully. The morning sickness was past. Grit had told her she reckoned the child would come after winter's first thaw. It would be an early spring child. God willing, she would bring no troubles to them and all would be well. But Lady Anna remained suspicious.

One day at dusk when food was served in the kitchen and Kristina ladled beef barley broth into a silver bowl to be taken to the chambers upstairs, Lura said, "What are words like?"

"What are they like?"

"Written words, I mean. They are like magic to me."

"No magic. Just thinking. Using the gift God gave us."

"But these words. How do they make up themselves from the letters that you put together?"

Kristina remembered how she had learned to read; so long ago it seemed now. Her mind went back to her mother, and her feelings followed her mind, and she was sitting on the warmth of her mother's lap, her head nestled against the soft, woven wool of her mother's bosom, and they made marks with chalk on a board—marks that at first looked like the print of bird's feet in dirt.

"My mother told me, a word is like a nest of thought. The way a bird twines straw into a nest, the letters are sounds that twine into words."

Lura took Kristina's hand. It was the first time they had touched. Lura's grip was firm and dry and urgent.

"What else did your mother say?"

"That of all things, she wished to persuade people against cruelty."

"Cruelty. It is a terrible thing."

"Yes."

"She was a wise woman, your mother. Do you miss her?"

"Very much."

"Do you think I might learn?" Lura whispered, as if they might be caught and punished for even speaking so.

"Learn?" Kristina looked more closely at Lura. She saw such earnestness in her face that it startled her.

Lura released her hand and shrugged with shyness Kristina had never seen from her.

"To know the reading of words," said Lura.

"Of course you can learn."

"Dim as I am?"

"That is the point of learning, to bring light into the dimness. But you must do it yourself."

"You can teach me?"

"I can and I will, if you wish it."

"It is my fondest wish, not to be left behind."

"Behind who?"

"Behind everyone."

WITTER

This villein's life was life in a time of its own, a spell of its own, life lived as Witter had never known it.

The harvest was almost done. Moving from one field to another, the villagers seemed to communicate mostly with looks. They sang in ancient measures, stepping off while they worked, chanting of good harvests and plentiful feasts in hard winters, versing to the scythe cuts, trading off verses across the fields, making the time pass, making the work get done. They all worked hard, unquestioningly, and long, from sunrise to sunset. When laboring, the villagers said little or nothing much to one another, and nothing at all to Witter, nor Grit, nor Dolf.

The sturdy villagers were hardened by work, and with a will to match—like one animal with many parts that were all strong in concert. Witter found himself envying their unity, their faith in what they were and who they were and why they were. When he was with them, he was one of them, too. He felt something almost like security at those times, even if only for a few seconds, until he mocked himself for it.

He would be chopping, and a man—never a woman— would step over the rows and take the hoe from him, and as if demonstrating to a mute, the man would show with exaggerated motions how the chopping should be done, then thrust the hoe back into his hands.

At first his back felt like it would break. But then, after a few days, sleeping every night like one dead, eating enough for three men, he began to gain strength. He began to feel his muscles swell and harden. Iron cords came up under his skin. The shovel and the hammer were lighter. Each motion became almost effortless. His palms were rough like tree bark.

Under the load of work he would experience a pleasant euphoria, slashing with the scythe, in a rhythm, paced to the songs sung by others across the fields in the cool, crisp air. A supreme indifference would take over and then he could work all day.

"They are not going to speak to us," said Grit. "We are under the protection of the estate, but no doubt the priest has warned them of danger to their immortal souls if they commune with so-called heretics such as we."

Magistrate patrols had passed down the main road through the estate, as well as the occasional low-ranker knight trying to find a position. But, after bread and wine from a wagon, they were farewelled without a word about the refugees.

Witter, who had run away from everything most of his life, at first had felt stranded here, on this island, this village, this estate. And yet he felt for the first time since he was on the run that he could rest in peace.

It was not that he trusted in life more than before. It was that he felt he must stop somewhere. His dream of reaching the Ottoman states was still in the back of his mind. But there had been too much fear, too much hysteria. He had lived on a chain of panic.

Now he needed this island. True, he had never felt more an outsider, and yet he felt he belonged, too.

He adored Kristina, but feared for her naiveté, her brave and foolish pacifism in this world of monsters.

Sometimes while he worked he was filled with an enormous sense of peace that almost overwhelmed him. At those times, still cutting weeds with a hoe or chopping away with a scythe, he would send up his prayers.

And sometimes he would hear the voice of his father, Judah, urging him through Proverbs to trust in God, but also to beware...

Then will they call me, and I will not answer; they shall seek me and they shall not find me...

Because they hated knowledge, and did not choose the fear of the Lord...

They shall eat of the fruit of their way, and from their counsels they will be sated, for the backsliding of the naïve shall slay them, and the tranquility of the fools shall cause them to perish...

But he was weary of running away.

When he was with Kristina, when she visited for a brief meal now and then, he felt so alive seeing her. Her belly was ripening. She was pregnant. And she brought fruit and bread from the castle, and sometimes even a jug of wine.

If omnipotent Jehovah has seen him safe this far, it must be for a reason. Why was he spared, a man so venal and cowardly, so doubting, when so many finer lives were destroyed?

Bitterly optimistic yet, despite all, Witter dared envision a future world in which freedom and equality might take root through the power of literacy, if individuals might ever think for themselves. And at the end of every thought, every fear, every plan, he sealed his mind with the knowledge that God controls all—whatever happened would be from that inscrutable source, and therefore, speculating was comfortingly pointless and illogical. You could imagine the worst; but why, if you could not believe it?

So he answered back to Judah, his father,

My sanity is such a tenuous agreement with myself, and I pray God to preserve it. But how close I am walking the edge of the abyss. How easy to fall out of caring whether I live or die now. In my growing up, I assembled my disguise, but now, here, in this place, I am who I am. Just a man cutting the earth to provoke from it bread in the sweat of my brow...

So, every day when first light sent them all into the fields with unspoken work to be done, Witter expected each day to be his last day on earth. And somehow he felt he belonged here on this island. Perhaps his capacity for fear had simply worn out.

For somehow, with the pact Kristina had made for them, he was no longer afraid.

That is, he was no longer afraid, until one chilly gray day, after the first snow, when the harvest was being tallied in the grain barns and people waited in their houses and huts.

Witter was at the fire in the house, eating his bread and cheese with Grit and Dolf—for they ate together, apart from the others who did not welcome them—that a big-shouldered man opened the door and stood there to stare at Witter. It was Merkel, the blacksmith.

"Witter," Merkel said, crossing his arms. His brow was black and grown together in one thick bar over his tightly close-set blue eyes. "You, come."

"Me?" said Witter.

He looked at Dolf, then Grit, who shook their heads.

"Yes you, heretic. Your name is Witter. The girl Lura was told by Kristina who you are. What you are. And Lura tells me everything. Get up."

The big man stepped closer and Witter shrank back on the edge of the log, his world shrinking in on him.

"He has done nothing," said Grit. "Please do not take him. Take me instead."

Merkel ignored her.

"Off your ass and on your feet," said the man, ignoring Grit. Witter looked at Dolf, but Dolf lowered his head, unmoving, and stared hard at his big toes protruding from the tip of his worn-out leather boot.

"He has harmed no one," insisted Grit. She started to rise but Witter took her arm and pulled her back down.

"It is all right," Witter said.

Witter got up. He pulled his cloak about him. The cheese and bread clotted in his mouth, half chewed, like a clod of earth, food that he needed in his belly but could not swallow. Witter fumbled for words, and felt like a fool. The big, wide face stared down at him.

"Do you want me to jerk you by the neck?"

"What will you have me do?"

Now the big hairy hand enclosed around Witter's arm and pulled him outside. Witter felt the cold bite his lungs and his feet skittered along over the thin snow.

"I am Merkel," said the man, and released Witter.

"Where are you taking me?"

"To the smithy. There we will begin."

"Begin what?"

"To find the truth."

Stumbling along beside the man, Witter reviled himself.

Why did you not run? Why did you not take your chances on one of the moonless nights?

Here he was, playing the heretic among the rustics, for being the Jew as God had made him to be. And if these crude men took him and stripped him for torture, they would see indeed that he was a Jew, one of the blood who had persecuted their precious Christ, even though the prophet they claimed was himself a Jew, and a priest of Jews.

"Stop dragging your feet and walk," said Merkel.

What madness awaited him in the smithy he could only imagine. Coals and tongs, hot irons, and this man was as strong as a beast and covered with scars of old burns from his forge. Would they punish the others, even Kristina, for harboring him?

Perhaps the Bible has been discovered. Or perhaps he is even insane...

It was too late to try to run. And run where?

Fool, fool, fool!

As he stumbled behind Merkel, obeying this fate, he heard himself laughing. In his weariness, Witter had thought that being on an island among illiterate rustics at the edge of nowhere was better than running. And that made him laugh all the more. He was a fool.

Witter, king of all fools...

"Why are you laughing?" said the blacksmith.

"I am laughing at a fool," said Witter.

He stopped and dug his boot heels into the glaze of thin snow and skidded to a halt.

"I am no fool." The blacksmith grabbed his arm again and jerked Witter along.

This made Witter laugh even harder. If Hell existed and were the Gehenom of unholy reason, as his father had believed, perhaps he was already dead and did not yet know it. His fear made that thought indescribably funny.

"Watch your tongue," said the brute. "Do not mock me or you will regret it, I promise you."

"I already regret it," said Witter. His laughter barked.

They reached the smithy. Smoke churned from the short chimney in the slate roof. Merkel pulled the big iron bar that opened the door.

"Now we'll see who laughs," said Merkel.

Witter was shoved forward; he stumbled inside and felt a blast of heat sting his face and ahead in the deeper dark he glimpsed the orange mouth of the furnace waiting.

Konrad

"Since there is no ransom, and you are not a first son, and you lied, we are at a quandary as to your fate. I planned to use my share of the bounty to fund more mining shares and to promote my press. I only confide this to reveal how seriously you disappoint me, and how grimly I now perceive your future."

Word had come to Bishop Lorenz by courier the day before that Mahmed was of no concern other than being a blessed child of Allah and a valued soldier; but it was a soldier's fate to perish in service of his lords, and the family of Mahmed had no treasure with which to rescue and restore him to home.

"I implore your Christian forgiveness," said Mahmed, bowing with that false humility that Konrad despised. "For delaying my death as long as possible, I admire your virtue."

There was nothing to say, and Konrad turned away.

Two days later, he visited again, and this time tried another approach. He walked in the bishop's garden with Mahmed. The day was very cold. Perhaps the air itself would work to advantage.

Below them, the river was frozen. The garden was walled and protected on the high bank of the river below the massive walls of the fortress. The ground was hard as iron, frozen now, and the garden itself was dead and sprinkled with snow.

They wore hooded fur capes—Konrad in ermine, Mahmed in rabbit fur—their breath frosty as they walked. Mahmed lost his usual poise; he stood hunched over and shivering.

"The cold affects you greatly, I see."

"I am unused to it," Mahmed said. "But the cape is a most generous and welcome gift."

"I asked you for stories, and you said you would not lie, yet you did lie, and now your fate is in question."

"I was dishonorable."

In the west the sky was dark again and the wind was picking up.

"You also made an oath not to attempt escape," said Konrad. "So why not break that one, too?"

"Without forgiveness, you could kill me and be done."

"You owe a debt for your life. Debts are not forgiven so easily as wrongs. Killing you would be easy in a dozen ways, but there is our investment to consider."

"Your investment."

"Exactly so. You have been expensive, not only in coin."

"It is cold," said Mahmed.

"For a Muhammadan it is cold, I know. An hour outside is good for health. Your dark skin does not love the chill, I see. More suited for sultry climes and the desert. Is not that so?"

"It is bleak here. In my city there are gardens that bloom indoors, under glass, where one can stroll and smell the beauty of spring year-round."

"You are good at making up lies."

"Regrettably, it is true."

"You are here now, and being here is what is true for you. But it is good that you can invent tales."

"All as you say."

"The sooner we have our talk the sooner we can do business."

"Business?"

"You see, the bishop is fond of you, though I cannot see why. He is embarrassed that you bring no ransom, for you are expensive to maintain here. I said why not burn you for the public to cheer and vent their spleens, but he said no. That to him incites vile sinful emotions. He is a soft man."

"Yet he sends others to war."

"As do your religious men send soldiers to kill and to die, in the name of Allah. Is that not so?"

"Yes. All as you say."

"Let us be honest. Leaders must often do terrible things in the name of their state and religions. For me, I will do as I see fit and not seek refuge in some conceit of goodly pretenses. My press will not hold back from what is necessary."

They came to the end of the garden where the rose bushes glittered in a prison of ice. The thorns were visible on the black, naked branches, like burnt bones imprisoned in the glaze. Konrad thought how strange, that roses grow from such ugliness. Mahmed's teeth chattered. Good.

Konrad looked beyond the bank of the river below, where the frozen surface curved away like the great bow. On the far side, down past the town shanties, a pack of children were playing on the ice like ants. Nearer the town, where filth ran from the gutters year-round, men were cutting blocks of ice with saws and loading them onto wagons. Konrad made a mental note not to use ice ever again.

His thoughts returned to the stranger standing beside him, waiting to hear his next words.

"Nor would the bishop dispose of you in a dungeon. And to release you after boasting of ransom would compound his embarrassment. Then I came upon a marvelous way for you to earn your keep."

"I will do my best to serve, if there is any hope I may someday return home."

"No promises. You will do well to keep your hide."

"All as you say."

"Do not keep saying that. You have a way of mocking while at the same time being perfectly compliant."

"How may I serve?"

"You may know that now I have my own print press. Quite a large one—two presses actually. I have monks to run it. All of them literate, of course."

"Congratulations. Reading is the coming thing and knowledge will change the world. You will prosper."

"We need good stories. That's where you can serve."

"And how? Stories?"

"Brother Basil will visit you regularly and you shall dictate stories."

Mahmed brightened. His mustache lifted and his white teeth were exposed in a brilliant smile. Konrad had never seen a genuine smile on Mahmed's face before. He looked younger, brighter, and hopeful.

"You like that idea," said Konrad.

"Yes, yes I like that idea. You see, there is so much to share. Things not appreciated here."

"Tell me," said Konrad. "That is just what I want."

Mahmed looked up at the flat clouds moving darkly and lifted his arms.

"Last month, on a crystal clear night before the first snow, I was gazing at stars from my casement window. Cygnus, the Swan, was flying with heavenly wings across the evening sky. I tell you, Konrad, few constellations offer such glories to the eye and the soul as Cygnus. When one beholds the Swan's center star, Sadr, that is where the Swan's wings stretch away from its magnificent body, westward to Zeta Cygni and eastward to Eta Cygni. Each star is a jewel of color and…"

"No astrology," said Konrad, cutting him off. "We can get any street-corner fop for that."

"Not astrology, it is astronomy, a science of the mechanics of celestial delight."

"Do not mince terms with me. I said stories. Though there is no ransom, you can help my press in another way. We need good stories that sell."

Mahmed sounded hopeful, even enthusiastic.

"Yes. None better than the stories of the heavens and how the stars are all related."

Konrad realized that Mahmed was far dimmer than he had reckoned him to be. Talking like a student about stars, colors, delights. What a fool.

"Then perhaps pricking for pox," said Mahmed.

"You talk of pricking people and they will storm the Marienberg and tear you apart with their teeth. We have just had pox and praise God it has passed now."

"But pricking is to prevent, not to cause."

"Pricking is known to be a Muslim trick to poison foes. Do not insult me by speaking of it again. I have personal loss from the pox. All do who live."

Mahmed was silent.

Konrad knew of the pox in the countryside and he thought of the letter from the courier. Dietrich was dead. He wondered how much he would miss Dietrich. But there was a good side. No word of Lady Anna, his cousin, and the thought of her warmed him in a male heat. Next spring he would go there when he could be certain the pox had passed, and Lady Anna had sufficient time to grieve. Perhaps rekindle what might once have been. The soft sleeping robe she had given him long ago was worn silken as her arms had once might have been. He had written his godson, Florian, in England, at university in Oxford, with condolences. There were many loose ends to tie up, in time. But now he must launch his press. His vision of this venture would bring him power and money and he would do it for the greater glory of God, and ensure himself a fine place in heaven. When he prayed, it all fit. And he was filled with a righteous certainty of its good.

"Enough cold," he said to Mahmed. "Let us retire within, to the fire and hot wine."

Konrad turned, and the bodyguards that followed them everywhere were bent over trying to warm themselves. As soon as Konrad saw them they straightened up and walked with their right hands on their sword hilts, as was proper.

Minutes later, Konrad sat with Mahmed in front of the great hearth in the fortress gathering room, where a log burned with such a roaring heat that they were forced to sit halfway back in the room from the fire's orange glow.

Wine was brought on a silver tray with silver goblets, as was always done when Konrad came here, without asking. Konrad saw Mahmed glancing at the servant girl. He marked that. Mahmed was young to be away from women so long. That would be easy, to send her up to him.

"Now," Konrad said, "we were talking about you."

"Your printing press. You need good stories. How can I help?"

"The stars are boring, always there, you see? We need stuff that sells. At the same time, it must persuade. In order for us to lead, the minds of our people must be continually shaped to our purposes. Our folk are simple and easily distracted. They clamor for more, more, more. We must train them, as dogs are trained, indeed. For the good of Church and of state, one mind."

"I see."

"Do you? I trust so. That is good."

"Ask and I will do all I can. But not against Islam."

"Of course not against your own religion. Basil will visit you to collect tales. Of heretic and Jewish practices. The more lewd the better."

"But why am I supposed to know of such people?"

Konrad had decided this was the best way to use Mahmed. Trick him into telling tales of others, then write and print the tales as Muslim stories by a Muslim. If some good stories about heretics and Jews came forth, those could be used also.

Konrad said, "You are well-traveled. You are exotic to our people. I know there were heretics on the wagon train from the march. You were with them. We want their heinous beliefs, their sinful lecheries, their vile apostate tendencies. Of those things the public cannot get enough. The broadsheets of that kind sell like hotcakes, and those kinds of stories serve to enforce belief in the state and the Church. Then there are Jews."

"Was Christ not a Jew?"

"Do not dare debate with me. Christ was the son of God. You have the Jew infestation, and we have them, like nits from lice. They hoard money and lend it to nobles who protect the state from their like. Of Jew and heretic, we need all the obscenities and weirdness you can recall. Of stories of Muslims, our monks will supply those from things you do or say. We need all the rich tales that you can imagine."

Mahmed was staring at him.

"All I can imagine?"

"Yes, of course. Exaggerate. Your name will be famous for these tales. Help me help you."

"Those would be lies."

"It is not lies when the end result is truth. When the people are led upon the correct path. Are the stones of a path lies, simply because they are stones?"

"You lose me," said Mahmed. "I am confused."

Konrad had enough of being with this foreign dolt. His way of seeming not to understand was too irritating. He could have the worthless bastard shrieking the stories out in the chambers beneath their feet. But Lorenz would not have it that way.

"The world is changing and we who rule must now fight for the minds of our people who are the sheep in our care, our flock. Reading has changed everything."

"Is the truth not still the truth?"

"Would you be less confused," said Konrad rather casually, "on a board with a white-hot iron plumbing your ass?"

Mahmed said nothing. He blinked, staring.

Konrad said, "Do not look at me like a child. We are men of the world. You are a killer by trade."

"Forgive me, I mean no harm, my mind is so full."

"Let me help you," said Konrad. "You will pay your board and buy your skin, and if enough of your stories sell, perhaps a coin or two can be put aside for you if you wish to purchase a girl. Or perhaps your taste runs to another peculiar vice that might be brought in, with no harm done. In Wurzburg these days, anything can be bought. After all, I am a broad-minded man of education, and your customs are not mine to judge."

Mahmed just stared, as one condemned.

Konrad took a deep quaff of the hot spiced wine. He turned and saw Mahmed throw his head back and completely down his goblet, his beard and throat pumping.

"The Veritas Press for the People," said Konrad.

"The Veritas Press?"

"Mahmed, do you purposefully annoy me, repeating my words? The Veritas Press for the People. The name I have chosen."

"You call your press truth and I call myself righteous, and yet I drink wine now." Mahmed lifted his goblet for more wine and the serving girl came quickly with the pitcher.

"Then we have clarity, you and I?"

"There can be no doubt. I drink to it."

"Excellent. Let us never require harsh words again. You start tomorrow. I will send Basil to visit you. Be thinking. If we do not tell the people what to think, others will. So now you understand."

"I drink to Veritas," said Mahmed, downing the wine.

Later, Konrad instructed Basil to supply a steady measure of wine to Mahmed's quarters.

"If we cannot seduce his soul, dissolve his fiber."

The next week was spent with the monks who were chosen for their skill in letters.

First, Konrad had Basil summon them, nine monks in all, to his town mansion, and flattered them by treating them not as equals, but at least as salon guests. Half of them had taught literature or philosophy at Wurzburg University. All were bright and ambitious men.

Konrad's servants gave them good wine in silver goblets at the long table, and he paced, instructing them.

"Truth is that which works best for good. Therefore, Veritas. The name of our press. You shall create stories to motivate our people for the common good. Create, I say, not report. There must be grains of fact, yes, but each story must make the point we most desire. That the state knows best. The state works best. All who defy the state are evil. Because you are talented in letters, each of you put forth by Basil, you are the chosen few. You shall begin a new way of reaching the public. The truth requires all your talents to shape it to our dutiful purposes."

He saw the surprise on some of their faces. And he let this all sink in while more wine was served.

"Truth is good. Can any of you deny that?"

The nine monks shook their heads, none daring to speak. At the head of the table, Basil's head bobbed like that of a marionette, agreeing and eyeing the others.

Konrad paced slowly, leaning to peer into each of their faces in turn.

"Truth is good, I say. Therefore we must create good by creating our own truths. You shall bend it and use it with all your talents, and you shall make our views public, with great power to persuade. The public will bend with the will of your thoughts. Therefore, you shall from this day be called *publicists.*"

WITTER

Out of the snowy day, they had entered the dark cave of the smithy house, Witter resisting, and Merkel's big fist shoving him inside. The air in here was burnt, dark and bitter with char smoke. The clanging of hammered iron came from somewhere in the back.

Iron. Fire. Scorched air.

Oh God, deliver me...

Witter stood there in an open spot between an anvil and a bed of coals where irons lay glowing. Merkel took a pair of tongs and lifted one of the smoldering irons and held it up to inspect it. Seeing the hot iron, Witter felt himself sway, and nearly fainted.

"These are not flat enough," Merkel shouted to the back, where the hammering rang out. "They must be twice as wide when beaten out flat. Then fold each and weld it to the next."

"As you say, sir," came a subservient voice.

Merkel waved the iron at Witter and spoke.

"You will teach me to read and to write," said Merkel.

Witter just stared. Merkel's eyes followed Witter's gaze down to the yellow-hot iron smoking in Merkel's tongs, and Merkel suddenly roared with laughter, throwing his head back, laughing from deep in his big chest, shaking his head.

"Why else did you think I would bring you here? To roast you a little, play with you? Make you dance and sing?"

Witter had thought exactly that. He had been too paralyzed with fear even to run.

But he said, "No, to work in the smithy, I thought."

"A weakling like you? To work iron? No, to teach me."

Witter felt the insult first, that he was thought weak by this blacksmith, for Witter had become much stronger than he could have ever imagined. Then he realized the good news. It seemed impossible.

"You want me to teach you…to read?"

"And to write, I said."

"Yes, yes, to write." Witter's mind was reeling.

"What good is the one without the other, man?"

A timid voice in the back said, "I am Linhoff and I also wish to learn."

"You work, I learn," said Merkel.

"Sir, I can listen while I work, can I not?"

"Shut your hole, boy, before your brains fall out," said Merkel. "You want to apprentice to me, that is one thing, and because your father and me is friends since we was wet-ears, I say yes. But do not press me, or your ass will be gone."

"Forgive me, sir."

Merkel winked at Witter. "I taught him to call me sir. But you need not do so."

Witter did not have any idea what to say. It was as if he had been locked in a cage with a bear. Saying or doing anything might cause it to attack. Merkel leaned closer to him and looked him up and down as if never seeing him before. Then he nodded and smiled. His eyes gleamed in the dark coal-blackened face. His beard was singed, and this close Witter smelled the burnt hair of his head.

Merkel spat on the earthen floor. "If that damned upstart Lud can learn this reading, by God, so can I. Can I not? I make tools and hinges and horseshoes and scythes and hoes and anything else. Am I not a smart man?"

"Anyone with a brain can learn to read," said Witter. "It is the thoughts in the reading that bring more difficulty to some."

Merkel went to a cupboard and swept away iron tools on top and pulled open a drawer. His blackened fist pulled out a dozen broadsheets.

"I want us to read these. I want to know what others are saying and what is in the world. I will be the first to read. I got these from Klaus, the road peddler. He gets them in Wurzburg, but they might as well be cinder burns, for all I can make of them. I like the pictures, all right, but I want the stories to go with them. Tell me what they say."

Witter took the broadsheets.

"Secret Ways of Coupling, Jew Infant Sacrifices Revealed, Cannibal Escapes from New World Ship…"

"You shall not leave me behind," said another voice.

Witter turned and saw Sig standing in the smithy doorway. Snow flurried in past him.

"He belongs to me," said Merkel. "Go get yourself one of the others. They all know how to teach this reading and writing, Lura told me so."

Sig stepped in and Merkel advanced and the two men butted their chests together, arguing nose-to-nose.

"Out of my smithy before I reshape your thick head on my anvil," said Merkel.

Now Witter saw Kaspar, Sig's son, leaning on a crutch at the smithy door and staring inside. Behind Kaspar were two others, both young men Witter had seen working in the fields, Jakop and Max were their names.

"I wish to learn," said Max, pushing forward.

Witter knew that Max had been considered a jester but not since Max's mother, Brigita, the cheese maker, had died of the pox, and Max had not kept the secrets of the trade, did not want to make cheese, but tilled as a laborer. At the door, Max's eyes were deep with serious intent.

"We all wish it," said Kaspar.

Sig looked at the young men at the door, too, and Witter realized Sig was embarrassed.

Now Sig was nearly slobbering, so red was his face with a frustrated fury. "You want all knowledge for yourself? No. I shall learn with you. You will not better yourself, not over me."

Witter lifted his arms and they both looked at him.

"Listen, listen to me. We cannot do it this way, to learn we must have a class."

He thought how Maimonides had centuries ago laid down the famous Eight Levels of Giving, the laws of giving charity to poor people. As brilliant as these people were in the arts of their farming and their crafts, their insularity was astonishing. And if worldly knowledge were the ultimate wealth—and Witter believed that it was—these villagers were as poor as any people Witter had ever known. This would be the lowest level of giving, if he taught them, the eighth level of the "unwilling" charity. But it would be real *tzedakah,* charity his father would certainly approve of, if he taught them to read. And if he were truly willing, if he did it from love of mankind, the level of giving would rise much higher. Witter felt pride. It was strange to feel it.

Sig and Merkel were staring at him, Witter realized.

"A class?" said Sig.

"What is a class?" said Merkel.

Lud

How he would spend this winter, at first Lud did not know. He only knew it would be lonely in his little house. Often now he went into the house rafters and brought down the lockbox and took out the leather-bound volume. He opened it now, and inside were the blocks of words that he could partly read, but they did not connect into thoughts.

Then he realized this—that when he was with the book, he did not feel alone.

No, he could not read the words, except the little ones that connected other words and meant nothing. Still, there were illustrations—knights and ladies and other scenes of manners and family life, and only a little of weapons and war. He could not yet read the title. Each time he held the book in his hands he thought of that day in the Wurzburg bookstore with Dietrich, and Dietrich buying him this precious gift, promising Lud he would be able to read it someday. And to himself he swore, yes, he would.

You will see, Dietrich, I will read it...

The harvest work had gone late into the big moon nights and the yield was good. He had used Huber's method of tallying, marking sticks for Father Michael to make account for the sharing out. The bishopric's share from the estate was half. And the estate share was a quarter of what was left. The villagers divided the remaining fourth equally. Their own crops were laid by, and those with trades like the smith or the miller were comparatively wealthy men. The seed for next spring planting was laid by and carefully stored high in the estate barn from rats and mice.

There was enough. They had avoided disaster.

There would be no fights or hunger. Some barley was bundled and stored for animal feed. The beasts liked it less than wheat because of the hulls, but in order to fatten the cattle over winter, the barley got hulled and hammered so they would eat it. Sprouted in water, the barley made good feed for winter chickens. And when the head of a bundle was soaked, the grains sprouted in five days.

The sprouted barley had another good purpose. Making malt for brewing ale was a sport undertaken in every hut and house, and ale parties would go on through the winter as each brew came to a head and was shared out by all. That would be the next time of fights and secret couplings that led to more fights. Lud had to get ready for that, for in winter the steward must act sometimes as magistrate. A dead farmer could not till ground for next spring's crop.

After harvest came the festival, and Lud avoided it. For a day and a night, want and troubles were forgotten. The pox became a memory and most of the village was one merry crowd. Around the linden tree the square became one big elaborately decorated beer hall. No ox was roasted this year for none was too old to plow, and the crop had not been so full. But they gorged on roasted sausages and chicken and the big white radishes that women cut in fancy forms. He avoided it because there was no girl he wished to dance with, and if there were, he had not the courage to see her face recoil from his.

And the sharing out made him uncertain of how to regard himself, in this new aspect of wealth.

Lud was astonished at his steward's share. Added to the fifty gold marks from Dietrich, he would be able to own a house and a fine horse of his own. Father Michael assured him the share was correct. In fact, Huber had taken more than that, the priest said.

He had not learned much about reading and writing, but he could write his name and he could read a few words. Each day he recognized another word or two. What he had learned most was how to manage around those who wanted more than their share.

Some had heckled, some had flattered, some had tried bribes. He could tell who was a cheat in the tally by how hard they tried to get more than was fair. But more and more they were getting used to the idea that Lud was steward and would be steward until he died or was killed or ran off, and that was that.

The first snow hit hard. It came on a driving wind out of a black sky that soon was a whitening wall, howling. Then the storm settled on the land and came sinking down in a smothering silence. Giebel disappeared under a pure white sparkling blanket. Every house and hut became a white hump that sent smoke slanting into the winter sky.

He made sure that the outsiders, Grit and Dolf and Symon and Witter, got their sharing out, based upon their labor in Ruth's parcel. And when all the sharings were done, he wanted to get drunk. But he did not dare.

He never allowed himself to lose control now. He trusted no one. Their smiles and seeming acceptance could be a ruse for ambush. He slept lightly and held his dagger tightly as he slept. He was like a miser with his gold under the blanket instead of a woman's silky warm legs twined in his.

Never had he felt so alone.

Sometimes when he reported to lady Anna, he lingered at the castle for a glimpse of Kristina. He tried to time his visits with Lady Anna's reading lessons, which took place every day after breakfast.

Kristina's belly was big now, and when she walked her slender body tilted backward to hold the pendulant weight. Often she walked with her hands under the precious new life she carried. Lud—at those times, seeing her so—wished bitterly that it was his child she carried. Not a desire to bed her, but something deeper. To join with her life. That her life might purify the filth that he felt he was, like a stain on his own world.

All was well in the village, he reported to Lady Anna. He made sure enough firewood was cut to heat the castle fires and its kitchen, and water brought and ice broken where the stone walks were dangerous, and meat brought from the smokehouse, and sometimes wine from the casks in the cellars for Lady Anna.

Christmas came and went and Father Michael made a great show of the Nativity in his church, with many candles lit by villagers praying for this boon or that. On New Year's Day, Lud avoided the drunken revelry. He heard the music but he kept outside of it all. There were only a few minor brawls. Several of the boys who went to war went off with girls, and there would certainly be bans announced soon, and betrothals in the springtime.

There was nothing to do now but wait for thaw and the spring planting, when the moon would be in second quarter and the time for bearded barley to be sown.

Then, at last, Lud realized that something else was going on in the village, hidden from him, besides ale parties and couplings and suchlike.

In the village, at the smithy and also in the mill, there were covert meetings. At first he thought that the group of men who followed Sig and Merkel were plotting some plan against him. Kill him and promote to Lady Anna one of them as steward.

But it turned out to be nothing like that. It was even more unexpected, more astonishing.

Reading classes were being held at night and some even by day, when labor was done. At least a fourth of the villagers were trying to learn to read and to write. It was Witter teaching at Merkel's smithy, and Grit teaching at Sig's mill. And Dolf and Symon were living it up as high guests at every ale party, where the host wished to learn a word or two.

Lud realized that it was not a passion for learning, but a reach for status—to not be left below or behind as others climbed above.

Learning of this all, he went back to Father Michael and insisted his own lessons begin anew, with much more concentration. That winter gave him much time to devote to this.

The priest had a big fireplace in his stone room behind the church, and during lessons there Lud sweated in his woolens. The priest indulged not only in wine, but also in heat.

"You have started something," Father Michael said. "A sudden passion for learning."

"If I can learn anyone can learn."

"More, they all have a pent-up hope of a better life. In confessions I hear it all."

"Better how? This life is what it is. How can it be made better? There will be no more sun, no more rain, no more land. And no less want, no less troubles."

"But with reading comes the minds of learned others, and you can join their thinking. There will be more questioning, and that is not always good, but not always bad either. A villager has never had much learning after a craft was taught. The rest of life was using the craft to earn. Now, there seems to be this new idea. I find it remarkable."

"Where will it all end?" said Lud. "If with reading, anyone can better themselves beyond their station?"

Father Michael looked at him in his sad way, almost with longing of some kind, and did not answer directly, or at once. He rose from his bench and threw more wood into the big fire and drank more wine.

"When you can fully read," said the priest, "what will you wish to read?"

"I must be able to read all communications, all tallies, all accounts, and all decrees."

"Yes, but I mean...what books of thought?"

"Books of thought?" said Lud.

"Reading is more than tallies and letters."

He had not thought on this. It was a good question. Then he knew the answer.

"Every volume in the library of Dietrich, I shall read."

"And how do you wish to be changed by reading?"

"How did it change you, priest?"

"It made me less lonely, but...more unhappy."

"How less lonely?"

"I have friends in the books when I read."

"That I cannot imagine," said Lud. He studied the priest's face to make sure he was not being mocked. The sad gaze flicked away like a discovered bird.

"You shall understand," said Father Michael, "when you have learned to read and discover books for yourself."

"Why unhappy?"

"I had hoped for more, that knowledge would redeem me from who I am. But it has made me more of the same."

"Is that why you watch me with such sadness sometimes?"

"You mean a great deal to me, Lud."

"In what way?"

"I hope you will see the truth."

"What truth?" said Lud suspiciously.

"You yourself must see it, for yourself."

"Where is it found, this truth?"

Father Michael stood watching him with that sad lingering gaze that always uneased Lud. "Lead can be painted with gilt, but it is still lead. But sometimes there is love."

"Love? Love is truth?"

"Yes, Lud. Only that. Nothing else can last."

"Have you witnessed this love, do you know it?"

"Oh yes, I have seen it, prayed upon it thousands of times, but I do not yet know it."

Lud hoped that he did not understand, and they said no more of that. But he never forgot what the priest said. You are what you are no matter what. His thoughts were ever more tangled…

Dietrich said that reading is one way to search for truth. But what is truth? Is it not different for every man? Truth for the soldier who must kill? Truth for the priest who must pray? And if there is no truth to be found?

The year ended as ever with Christ's Mass, and the outdoor festivals of bonfires, and homemade gifts for sale, and hot wine. The children were excited, and the linden tree was festooned with candles and ribbons representing prayers from ancient times—secret pagan charms for fertility, good crops next year, and success in love.

Where is it found, this truth? Have you seen it?

During his reading lessons, sometimes he began challenging the priest about how thin was the covering of the Church over the heathen beliefs that set the crops and the harvest.

"The old crones still worship the linden tree, you know."

"When the new God fails them they seek the old ones," said Father Michael, surprising him.

A turn had taken place, little by little. The priest had softened, had relented his pedantic authority in the lessons. Lud felt a new equality with Father Michael that he did not understand. The priest seemed to actually respect him.

And in the spring there was more news.

It was on an early March morning, when the first birds were coming and the sun came out full and the ice hanging from all eaves and thatch ran with water, that he heard that, in the castle, Kristina had borne her child, and that it was a boy.

Kristina

Near time to deliver she had been getting up a half dozen times in the night to pass water, her feet on the wintry cold stones of the tiny castle room where she slept with Lura.

The reading lessons with lady Anna were shorter, for Lady Anna had birthed a child and sensed Kristina's distress. Kristina played the harp less often, too, even though that had soothed them both. The greatest change was that now she never went out and visited and prayed and sang with her brothers and sisters. Often, she asked Lura for news of them.

She prayed for Witter, and she thought how Berthold had cursed Jews for murdering Christ, and how she had retorted that Christ himself was a Jew. Sometimes she feared and wondered if Witter would be discovered, but he had not been.

Alone, in a fitful half-sleep on her pallet, she prayed for Witter's safety, and for Grit, and Symon, and Dolf. She prayed for Lady Anna and for Lura and for Arl and for all the villagers. She prayed for the priest and for Lud. She prayed for all who were suffering, all who were lost, all who were forlorn.

But more and more, she prayed for the health of her child. She felt ready to burst with such ripeness.

And then the pains began to cripple her, and Lura sat her down on a pile of bedding in the corner and lit a candle.

"Arl is trusted," said Lura. "She has whelped many, when she is not weaving, and her mother was baby catcher in her day, too, before the ague took her."

"Do you think she will come?"

"Arl? Miss a birthing? The way she loves babies? Ha!"

"Please hurry, Lura."

"I will be back soon, very soon."

And so Lura ran for Arl, and Kristina waited alone.

Waiting, Kristina's thoughts raced. Many times she had heard that what a pregnant woman saw might distort the body or bind the fate of her infant when it grew inside her. And though she resisted and indeed believed it superstition, fear overwhelmed her:

Will my baby be born with the cord around its throat, the way I did see Werner Heck hanging? Or will my baby be afflicted in the arm, for did I not see the great black dog tearing at Witter? Will its tiny throat be afflicted, for did I not see the baby's father, Berthold, bolted in the neck?

She had her eyes closed and her teeth gritted and felt hands on her belly and opened her eyes and saw Arl; Arl kneeling, looking sweeter than she had ever seen her look; Arl, who had lost both her twin boys Hermo and Fridel; Arl now firm and kind and steady, working with Lura to deliver her child.

Kristina prayed and did not scream in the astonishing waves of pain.

"Warm this room," said Arl to Lura, and Lura stoked up the small fireplace with split oak until it roared red-hot. "Go and fetch the birthing stool. And kitchen sleeves for both of us."

"Please, I want Grit," said Kristina.

Lura was gone and came back quickly, with wide-eyed little Leta bringing linens and kitchen sleeves and hefting an ornate, short-legged stool carved beautifully with the design of a woman with open, welcoming arms. Kristina had never seen it before.

"That is Lady Anna's stool," said Arl, pulling the sleeves over her arms. "The carving is Margaret, patron saint of childbirth. Did you ask?"

"Indeed, the lady sent it, saying she will never bear another child, with Dietrich gone from her life."

Arl and Lura helped Kristina up onto the short-legged stool with its open front seat, where Arl spread Kristina's legs wide, and Lura lifted Kristina's sleeping gown away, draping it over her back.

"I am here, Kristina," said Grit, kneeling beside her.

"We have enough with you two godsips; we need no more," said Arl to Lura.

"I will keep others out," Lura said.

Grit said, "We must stop up the window and keyholes and light all candles. Put straw under the birthing stool."

Kristina knew that godsips were women witnesses to birth who would tell of it later. In Kunvald they were called gossips, these women experienced in birth and close to the new mothering woman.

Grit began massaging her belly gently with warm olive oil. She smelled it, and knew Grit was soothing the baby.

"Leta," said Grit, "support her back."

It seemed that days passed, not mere hours, and the pain came in white-hot sheets and went away and came again, as if the world would never end. She was shocked at the intensity of the pain. Did her baby feel it, too? Did her baby writhe at each bolt of fire that made her writhe?

Lura held her hands and whispered sweet things in her ears. Behind Kristina, supporting her back with firm strong hands, Leta knelt, praying almost silently—Kristina could hear whispering, like the sound of bird wings fluttering.

When the pain was worst, Lura whispered, softly, over and over, "Only our Blessed Virgin conceived without pleasure, only she birthed without pain…"

After hours of pain and fear, Kristina began to pant, and her sweat poured. The hearth fire was kept going, and now she feared for her baby more and more. She could hear Arl and Lura and Grit whispering among themselves. Kristina heard how they sounded like lifelong friends now, sisters in birthing, women bonded in the new life they were helping bring forth, and she was comforted by this.

"All men," said Grit, "all come through the same door to this world, which is the body of woman."

"And they cannot wait to get back in," said Arl. There were snickers but Grit hissed impatiently at the jest.

Lura said, "Lady Anna has sent hot spiced wine and sweetbreads. On her own *desco da parto*. For refreshment after the birthing is done."

Kristina glimpsed an ornate tray, hand-worn with many polishings, and painted with cherubs.

"Look how fine," said Arl. "The lady wishes to help."

"In birthing all women are women," Grit said.

"Keep the wine jug nearer the fire so it will still be warm when the child comes," said Arl.

"But my baby, my baby, it will not come," Kristina said.

Grit said, "The birth is delayed. We must open drawers, open doors, untie knots."

"Yes," said Arl, "open all spaces to encourage the birth."

This was done, Kristina dimly realized, as she heard locks and bolts and the scrapings of wood, and then she smelled an herb being rubbed on her face around her nose.

"Coriander," said Lura, "to entice the baby forth."

"Chew this," said Arl, and Kristina tasted hot pepper in her mouth. Arl said, "It will help speed the baby out."

Hours more passed, and she saw the candles burn down and being replaced. With the casements closed, she knew not if it was day or night.

Suddenly, without warning, she felt a compelling urge to bear down. The quick urge came again and again, and with her pushing came the worst pain of all. She heard screaming and realized it was hers. The women were massaging, comforting, urging, all around her.

"Sweet child, sweet child," Arl kept whispering in her ear. "Sweet child bringing a sweet child…"

At last the baby came. She heaved and groaned and the baby burst from her body. Arl's hands were under the stool on the straw, waiting to catch him. There was a final molten pain and then the baby fell into Arl's hands.

"A boy," said Arl.

Like a dusky, blue, angry pup he shrieked and writhed, and Lura and Arl wiped him. They pressed him to Kristina's bosom. His hands and feet were purple, miniature, perfect.

Grit swaddled the red squirming infant in a washworn blue birth blanket brought by Lura. Kristina swayed on the stool and felt a surge of deep joy. Cradling her newborn, she smelled the blood and tears of his fresh new squalling life and she was panting and drenched and astonished and rocking on the stool. He was the color of earthworms turned by a plow. He was hers.

"Let us get everyone and everything cleaned up," said Arl. "Keep this room hot."

Lura reached for the birth cord but Arl stopped her hand.

"Shall we not pull the cord to drop the afterbirth?" said Lura.

"No," Arl said, pushing Lura's hand away from Kristina. "Never pull the cord. Such force can cause the womb to come down and terrible bleeding would follow. Many women have perished from the impatience of others attending."

Finally, of its own accord, came the afterbirth.

Then, Grit helped Kristina down onto a bed of straw in the corner and began to wash her with water from a bucket.

"Now the wine," said Arl.

A goblet was pressed to her lips and she sipped the warm, pungent tang of the wine. The life of the grape went warming deep into her, spreading everywhere.

"Let us give thanks and pray," said Grit.

Arl and Lura stood and stepped away.

"What words will you say?" said Arl.

Said Lura, "Who will you pray to?"

"To the One who made us all," said Grit.

Kristina felt Grit take her hands. She saw Lura and Arl stepping back, away, as if suddenly afraid.

"Dear Lord, may this child be blessed with good health, may he grow in the ways of righteousness and live in the peace of love and charity. May he never be afflicted by wrath, nor take up arms against his brothers. May he walk in the ways of our lord Jesus, and always on the path of love and good for others."

"Praise God," said Kristina.

"Praise Him," said Grit.

"And bless Lura, and Arl, these good sweet ones who have helped me so," said Kristina.

"Forgive me," Lura said, "I was afraid."

"Afraid of what?" said Grit. "That I might pray some heretical spell?" There was more pity than anger in her voice.

"We are simple country folk," Arl said. "There is no evil in your words. But all our lives we have been told to fear heretics and their influences."

Kristina felt a leaden weight of fatigue enveloping her.

"Let us say no more of this," said Kristina. "Please."

A few hours later, around the first light of dawn, Grit slept beside Kristina, with her baby at her bosom asleep, and Kristina woke, hearing whispers, recognizing Arl's voice and that of a man.

Kristina looked up; the priest named Michael came in.

"Lady Anna sent me, in fact, insisted I come for the sake of the soul of the new child."

The priest stood there looking shy. There was snow on the hood and shoulders of his dark cloak and he removed it.

She blinked, surprised to see him. She covered her bosom and he sat down in front of her on a stool.

Lura and Arl stood back, watching silently. She realized one of them must have fetched the priest.

He said, "I have come to perform the sacrament of baptism for your new child."

No, she thought.

It was primal and unreasoning, her mother's fear of him, and she did not want him here near her newborn.

"I see your face," he said, and his eyes looked sad. "And I know what you think. You want him to grow and learn to read and discover God's word for himself and then decide as a man whether he wishes to vow faith to Christ or not."

"How do you know that?" said Grit, her voice wary.

"I, too, can read," he said.

"Please, I am too tired," said Kristina, evasively, unsure what to say, how to avoid him without offense to Lady Anna.

The priest knelt, trying to see the baby, and he spoke gently. "I know you are teaching Lady Anna. And I know that others are now teaching villagers. I may be a drunk and a coward, but I am not blind."

Said Grit, "Why have you not denounced us? Or have you sent word to the outside?"

"Grit," said Kristina, trying to calm her.

"These are my people. As I belong to them. You serve here and so do I. I denounce none but my own weaknesses."

"If you did any denouncing," said Lura, "you would soon deal with Lud, and you know that, too."

"Without doubt, I deserve your rebukes." Father Michael said, and he winced. "But in truth, I am here because Lady Anna insists that Christ made it clear that baptism was necessary for your babe's salvation."

"When Christ spoke to Nicodemus," said Grit.

And Kristina said, "John, third chapter, verses one to twenty-one."

"How do you two know that?" said Lura.

The priest lifted his brow in surprise. "Indeed. You know it well. Let me persuade you that what I do cannot bring harm, and the villagers will bless you for it, and anyway, your son will be free to come to whatever faith he wishes in years to come."

"I mean no offense," said Kristina, "But do speak it in our plain language, not Latin, please."

"As you wish. His name?"

"Peter. For the apostle Peter, and that my child may become a bringer of light and hope. His father would have wanted that, I believe."

"Wonderful," said Grit. "Peter, oh yes."

So Kristina permitted the ceremonial christening. Grit, beside her, watched without comment, but seemed ready to fend off any unwelcome or unforeseen act by the priest.

"Amen, amen I say to thee," he said, "unless a man be born again of water and the Holy Ghost, he cannot enter into the kingdom of God."

The baby wailed at being sprinkled.

"Did you warm the water?" said Lura.

"Sorry, I should have thought of that." The priest bowed and gathered himself and his implements of ceremony, looking sheepish and pleased. "Kristina, bless you for accepting this. It meant much to me. Good-bye little Peter. May Christ bless thee with all good gifts."

When the priest was gone, Arl said, "He means well, though he is a coward and a drunk."

Said Lura, "Just as he himself said—not a very bad man, just not a very good priest. When I was a little girl we had a good one, as good as any saint, but mother said he starved himself to death, giving away his food to others."

Grit stroked Kristina's face and said, "The priest did no harm. May God bless thee both, mother and child, indeed, with all precious goodliness."

The baby mewed and wriggled close in Kristina's warmth. Again he was seeking her breasts.

Said Lura, "He wants back where he was, but he belongs to this world now."

"This will put an end to the rumors," said Arl, washing her hands in a bucket.

"Rumors?" said Grit.

"Nothing," Lura said, touching Arl to shush her. "Foolish talk from foolish tongues."

"I want to know," Kristina said, "what rumors?"

"Rest," said Grit. "You are too tired for such."

Kristina shook her head. "Let us have it all."

Arl shrugged. "That a heretic consorts with demons and would bear a monster of some kind."

"May God forgive such evil thoughts," said Grit.

"I did not say them," said Arl, offended.

Hearing all this, Kristina shrank back with her baby into the stone corner, the straw shifting under her. Into her hips now came mild cramps, and Arl seemed to read her mind.

"A little cramping will plague you still, but it is normal, God's way to restore your girlish waist."

But her fear now had resurged. Kristina thought of how they had feared Grit's prayer of blessing for the child. She lifted her sleeping baby and pressed its face to hers.

Please, dear God, protect my little son from the evils of hatred and fear, do not let him be infected with the violence of this place nor the ignorance that breeds evils, Lord, help me protect him...and save me from my own weaknesses, and from judging of others in my fears...

She lifted a hand and reached out to take Arl's hand.

"Thank you, and bless you, Arl."

Arl's face broke into a smile with pleased surprise, and Arl knelt and hugged Kristina, and then Grit and Lura embraced, and then all embraced as one around the newborn infant.

Said Arl, "When first you came, many of us feared you, wished you were gone. Now you are one with us."

Kristina struggled to make her passion into words.

"I do not know how to say what I feel..."

Grit said, "Only women understand what we know, for what we feel is beyond understanding."

Witter

More and more, there was a sense of permanence settling upon Witter. Living here in this illiterate abode of villeins was a new kind of parallel life. Here, where the reformers covertly sang their prayerlike hymns, and the village men and women squatted to openly pass dirt in the fields and sang bawdy songs while struggling with animals and plows and axes, he felt safer than he had in years, isolated on an island of ignorance and drudgery. At the same time, he felt ever more trapped.

Perhaps it was because he had attained a surprising new status. His reading class had begun, every late afternoon, before dinner, in the back of the smithy.

His father, Judah, had been a great teacher, and it seemed Witter had inherited a gift for teaching, too. The sense of expressing logic and offering it in digestible bits, one upon another, to make a full meal in the mind of the student, was a tantalizing prospect. And wonderful to behold, when the students understood, and lavished him with their gratitude. Here, in the land of the blind, he was one with sight, and more and more of them craved to see what he saw.

Sure, there had been fear in plenty—that critical test of village loyalty when the bishopric's wagons came through to collect the crop share from the estate, and he feared they would be denounced. Witter almost panicked and ran, but he was learning to wait and to watch, and that dread incident had come and gone without disaster.

He wondered how far to go with what he taught the villeins to read. Despite their lot in life, they were proud. If they ever learned too much and realized how unjust their lives were, there would be unrest. He had to avoid that at all cost, and stay with simple readings. Certainly he could not teach Erasmus or other such liberal works of enlightenment.

Since villeins had no rights except those granted by their lord (who had all power over them and received their labor as payment for the land upon which they lived and toiled for food) all depended upon whether a villein was born upon an estate with a good lord, or one with a bad lord. But apparently few wrongs had ever been practiced here. The villeins were even permitted to fish in the streams and hunt in the woods with snares and traps, unlike on any other estate Witter had known of before.

As the months passed, then a year, then two, and the same work, the same cycle of planting and reaping, the same festivals, the same people came and went, his fears began to give into the routines. No one was denounced, and it seemed that the villagers were all the same. They were born villeins, in bond to their lord, and were raised here and married and birthed and died here. They were all one. They fought among themselves continually, but when it came to outsiders, they were like a wall. The hard thing was to become accepted. Or, if not really accepted, at least ignored. For that, he knew, one had to become essential.

To read, to teach, to own the secrets others desire…

Merkel and Sig and others, one by one, began coming to learn, in the warm smithy after a day's work. Sig did not want Grit to teach him, for she was a woman. Grit had women for her own students now, and at night, she and Witter often compared methods, deciding which methods worked best.

"The men want to leap over the basics," said Witter. "They demand to know things quickly, and yet they cannot make those leaps, and each time I must help them make small steps, learning their letters one by one."

Said Grit, "The women are the opposite. Often I do not know how much they learn because they are too quiet. Too humble and shy. Then, when I have them write something out, often I find some have learned much more than I thought. And others have learned nothing."

"It is clear the women are more patient," said Witter.

"When ever was that not so?" said Grit.

Merkel welcomed the men to his smithy, for this association with Witter and with new knowledge obviously gave him more stature. Sometimes Merkel, or another, brought a big jug of ale to share. Sig, not to be outdone, brought fresh buns. When Witter told them each student needed a small slate and chalk, Reuben the carpenter became part of the class, for he brought roofing tiles of slate and broken pieces of carpenter chalk.

Witter had seen primers for literacy on sale in a dozen market square stalls in every big city, and so he imitated their simple routine of learning letters first, then memorizing the sounds of each letter, and then combining the letters into words.

The students complained bitterly that Witter wanted them to learn Latin. Grit told him she had the same problem with her female students. Nobody wanted to learn Latin. Then he heard that the priest was forcing Lud to learn Latin, too.

Over and over again he heard, "Why is there no learning in our own good language?"

"Because many lands speak many languages, but when men of many lands come together, they speak Latin."

"We do not live in many lands, we live here."

Then Merkel brought out a small cheaply printed book he had bought from a peddler years ago with no idea what it was, except that he had liked the woodcuts of knights and ladies and farmers. He brought it out for Witter to examine.

Witter recognized it: *Meier Helmbrecht.* It was an epic poem of the thirteenth century about a young dandy's attempts to become a knight and rise above his station, only to find that knights were reduced to highway robbery and hunting for bounty.

"It is in Latin," said Witter.

"Can you read it to us in our language?"

"This is not for entertainment, this is for you to learn to read and write."

"How many languages do you speak?" asked Sig.

"A few," Witter said.

"A few? Why more, when one will do?"

But they insisted he read it and so he did, translating into German as he went.

Then Sig the miller brought out a book, as not to be outdone. It was *Der arme Heinrich,* another old sentimental epic poem. This one was of villein life, about a virgin villein girl who sacrifices herself to cure a leprous knight.

Knights, thought Witter, *always knights. Always the sword swingers, but so rarely the wielders of intellect...*

This one was in German, not Latin.

So Witter sat on a stool and read to them from each book, and they sat around him like children and listened enrapt as if he were casting spells of great magic, and more than ever, they wanted to know how to read things for themselves.

They laughed when the fop put on airs and they wept when the girl tended the knight, and they stared impatiently, always greedy for the next hilarious or heartbreaking revelation of the story.

Little gifts of food, cloth, a comb, began to appear on the stoop of the house where Witter lived with Grit and Symon. Gifts from Witter's students and gifts from Grit's students. Dolf and Symon soon had their own students.

There was never reading or talk of reading or learning to read when strangers passed through the village. It was well known that in many other estates, learning to read was forbidden and punishable by law.

Increasingly, this angered those who wanted most to learn to read. The more they learned, the more resentful they became.

"Are we beasts," said Merkel, "that we cannot be trusted to learn? Did not God who made all things make us with a brain to learn?"

Said Sig, agreeing, "Knowledge is a tool, like any tool."

"What do they fear of us learning?"

Witter knew well enough what was feared by authority, but never fanned those flames, lest a fire rise up to burn him, too. If they could read they could one day perhaps see through the political structure that oppressed them.

Witter saw the impact of a little learning, as they began to learn the letters of the alphabet, and then put a few short words together. They were ever more anxious to learn.

At the forge, Merkel sang out the letters as his hammer rang in time.

Now Witter worked in the smithy and helped young Linhoff break charcoal into small cubes for the bellows forge. And with a charred stick he tried to teach letters and to help Merkel know how a certain mark could be a certain sound and how several marks could combine into sounds that made a word to be spoken.

Sometimes Merkel would go into rages and throw iron, unable to quickly understand. Sig might come by, bragging of a new word he had just learned, and this made Merkel become even more enraged.

"You must teach me harder," said Merkel. "Not all the village wants to learn. I am your friend. Others say only the priest should know letters. Some say the letters can be the words of demons just as easily as the words of saints. So teach harder, Witter, help me learn better. We will show the others what intelligence is."

Also, preserving the Sabbath days was always a problem, for Merkel thought Saturdays were days of work, good for teaching and not rest. Witter resorted to many excuses of health and invented miseries for himself. Then he would find somewhere private, even far-off in some field, to worship and pray alone. That was the one time he could most likely hear love in the voice of his father, Judah.

You are becoming stronger here, my son, in a way most pleasing to me... yet still you hide from the truth of who you are, and the others now under your care, they toil in blind ignorance, though you teach them to read...

In the fall when the villagers had their harvest feast, he had gone out alone to the haycocks to kneel and chant the Kol Nidre song as best he remembered it, to begin Yom Kippur, and then the Al Cheit prayer of repentance, and he had a life full of doubt and failings to repent.

He ate salt first and abstained even from water during the fast. He suffered and attempted prayer, and in his mind he visualized the Torah and read from it, all the while remembering the ones who had birthed him, who brought him into this world and were now murdered and gone.

He saw Grit and Symon and Dolf less and less now, and Kristina hardly ever at all.

Sometimes on rare occasions, and on Sundays, they gathered in the little house to pray and sing, but more and more they did not sleep there together. The village was taking them for their own. It was understood that, for now, they would keep their ideas to themselves. But they argued the point of life here, and the vows they had taken.

Witter did his best to steer these secret debates.

"For my baby's sake," said Kristina, "I have given my word to keep private faith, for now."

"But, when they become able to read," said Grit, "are we not bound to show them the Scriptures, for their souls' sake?"

Dolf said, "If they learn. Some are slower even than was I, and that is very slow indeed."

"Then we try harder and longer," said Grit.

Witter said, "But then there are all those who fear us, who fear reading, and who keep warning the others not to learn. Is it good to create dissent among neighbors?"

"No," said Symon, "but it is wonderful to share words with the ones who do wish to learn, and see their eyes light up. I, for one, never dreamed my life would have such importance to others."

"Nor I," said Dolf.

Witter saw where this was going, and did not like it. These rebaptisers had kept their heads low so far, because they were so terrified when they first came here for refuge. But now they were getting restless. They had not come all this way to teach reading without also teaching the Scriptures that naturally and surely followed.

He was not on the path they had all taken, with vows to pursue it to the end, even to a horrible death. But only Kristina knew this. Only she knew he was a Jew. He traded looks with her sometimes, and knew she would not reveal him. And he knew he had to try to redirect them, or at the very least try to delay them, from their urges of self-destruction.

So Witter said, "But those truths are in the Bible, and reading the Bible is forbidden, a crime punishable by death. Can we lead them to that end? Let each of them make that choice when the time comes. Assuming they even do learn to read. For now it is all the fashion, to say one is learning. But how many will follow through?"

"It could take years," said Dolf, "if ever."

"It took me four," said Symon, lowering his head sheepishly. "Four full years and still I am weak."

"How long does not matter," said Grit. "Christ is our light, and love must guide us."

"Love must indeed guide us," said Witter. "But many in the cities can read, and yet observe how they live, wanton and cruel and shallow, full of vanities and pleasures of the moment. Reading has certainly not been the salvation of most who have learned."

Dolf said, "Nor has it led to wisdom."

"Nor the stake," said Symon.

Witter said, "We need not expose ourselves for now. They will themselves discover the truths that they shall read, in time. So let us be patient."

Grit frowned. The lines of her eyes and her mouth reached and connected. Her eyes bore into him. "Each one needs to find his own understanding with God. Reading the Holy Word is the gateway."

"Not until they are ready," said Dolf.

"Then let us teach and be patient," said Witter. "And as long as we provide the learning they desire, we are safe, and the longer we teach, the more we shall be respected and the more they will consider us part of their lives and the village itself. After all, Kristina is under the command of Dietrich and has undertaken Lady Anna to teach."

"Very well. Teach and wait," said Grit. "In time, we will let them read for themselves, and then the Scriptures shall be self-evident."

So they voted and it was unanimous.

They prayed and sang and Witter felt relieved, for now.

Hanukkah came when the villagers were praying to their ancient linden tree and pretending to be good Christians. It became almost impossible then for Witter to make excuses. They wanted him with them in the church or in their revelry.

And Linhoff and his friends wanted more learning after work, and pestered Witter to no end. The young men cornered him when he was drinking water from the well bucket. He looked up at them, warily, and felt a crawling of sudden fear.

"What is it?" he said.

They traded deep looks, and Linhoff swallowed, obviously trying to frame his words carefully before speaking."Why should only the older ones learn to make out words and such?"

So that was it. Witter felt such relief. He dipped more water from the bucket and sipped from the wooden ladle. It was chill and musty but quenching.

Witter swallowed and said, "Stay ignorant, it is easier."

"No," said Linhoff. "It is not easier. We were told to go fight a war and we were boys and wanted praise and so we took the coin and went. Now we are home, those who live, and we know nothing. Less than before. Somehow we must make sense of all this folly."

"All of you wish to learn?"

"Max, Ambrosius, Jakop, Golz, all of us, even Kaspar."

"What good will it do you here?" asked Witter. They were glaring at him like hungry animals, as if they could tear him open and devour that which they craved from him.

Now it was Ambrosius who stepped forward. Witter dropped the bucket ladle and took a step back.

"Our whole lives are ahead of us. We do not trust the elders. Some want reading only for themselves. Others fear it. But we who are young, we want to read and learn a better way of life if we can. Or at least understand why things must be the way they are. We will bring food and gifts. Just say you will teach us, too."

Witter was beyond astonished.

"But it is impossible, I have no more time."

Ambrosius put his rough, red hands together and raised them in supplication. "All my life I have yearned to know how to read, since I first saw a priest staring at a book. I knew magic was there. Magic of thought and the secrets of life. I do not know what. If only I could read."

Finally, Linhoff pushed forward past Ambrosius.

"Your charcoal will be broken and gathered and your tool cleaning will be done. Make us a class just for us, Witter."

"I work, I already teach Merkel, I have no time."

Ambrosius knelt before Witter, as one kneels before a priest. It was embarrassing, and a little frightening, the urgency in the strong young face. And it was endearing.

"Witter, listen to me," said Ambrosius. "It can be at night, Sunday, any time you can spare us."

Said Linhoff, "The old will not bend easily, they break like brittle iron before they change. It is the young who seek new ideas, new ways. You need us to value you, as much as we need you to give us value."

Ambrosius was more earnest and Linhoff was brighter than ever Witter expected.

Staring at them—at their urgent waiting eyes—Witter thought of the ease of knowledge that had been lavished upon him by Judah and the other elders. So much knowledge had seemed a burden, an unfair responsibility. And here were these youths who begged for even a taste of literacy, which was merely the gateway to the thoughts of strangers. Witter knew he could not be the gatekeeper and keep that gate closed.

"All right," he said. "Very well then."

Ambrosius bent forward and took and kissed Witter's hands and Witter jerked back in alarm. His face burned. Suddenly, he felt ashamed, unworthy to harbor knowledge that he had not really wanted nor valued highly enough.

"You must study as I say," said Witter, becoming gruff and pedantic now, standing away from them. "Learning to read will require much time and diligence."

"Yes," they all said, "yes, anything, yes, yes."

They were humble before him and he felt the power of that, and the value of his knowledge, all that his father had poured into him, all that he had poured out like blood into dry soil, all wasted until now.

So, that was how it got started—the teachings of Witter to the raw young men who had survived the recent war.

For the first time in his life, he felt himself of great value to others. For the first time in his life, he felt he was beginning to try to live fully, as a man.

Kristina

The first three years of her child's life were filled with what seemed an endless series of incredibly beautiful moments. Suckling, toddling, the joyous first sounds, the delight in everything, learning to walk, sleeping together, and teaching all the things a little one needs to be taught. Lady Anna pretended to be annoyed by his cries and motion when she was near, but Kristina saw her secret delight in the new child's joy of life.

Several times a week Kristina found time to go with Grit to visit the frail and old, the widows, and the orphans of the pox. Arl gave woven cloth, and Lura helped by keeping Peter, and by giving bread from the castle kitchen when she could spare it. And all leftovers were saved in a gruel stew.

Said Grit, "We shall not preach to those afflicted, and thereby make them pay for our charity. Nor sing our hymns that boast of our sufferings and faith. Let us tend their misery and their hunger."

At such times they helped with whatever hard labor they could, cleaning out a house or washing or sewing or making charcoal. The little children worked alongside their folk, even the cripples and sickly, and their little bodies needed washing and picking of nits and lice, and their ragged cloth needed mended or to somehow be replaced.

Sometimes their ministrations were refused, for fear of offending the ghost of ancestors by strange rumors of heresies, but food was never turned away. Kristina saw the wisdom in Grit's admonition not to sermonize these visits, to let the work speak for love itself. And in time, they were welcomed.

"I hear praises of your charity," said Lady Anna.

Kristina steeled herself for anything. But the lady seemed pleased.

"I have waited to see whether you were devising means of influencing my people, but you have not done other than to help the weak and infirm. From now on, I will see that you have more to give them. It is I who have been remiss in charity, and I am obliged for you in demonstrating Christian love."

The reading went on with Lady Anna, and now broadsheets were turning up in the village. Kristina wondered how this was possible, until Lura explained it.

"Klaus, the road peddler, used to bring them for Father Michael, who was his only customer. But now Klaus has many more customers, and he does a lively trade. Thanks to all learning to read."

And now, also, broadsheets were coming down from Wurzburg with the drovers and traders bringing hard goods and supplies. Some looked tattered as if read a hundred times, others were packed like new. Most had crude woodcuts illustrating the words for those who could not read. The most worn ones were those most lewd.

Kristina was appalled at the wild tales they brought, filth and lies and trash to lure weak minds, with lust and spells and all the evils of superstition. Lady Anna soon developed a thirst for their sensationalized reporting of alleged news, and Kristina had increasing difficulty reading them without challenging the lies and half-truths. If she did, it would seem to be preaching, which she had solemnly promised not to do.

But one day Kristina could no longer hold her tongue.

It was a reading session in the antechamber and Lady Anna was excited. "What of this one, concerning a practice by the Turks, said to poison the souls of good Christians?"

Lady Anna had a broadsheet from Wurzburg, with the title "Turk Describes Evil Pricking of Christians!"

Kristina read it through. Her eyes widened. It was printed by Veritas Press and purported to be the confession of Mahmed the

Turk, prisoner hostage at Marienberg, describing warfare by pricking to infect Christians with pox.

"Lady, this is false. I know this Mahmed and tended his wounds."

"My god, you know this Turk? You know him how?"

She described to Lady Anna how Mahmed had pricked her, indeed giving her a light case of pox from which she quickly recovered. And how that had given her the immunity to be able to treat Lady Anna and others in the village during the epidemic.

"But," said Lady Anna, "my own cousin Konrad sent me this, from his own press. He does this instead of ever visiting me, I am sure. Though once he quite doted upon such visits. Now that my beauty is ruined, I doubt I shall ever see him again. But I will never forgive him for neglecting my husband's ceremony."

"I am sorry, lady."

"It is a lie?"

"Yes, lady."

"You say this knowing you may vex me and make me want to punish you?"

Kristina spoke quickly, before she might lose her nerve and her honesty: "It is a lie, and I have no gain to say so, other than to say the truth to you, to one to whom I am grateful and loyal."

Now Lady Anna paused to think, and Kristina felt Anna staring into her eyes as if trying to see what dwelled there.

"For what possible gain would such a lie serve?"

"I can think of only one purpose, and that is to create hatred and fear, lady."

"This pricking…it would have saved many lives."

"I can only say that it saved mine."

"Then this is a calumny, and harmful fear-mongering."

Lady Anna took the broadsheet and threw it into the hearth atop glowing embers; it caught in a flash and was gone, like a demon banished.

Time passed in seasons, as quickly as did the seasons in the rural life of a small estate peopled by villeins. The rotation of the seasons were mated to the rhythms of planting and harvests, and the festivals and ceremonies became a routine that was as dependable as the seasons taking their turn upon the earth.

But Kristina's child did not follow the set pattern of life.

Little Peter did everything later than other children. He was a listless baby, and while others walked by age one, some talking by age two, Peter lay in his swaddling and stared, and finally began to sit up.

Kristina carried her child on her hip about in the sun, when other toddlers were crawling in the damp dirt about the well where mothers carried buckets of dripping water. His hair was blond as flax, but by age two it was fast turning brown. His lips were full like Berthold's and yet his blue eyes were impish, nothing like Berthold's, the eyes of her mother, and he was himself in other ways; a strong delight in things that gleamed, like a cooking knife or the coals of a fire.

Kristina hoped that prayer would help him as soon as the child were truly able to understand and be taught the Scriptures.

She began with the hymns.

When alone with him, she played the harp and sang the forbidden hymns to him, but the little boy was so easily distracted. She wanted the hymns to instruct him, she wanted the stories in the songs to inspire him, but he grabbed at the harp strings, and he poked his fingers into her mouth when she sang.

Perhaps little Peter was too young. She hoped that was why he did not easily learn. It distressed her, how she saw other children in the village quickly learning other things, like how to chase and spin a barrel hoop, how to sing children's rhymes, how to play games with sticks and stones.

She prayed that she would be more patient with him. He was slow, very slow, in training to go outside to relieve his little bowels. She fretted as Peter became older and filled his pants. It annoyed her most that he could not read at all, and that he giggled and openly enjoyed her embarrassment when, red-faced, she had to clean him.

On a late spring morning she took him far out into the fields. When he tired, she put him on her back and bounced him along, making him giggle. It took two long hours, plodding in the rising heat past the tilled fields and new flowers along the pathways, beyond the flowering apple and peach orchards, to come to the place of Berthold's grave.

The little circle of fieldstones was nearly hidden now by daffodils she had planted two years ago. They were blooming late and had greatly multiplied already. Peter pulled at the yellow blossoms and tossed them at her. They ate bread she had brought, for the apples and pears on the trees were green. She sang hymns for Berthold. She gave thanks for the care with which Lud had buried him four years before. She prayed for Peter to be wise and to seek the truth.

Peter grabbed for everything. He was fidgety, always impatient to hurry to the next event in his new life.

We are here, she wanted to tell him, *to visit your father...*

But the child would not understand. And anyway, that would be a lie. Berthold was not here. She tried to imagine him walking with Christ, but that was a false feeling, like a painting in a church. She did not know what to imagine. But she felt he was not here. So, not knowing what to say that she could be sure was true, she just smiled and picked up Peter and carried him back home. There were years ahead when he would understand more. She hoped.

The seasons had crawled past when she had no child, but now they seemed to fly.

For all this time she and Lady Anna had struggled to read the little volume of Erasmus's *In Praise of Folly,* laughing all the way through at the hilarious mocking of pomp and vanity. Sometimes they were almost like two village girls teasing one another, and then they would catch themselves, and resume the old proprieties of rank.

Lady Anna had grown to love the harp and sometimes wanted Kristina to play and not even have reading lessons that day. Kristina was startled one day, when Lady Anna lifted a hand to stop the harp playing.

"What is it you are singing?"

"Singing?"

"Your lips are moving as you play that melody. What are the silent words you are mouthing?"

"Just a village tune. I forget," she lied. The stain of the lie sank in and made a blot of shame in her.

Kristina realized it was a hymn that she was almost making audible, and she tried harder not to move her lips.

At first, Kristina had kept Peter well away from sight of Lady Anna, but then during reading lessons, Lady Anna began to send Lura to bring the boy. And it was obvious that Peter was a delight. Lady Anna insisted little Peter wear the finely sewn linen and woolen toddler garments saved from her own child, Florian.

And Anna spoke proudly of Florian, now a young man of age and still away in England, learning law, to become a lord of letters, perhaps even in the court at Vienna.

Four times a year, as if also governed by the seasons, Florian's letters came from England. They always arrived in a fine leather rain wallet, brought by horse courier from the Wurzburg Bishopric. Always there was an outer missal, a brief note from Prince Konrad von Thungen, the boy's godfather. The letters were forwarded through diplomatic channels and bore Konrad's green wax signet seal over another red seal underneath, and had obviously been read and sealed twice.

Lady Anna would first quickly read Konrad's note.

"Again he asks to pay me compliments. Again we must write to refuse. You must help me word it well."

"What do you wish to say?"

"Understand that Konrad is Florian's godfather and my cousin and as a young girl he was always so fond of me. He was against Florian ever going to England, fearing a liberal education there, but that was Dietrich's desire for his son, so Konrad may argue with me to bring Florian home before his education is finished. That I shall not do. And Konrad cannot ever see me again, not disfigured as I am. Yet in refusing Konrad, I must not give offense. He will be the proper one to promote Florian at court, when my son's full maturity has ripened."

"Shall we begin, lady?"

"No, let me first read my son's words to his mother." Lady Anna broke the seal with an intense anxiety. "Help me where I falter. Please God, it be good news."

Kristina always assisted Lady Anna in reading the letters. This one was even more difficult. The fashion in handwriting was becoming ever more elaborate and floral. Florian's letter, with its many juvenile flourishes, took much time to decipher into spoken words.

"Dearest Madam, Mother, No day goes by without grieving for my father and my regrets that I was not at home for you, nor home now for you. As heir to the estate, I am now on the verge of manhood, and yet my studies carry me forward into the very future of the thoughts of mankind. England is astir with law and philosophies and sciences and discoveries. My mind wakes as one reborn."

Lady Anna stopped Kristina. "What would he mean by that do you think? What philosophies?"

"I cannot rightly assume what your son would mean."

"Read on, please."

"No one can even imagine where humanity is going, but it is forward, I can assure you of that. Upon my return we shall do things differently than before. My father insisted I be educated here, and I did not want to leave my home, but now, for his foresight, I am blessed, as I pray that in some glorious day to come, all shall be blessed, all equal, all sharing the honor all men are due."

Always, Lady Anna would be perplexed over Florian's letters, as they took more and more of this tone.

"All men equal? How is that good law? How can all be equal?" she said. "How can all be blessed equally? Is there not a right structure to things?"

At first, Kristina did not answer.

Said Lady Anna, "I asked you a question, I expect you to answer. Do not hold back. Give me honesty."

"In the eyes of God," Kristina dared suggest, "are not all equal in His sight?"

"Did God create men so? Is the tiller equal to the knight? Is the priest equal to the bishop? How can all be equal to God when God has created all unequal, giving power to those who rule and obedience to those who serve?"

Kristina was overflowing inside, but held it in check.

"I see," said Kristina, for she had learned evasion, and when to say no more.

It was unsatisfying. But safe. She had to live here and she had a child to protect. The lady would demand honesty, and then often she would punish it.

"What I wish to learn most," said Lady Anna, "is to write my son letters, in my own words, so that I may address his letters from England. I do not wish to question his ideas as impossibly unsound, though they seem quite odd. You must help me answer cleverly, to learn more of his mind."

That was how, in the fourth year, they began to write the letters, together.

Lud

Three years of good harvests. A dozen marriages and a crop of babies, and good times. The pox was a receding memory, and the village again was prospering. Yet in all this good luck, there was one truly fundamental change.

Reading. There had become divisions among the people: those villeins who could not read, those learning to read, and those who could now read. And between were those who were against reading and those who were for it.

New broadsheets began coming down from Wurzburg, sometimes with passing peddlers, sometimes brought back by a returning grain shipment. Lud dreaded each new one, for they were designed to stir up trouble.

The worst ones came from Veritas Press in Wurzburg, and Lud had enough reading sense now to work his own way through them. Even with all he had seen in this world, he could only marvel at the audacity of their lies.

Each one always had at least two sensational stories. One would feature monstrous practices of Turks, supposedly revealed by the Turk noble taken hostage in the late war. The other would expose shocking secret evil ways of heretics, sometimes including titillating sexual deviances. They were reported from signed confessions of the condemned.

The trouble was, a number of the villagers now could also read the broadsheets. And there seemed now an unquenchable thirst for each new one that came. Even when several copies came along, those would be worn out from being passed on and on and on, from one to another to another, sometimes resold for more than their original cost, so that passing peddlers and travelers were constantly badgered for any new printings from the city.

It was late spring and the seedlings were up in the fields, the crops well under way.

Lud sat on a root of the linden tree, reading the broadsheet he had bought that day. Crows cawed somewhere as if mocking him. Or what he was reading.

"Bats Fly From Heretic's Mouth When Burned!"

He read it over and over, to make sure he was not reading it wrong. Later, passing the smithy, he heard Merkel and Sig arguing about the same broadsheet.

Sig said, "Heretic at the stake. Heretic is being burned, you see, and opens his mouth to yell for Satan's help, and demons fly out of his mouth in the form of bats. You see now? Satan triumphs again. The demons fly to find another victim. Myself, I sleep with my mouth closed, or covered."

And Merkel said, "You miss the point, Sig. The demons that possessed him and made him do heretical things, they fear fire and took flight as bats and abandoned him. Satan was no help at all. His demons can be defeated."

Sig said, "I go to Mass every Sunday. I did not see you there all this month."

Lud spoke, surprising them. They had not seen him. "So how do you know these heretics? You have to burn everyone and see if bats fly out?"

"It is in print," said Sig, "read it for yourself."

"If it is printed it must be true?" said Lud.

"Lud," said Merkel, "you know how to read, a little, I grant you that. And you have been fair as steward so far, and that surprised everyone. But do not play the wise man with us, we who have known you all your life."

"Your teachers, Witter and Grit, and Dolf and Symon too, and Kristina who teaches Lady Anna, we are bound with them by Dietrich's word. And have they harmed us?"

Merkel said, "None has said so."

"As long as they speak no heresies," said Sig.

"What evidence of heresy has ever been seen?"

Merkel frowned and said, "None. Except they can read."

"Many can read," said Sig.

Lud said, "Only Kaspar has ever called them heretic, and he heard it from some other fool on the wagon train, no doubt."

"Truly, they have done no wrongs, and even very much good," said Sig.

"Has Father Michael ever spoken against them?" said Lud. Sig and Merkel traded a look.

"No," said Sig, "but he is a strange priest, anyway."

Merkel said, "Father Michael speaks more of his own weaknesses than of ours."

Now, from the back of the smithy, Lud saw Linhoff emerge from the shadows, his young, sooty face peering at a distance.

"So if this story is believed by some in our village, what will you say?"

"That bats would only be found in the mouths of true heretics," said Merkel.

With that, Lud left them, shaking his head in wonder at how such men could learn the elaborate crafts of smithing and milling, and yet be as dull as the stones in the village wall. Then he realized that Linhoff had come along behind, catching him.

"That bats," said Linhoff, "would be found only in the minds of fools."

Lud looked at the young man. He had taken him to war and back, and now he was steward and Linhoff apprentice, and again Lud was in the superior role, not to mention that, man to man, Lud was stronger in a dozen ways.

"You are learning to read," said Linhoff.

"Trying."

"I also. And some of the others who were on the march with pike. I wonder where it will all end? The big men in the village, I think, want reading only for themselves."

"Maybe they're afraid you will get ideas. In many places it is illegal to learn reading. Did you know that?"

"No." Linhoff looked shocked. "But I only wish to better myself."

"To better yourself means to rise above your station. That means to rise above others. Learn if you will. But keep things to yourself, and never brag."

Linhoff smiled, and was off. They did not speak of reading again for a long time.

It was in the winter of the third year of his stewardship that Lud, with no help from Father Michael, finally was able to parse out the title of the book that Dietrich had gifted him. The priest drank more now and seemed to try to avoid Lud, often making excuses to skip their lessons.

Handbook of a Christian Knight by Desiderius Erasmus...

The title alone paralyzed him. Why would Dietrich taunt him so? Did he expect him to aspire to knighthood somehow? It was like a slap in the face from one now long dead, one as revered as a father ever was.

He rode the wintry fields and woods on Ox, and pondered this for days. He sat alone in his house and built up the fire, and one night he drank ale and wept and loathed himself for the self-pity that was foolish.

If Dietrich had wanted him to live the life of a knight, why had he not raised him so? Was this gift book—precious as it was—supposed to take the place of a life of learning from others?

A knight was only one step on the social ladder below a lord. He would have been taken into Dietrich's house, the castle home, at the age of six or seven, and raised there to become a page boy to serve Dietrich himself. He would have had basic education under a hired tutor, and lived seven more years under Lady Anna and her maids, who would have taught him courtesies, dance, dress. And at thirteen or fourteen years he would have become a squire to Dietrich, hunting with him, riding, hawking, serving at jousts or if the knight went to war.

Then, like Florian, he would have been sent off for higher education. But that was not his fate.

He thought how bright little Florian had been, how he could be taught something just one time and he got it, and never did he forget. He had helped Florian learn the ways of horse and hunting by age eight, of tracking and the bow and snare and skinning, and how to fight with bare hands and with a knife, and how to grapple and how to fight to kill and how to fight to not kill. The child was a quick learner and did not whine when hurt.

Florian was like a son to Lud, like the sons he had lost when the pox took his wife and children. All the rough things of life and survival that Dietrich wanted little Florian to know, the bestial things, Lud had taught him.

Lud adored the fine-spirited boy, and had loved every minute of every day with him. But then, at last, Florian was brought into the castle and tamed—dressed up, practicing dance and courtesies. He missed little Florian then, and heard from Lura and the other serving maids how the boy took to castle life, reading everything in Dietrich's library. Learning.

Then came the day when Dietrich took his son away, and Lud had not seen him since. Dietrich returned, months later, and explained that his son was in England, off to some green wet island of fogs, far from here. Everyone in the village knew it was the ambition of Lady Anna that Florian become a fine lord, a creature of the court in Vienna perhaps.

There was a celebration at the castle, with free ale in the village for the villeins. Lud heard from Dietrich that a young daughter of some lord, named Barbara, had been promised to Florian when both came of age. Lud hoped Florian would not become a noble too educated for life here in the raw countryside. But such bookish and mannerly things could be learned at Wurzburg University, and no one understood why Dietrich wanted to send Florian so far away to be schooled.

So, Lud missed Florian and the times they had adventured together in the woods, almost like father and son, or, like he had sometimes fondly imagined, the elder brother and the younger, under the eye of Dietrich. But Florian had been gone for years now.

Who knew what he would be like when he returned. And besides, he would return as master, not man.

Lud passed his winter days in such reverie. His moods rose and fell like the winds outside. And his sense of dismay grew like a festering thorn. Thinking on all this, he realized he had indeed been raised as a knight, but only on the manly side. Dietrich had taught him all those things a man should know, but the education and the courtesies and all the niceties were lost on him, and he had never been welcome inside the castle by Lady Anna.

All this came crashing down in a single revelation, and Lud—confused, angry, and wounded—fell to reading the book with a voracious appetite, as if the pages held all the secrets that Dietrich had withheld from him in life.

So that winter he began to read, and it all began to fit together, and he read and read, and it took him a full month to find his way through the first page of the book.

The thoughts in the book surprised him. He had expected them to be obtuse, complex. But they struck him at once as thoughts so much like those of his own, the private thoughts he had kept to himself, the thoughts he most doubted…

"The life of mortal men is nothing but a certain perpetual exercise of war: as Job witnesseth, a warrior proved to the uttermost and never overcome. And that the most part of men be overmuch deceived…"

This monk Erasmus compared the life of a man to that of a juggler, and this idea Lud wholly understood. Some of the thoughts made him laugh out loud as he read. Lud found treasures again and again, so much in agreement with life as he had already observed it. His reading kept improving as he pried the words from the pages, one by one…

"…whose minds this world as a juggler holdeth occupied with delicious and flattering pleasures, which also as though they had conquered all their enemies, make holiday out of season, none otherwise verily than in a very assured peace. Peace, peace, and yet there is no peace at all."

This passage alone took three full weeks to work out, from Candlemas through New Year. He was confounded.

Was this what Dietrich wished him to discover?

And if so, what else was in the book? And why had Dietrich told him to find truth? Was truth to be found in books? If so, how?

Then one evening, late, Lud felt himself overcome with the need to know more, much more, and he could wait no longer to dig the words and meanings out for himself.

On a snowy night he stomped through ice-crusted snow, his head bent into a knife-edged wind, with the book inside his cloak as if it were a shielded newborn, and he took the book to the church.

Lud expected to find Michael in the priory, passed out, vomit on his surplice. But he was not there.

He found the priest in the sanctuary, on his knees, praying under the wooden Jesus whose pearly eyes followed one everywhere. Lud's footfalls on the worn stone floor were nearly silent, but the priest seemed to sense him there. He lifted his head, nodded, and smiled. Perhaps he, too, had been alone too much and welcomed any company, even a pockmarked beast of a man like himself.

"Come take hot wine with me, Lud. It will be my first of the day. Come, back into the priory."

The priest threw some split wood into the fireplace and the embers smoked and sparkled into new fire. He filled a clay jug from the warming pot on the iron ring at the side of the hearth and poured out goblets for them both.

Lud drank. The spicy wine was rich and burned a welcome path into his chill.

He considered this man, no older than himself, who seven or eight years ago had replaced the old priest under whom Lud had grown up in this village. The old priest said little and mouthed the Latin and was kind and dull. Nobody wept much when he died, and Lud had a thin and faded impression of that man.

This Father Michael was very different. It was rumored he was sent here to a dead-end rural village as punishment for some insubordination at a higher-rank monastery where he had taken his learning to become priest.

"Good wine," said the priest.

"All wine is good," said Lud, "when you can get it."

"You dislike me. May I ask why? I can think of many reasons. I just wonder which it is."

"Dietrich liked you."

"We saw eye to eye on many things."

"Perhaps I am a little jealous."

"Perhaps, Lud, he liked me. He loved you."

Lud looked at him and said nothing. He wanted to ask, *did Dietrich tell you that?*

But he did not dare. He let it lie, as it was said. And the priest drank and watched him, also saying nothing now.

Then Lud carefully brought the book out from inside his cloak. It was in its leather wallet and he handed it over to the priest.

Father Michael took the book with great reverence and opened it gently.

"Erasmus," said Father Michael.

"Do you know it?"

"I love Erasmus. And such a beautiful binding, and the print is crisp, deep, lovely."

"You have read it?"

"This and others. He wrote more than one book."

"And you have read all?" Lud felt dismay.

For the first time today, the priest smiled.

"Yes. Many times, all. You seem disappointed when I say that. Is it because I am not such a good priest, or man, and you find that reading has not improved me?"

"Yes. You read my mind." How could the book hold such truths if this man had read it and yet had remained as he was, this sorry excuse for a priest?

The priest winced, as if Lud had reached out and touched him.

"Lud, please do not judge. You do not know me, yet you think you see me clearly."

"I think not on you. I am here about the book."

"Tell me about this wonderful book. How did it come to be in your hands?"

"Dietrich give it to me as a gift. He told me there is truth inside. That I must learn to read and to find that truth."

"And you kept it a secret from me all this time you have been learning to read?"

"Yes."

"I see. You did not wish to share such an intimacy that Dietrich bestowed upon you with this gift."

"Tell me what it says, all of it."

"You have tried on your own?"

"It takes too long."

The priest looked at him, long and deeply, and with boldness that Lud had never seen the priest display before. With the book in his hands he seemed a larger man, a stronger man, a man of conviction, suddenly transformed from the drunken coward Lud had always thought him to be.

"I am beset," said Father Michael, "by diverse enemies from above. Inflicting upon me struggles...wrestling with my own corruption. Do you understand me, even a little?"

Again there was the old lingering gaze. Lud felt it strongly, as if the priest were trying to touch him.

"Enemies?" said Lud. "From above?"

"Yes."

"You say God is your enemy?"

"Listen, and hear what Erasmus is saying."

The priest sat up more straight, and ceremoniously, he flipped through some pages of the book. He paused, and then he read:

"Behold over thy head wicked devils that never sleep, but keep watch for our destruction, armed against us with a thousand deceits, with a thousand crafts of noysances, which enforce from on high to wound our minds with weapons burning and dipped in deadly poison... except they be received on the sure and impenetrable shield of faith."

The priest paused, and Lud said, "There are plenty of enemies here, enough to go around."

The priest closed the book, and looked at him. He seemed to be waiting for Lud's reaction.

"What does it mean?" said Lud.

"Do you know why I have not reported that there are people learning to read? Or that there are those teaching reading, possibly heretics, here in our own village? Do you know why I have not reported this to Wurzburg?"

"Because Lady Anna has forbid it."

"The Church is my order, not Lady Anna."

"I could cut your tongue out, then your throat."

"Yes, there is that, too. But fear of you nor anyone else is not why I haven't told. My fear of life is far greater than my fear of death. You might be doing me a favor."

Lud felt a queasy notion, his mind seeing the throat where the edge of a blade so easily slipped in to steal a life. Such thoughts were always unwelcome. But a man back from war must expect to suffer them, and always be alert to quickly smother them with other better thoughts.

The priest said, "But you need me to help with your reading, and to tell you what is in this book, and others, in time."

"Why then have you not told?"

"There are many wrongs. More than rights. There is a great imbalance. You do not know this, but Dietrich and I spent many a long night sitting up with wine or ale and wishing together for a better world. Imagining how that world could be. How it could take shape and become. The only way we ever agreed upon was through the banishment of ignorance. And that could only come from learning."

"I had no idea."

"We read the same books. Our beliefs were the same. But he was brave and I am not."

"The banishment of ignorance, you say?"

"Dietrich would say that all evil comes from the desire of men to control one another. I would say that all evil spawns from ignorance. We often debated this, and many times by dawn we agreed that the two were somehow much the same."

"You must share with me everything about Dietrich."

"Must I?" Father Michael threw his head back and downed his goblet, and Lud watched the priest's gullet oscillate with the bony lump bobbing at each swallow, his white flesh exposed under the fringe of beard.

Then the priest dropped his head and leaned over toward Lud. He spoke low, as if spies might be listening, and he looked silly that way.

"Yes," said Lud. "You must."

"Very well, I shall show you some things."

The priest went to a wall closet and opened it and brought papers from a shelf. He laid them out on the bench.

"What are those?" said Lud.

"Lies, mostly. The Veritas Press at Wurzburg. The monks who create such inventions are now called by a new name, 'publicists.' Their mission is called 'propaganda.' The word once meant to dispel lies, but now it functions as the opposite—to create illusions in the collective public mind. And those so-called publicists are making a great success of telling the lies to anger people. It only works with ignorant people with little learning. People who have only learned how to read, or how to hear others read, but not how to think. No doubt the publicists mean well. They may even believe they do God's work."

Lud picked one up. There was what looked like a horned beast in a turban riding a fire-breathing horse. Lud could not read all the words.

"Turk…secret…devil-something…?"

"Turk Secret Devil Worship Sacrifices."

"What does that mean?"

"It says that the Turkish hostage, a Muhammadan, has revealed the loathsome practices of making war to seize innocent Christian children to sacrifice to their God, whom they call Allah, which is a secret name for Satan."

"That is absurd."

"Is it? Yet here it is, in print, given out as truth. The Veritas Press. How can it not be true? It goes on to make the case that new taxes are necessary, so that the border regions can be assisted by mercenaries."

"New taxes?"

"That is what it says. We village priests are to collect even more new bishopric taxes from those we are sworn to protect and save from evil. Lud, do you not see the necessity of new taxes, when monsters are threatening our children?"

Lud heard the tone; knew he was being tested.

"Turks are men. I have fought them enough to know what they are—the same as me. Stop being ridiculous."

"When life itself is ridiculous, a little humor protects the truth. And the truth is, you do not wish new taxes? Are you not loyal? Do you not love your country?"

"I am loyal to my own. Do not insult me, priest. I dislike mockery."

"Mockery? Are you doubting the Veritas Press? Are you a Turk lover?"

Now Lud stood suddenly, his face stinging with fire. He stood so abruptly that the bench tipped backward with a boom on the floor stones. Father Michael gave a boyish grin, a grin of delight in baiting Lud, and Lud knew it, and it angered him.

"You want to hit me, cut me, make me shut up," said the priest. He said it with a kind of triumph, as if proving a point.

"Yes." Lud stood trembling, forcing his hands down to his sides. The priest swayed lightly before him.

"The very words on that paper make you furious."

"Yes."

"That, my friend Lud, is the power of print. A mere piece of paper. Words printed upon it. And your rage."

The priest, having made his point, sank down onto his bench, apparently exhausted by the effort.

"Of course," the priest went on, "there must always be a grain of truth upon which to base the larger falsehood, lest it be denied. They cite testimony they say is by the hostage Turk Mahmed. Who knows whether he said any of it, or perhaps one shred to exaggerate?"

"What part of it is truth?"

The priest laughed. "I wish Dietrich were here to laugh with us now. Yes, Turks do sometimes invade and make war. So do we attack them and invade and make war. They probably lie about us being devils, too. This is how you make people hate. You make them fear, first. Then the hate naturally comes, as night follows day."

Lud sat thinking on it all.

"What is in the other papers?"

"More of the same, with variations on the theme. Some about heretics. Some about Jews. Always the same, that the state and Church protect us from terrible evils, that they know more than we, terrible things, and that we should be grateful to send our young men and our grain and our labor into their keeping, to protect the good. To keep the world safe for Christ."

Lud felt dizzy with it all. His mind reeled back to so many rumors on the marches to war, and how evil the Turks were said to be. He thought of Mahmed and his civility and courage in capture. He wondered what they were doing to him to extract such tales.

"Forgive my anger, priest."

"I meant no harm."

"It was that you mocked me. Taunted me. It is not just since I had the pox that I react so quickly. From being a boy without a father, perhaps, as long as I can recall. Always I was too proud, with no reason why."

"They say that pride makes a fine breakfast but a poor supper. I lost mine long ago. Or perhaps I hid it and can no longer remember where."

Lud saw that the priest had confessed something rare and precious to him, and he felt compelled to give something back of equal value.

"Sometimes," Lud said, "you fight with nothing left but pride. It sustains us. Whatever fight we are in."

Father Michael paused, and Lud saw that he thought long before speaking.

"When the people of this village have learned to read, and they read lies, what will they believe?"

"Dietrich said we must learn to think."

"Lud, listen." Father Michael's eyes blinked, and he spoke with dread. "When they learn to read, and they read truth, what will they believe? What will they do? If they indeed learn to think, how will villeins' minds react to the truth? Will they rage and rise up against their own?"

Lud felt the thoughts slam into his mind like rams battering against a great door, its hinges bursting.

"What would make them do that?"

"Lud, when you have filled your mind with all the reasons you discover, why things are the way they are, what will you do about it all?"

"What will I do? Who am I to do anything? I do not understand. You twist my thoughts, priest."

Now Lud saw fear in the face of the priest, fear of Lud. And Lud realized his own stance appeared aggressive, and that he had placed a hand on the thin, bony, robed arm of Father Michael.

The priest had pulled his arm away as if burnt. He cringed back from Lud. Father Michael lifted both his hands in defense, as if expecting Lud to strike him down.

"Forgive me," said Lud. "I mean no harm, but never twist my thoughts so. How do you mean, the way things are? What would I discover in reading that I have not already seen with my own eyes?"

The priest would not now look at him. He averted his eyes, and Lud felt hideous, remembering his mask of scars, thinking at first this is why the priest looked away. And yet he knew somehow that that was not true.

The priest said, "It is probably from too much wine. If you will forgive me, I am to bed."

Life was always like that. It was dangerous to become too close to another person. One weakened by loneliness might reveal too much.

Then, later, Lud lay in his own straw bed, alone in the dark, alone with his heartbeat, alone with his loneliness eating him alive, confused, alarmed, with a sourceless regret. He was as much a loveless monk as was the priest living alone in the stone cell of his church.

Thinking of Kristina did not soothe him to sleep, not as it sometimes did. Caressing himself and thinking of her that way only filled him with self-contempt and increased his loneliness, always leaving him emptier than ever before. If he enlarged his mind perhaps he could win her that way, he sometimes dared to hope.

Dietrich had loved him and believed in him. Even if he did not love himself, nor believe himself capable of anything much, he would try.

And so he vowed to work harder to learn to read, for Dietrich had told him it was the key to everything he must be, and everything he could ever become.

Witter

It was when many in the village had learned the crude basics of reading and writing, and when they could themselves, alone, read basic words and begin to piece together meanings from large blocks of print, that the troubles began to happen. And with the troubles came the first terror.

Witter had allowed himself to fall into a kind of pleasant suspension of wariness. Years of living as a hunted animal had worn him out. Living here, teaching his literacy class, reading the old epic poems with his villager students, seeing them learn to read and write their names, becoming a valued person—a teacher—enjoying the respect of those who were lowest of the low in rank, all had made him feel cherished.

His class continued to gain members, outgrowing the back of Merkel's smithy, moving over to the grain barn of Sig's spacious, musty mill, where people brought their own small stools and benches to sit around the big heater that dried the grain to warm winter days and nights. They sometimes brought a run of ale to smooth the classes.

Grit's class had grown, too, from a few women and youngsters, to nearly filling the big room in the back of Arl's weavery where the looms stood to one side.

When they compared their classes, always some things were certain. All the students were slowed by the slowest learner. But most were learning, except a few who quit in frustration, saying the low were not meant to learn the high things like reading.

Witter had never expected such a following. He forbade anyone to mock the efforts of another, and this gave him a reputation for fairness. He had even gained a few pounds. Now and then a village girl flirted with him. But he was careful not to return such attentions, for he knew that every girl had a man, older or younger, ready to act upon any slight or advantage taken.

But the world outside was changing. That was evident, if only by the advance of the printed word itself. Like blood circulating throughout a body, the change came down the road even into the most meager of villages and estates.

More and more, the broadsheets from the city began to pass down the trading route, brought and sold by peddlers and travelers on the main road from Wurzburg. And more and more, the broadsheets brought their outrageous lies and defamations to Witter's class. He tried to keep such trash out of the lessons but it was unavoidable. They were just too popular.

"Tales from Foreign Lands" was basically an excuse for woodcut scenes of cannibalism and tortures. Then there was "Slaves of Babylon," little more than pornography, which supposedly revealed the alleged sexual practices in the harem. Then there were those like "Jews and Heretics," a treatise on a secret war against Christianity by the forces of darkness combined; fear-mongering for the ignorant. All such printings were based upon fear of anything that did not support the ruling class. Witter felt contempt for them, for in their lies, few were even very clever.

Merkel was among the few with money to buy such broadsheets, and he and several others like Sig, had become addicted to the latest spewings from the skilled monk publicists at Veritas Press in Wurzburg. And worse, Merkel lent them out for a pittance, and the copies became worn until unreadable.

It was during the lull just before harvest, one fall night in the evening class, when Merkel insisted that Witter present a certain new broadsheet to the reading class.

"This tells of secret plots to destroy us," said Merkel at the beginning of the class. He had stood and waved the paper, showing it to one and then another.

Witter said, "What do you have there? We need to begin our regular lesson. Be still, please."

"This is important. It warns us to beware of those who sneak among us and spread doubt and distrust of the Church. It rouses all true churchmen to weed out the evil ones who worship false idols and charms and spells they would use to persuade us."

"Merkel cannot read well," said Sig.

Merkel handed the broadsheet to Sig, who frowned at it, holding it out at arm's length, leaning toward a candle.

"Fine," Merkel said, "Read it for yourself. It says to watch for those who say we need not defend our sacred country from outside evil, and it says that the worst evils are those among us. Heretics and liars who twist the holy words of God to weaken our freedoms."

"Freedoms?" said Linhoff. "How are we free?"

"Who are these heretics and liars we must watch for? What are these spells and charms that deceive us?" said Ferde.

Sig said, "The pictures show demons and such."

Then from the back of the room, Kaspar spoke out. He had been half hidden behind the shadows of a loom.

Leaning on a crutch, Kaspar said, "You are all breaking the law. Reading is not meant for such as us. These heretics are stealing our souls and filling you all with evil doubts."

"What doubts?" said Witter.

"Read the paper in Merkel's hands," said Kaspar. "That will persuade any who doubt the real truth."

"Persuade us of what?" said Grit.

Witter looked around and saw Grit holding an iron cooking kettle.

"This class is for the men," said Merkel.

"This pot has a hole for you to mend," said Grit. "And I have been meaning to visit one of the men's classes, to learn so that my classes might improve."

Witter smiled; Grit was clever enough to flatter the men, stubborn enough to come here where she knew she was not welcome by the men.

"Leave the pot and go," said Merkel.

"Who are these deceivers you speak of?" said Grit.

The other men were all looking at Grit now.

"You tell us," said Kaspar. "Who is the deceiver?"

Witter thought, *here it comes...*

Then Grit spoke up and made it ten times worse.

"The Bible says that all are created equal in the sight of God. Christ said that we must love one another. Never to judge one another. Love thy brother and love thy enemy, all the same."

"You have read the Bible?" said Sig.

"Reading is not a crime," said Grit.

"Reading the Scriptures, that is a crime," said Kaspar. "Only priests are allowed to read the Scriptures. And in their learnedness, they tell us the true meanings. So that we in our ignorance do not mistake what the Scriptures mean, and fail to obey them correctly."

Witter hoped it was over, that surely Grit would back away and leave, but he was wrong. Grit's face was red and she stood her ground.

"No," said Grit. "Only by reading the Scriptures directly can you each know the truth, as it is truly written, and decide each for yourselves what you must be, what you must do."

Now Kaspar was hobbling on his crutch toward Grit, the worn wood tip scraping across the floor of the smithy. Kaspar stumbled between the men, his face in a rage.

"I said reading the Scriptures, that is illegal, a serious crime," said Kaspar. "You say you have read them yourself?"

Witter cringed; he felt thrills of fear, and he fought an uncontrollable urge to run. It was the urge that he had almost forgotten in this place that had seemed such a safe haven. It was the urge that had so often saved his life.

But he stood there, fixed, staring, as the storm broke.

But Grit stood up to them, and said, "The Bible is the proof that the broadsheets promoting war and killings, they are false. That is not what God wishes his children to do, to fight among themselves, to hate one another. Christ said to forgive and love. It is that simple."

Kaspar had reached Grit and now began shouting.

"You see?" said Kaspar triumphantly. "Condemned from her own mouth! Only priests should read the Bible and tell us the true meanings! Would this evil woman say that I lost my leg for nothing? Did she support our troops? Dare she claim that we sacrificed for nothing? That those dead friends and sons whom we buried out there, they fell for nothing?"

There was a shocked silence.

Witter would not have been surprised if the whole of them rose up in a seething mob of devils and tore Grit and him apart limb from limb.

"How can love be evil?" said Grit. "How can the commandment of Christ, His one and only commandment, to love one another, be evil?"

Then Grit looked around at all of them, with a sad sweet kind of sorrow, as if she had failed, and she left the smithy.

Kaspar smiled coldly. His young face looked incredibly old now, Witter thought. The candles in the weavery threw strange shadows as Kaspar moved on his crutch among them, in jerks like an insect with one missing leg, scraping his crutch along.

"I too have learned to read and to write, thanks to these heretics. And I have written to the church magistrates in Wurzburg Bishopric, denouncing those who have come among us."

"You have what?" said Arl, standing to confront Kaspar.

"My letter went with a peddler last fortnight."

Peddlers are notoriously unreliable, thought Witter.

The thought was ludicrous, and its very weakness told him how little hope he held out from this suddenly unfolding disaster.

Lud

"Did I not warn you?" said Father Michael.

"Gloating does not suit you well. This is an emergency. A magistrate's deputy and men could show up here anytime."

The harvest was in full swing, the classes of reading had been suspended, the villeins were hardly talking to one another, and they had divided into opposing camps: those wishing to continue learning, and those who wanted to burn everything written. If magistrates came and found forbidden books or documents or writings, all could be judged and arrested.

A bad beating would have been better than reporting this mess to Lady Anna, as a steward should do. She would be furious—both at Kristina for her teachings, and at Kaspar's disloyalty in writing a letter.

No, that would do no good. The lady could do nothing to help. One way or another, it was on him now, the steward.

Lud was going mad over this, and he had invaded the confession box where Father Michael waited during confessions and dragged the startled priest out.

"Please, those waiting to have their sins absolved must be served," said Father Michael.

The priest was suddenly reasserting himself. Gone was the deference that had grown between them. Lud wondered why.

He saw no one waiting. He pulled open the little wooden door of the confessional and saw Jakop sitting there, looking up sheepishly. Lud grabbed his collar and hauled him out.

"Go, Jakop, stop abusing yourself and get married and say ten Hail Marys."

"You are wrong to ridicule," said Father Michael.

"Did you have any part in this?" Lud said. "And you know what I am talking about."

"Why would I make trouble for myself?"

"That is not what I asked you, priest."

"Every estate has judicial power over its own vassals. But Wurzburg will investigate whether reading the Scriptures has been done here by laymen and not by the priest, which is a crime actionable by bishopric law."

"Is that how you keep yourself in wine, being the only one legal for reading Scriptures?"

"I did not make the law, nor do I love it."

Lud rubbed his face and felt the fibrous grain of scar like tree bark. He said, "Maybe they will not come. The letter would be as from the hand of a child, or simpleton, probably barely readable."

"Kaspar's letter will surely reach them before harvest sharing out," said Father Michael. "Or as you say, the letter is so inarticulate they will laugh and toss it away."

Lud considered. "Perhaps Kaspar even lied, and there is no letter. He has gone quite mad since coming back without his leg. Greta has ended their betrothal, saying Kaspar is not who he was when she promised to wed."

"We will know," said Father Michael, "one way or another, after harvest sharing out, when the Bishophric sends its magistrate deputy to account and take their share. They would investigate, at the least, perhaps arrest and torture some of us just for the sake of appearances."

"Waiting is not good enough. Anything can happen when a village divides with fear this way."

"We must pretend all is well. And wait and see."

Lud glared at him. How could he expect this soft man to understand? "That is what you would do? Nothing?"

"What will you do?"

"The only thing I can do, priest. I am steward. Do you have no better advice for me, with all your learning?"

"Only one thing, Lud."

"What is it, then?"

"Tonight, open your book that Dietrich gave you, your *Handbook of a Christian Knight,* and find the passage, 'Rule Number One, Against the Evil of Ignorance.'"

"Priest, I am exhausted."

"And yet, Lud, what you seek to know is there."

Kristina

The tiny air vent in the recess at the ceiling threw a single shaft of bluish fall sunlight down upon them. The stone room was dank and smelled of mold and decay.

If ever you become too afraid, sing, and God will hear you...

She had sung earlier, in the dark hours of the night before, but now her heart would not lift high enough to make song.

Grit sat beside Kristina in the straw, holding her hand. Across from them sat Dolf and Symon, looking forlorn with their backs to the wall.

Lud had taken them one by one, down the stone stairs, deep into the belly of the castle, into darkness as if into a stone pit. None had resisted.

Only Witter was not here. Lud had not found him. Kristina wondered, would she ever see him again? He was probably miles away by now. She hoped he would not be hounded and killed by dogs. And she tried to force her mind away from what he might even now be enduring.

Beside her, Grit was trying to sweeten things.

"Fresh straw," said Grit, "that is nice."

"Very nice," said Dolf, standing up. He was seething, and started pacing the small center of the stone floor. "Quite a reward for helping them."

Kristina ignored his anger and said, "The candles, too. They give good light."

Grit said, "They mean us no harm. Lud said he took this precaution to protect us."

Dolf sneered. "That pock-faced bastard. We were fools to trust him. That killer."

Said Grit, "Stop it, brother. Anger does not help. Not you or anyone else."

Dolf looked down at her. "Teaching them to read is like teaching a bear to tend a baby. Now they are prey to all evil thoughts, more than good ones. And I thought my mind was small. Here we are prisoners now, behold their gratitude."

"Did you help them to obtain gratitude?" said Grit.

"Not for this did I help them, either."

Symon said, "Villagers can go mad with fear, I have seen it myself. Better here than in their hands if they lose their minds and want to take it out on those who are from the outside."

"Half the village is for us," said Grit. "You heard them defending us. It is only the ignorant, and the believers of those lies from Wurzburg, who denounce us."

Kristina said, remembering, "Lud told me that the last time anyone was put here was a man for his own protection."

"I heard that story," said Dolf. "It was a butcher who went mad and pulled out his eyes, and they chained him here, for the protection of the village, not him."

"We are not in chains," said Grit.

"At least Witter was not taken," said Symon. "He must be far from here by now."

Dolf punched the air with his fists. He looked up into the air shaft, and his blind milk-eye gleamed with tears. "It is I who have a blind eye, and yet I do not turn it to the truth when the truth must be faced."

Grit stood up and tried to solace him but he pushed her hand from his arm.

"Brother Dolf, it will be all right. God's will be done."

"Stop calling me 'Brother.' You cannot pretend we are safe and well. This is the end."

"Not the end, the beginning," said Grit.

Said Dolf, "There is only one way out of this, and that is when they unlock the cell and take us back up those stone stairs and out into the square to a stake, or to Wurzburg for torments first."

"There is another way," said Grit.

Symon said, "You have friends who may come?"

"Prayer," said Grit. "To enter the light."

"You think prayer will unbolt that door?" said Symon.

"Yes," said Grit.

And Kristina felt Grit squeeze her hand, and together they prayed, and in her prayer, Kristina begged God to save her child. She felt the solid presence of Grit but she herself felt transparent, weak, like a fading memory.

"Lud," muttered Dolf. "Pock-faced bastard. I should have fought. I should have killed him."

"Too late now, so shut up, Brother," said Symon.

Kristina kept trying to pray. She had no heart for anything but the thought of her baby. When her prayer felt hollow, as if the stones did not permit its passing out of this dank tomblike hole, she wanted to sing. Perhaps God would hear her song.

Dolf glared even harder at her as she began to sing.

"Descend celestial Dove,

With all Thy quickening powers..."

Then Grit sang with her...

"Disclose a Saviour's love,

And bless the sacred hours,

Then shall my soul new life obtain..."

Then Symon, too, sang, in his frog's voice, cracked and rising, like an exuberant boy.

Dolf sat and held his head down between his knees and put his hands over his ears. Between verses, when Kristina took in her breath, she could hear Dolf sob, then he was weeping, and Grit rose up and went to hold and pet him like a child.

But in the singing, her mind and spirit would not rise up. She was fixed to this earth, for she was a mother, and her heart belonged to her child. She stopped singing and Grit went on with the words, holding Kristina's hand.

All her thoughts came to little Peter, whom she had left in the arms of Lura, and she wondered what Lud would tell Lady Anna of this all, and what the lady would say must be done with a heretic's little child. Lura had brought blankets—for the night had been cold—and fresh candles. But Lura did not know what the outcome would be. There was no doubt now that Kaspar had sent a letter to the bishopric magistry.

"Our reward for teaching them to read," said Dolf.

Now, as the light in the air shaft waned with sunset colors and then faded away in nightfall, and Grit lit the new candles, Kristina did not want to sing for joy of the next world, for that meant leaving this one.

Giving birth had utterly changed her life. Now death seemed like a cruel exit, a tearing of life apart, for it was exile from the child she had borne and loved. And being forcibly separated from her little boy felt like something was tearing inside her. There was no triumph in death, not now.

Grit stubbornly kept up the songs. All she could remember, she sang. But after a little while, as the chill seeped up through the stones, and everyone wrapped themselves in the good blankets, they became isolated pods, each alone, and Kristina looked about and saw her brothers and sisters isolated, each cocooned in wool and no doubt captured within their private fears and thoughts.

After some time, Kristina looked up and saw moonlight in the air shaft, realized she heard something, and then she knew what it was.

Dolf was bent over, quietly sobbing again. This time no one went to console him. She looked over at Grit and thought she was asleep, but then in a flicker of dying candlelight she saw Grit's eyes, open, and gleaming wet.

She wanted to beseech her maker, but the thought that now filled her mind was utterly human, and it astonished her that her prayer was not directed to God:

Lud, Lud, why hast thou forsaken me?

And she knew that was profane, and it was foolish. Lud was steward. He was not his own man. He belonged to the estate. And he would do what he had to do to protect the estate. And that was what most filled her with fear. Then she heard the cell door.

Everyone sat up. The door was being unlocked.

It groaned open, and into the dimness poured yellow lantern light, and she saw Lura with Lud in the cell door.

Lud held a lantern and a bucket that was steaming. Kristina smelled hot barley. Dolf and Symon both sat up sharply as if expecting to be attacked. Grit stood. Kristina stood, too. Symon shifted back, behind Dolf.

Grit greeted them like honored guests for a family gathering: "Welcome, Brother and Sister."

Lura said, "We bring fresh water and food. Wooden bowls and spoons, a joint of smoked goat, a wedge of cheese. Lud has hot barley."

"God bless you," Kristina said to them.

In the scant lantern light, Lud's face was grimmer than ever. His countenance was hard—whether from anger or shame, she could not know—and his eyes avoided hers. Kristina turned from him to Lura.

"What of my child?" said Kristina, taking Lura's hand.

"Well and loved, with me and mine," said Lura.

"Will you let us out?" said Dolf.

"No," Lud said. "It is too late for that."

"Will you not let us run?" said Dolf.

Lud shook his head. "It is dangerous out there."

"Who wishes us harm?" said Grit.

"The village is too strange," said Lura. "They do not know what to think. On the one hand, they like you, many of them, and want what you have given them. They also fear you, and what you have given them. They are confused."

"When they are confused they are dangerous," said Lud. "And worse when they are afraid. If magistrates come and accuse, anything can happen, many may be taken."

"What of Lady Anna?" Kristina said.

"She does not know," said Lura. "She thinks you are to bed with a chill. Best leave it so."

Lud gestured to Lura and they went to the cell door. Lura went out first, and Lud looked back at them.

Lud said, "The magistrates will come with deputies guarding their bishopric wagons for their harvest levy on the sharing out. If they come to investigate Kaspar's letter, it will be then. That is in two days. Tomorrow is Sunday. Monday is their day to collect our grain share. Then we will know, one way or another. Until then at least, you must stay here."

"And Kaspar walks free," said Dolf.

"Free?" said Lura. "He is in the next cell."

Then the old cell door closed, the warped wood groaning on the rusted hinges, and suddenly the warm lantern light was gone. Kristina felt trapped. The lock rattled, and their footfalls faded away.

Quickly, Grit took up a dying candle and lit new candles.

Kristina withdrew, went back to her blanket in the corner, and she sat enwrapped and watched Symon and Dolf fall upon the food like wolves.

Then a candle came dancing like a fairy through the dark toward her. It was Grit who came to sit close, and Kristina opened her own blanket and Grit set the candle on a stone before them, and they enfolded themselves together inside both their blankets, like two little girls playing a game of hiding.

They did not pray or sing. Their hands found each other, fingers entwining.

Kristina stared into the little, twisting golden candle flame, and her soul reached into that light and held on tight. In fire she would die. Only in fire would she escape this world. She knew that now. And if fire was the portal through which she must pass, it was only by faith that she would endure it.

But what she felt she could not endure was being parted from her child. And for the first time, she realized what her own mother must have felt when her judgment had come, and they had torn her away.

"Do not weep," whispered Grit, holding her close.

Kristina had not realized that she wept. But, realizing it, her tears burst out harder and she pressed her face deep into the abrasive weave of the coarse woolen blanket.

Grit held on to her ever more tightly, as if saving her from demons clutching at them both. "Do not weep, dear sister, for we are never alone."

Then a key scraped in the old lock. They all looked up. The door groaned open. It was Linhoff.

"I brought you new broadsheets to read, and fresh bread. Do not worry, Lud told me to do it."

In the pale shaft of light they divided the broadsheets among them. At first they looked through them listlessly, clucking a tongue, sighing at the cheap stories.

Then Grit hissed.

Kristina turned and saw Grit's mouth hanging, dumbstruck. Grit stared at the broadsheet.

"Kunvald," she said.

"What? News of Kunvald?"

Kristina moved closer and leaned over the broadsheet.

The others did the same.

The paper dropped from Grit's hands, and Grit put her face in her hands and she shuddered, then she simply broke down and wept. Kristina had never heard Grit sob with such emotion before.

Dolf and Symon were reaching for the broadsheet but Kristina grabbed it.

"Read it," said Dolf, "out loud."

But Kristina could not read it out loud. The words came from the paper to her mind but stopped there. Her mind would not send them to her mouth.

The words were unspeakable.

A campaign of "purification" had swept Bohemia. Listed among the towns "cleansed" was Kunvald. The names of those burned in each town were listed after the town.

Tears scalded her face. The words blurred, but she read them. There, on the list of those burned at Kunvald, were "printers of heretical and demonic beliefs"—Rita and Johannes.

Witter

Only Witter had known absolutely that Lud would arrest the Brethren. He had argued with the others not to sleep in the same house. He had told Kristina to trust no one, ever, that they must run while they could.

But with their habitual faith and stubbornness they trusted Lud, and would not budge—

Where would we go?

And if we run, will not the magistrates blame the village and take a terrible revenge, and would that not be on our heads?

Has the Lord not sent us to do this work?

If we run, does it not prove guilt?

They would not budge, they would not listen, not even Dolf or Symon, who were obviously terrified. So Witter had disappeared himself. It was the one thing he had become good at. Hiding in plain sight. Hiding where searchers would least expect to ever look for him. Here in the church.

Now he lay somewhat comfortably within the rafters that bridged the slanted roof beams within the ceiling of the church. It was warm up here, the heat rising from the two hearth fires below at either end of the church. He had found a heavy curtain rolled up, and it made a good shroud for sleeping and for waiting.

Last night, Saturday night, he had stolen down to the main floor to steal wine. He had looked up at the glass-eyed Jesus and felt an intense sorrow for the mystic whose nonviolent compassion had brought his death from those who were jealous of all challenges to their power.

It was Sunday, and Mass would come soon, and he would lay up here and listen to the priest condemn him and Kristina and the others. It would be the priest's perfect opportunity to seize upon the confusion and anger in his parish. To bring them back under his wing.

Then they would give over the heretics when the magistrates came, or perhaps even kill them in the cell, or take them out into the square to burn them. If they burned the heretics themselves, the magistrates would certainly approve and be appeased. The village would be saved.

When all the speeches and arguments and talk and preaching were done, today or tomorrow or the next day, the heretics he had grown so fond of would be gone, and he would face himself and end it or be gone, too, on to the next random place of refuges, before winter set in. He would weep, yes, and his heart already felt sick. But he was not one of them. And he knew that, even if he had dared beg Kristina to run away with him, she would never leave her child, nor would she risk little Peter's life running from village to village, living like wild things, hunted by dogs again, or worse.

Yes, he would wait and see, and despise himself, and then when it was time he would see to his own punishment.

So now Witter lay up high in the rafters, peering down through a wide crack in the ceiling boards, and watched the sanctuary fill.

Father, behold me, your beloved son, the fool, see to what pass I have come, like a rat, hidden and observing the world and hoping it will all pass away soon…

Beneath him, the villeins poured in until they were packed inside like sheaves in a barn. He felt the animal heat rising and smelled their many unwashed bodies packed into this barn of a church. Gathering here, they came to celebrate the cruel death of a Jew long ago. They hated and feared all Jews except this dead one, and they worshipped the cross, that implement of death by torture; they praised it, made its sign over their hearts. The belief itself was a kind of madness and it bound them together down there.

Witter saw himself, too. Once he might have taken solace in a feeling of superiority, seeing these people as they did not see themselves. But he knew his own shallowness. And the irony was too crushing to contemplate, too cruel, and the bitterness too sharp, making him take deep breaths.

His father, Judah, had often spoken of eternal justice, and evoked Isaiah's wisdom: and he heard those words now…

The way of peace they know not; and there is no judgment in their goings: they have made them crooked paths: whosoever goeth therein shall not know peace…

And, looking down at the mob, Witter thought of words spoken long ago by a Jew, a rabbi named Jesus, upon which this very religion called Christianity was based. The irony was too severe to be delicious; too cruel.

Judge not that ye be not judged…

Finally, he saw the priest enter from the sacristy and climb the wooden steps. He made some ceremonious tokens to the wooden Jesus staring from the wooden cross, and then he went up onto his pulpit to stare down at the waiting mob.

"Today I speak to you as a man, for you know I have not been a good priest. But today, the time for evasions, the time for foolishness, the time for falsehoods, that time is over. Let us be done with it."

Here it came, Witter thought. The priest had them now.

"If I were a good priest, here is what I would do today."

The priest paused. He leaned forward and looked down at them.

"A good priest would bring you, my prodigal parishioners, back to my power. First, I would banish all reading. I would terrify you with accusations that you have danced with demons. You flock here today and fill this church and beg me to intercede with the Holy Virgin. And I should let you confess the sin of your pride in learning to read. And forswear you never to read again. Then would I be a good priest. A good servant to the church."

There was a leaden silence. The faces below the priest shrank from his gaze. He grinned down at them.

"But I am not a good priest. You all know that only too well. If I cut you off from reading, you would know only my words, only what I say the Scriptures command. I could say anything I wish, and you, who could not read for yourself, must believe that what I say is from the word of God."

Witter felt his spirit stir. Frowning, he wondered what trick the priest was up to. Why be devious with this backward village? Or was he being devious?

Below in the mob there was a stirring, too, for the people did not know how to take all this from the priest.

"These people in our cell, they met our men in war, and they could have run away, but they risked their lives to heal them, and some were slain. They did this because they can read. Because they have read the one commandment of our lord Jesus, which I have also read, and tell you now—love thy enemy, love thy neighbor, love thy brother."

Father Michael paused and he stared out at them as if his gaze could penetrate their minds more deeply.

"Yes," he went on again, "I say you, and you, and you. Because those who some of you call heretics can read, because they read directly from the Scriptures, they went out and were taken and hunted by men and dogs, and here they came, and found pox, and again they did not run, they stayed long after they helped the diseased of our village."

Again he paused, and again he glared at them.

"Yes. You know it is true. They stayed to teach all those to read who so wished. Every day they stayed, their lives were at risk. Yet they stayed. Even when you read the vile lies from Wurzburg, they stayed. Lies you could not have read if they had not taught you. And now because they stayed to liberate you from your darkness, your ignorance, they are condemned by a letter. By a letter, I say! A letter that could never have been written in the first place, had not that person been taught by them how to read!"

The priest paused to gather himself and to let it all sink in. Witter was stunned; could he be hearing this right?

The priest's voice sank lower again, as if he struggled for the next thoughts.

"No, I confess to you all, you well know I am not a good priest. I did not teach you, nor do for you what some strangers came to do. And now, because the so-called heretics did what I should have done for you, they are waiting in a cell to be taken by magistrates tomorrow, when the bishop's sharing wagon arrives with deputies. My shame is drowning my soul."

Whispers ran crackling through the mob of villagers, arguing, shoving, below him.

"Now let me ask you. Have they ever spoken against God? Have they ever spoken against Christ? Have they ever shirked from giving aid or charity whenever they could?"

The crowd was moiling with arguments, and now the priest began raging at them, pointing his fingers at one, then another, then another—

"It was you who asked them to teach you to read! You who brought them to this pass! You who then condemned them for what you yourselves begged them to do for you!"

Now some of the villagers were crossing themselves and hurrying out the church doors. Witter had never seen anything like this in his life. He crawled quickly down the rafter to an opening where he could better see it all.

Below, the priest leapt down from his pulpit like a madman, with spittle at his beard. His eyes were as wild as a beast suddenly released from a cage.

"I tell you, yes, you wretches, that it be a plague on your souls," he screamed at his fleeing flock, "if these harmless ones be sent for torture and burning! He who is without sin, let him cast the first stone!"

Lud

He knew the church would be packed today. Mostly absent for months, the villagers would pack the church, each to rid themselves of any stain or gossip of siding with heretics. In conviction, their presence would mean nothing. It was all about appearances. And in a village, appearances were always important to maintain. But he had never expected the show he was to see in the church that day.

Last night had been sleepless—spent with his treasured book, finding the section the priest had directed him toward: "Rule Number One Against the Evil of Ignorance."

The hours had passed, irritably at first, three candles burnt down to guttering stubs, as he bent over his wooden table and made out the words of the monk Erasmus, and labored to parse out their wordy connections.

As if in battle, he fought on and strove with the fever of one finding an opening through which to pass alive, and his hunger for meaning came on, stronger and stronger...

"If thou believe He is God, thou must needs believe that He is true also, and on this wise think without wavering, nothing to be so true, nothing to be so sure, and without doubt of the things which thou hearest with thine ears, which thou presently beholdest with thine eyes, which thou handlest with thy hands, as those things be true which thou readest in the Scriptures, that God of heaven, that is to say verity, gave by inspiration, which the holy prophets brought forth, and the blood of so many martyrs hath approved..."

Now, Lud stood watching the Mass from the back of the sacristy. It was astonishing. He had never expected the soft priest to preach that fervent sermon, nor to throw off such a yoke as the one placed upon him during training to promote his religion. He realized he had never liked the man before. That he liked him now.

This priest has grown some balls…

Lud watched the crowd boil and bolt. Father Michael's unexpected ideas and his chastisements panicked them as much as it had surprised Lud himself.

Not all of the flock ran away. There were a dozen on their knees at the prayer bar, crossing themselves, some in tears. Father Michael went down and blessed them. Lud saw that the priest's hands were trembling as he went from one to another, kneeling, bowing, chanting.

Nothing had been the same since Kristina and her friends had come here. Everything was dividing, changing. And now, even Father Michael had taken a stand.

"As those things be true which thou readest in the Scriptures," the book had said. The passage the priest had told him to read, to help him understand. The book that Dietrich had given him, to help him understand.

His mind reeled with it all.

"Learn, find the truth, your own truth," Dietrich had said. Lud remembered begging God to spare Dietrich, bargaining that he would become a monk, anything, if only God would relent. But Dietrich had died anyway. And in truth, Lud knew he had felt no connection to God, and had been begging for himself alone. But Dietrich had commanded him and set his future with those last words.

Is this the truth? One must read, to know? One must know, to judge? One must know how to read, to believe?

This priest was no coward, to lash forth this way. No amount of sacristy wine could quench the molten fact that the priest would be condemned with the others when the magistrates summoned witnesses and the denouncing came. All here were witnesses to his defense of heresy. And Lud loved him for all of that. The contempt was gone.

He left the church the back way. Now it was past time to go report to Lady Anna. He was steward. He had to report. She ruled the estate. She had to listen. And soon, his duty would be done, one way or another.

He went straight to the castle. On the way there, several villagers tried to stop him to talk—Merkel, Ferde, Deet, Sig—wanting to know what he thought, what he would do.

"Will you denounce the priest? What does Lady Anna say? Will we all be questioned?"

And Sig the miller, father of Kaspar, the causer of so much trouble, stopped Lud near the huge, old linden tree in the square. It hurt Lud to see the good man so hurt by such a bad son.

"Lud, please, why have you arrested my son?"

"Kaspar is held for his own protection."

Sig's eyes widened with fear. "Protection? From who?"

"From himself. From his mouth. From many who are afraid now. Kaspar is not arrested. Take him food, anything you want, but not ale or wine. He is yelling enough as is."

"Take care with him, Lud. Do not forget his is lame, nor how I let you take flour from the mill when you were but a hungry child yourself."

Without answering anyone else, Lud pushed past them all and went on. At the castle, he ran up the stone stairs.

On the stone rampart outside the portal to the bedchambers, Lura blocked his way and did not want to admit him. She was all questions.

"How can this help? Why have you come? She keeps asking for Kristina. What will you say to her?"

"You are my friend, Lura, but I will enter past you, by force if I must, and you know me well, and you know I mean that."

"Wait then, damn you, and I will advise her and prepare her."

Minutes later he was admitted.

Lady Anna wore her veil and a winter dressing gown that covered her as effectively as a satin blanket. She sat in a chair with needlepoint in her lap.

"Where is Kristina? What is happening? Why has my steward not advised me?"

"That is why I am here, lady."

So he told her the whole thing, and even through the veil he could glimpse her eyes flashing with indignation.

"My villagers? My villeins? They are all learning to read? I cannot have it. I forbid it. I will not have it!"

"Dietrich said for all to seek the truth, my lady."

"Truth? How could villagers know truth unless it is explained to them by a good priest?"

"I think they did have it explained to them quite well today in church, my lady."

Lady Anna looked at Lura. "Were you there?"

"I was, lady. The priest spoke fire today. He was like one possessed. Defending reading, he did."

"Our priest? That young, cowardly sop?"

"The very one, my lady," said Lura.

"My husband liked him, God help us. They read the same books and had long talks. I would have sent that priest away but I was sentimental, because of Dietrich's memory."

"The magistrates come tomorrow for our grain share to the bishopric," said Lud. "You know, lady, that at this time they collect prisoners from the estates who must be sent to Wurzburg for capital crimes. There will no doubt be deputies with them, perhaps others."

"What is that to me?"

Said Lud, "Just this, lady. The church magistrate may act on the letter and call witnesses and make arrests. What shall you have me do?"

Lady Anna pushed herself out of her chair. She stood seething, waving the needlepoint needle in Lud's face like a dagger. He took a step back from her, surprised.

"I have a mind to give them all over and punish them all, all who have learned to read are ruined, spoiled, rotten. Villagers have weak minds and it is not suitable for them to learn too much! Who do they think they are, writing letters to outside magistrates?"

Kristina

Awaking and opening her eyes, seeing the dull light on the dead gray walls encased around her, Kristina was struggling against chills, as if suffering under a cold rain.

Kristina sat up on the rough wood pallet, pulling the heavy woolen shawl about her, and feeling helpless. Then she remembered where she was, and why.

Her mind raced. She waited until it stopped, and then she held still and tried to be strong.

It was the cell beneath the old castle tower; the pit where once a wretched, mad butcher had pulled his own eyes out after dismembering his poor wife and children.

I pray that their souls are all at peace...

She tried to pray for them. When she did this, it was easier not to dwell upon herself and her dread.

Everyone she loved died. She thought of poor Kunvald, and all of the people she had known there who had saved her life and nurtured her to womanhood. Patient Rita and hardworking Johannes, so like parents to her. People who lived to teach and share all equally with others. How they must have suffered so terribly. And their fear, seeing their loved ones in torment. All gone. All of them.

Dear God, why is love so feared and punished? They only tried to bring good to all. Why were they so hated? Why must it be so hard?

Her child was everything now. Her prayer could not penetrate her dread nor lift away the thick weight of her fear. She shivered and hated her weakness, this waking to fear, for fear was the denial of God's grace, fear was belief in the body more than the soul, fear was belief in this world more than eternity.

Her mother's admonition to sing to God in her fear felt weak and false now. She refused to sing. It was as if she were encased in an evil shroud through which she could not reach God and God could not hear her.

I am so weak. So afraid. So faithless…

"Goddamn them all," she heard someone whisper; it was Dolf. The words were terrible ones.

At first she did not believe she heard right. Then she heard someone whimpering. Possibly Symon? She knew that she should go try to comfort him, but she held on to herself, with her own arms wrapped around her.

Ever since she had been a little girl—ever since losing her mother and father and older sister—her fear had crippled her, embarrassed her before God. It made her small and pointless and too often it possessed her. If she did not have the child, perhaps she would find that sublime indifference that saints were said to find in extremis.

"Do punish them, O Lord," said Dolf.

Grit's voice said, "Hush, Dolf. You harm yourself."

Dolf moaned. "How can I be more harmed? If God would let our great teachers at Kunvald be burned, how can we wretches hope for anything better? If God does not love us, what is the use?"

"They walk with our Lord," said Grit.

"You say it so sure," said Dolf.

"Pray with me, Dolf," said Symon. "I too am afraid."

"No, damn you, get away."

"I will pray with you, my brother," said Grit.

Kristina looked at Grit. "We are not all saints like Johannes. Even bent from their cruel torments, he never weakened, going about his life work, not even speaking of the things done to him. Yet even one so free of fear as Johannes, they destroyed."

"Child," Grit said. "Johannes was no saint, he was much more, he was human. All more worthy of the courage he kept hidden. You think he never felt pain? Never felt fear? Before he and Rita sent Frieda off into the world that day, a day now that seems lifetimes ago, I found Johannes alone, on his knees and weeping like a baby in the back of his print shop."

"Weeping?" said Dolf. "Not Johannes, never."

Grit took a long deep breath and released it slowly. "He held onto me and my hands comforted him and I felt the lumps of scars on his back, even through his cloak. He prayed with me and sobbed it out, said he was never certain whether God listened to us. Johannes was human. As are we. As are all God's children. Just human."

Now, Kristina's mind turned inward. She could hear the others speaking, but her thoughts were not here.

Little Peter. What would happen to him if she were destroyed? And had her fear of the magistrates, of their dogs, harmed him in her womb? Had her fear constricted him, made him slower than other children? Did she bear that mother's guilt, from the harm of her lack of faith? Had fear damaged the child, stunted him? Made him doglike in his slowness? Who could know such things, but God?

Forgive me for my weakness, for my sins, I pray for the souls of all lost, all in war, all in madness, all in injustice, I pray for my child that he be saved, I pray for my brothers and sisters, I pray for myself that I am worthy of the sacrifice of our Saviour...

But prayer did not smother her fear for her child. She had thought that if she attained enough faith she would break free of such fear. But when she was weakest, she thought that fear itself was a trick, sent to test her. She knew now that was not it. The truth of fear was that she had not enough faith.

Perhaps God created evil solely to test faith. But did that mean that God had created man from a need to be loved? To force that love by fear of evil?

But such doubts, such accusations against God, had to be the work of Satan.

I sought the Lord and He heard me and delivered me from all my fears...

There were steps on stones outside the cell, and voices whispering somewhere, and she opened her eyes and first realized that dawn was breaking, the light coming through the air shaft in a blue and pink slant where dust motes turned like stars, and Grit and Dolf and Symon were all sitting up, sleepy and startled. Dolf's milk-eye dripped tears.

"Goddamn Lud and all of them," whispered Dolf.

Now Grit put one arm around Dolf, and her other arm around Symon, just like a mother might, and squeezed them close.

"No more cursing," she said. "We may be very close to God now, closer than we have ever been."

Then Grit began to sing softly. Her voice was shaky at first, then steadier as the words came…

"I'll praise my maker while I have breath…"

Grit nudged Dolf and Symon so they would sing the line, and Kristina now forced herself to sing it with them…

"I'll praise my maker while I have breath…"

Then Grit sang the next line, and the next, and Kristina sang each line after Grit had sung it…

"I hope to praise Him after death,
I hope to praise Him when I die,
And shout salvation as I fly…"

Kristina tried to seem unafraid, when they glanced at her. Still, more fear came with not knowing who was coming, or why. The singing made it better somehow, as if she could not sing and be afraid at the same time.

Now she heard the cell door rattle; it was being unlocked. Fear ran through her and she pulled her knees against her chest and cowered like a cornered rat.

She wanted to pray—*Remember, I am with you always, to the end of the age*—but prayer failed her. She could not rise up from the unclean, possessing sense of dread. The fear for her child was greater than her fear for her soul.

Then the cell door scraped open and she saw old Vogler, the gatekeeper, with Little Golz, his new key bearer. They looked in, their faces full of apology, and then they moved back.

"Move, make way," said Lura's voice.

Kristina almost laughed with relief, seeing Lura with a lantern glowing yellow in the dim stone passageway. Lura's sweet face, tight with concern, was radiant in the lantern light.

Kristina's fear hung upon her like a dark chill, a damp foulness from which she needed to bathe.

Dolf said, "Symon, wake. Maybe breakfast is being brought, and perhaps some news, good or bad."

But then, just behind Lura, Kristina saw a smaller figure with a veiled face. It was Lady Anna.

"Kristina," said Lady Anna.

"I am here, lady."

"I know you are there. Come out."

"Come out?"

"At once. You are neglecting your duties in my service. We have an agreement, do we not?"

"Yes, but…" She looked at the others.

"Come out I say, come out at once."

Grit, Dolf, and Symon all moved, but Lura lifted a hand and shook her head. They all stopped.

"She only wants Kristina."

"I have no bond with the others," Lady Anna said. "Be brisk, the smell is not to my pleasure, nor the dankness here."

An hour later, Kristina came from the tub, her body steaming and clean, and Lura handed her a clean serving gown.

"Where is my child?" she said, dressing.

"Your sunny boy is with my own boy, Klops," said Lura, "safe and happy. They play like brothers."

"Thank God, I have been so afraid."

"There are tiffs, boys will be boys, but no one would harm little Peter. His laughter cheers us. He delights in everything, great or small, all things are such discoveries to him."

"I am so afraid of what that letter may bring."

"Many are angry at Kaspar for the letter. You never did him harm, but Kaspar was always a bitter sort. Some are angry at Lud for jailing you, but others are angry at him for jailing Kaspar. The village is full of fear of the magistrates coming, if they come. It is a very bad time, and all are confused. All, it seems, but Lady Anna."

"In what state is the lady?"

"Most quiet, burning in a rage. Saying I lied to her. Lud told me not to upset her. When she found where you were, she was livid. She missed her readings and your harp, and I actually believe she missed you. But most and worst she resents any pin upon her authority."

Then she went up to the lady's chambers and nothing was said, and she played the harp and they read *In Praise of Folly* together, Lady Anna having mastered several passages accurately now.

At the reading desk, Lady Anna read ploddingly but well. The lady had chosen a new passage. It was Folly speaking in the first person, Folly commenting upon the knowledge of mankind—

"And now I think you see what would become of the world if all men should be wise; to wit it were necessary we got another kind of clay and some better potter..."

But this morning they did not smile together and Lady Anna did not make her usual smirking sounds when amused. Kristina knew the lady had chosen this passage to read for it had meanings that seemed to chastise Kristina—

"But I, partly through ignorance, partly unadvisedness, and sometimes through forgetfulness of evil, do now and then so sprinkle pleasure with the hopes of good and sweeten men up in their greatest misfortunes that they are not willing to leave this life, even then when according to the account of the destinies this life has left them..."

Kristina felt the lady's cold temper seething and she dared not interrupt, nor speak of anything that weighed so heavily upon her own heart. So she listened and kept still, exposing nothing until the reading was done.

"And by how much the less reason they have to live, by so much the more they desire it; so far are they from being sensible of the least wearisomeness of life..."

But the whole time, all her thoughts were with her child. She yearned so to see him, smell him, tease him, feed him, hug him, love him. What did it matter if he was slow? Was life a race between children of God? Was that not why God had created man, to be loved and to love? How had she been so foolish, so evil, as to ever feel disappointed in Peter?

Said Lady Anna, "In the words of Folly, there are many lessons to be learned. Do you see the relevance, Kristina?"

Kristina looked at her blankly; she had not heard, but she knew what to say.

"I do see, lady, that you have become the teacher."

"If all men were wise, would the world do better?"

"Folly says no," answered Kristina. She felt she could not give a better truth to her answer.

"You vex me," said Lady Anna. But, even through the veil, she saw Lady Anna smile for the first time that day. "It is difficult to be fond of one so clever."

"Reading, lady, does not make one clever, it is the desire to read that is born in wit and curiosity."

"When I came for you, down in that horrid cell, you were singing. Tell me how you could be singing? Did you not imagine many terrors? Were you not afraid?"

"We were afraid. That is why we sang."

"Fear is worse almost than pain. It is pain."

"If one loses faith, only fear remains."

"Where does so much faith come from? You have no priest to inspire it. How does it come?"

"My faith is weak. I am not one to say."

"Your faith? Weak?"

"In that cell, I despaired. I tried to pray but failed to clear away the fear. The fear is like fog and you cannot see through it, nor feel your way."

"Yet you sang."

"Sister Grit sang, to lead us out of that fog."

"But she is not your sister."

"She is the sister of my soul."

"Am I also your sister?"

"To say so would offend you. Presuming we are equals."

"Are not all equal before God?"

Kristina did not answer. There was no answer that she was brave enough to trust, and perhaps it was a trick.

"Lud meant well," said Lady Anna. "To protect you."

"I know."

"He is an ignorant man."

"He will not always be ignorant. He is learning. And he has what cannot be taught. He has a good heart."

"Lud? You think so?"

"I am sure of it."

"You amaze me. Idiot or savant, I know not which."

Lady Anna nodded. Kristina detected a smile. Kristina knew when Lady Anna smiled, even though she wore a veil, for she could see the gleam of her eyes. They glittered when she wept and when she smiled. And when smiling, Lady Anna also nodded.

"Perhaps," said Lady Anna, "we shall sing when afraid."

Then they were interrupted.

Lura came hurriedly, and spoke between breaths: "Lady, you instructed me to advise when the bishopric sharing wagons arrive. Lud rode out a while ago and has returned to say the wagons will be here very soon."

"Did he say there are magistrates?"

Lura's voice trembled a little. "Yes, lady, I saw from the rampart, there are armed deputies, magistrates, and monks."

Kristina's mind stopped; she felt her insides go cold.

But Lady Anna rose up stridently.

"Very well. I shall wear my high collar and the black velvet cape."

"The wide black hat with trailing ribbons?" said Lura.

"No. We do not travel to court. A plain sun hat will do. I am of this village and will not put on a show. Then we must meet them properly."

"We?" said Kristina.

"You shall accompany me. Are you not my serving maid? Would they not see that I am a lady?"

Lura said, "You look all the lady today, truly."

"Then let us go down and do this business."

Lud met them out in the courtyard. Kristina stood back with Lura. The sun was up, and shaded under her wide-brimmed straw hat, Lady Anna listened to Lud's report. Her finely shaped face was a whitish oval through the veil.

"We have loaded their grain shares into their wagons. The levy was fixed but they have raised it again."

"Raised? Again? You allowed it?"

"Nothing to be done. I read the bishopric decree and the tally and the lead was set."

"You read it yourself?"

"Yes, lady. Now a monk and his magistrates approach the village gate. They mean to make arrests, I fear."

"Stay close beside me," said Lady Anna to Lud.

Lud escorted them out through the square, past the linden tree, where the villagers were gathered in a crowd, silent and watchful.

Now, Kristina realized that Lud wore his Turkish sword. It hung from his leather belt, long and curved. She had not seen him with that sword since that wagon march from Wurzburg four years ago. But he wore it easily, as if he had been born wearing it. The hilt was chased with bronze, and the long, black leather sheath was scuffed, swinging a little with every one of his steps. Somehow she felt better that he wore the sword.

Realizing this, she felt shame. Shame and fear for him was what she should feel now. Fear for all of them to whom she had brought this danger. The sword was sinister, a deadly instrument of murder, with no other function. She knew she should not admire anything about it or about Lud wearing it. She knew Lud, knew he would not wear it for show, for nothing. Perhaps he would protect her. And in protecting her, he would protect her child.

Help him, and forgive me for asking it...

Approaching the village gates were a dozen riders.

Kristina, standing just beside Lady Anna, saw the little monk at the front of the riders, and she felt her heart seize in her chest. It was the monk from the market square in Wurzburg. The monk who had caught her handing out broadsheets. The monk who wanted her under arrest. The monk from whom Witter had saved her. He was here.

Please God do not let him recognize me…

Lady Anna greeted him as if he were an honored guest, but Kristina heard the false welcome in her voice.

"It is Anna von Seckendorff Geyer who welcomes you. Greetings to you, Father Basil, is it not?"

"You mock me with sarcasm, for we both know I am Brother Basil, not so learned as a priest, merely a humble servant on bishopric business today."

"Why assume I mock you, and not honor you?" said Lady Anna. "Is that true humility?"

Kristina watched the monk narrow his eyes. He was obviously not expecting such a vigorous challenge, especially not from a woman. Now the monk became officious.

"You do remember me, my Lady Anna, dear child of nobles of the Holy Mother Church. Greetings." The monk closed his eyes and made the sign of the cross and waved his arm as if casting gifts upon the village crowd. "Blessings upon you all, I say it in the name of the Holy Virgin, and her son, our Saviour, Jesus Christ."

"May God preserve us all," said Lady Anna. "It has been years, Brother Basil, at communion in Wurzburg if I recall."

Looking at Lady Anna, the monk said, "Yes, I recall your last visit to Wurzburg cathedral with pleasure." Basil's voice was even more false and kind. But there was condescension, too, an assumed superiority.

The younger monks, flanking either side of Basil, their master, watched him upon every word; Kristina saw how obviously they revered him, and studied him, and wished to learn from him. The armed deputies on horse were different. Their alert, hard eyes showed they were here to do harm and they had seen too much harm to care for such formalities. They were more bored than eager.

And then she heard the dogs. Handlers with dogs on chains were afoot behind the horsemen, and she could see them sometimes under the legs of the horses in the rear.

Her mind seized with the old fear: *Dogs...*

Was it just like this at Kunvald? Magistrates and monks come and read charges and then torture all until all confess. And then all are burned or beheaded? Then the Church seizes their land? Was it just like this? And will this happen now? Here at Giebel? Will this be the end?

If the magistrates took investigation into the village, the nightmare would have caught up with her, and surely she would not be able to bear it this time. She stood beside Lady Anna, trembling inside, forcing herself to act, to appear calm and innocent. Then she realized she felt guilty, and this angered her.

I am innocent. I have done no wrong!

And from this anger she took heart.

Said Lady Anna to the monk, "I am sorry that my cousin Prince Konrad has not arrived to attend with you. Since our village suffered pox, four years past, we have not seen dear Konrad."

"Dear lady, Konrad did not know of your beloved husband's death until late. So many perished. The prince sends his most dear greetings but regrets that state business requires his duty elsewhere."

"I have heard of his success with the printing press. Are you not involved in that as well?"

"You have good ears, lady."

Now, Kristina saw the monk staring at her suddenly. He frowned as if trying to remember. Kristina shrank back slightly, praying that the monk would not remember her from the market square.

But Lady Anna spoke, breaking the moment.

"Sir, I have eyes as well as ears and a brain. And I have seen and read the trash from your so-called Veritas Press."

"Trash?"

"For simpletons, yes. Trash, I say. You may tell my cousin so. He disappoints me."

The monk smiled and cocked his head. "Lady, I did not know you could read."

"Who told you I cannot? Add that to all else you do not know. Astonishing, that my dear cousin, a prince, would stoop to such tradesman business."

"Not trade, but soul preserving, lady. You call it trash? We do the work of God, the Holy Mother Church, battling for the minds of our flock. You surprise me, for I know Konrad believes you a most devout Christian."

"You are not my confessor, Basil. God sees clearly into all our hearts, and knows who we are. And now that our sharing is done, take your bishopric business elsewhere. Farewell, and good day."

"The sharing out was but our first business today."

"Oh? Have you come to do Mass over my dear husband, departed these four years? If so, monk, you are somewhat tardy in your ministrations."

"No, dear lady, I regret it is upon Church business I travel here today. Laws may have been broken here in your village. Many may be questioned, and I have brought my monks and magistrates of church law to secure such testimony as may be fit for trial."

"You have seized your grain portion, the lion's share of our bounty. The vitals that must need see our village through winter. Taking that much will cause many to suffer. Then take it. But that is all you shall take from Giebel this day, sir."

"Lady, perhaps you do not know. We have a letter of serious content, most serious, obliging us to investigate. It is said that for years, grain stores have been tallied low, so that the villeins here might receive greater shares of God's bounty, reducing the lawful bounty to be given to the bishopric church-state. That this was approved by the late knight Dietrich to improve the lot of his villeins, against all right order and sacred law."

"You dare defame my late husband's name? And where is your proof of such charges?"

"Also, that the Scriptures are being read in this village by some who are not priests. That in itself is a criminal act."

"I am the law here. I know of no such crimes."

"Nevertheless, we must be thorough. Make way, please."

Lady Anna stood her ground. Lud, beside her, did not move. Kristina did not move. The villagers did not move. They stood together, a wall that was Giebel village. It was as if they were held together by an invisible spirit that unified them, a force that all felt as one, and Kristina felt it, too.

Said Lady Anna, "If I give way, you will enter my estate, seize any of my people you wish, do with them as you wish, torture and break and make madness. You will make them say whatever you wish, about whomever you wish. You will ruin any you wish. Charge any you wish."

"With no pleasure, such duties must be done."

"Then with such a story you will sell many broadsheets from Veritas Press, no doubt. And who will plow and sow and reap next year? Who will raise their children? Who will bear boys to become men for your next levy of war? No, Basil, the law is the law. And the law is mine. Every estate is its own law, and the Holy Roman Empire is built upon that law. I shall not let you violate my keeping, and ruin it with nothing more than vague slanders."

"You speak law of the state, lady. Secular law gives you those rights. But I am the law of God, of the Church."

Lady Anna said, "Has my dear cousin Konrad empowered you to disrespect me so publically, on my own estate, where all villagers and your own monks and men of law are full witnesses to your act of insult and offense?"

Basil looked down his little nose at her. "Lady, no disrespect is meant nor proffered, I assure you."

"My cousin Konrad will hear of this."

"I assure you, lady, it is Prince-Bishop Konrad's desire to extend his protection to you and your estate, as godfather to your son, Florian, and dear friend of your husband, and as your own cousin, for these words he has given me to address you."

"You should have said so to begin with. I desire no such protection. I will not hand over the estate of my son the heir."

Kristina saw the monk becoming impatient. The magistrate deputies behind him bore arms and sat their horses waiting for orders, sweating in the autumn sun. The monks pulled their capes off their faces, wincing. Leaves of many colors blew down from the great linden tree, flew across the dirt square, through the waiting men, with dust that made them spit and grimace.

"But we must investigate such letters, just as a matter of course. Heretics have escaped this way in years past. Crude as it was written, the letter was quite explicit."

"Who wrote such a letter?"

"Kaspar, it is signed by that name only."

Lady Anna said, "Produce this Kaspar, then, sir."

"By law we can assume he will be here," said Basil, as if explaining it to a child, "as is written in the letter to court."

"Then you have my permission to call his name to this crowd that he may come forth."

Basil motioned to one of the attendant monks on horse behind him, and the armed horsemen at either side watched the crowd. Kristina looked upon them with fear, for they seemed the same men who had hunted her in the woods, killed Berthold, run them down with dogs, and she heard the dogs snarling anxiously behind the horsemen, and the jangling of their chains as the handlers controlled them.

"Kaspar!" shouted the attending monk. His face was young and earnest. "Kaspar! Come forth, Kaspar!"

The crowd of villagers stared, all stiff, not even trading looks. Some turned this way or that, but not one foot stirred from its spot on the ground. And no one spoke. All muttering had ceased, as if all were wary of being thought to have answered to the summoned name.

"So you see, we have no Kaspar," said Lady Anna.

"My men shall search and ask about, then."

"You will not, sir. One man or another has ordered me about all my life. Now I am mistress here. I am the judicial authority on my estate. Not any Wurzburg cleric. I will decide punishments and outcomes, none other. And you shall not confine us with Konrad's protection."

One of the magistrate deputies said, "Four years ago, we hunted heretics out of the city, down this way for a night and a day, but turned back from the pox."

Basil looked out at the villagers. His hand suddenly pointed at Merkel.

"You, man, who and where is this Kaspar?"

""Sir? I?" Merkel smiled like a fool, like the fool that he was not. "Perhaps from some other village or estate?"

"You!" said Basil, pointing now at Arl. "You, woman, where is Kaspar? Answer truly or God shall punish you."

Arl just shook her head and shrugged. Kristina saw that she was angry. Arl said, "I am just a woman, sir."

The villagers moved closer together and made a single wall that was the living village of Giebel. Many took hands now and some stood straighter, and others bent as if ready to receive punishment, but they were one wall of agreement. And that wall blocked the way into their village.

Lady Anna lifted her hand and walked forward so that the monks and deputies would be forced to ride their horses over her first. She stood in front of her people.

Kristina realized her time had come. There was nothing else but to give herself up, to step forward and save these brave people. She tried to force herself to move, but her legs would not move. She tried to find the power to force herself to move, to shame herself, to impel herself...

And ye shall be hated of all for my name's sake: But, he that endureth to the end shall be saved...

But it was Lud, not Kristina, who moved forward.

She watched him, amazed.

As if this were perfectly normal, he went past Lady Anna, straight to monk Basil's horse, and with his left hand he gripped its halter and bit, taking hold of its nose. The beast snorted, startled, but two of Lud's fingers slipped into the nostrils, controlling the animal. Its hide shivered and its hooves stamped but it was prisoner of Lud's two fingers. Kristina saw it almost as a miracle.

"Stand clear," the monk said, "what are you doing?"

Lud's right hand lay on the hilt of his sheathed sword, and Kristina saw that Lud was staring straight up at Basil, and there no was mistaking that if Lud pulled his sword, Basil would be first to die, no matter what else happened.

"Is that a Turk sword?" said the monk. "Does your hand dare lay upon it as threat to me?"

Behind Basil, a magistrate said, "We can ride the poxy bastard down. Shall we not get on with it?"

"Say yes to your man and we die, you and I," Lud said, looking up calmly at the monk. "You can guide me to the next world."

"You bluff," said the monk. His eyes twitchy.

"Do you think hell be hot, or cold?" said Lud.

"Hold, stay back," Basil blustered. His face was bright red. Kristina saw he was afraid and angry that he knew it could be seen, angry that he was not having his way. "I warn you that you are in danger of losing your immortal soul. I compel you in the name of God, stand clear."

"It is a fine Turk sword, sharp enough to shave hair, taken by me in battle." Lud's fingers twisted deeper into the twitching nostrils and the animal shuffled. "Let you and I go before our maker, with you leading my way, holy one."

Basil, his face red and sweating, lifted his arm to his men, holding them back. Kristina marveled at Lady Anna's courage, her proud dignity, and she saw the faces of the villagers agape at the defiance of their lady and of Lud against all these armed men.

"Lady, will you give me your word there is no Kaspar here? If so, we will retire with our deepest apologies."

Said Lady Anna, "No Kaspar has answered you. You have your sharing of our grain, and may God forgive you for taking such excessive portion of our toilings. So now you have my leave to depart with your booty, back to Wurzburg, sir."

And that was the end of it.

Basil turned his horse, and all the Wurzburg monks and magistrates turned behind him, and the wagons rolled away, and the villagers stood there and watched them go.

At first they all stared. Then some began to laugh. Then some began to cheer. Then some began to shout—

"Lady Anna! Lady Anna! Lady Anna!"

Then more and more shouted and then all of them were cheering, with the unleashed force of the fear that had so seized them before. The fear turned to exultation and relief, as water turned to wine.

Kristina saw enough through Lady Anna's veil to see that Lady Anna was as embarrassed as she was intensely pleased, and quickly the lady turned and waved to be accompanied back to the castle.

But the villagers—so fresh from their terror of the magistrates, released from their fears by the bravery of a woman they had never expected to stand firm—kept cheering.

"To work!" said Lady Anna to the cheering crowd. "What are you all staring at? Do you not have tasks, to prepare for winter?"

The crowd broke up. Kristina saw a sense of embarrassment as people passed her, avoiding her eyes. It was easy to see who had sided with her and against her. But they were all changed by this day. That, too, was easy to see. But what was not plain and evident was how they would behave next.

Kristina moved beside Lady Anna as they crossed the square back toward the castle. Lura walked on the other side of the lady. There was a grim hush like a pall of worry about Lady Anna, and then Lud was there, walking with them.

There had been no Lud at Kunvald, thought Kristina, *no one strong to stop them there...*

Lady Anna stopped at the castle gate in the dark, cool shade of the orchard across the moat from the castle walls. The moat below them was green with autumn water ferns, and the many colorful falling leaves lay on the dark water.

"Kristina, go see your child," said Lady Anna. "Lura will see me to chambers. Lud will release your friends. There will be no more weak minds learning reading. No more temptations."

But Kristina did not move; not yet. There were too many unspoken words waiting to break on the air. Too much had happened. Too much was yet undecided.

"What of Kaspar?" said Lud.

"That is steward business. Make your own decisions. That fool is the least of my worries."

"Your worries are my worries, lady."

"You are my steward. I value that you acted like one."

"From this day on I am a marked man. But that is nothing new to me. You may need appoint a new steward who has not given such offense."

Lady Anna looked harder at Lud. She leaned closer to him. "I need you more now than before this day, Lud. Do not think to escape the duty Dietrich laid on your shoulders, whatever its cost."

"I think no such thing, lady. All I am is here."

"God save us," said Lady Anna. "Am I the only one here with any wit to see what has just happened?"

Kristina heard exasperation, and something worse. Lady Anna was afraid, and her voice quivered with emotion that she could not well control.

"Lud, do you think this day was won? Do you imagine that all of that was about heretics, or some rag of a letter? No, Lud, they want my estate. Our stretch of fertile plain. I did not know it before today. That is what protection means."

Witter

Coward. Always the coward. Like a soul half formed that could not shape itself to courage.

Witter yearned to be with Kristina, to help her endure whatever happened, and yet he had fled away as he always did. He had fought the dog that one time. He had courage that one time. But the dog had given him no choice. When he had a choice, he fled.

He had seen it all. Like a ghost from the church bell tower, he saw the whole spectacle of it, and marveled at what he saw. Of course, it was not an end, more like a beginning. But of what, he could not say. Anything could happen next.

Each night in the deep hours he had slipped down from the church rafters for wine and bread and cheese, and when surfeited he had returned to sleep during the day up high like a night creature, a cat or a demon.

Then from a window casement, he looked down and saw Kristina and Grit and Symon and Dolf come out of the castle, blinking in the daylight, welcomed by a horde of villagers like long-lost relatives.

Seeing Kristina put a pang in his heart. But he stayed put. Wait and see. That was always the best plan. Watch and wait and see. As long as he was alive, and free, he had choices. Those choices were all he owned.

Down there, they stuck together, most of them. They were as different from him as night from day. And of course, he did not deserve Kristina.

Witter marveled at the change in his world view. He had never spent time in a village before, and never among villeins he knew by name. The village was a puzzle, but what bound it together was the glue of circumstance. Their fortunes rose and fell together as one. Some like the smithy and the miller had more than others, but not that much more.

All was shared: their fate and their harvest and even the water from the well, and all their collective goodwill, it was all property of the village and it was all shared. Yet the estate drew from them all its wealth. So even the estate itself was sharing in the village and fields and all its people, people whom the estate must sustain and protect, for its own survival. And yet, some who had learned to read were questioning it all, he knew. They did not do it openly but they were reading in secret. The young ones, especially, like Linhoff, were beginning to wonder why, if God made people, that some were high and others were low.

Once, Linhoff had come up to him privately, and said, "The book says that man must eat his bread by the sweat of his brow. And yet, only the low of men labor so."

"The book?" said Witter.

"The holy book. The law of God. Why do the rich not sweat? How can they take what is not theirs from those who do sweat? Is that not evil? Is it not wrong?"

"You have a Bible?" asked Witter.

"Not I, but a few others do," said Linhoff.

"Do you know the danger?"

"Reading changes a man."

So they fought and feuded, but shared secrets from outsiders and had their own code of conduct.

When things went bad, they stuck together, like now. Here they were. All were one.

Witter had not seen it since he had left Spain, his home, since all his own people had come together just this way, his father and mother and all the others, his once-betrothed Bianca, all gathering together in the synagogue, and they were locked inside and burned. And this set up a fearful longing in him, an anguish he had not felt so intensely in a long time.

Do not deceive yourself, fool. You are not part, nor can you ever be part of this. You are outside and will always be outside. So have your fun while it lasts, or make yourself undeniable, make yourself essential...

Now it was night again, and time to come down from the rafters for wine and bread and cheese, and perhaps to go out now that it was safe, and go to the little house and meet Grit and Dolf and Symon, and be one with them, too. Or run. Those were the choices.

Kristina, he had seen, was back in the castle. She had the lady and her child, and if he ran he would never see her again. He had stayed because he loved her. He had to face that fact. He had stayed because he had saved her before and, if he could, he would save her again.

And the Song of Solomon. The dreams came to him still, when Kristina would be alone with him, their bodies entwined, and he longed and hoped for those dreams, and they made life worth living...

"You have ravished my heart, my sister, you have ravished my heart with a glance of your eyes..."

Coming down from the rafter beams, down onto the bell tower casement, then onto the landing where the spiral stairs went down and down to the sacristy floor stones, he heard voices. He froze halfway down.

Then he recognized the voices: two voices, both men, echoing off the stones up at him—the priest, Michael, and Lud.

"But her son is heir, and he is in England for his education." That was Lud's voice.

Then he heard the voice of the priest, saying, "Prince Konrad is Florian's godfather, and he is Anna's cousin, and he always wanted her. I heard this often in confession, for when Konrad visited, Anna was ashamed for she sensed that."

"How can that be?" said Lud.

"She loved Dietrich with all her heart. Konrad was always jealous of Dietrich, for his manliness and courage and his sweet heart, too, she said. For all the things she loved most dearly."

"Konrad has not come since the pox. He would not want her now, for that," said Lud.

The priest said, "But to protect the estate means in reality to own it. To be protector and godfather of Florian. Not just godfather, not just cousin, but protector, one who can borrow a great deal against such an estate."

"Borrow? Would a prince need money so? He has the press, and other estates, and will be bishop someday when Lorenz is gone," said Lud.

Then the priest said, "The prince's debts are legendary, and he seized the press he now owns. That is common knowledge."

"Such things I do not know nor understand. I only know that if Dietrich were here, it would all be very different."

Witter had reached the floor and he saw them in the light of candles, both leaning on the table beside the wine cask, with its dripping bung.

He moved silently, slipping his steps softly over the stones smoothed by a century of human motion. They talked without seeing him, so intent were they upon their words and one another.

When Witter stopped a few feet away and spoke, the two men turned with a start to see him, as if he had speared them both.

"You must bring the heir back," Witter said.

They stared at him—the priest in wonder, Lud in anger. Lud stood up, too sharply, and he swayed and his hand gripped the table and tipped over his wine.

The priest said, "Is that Witter? Where have you been all these days? We thought you ran off."

"Were you listening?" demanded Lud.

Witter saw Lud's spilled wine drip onto the pavers, like blood, making red stars on the stones.

Witter said, "Yes, listening, and thinking."

"What business is this of yours?" said Lud.

"Throats have been cut for less, right?" said Witter.

"You say it better than I could," said Lud.

"What is it you wish to say?" said the priest.

"I like it here in Giebel. I do not wish to see bad things happen. I like the people here. And I have a part in this village, for all that. The key is Florian, the heir."

The priest and Lud traded a look, a pause.

"Florian? What good would he be here?"

"He is the heir," said Witter. "He is male. Is he not near of age?"

The priest said, "He should be coming on seventeen, maybe eighteen, if I reckon right."

Said Lud, "But they keep them till twenty in letters there. Dietrich told me so long ago, when he himself escorted Florian to England."

"Florian," said the priest, "Florian…"

Said Witter, "Go and bring him back from England. As godson he has privileges. As heir he has rank. He is now near enough of age to protect the estate."

"Dietrich is not here to make that journey," said the priest. "Forgive me for stating the obvious. But, you see…"

Witter thought of himself, Judah's heir, doing nothing to try to stop the burning of the synagogue and all within, instead fleeing across the hills—with the black smoke of death moving faster, pursuing him, catching him as he fled, choking, breathing the stench of beloved burnt flesh.

Said Witter, "Only the heir can stand against them now."

"Witter is right," Lud said. "Only the heir can press his rights and hold off the bishop."

"Again I must say, Florian is in England," said the priest. "His own mother's letters have not brought him back."

There was a silence.

Lud's voice broke it.

"Then we must go, and go as best we can, however we can, and bring him back."

Kristina

This fall, the leaves turned early. They were tinged with gold the way the icons in great churches were gilt-framed. Sometimes a sudden rain came up in the night. The evening glow was lingering long, with the barley harvest soon to come. On such nights, sometimes, she would sneak out and walk along the huts with the need for sleep dulling her day of fatigue, and then hurry toward the hut where her Brethren lived with her treasure, her child.

On such a night, when the rain cleared and clouds broke like something had torn them open, the moon was so full the twilight glowed later and later as if the sun had stuck just beneath the horizon.

Villagers called it the "barley moon," and when the barley was ripe they worked to harvest the fields half the night through, until the wagons and carts groaned under the high-stacked sheaves. Everyone except the castle folk helped. Tillers, miller, blacksmith, cobbler, candler, herdsmen, the Brethren, too. Starting at both ends of a field, hours later they met in the middle. Many would laugh and embrace and some would dance with relief it was done, exhausted as they were.

Sometimes on her way to the hut, she would stop on the silvery path, looking at the firelit windows of castle and house and hut, all seeming the same in the dark, and often she felt the smallness of being human and the enormity of the wonders moving above her in the sky.

What is my purpose? Why am I sent here?

It was so wrong how Witter thought himself a coward, when he seemed the bravest man she had ever known. But now, no one knew where he was or where he had gone. Was he out there somewhere, cold, alone? And why?

In the little thatched house Ruth had given them—after embracing Grit and Symon and Dolf, after all the greetings and awkwardness together had passed—Grit took their hands one by one. The hearth fire sputtered under their pots of beans and greens simmering on the iron hook.

"I fear for our brother," said Grit. "Let us pray for him."

"Witter is not our brother, if he has run away," said Dolf.

"Judge not," said Grit.

Kristina's heart stiffened, remembering the magistrates' dogs in the woods, and how bravely Witter fought for her. She missed Witter terribly now.

Help him, guard him, please…

Dolf grumbled, but they did pray, and while she mouthed sweet urgent words beseeching God, little Peter babbled nothings and bounced on her lap, pulling on her hair as though it was the reins of a horse. Pretending he did not exist ruined her sense of the prayer, and then it was over.

The prayers were done and they sang a bit. And then they ate with wooden spoons and clay bowls from the bubbling pot on the hearth hook.

Looking at the weary faces of her Brethren, Kristina thought wistfully of how it had been in Kunvald, reading, studying, debating in clean stone rooms where thoughts resonated like swallows in flight. Here the work was leaden and stoic and unending.

"Let me have the boy," said Grit.

She nuzzled her child's neck and set him down. He ran to Grit's arms, where he banged away on her porridge bowl with the wooden spoon.

"Such a fine boy," said Grit.

Kristina often caught herself thinking just the opposite. Why could she not accept him for what he was, God's gift, just as he was given to her?

My child is my only purpose?

His eyes were deep green, and his hair, golden at birth, was now deepening to brown. And she saw how Berthold's face was emerging slowly from the face of an infant, becoming the face of a little boy. And yet somehow he was slow, taking long to crawl, long to walk, too long to make word sounds.

"I never thought," said Grit, "I would be happy to be back here in this little house. Each fall we pack straw and clay into the cracks to ready it for winter. Each winter we huddle and pray, and yet it feels good here."

"We must plan which way we go," said Dolf.

"Go?" said Kristina.

"Yes, go. To escape this place before they change their minds and take us again," said Dolf.

"Maybe south?" said Symon.

"What about Witter?" said Kristina.

"Toward Switzerland?" said Symon.

"No," Kristina said. "We must stand for reason. And we cannot just abandon Witter. He may be hurt somewhere. And if he did run, he will come back. I know him."

"Maybe too well," said Dolf.

"That is a wrong thought and wrongly spoken," said Grit. Dolf nodded and rolled his milk-eye toward Kristina. "I am sorry for my wrong words."

"Witter is our brother," said Kristina, stung, for there was truth in what Dolf had said. She did care; perhaps too much, perhaps not all in a sisterly way.

Grit looked at her. "But Lady Anna has forbidden all teaching of reading now, you said so yourself. What more can we do here?"

"We must print the truth. I have thought on this all the time in that cell. We have been remiss. We have forgotten our mission."

Said Grit, "But we have been teaching."

"Reading only. Not the true word."

"Print how?" said Symon. "With what?"

"You will get us all killed or worse," Dolf said.

"We must go bring up the press from Wurzburg. The press we drowned in the creek, where the great oak roots enter the water at the meeting of the two creeks."

"You are mad," said Dolf.

"Let her speak," Grit said.

Kristina looked into each of their faces. Grit's sharp eyes sought hers, with determination. Symon's eyes were darting, seeking their own center. Dolf's eyes were afraid, distrustful.

She reached out and took their hands. She said, "We must find it, bring it back here, and restore it to the use it was made for. That is our work and we live in neglect of our sacred purpose."

"Sister Kristina," said Grit. "You have your child now."

Kristina took Peter onto her lap and began his daily reading lesson with chalk and lapboard. It was the second year of teaching, and yet he could hardly speak, much less make a letter with chalk. She prayed and she hoped he would leap into awareness of words, if she taught enough, and prayed enough.

Was she too impatient? He was only just past three, and he did not learn. He hardly responded. Often, his lower jaw relaxed and his mouth fell open, the tongue sliding out and dripping pearly drool from the pink velvet tip. Tiny scabs formed on his chin over time, and so Kristina had begun firmly stuffing his tongue back inside his mouth and then lifting his chin gently to shut his jaw. Time after time she did this, and one day Grit grabbed her hand to stop her.

"You are hurting him, Sister Kristina. Look, he is crying. If you cannot teach him gently, do not lose patience, or stop trying, please. Perhaps he is yet too young to learn."

"Others learn at this age. He is almost four and Berthold's child."

"He is only three, a child of God, he is Peter, not Berthold, a child as God made him. Let him be who he will be."

Little Peter shoved the chalk and board away and they clattered on the floor. The chalk broke into bits. Peter banged on his porridge bowl with his spoon, then dropped them, and ran outside to play.

She went to watch at a distance. Other children laughed and Peter laughed with them, their laughter circling the house outside as they chased and played. She saw him chase after them, all quicker than he was, Peter stumbling, awkward, but laughing. They picked on him, taunted him.

Her heart sank. But when she went to try to take him away, Peter squealed and fought her and ran away with the others.

And then came the day she was searching for Peter, and she found him with Lud and a pack of shouting, cheering village boys, out in the shadow of the linden tree. A cloud of dust was being kicked up and she saw why.

Peter was in a fight of fists. The other boy was no bigger, but a scrappy child that spit and kicked. Lud was urging Peter on. She saw Peter get knocked down and Lud get him back up, pumping his little fists to encourage him. And as she stared in disbelief, Peter leaped at the other boy and flailed him to the ground.

"Peter! No!"

She ran in to grab her son. He was bloody and happy and wild as a cat. The other boys were cheering his victory. Peter grinned proudly, his lips bloody.

"Me," he said, "me win."

"Leave him be," said Lud. "He does well."

"Does well? You teach him to harm!"

"He wants to be like the others, and now that he can fight he will be one of them. If you do not want him with them, keep him locked in a room somewhere. For Peter, this is the real world."

She tried to pull Peter away but he jerked free and ran away with the gang.

"See what you have done?" she said on the verge of tears.

Said Lud, "Would you rob him of his pride? Sometimes it is all a man has left to keep him going."

One day in the scullery, washing pots with Grit, she tried to tell Grit of all this.

Grit nodded. "Lud means well. Peter is himself. He is not you, not Berthold, not me. Each of us must learn to survive somehow, and come to our own belief, alone."

"But not with harm to others."

"Would you have your boy learn hate for others because they torment him? And would you have the other boys learn to bully because Peter permitted it?"

"Turn the other cheek."

"But Peter is just a little child, and he lives here, not in a fairy tale. Should he curl up in a ball and weep?"

"He fought. He beat the other boy down."

"Then he has a fire in his belly."

"Where did that come from?"

"God put it there, surely. And it will be your task to temper it with justice and love, when he is old enough to understand why. For now, he must survive. Do not judge Lud for helping the boy defend himself. That is all that Lud has ever known."

And Kristina thought farther back, and she told Grit of how she had been so terrified of the magistrate dogs when she was but a child herself, when her family was taken. Her fear was like a curse. A cross that she carried with her, which had now ruined her son.

"I fear it was the dogs," said Kristina. "When I carried my child inside me, my terror of the dogs impressed itself upon my baby, and now he is so, for all his life."

"If he has taken maternal impression," Grit said, "and if he took the impression of a dumb beast, it is God's will he is so."

"Was my fear a sin, and the impression a punishment?"

Grit took Kristina aside and sat her on a bench. They were both sweaty and the scullery air hung with steam.

"Kristina, hear me, for I love you and your child. Peter can be like a sweet dog that obeys and guards and protects, or Peter can be like a bad dog that bites and skulks and kills. How he will be is not in your hands. That is God's will, it is not your choice how he will be. Raise him as best you can, to be a sweet boy, loving and kind, and hope that he will choose your way, and not the way of the world. But it is this world in which he must survive."

Dolf came in with more wood to heat the scullery water. He had overheard them.

"Here is another question," said Dolf. "What would happen to your boy without you?"

"Why should he be without me?"

"Can you risk arrest by this printing and reading?"

Kristina helped him with stacking the wood, and together they stoked up the water-heating furnace.

Finally, she said, "What kind of world is there for my child, if we do not do the work to try to change this world from violence and fear and hatred?"

"We must try," said Grit.

"We are hardly protected here on this estate," said Dolf. "Have you forgotten how we were hunted out there in those woods?"

"Forgotten?" Kristina laughed. It was not like her to so bitterly laugh. "I wish I could forget, Brother. And you say we should abandon our brother Witter, when he saved me from those very dogs?"

"I will help," said Symon, bringing in more wood.

"To any who will help, I give thanks. To any who will not, I understand. There has been so much fear. We are all crushed by it. But I cannot stand living under this dread any longer."

"So you increase the fear?" said Dolf.

"I break the fear," Kristina said.

"Yes," said Grit. "We must answer the lies. More, we must print the truth."

Said Kristina, "We must bring home the press."

"Home?" said Dolf. "Is this home now?"

"Home is where we are together," said Symon.

"But our printings will quickly point to us here," said Grit, "and then we will be through. Facing the danger is not enough. We must have a plan."

"There is another way," Kristina said. "We will print the things we believe, and when market time comes we shall go back to Wurzburg with the market wagons."

By then, surely Witter would have returned, and she would know his reasons, and his courage and wisdom would be with her again.

Yes, he was a Jew. And only she knew that. She did not trust the others, not even Grit, with that knowledge. And in her protection of Witter's true identity, she had put herself outside her brothers and sisters, not trusting them. In that, she had sided with Witter against them, in trust. She did not feel the need to make him believe as she believed. She feared they would condemn him, fear him, reject him. And if they did, she would be forced to choose. But he was a good man. And part of her felt one with him, wherever he was.

"Wurzburg?" said Dolf, as if Kristina were mad.

Symon said, "And do again that which we ran from before?"

"Yes, Wurzburg," said Grit. "Kristina is right. If we do not do this, if we do not fight for our faith, what good are we in this short life? And we must give them better stories than the evil deceiving trash from Veritas Press. We, too, must do our duty, and become publicists."

Lud

Lud had wanted to help little Peter, for Kristina's sake. Each time he saw the boy being beat down and taunted, he took him aside and showed him how to fight back. On his knees he had pretended the child's frail blows hurt him, and this delighted the child and emboldened him to throw his little fists harder. It was skill more than confidence that won fights, but both were needed, and when Peter won his first fight, and thus won the admiration of the other boys, here had come Kristina, shouting and almost ruining it all.

Lud lay on his pallet, wrestling with his longing.

Some nights were harder than others, and many nights he woke, sweating, with his tool hard as a spike. He lay alone in his low bed with the fire burnt down and he ached in misery; and sometimes even, he wept for the need to hold a woman, the need to be held, the need of sweet succor.

His loneliness walled him in and the village itself was like a prison with no walls. Everybody knew everything, saw everything. A man could not buy a woman here, except with favors and promises, and anyway, that was just as empty, and also sad, for she sold nothing of her heart.

He could not sleep with a woman here even if one wanted him, for it would be known within a day by everyone in the village. And it would be just as empty, without love. And ever afterward he would be accused of bias or some of her kin would expect favors.

He starved to be wanted, inside a woman who loved him, to be enwombed by her love. He tried to remember his wife but he had long ago worn that out. And he always looked forward to any business at the castle, for that meant seeing Kristina, if only aside, in glances, to capture covert glimpses of her that he could keep and save for later, when he was alone.

Her sad, sweet smile, when she looked sometimes at him, did not mean love, he knew. Not the way he wanted her to love him. He thought how she had once looked at him with only fear in her eyes, a defiant kind of fear, but fear that a woman shows when she fears a man. When she smiled sometimes now, he was sure that it was the smile of a friend, or worse, that of a sister.

No woman would ever want him again. When he took relief from his own hand it was worse, a plunge into deeper emptiness. The loneliness then enlarged about him like the bottom of a dark sea. It hurt where he could not reach.

Sometimes, when the longing was nearly unbearable, he read the *Handbook of a Christian Knight* and found a passage that he had read over and over, when the lust was at its worst.

"*... how thou mayst resist the lust of the body... of which evils there is none other that sooner invadeth us, neither sharper assaileth or vexeth us, nor extendeth larger nor draweth more unto their utter destruction...*"

Why had Dietrich chosen for him this book? Did Dietrich expect him to live up to such impossible ideals? They were not meant for a normal man with such drives of the blood, the loins.

"*If at any time therefore filthy lust shall stir thy mind, with these weapons and armour remember forthwith to meet him: first think how uncleanly, how filthy, how unworthy for any man whatsoever he be that pleasure is which assimuleth and maketh us, that be a divine work, equal not to beasts only, but also unto filthy swine, to goats, to dogs, and of all brute beasts, unto the most brute, yea which farther forth casteth down far under the condition and state of beasts...*"

Reading this, Lud felt deep resentment, not toward God, but to this writer, this prude. And he knew that the writer, this Erasmus, struggled with his own lust, too. Lud wished Dietrich were here to explain this book, to defend it.

Lud knew what he himself believed. God made all beasts and God made male beasts crave sex. He thought of women at home who, despite his scarred face, had secretly taken his hand or given him an apple or otherwise shown to him their loneliness—Leta, even Lura—and he felt only brotherliness toward them. Not the hot wild urge he felt sometimes for Kristina, forcing himself not to stare at her. She loved God so. And God drove all males to hunger for females. And if God made it so, how could his lust for her be wrong?

Abstinence was for monks. And how many monks were truly celibate? Those who did not have love with one another had parishioners who adored them, or exploited them. Lud hated this book. It was unnatural.

But he was pockmarked, and he wore his mask, his face, like a curse. The nights would pass, if he could be strong. Perhaps someday he would dare to take Kristina's hand or touch her face. But he knew he would much rather fight a knife duel than risk her rejection.

At last, it was morning again.

When the sun was up, he dressed and slicked his hair, and went to the castle as he had promised Father Michael he would do.

Lud asked Lura to request Lady Anna to meet him in the antechamber, where they discussed estate business. He told her it was urgent.

He watched Lura leave him, saw the shape of her work-hardened body moving in the wash-worn serving gown, her hips wide from childbearing, and felt no lust, only the love a man feels for his sister. Lura was good to him.

Then he sat and waited.

Finally, Lady Anna came and stood there waiting.

"Has a cow died? Or a horse come lame?"

He stood quickly. "Lady, Father Michael, wishes to speak with you."

"I will see him at Mass."

"The priest says it is a serious matter of concern to all."

"Very well, apparently he could not wait, for he is already here, too, in the other antechamber. What revelation does he bring? Is it the end of days again, or some miracle printed in a broadsheet?"

Father Michael had been just outside the parted door, listening, and now he entered meekly, bowing, crossing himself. Lud saw that the priest was pretending this humility, and was anxious to proceed and persuade. Father Michael had become solid again, as if having a mission, an urgent duty to perform, had rallied all his core defenses and strengths.

Lady Anna crossed herself but was stiff with impatience. Lud watched her and thought of her as a woman, how beautiful she had been before the pox. Her form was still slender and fine in her elegant gown. It was insane, but he wondered if a pock-marked woman would have him, or if he would be repulsed by such a face as he himself wore; for life was mad like that, and unjust. And he thought how fortunate it was that minds could not be read.

Said Lady Anna, "The two of you have been up to something, I see. What must be said so urgently?"

Father Michael said, "Lady, we need to bring your son Florian back to head the estate. Under your guidance, of course."

Lady Anna took a long moment before speaking.

"Actually, I have thought on this at length. But he is in England."

The priest faltered: "If he stood as heir—and I mean no disrespect to you, lady, for you are brave and bright—but..."

"But a man is more respected. Even a young man."

"Lady," the priest said, "do send a letter please, at once."

Lady Anna threw her head back and her lace veil shifted and her ruined face was momentarily visible.

"Send a letter to whom? To England? By courier or by tradesmen? To fall into Konrad's hands? No, I think not."

Lud looked away, not in disgust, but in respect of her embarrassment, for she was not forced to wear a veil, but obviously did it from pride and from dignity. Dietrich would have loved her anyway, thought Lud, and inwardly he smiled. But he kept his manner stiff and formal.

She said, "What if my son will not come yet? I told him long ago of his father's death and ordered him to stay and finish his studies, as was his father's wish, though he wrote begging to return. And now I am to summon him home?'

"Florian must come."

Lady Anna looked straight at Lud. She nodded. "Lud, you then. If any can, you can."

"Lady?" Lud regarded her, confused.

"Lud, you, I say. Go bring Florian home. Tell him it is time to be a man."

"To England? Me?" Lud was astonished, almost laughing out loud, shaking his head.

Lady Anna was not amused. "Are you being stubborn or can you not hear? No letter alone will do. You must go."

"But, lady," said Lud, stammering, '"I have never been so far through foreign lands except in war on march. I do not know the customs or the languages. I have no safe pass for travel."

Said Lady Anna, "Priest, what do we know of France?"

Father Michael said, "England, Spain, the papacy, and we, the Holy Roman Empire, are allies, and the French are for the present subdued. The monks who minister abroad say that France has good roads with bad people on them."

Lady Anna nodded.

"For safe pass through France, I shall write Bishop Lorenz directly and bypass Konrad. You will take the letter to Lorenz first, and travel on from Wurzburg with his blessing. A simple trade pass will do for the port itself and passage across the channel, as that is international travel."

"I am to see the bishop himself?" Lud knew it was impossible and had to make her see that. "And then the travel? The languages? The French and the English?"

"Latin is spoken everywhere."

"But I have no Latin, or so little…"

"Lud, you are going. For languages there is Witter, who has many languages, I am told. Witter is obviously well-traveled. And, since Witter will no longer be teaching the weak minded to read, he is of little use otherwise."

"What about Father Michael? He can go."

Lud looked at father Michael for help, wanting him to intervene, to say something, anything, but the priest had withdrawn into the shadows like a cowering puppy.

"Witter, I say," said Lady Anna.

"But why Witter? I dislike Witter." Lud stiffened. By no means would he spend months traveling strange lands with Witter, totally dependent upon Witter to tell him what people were saying, what custom was being observed, which way was ahead. This was like a prison sentence, or worse. The very idea made him cringe.

"Lud," said Lady Anna, "your likes and dislikes are irrelevant to your duty."

"But lady, please, Witter is too clever by half for me, always watching, covert and smirking as if knowing all things but never saying."

"Because he is traveled, and with languages, you will take him." No matter what he said she had an answer.

Now Lud pointed to Father Michael, who stood silent as a statue, head lowered.

"What about him, the priest? He has learning."

"What about you, priest?" said Lady Anna. "I heard you gave a fiery sermon, at last."

"Like a falling star, I fear, that burns out quickly. Would that you attended church again."

"Would that you had attended my husband's deathbed as well. Look at him. He will not speak. He knows he is a drunk and dissolute. Speak up, priest."

"I would not last a day without wine," said the priest, as if in confession. "I am dissolute, and as you say, neither worthy nor reliable. Please release me to return to my church."

Lady Anna waved a dismissive hand and said, "Go, with our thanks for your honesty."

"Witter is waiting there," Lud said.

"I will entertain him until you come," said the priest. "But you will have to tell him all of this, I cannot begin now to phrase it or convince him."

Then the priest bowed and was gone.

"This Witter," said Lud, "why trust him?"

Said Lady Anna, "Witter can be trusted because his brothers and sisters live here hostage until his return."

"But why me? I am so low, so crude, and my appearance…it repels…"

There was a pause of silence. Lady Anna shook her head and made a sound that was perhaps a sob.

He realized why. She was not reconciled to her disfigurement, not as he was used to his. Hers was still an open wound in her vanity. His scarring was merely a fact. They were both scarred. It was a bad thing to say to her, and he had not thought before speaking.

He could think of nothing to say that would not compound the error. So he stood very still and silent, waiting until the lady gathered herself and sent him away or spoke again.

"Your face, yes. It repels. Only too well do I understand," she said at last. "But there are many others as scarred, Lud. Few will mark your passage."

"I meant no harm, my lady. I would cut my hand off before I would give offense to one to whom I owe everything."

"I know it and I believe it. But we need both your hands, and your courage and your wits now. It is you who must go, Lud, for aside from Dietrich, Florian has never loved another man better."

"But…I am just a villein."

"You taught Florian much about becoming a man, when he was small. If my son will listen to any person alive, he will listen to you, and you will make him understand and he will come home with you."

"Words do not serve me well, and I may falter in obliging Florian, for he has a sharp wit to reply."

"He will answer to his duty. I know his blood, from Dietrich and from my line. And you shall bear a letter from me, a letter that will help persuade him of the gravitas of all we face here, I pray."

Alone, Lud returned to the church, through the dark square, toward the warm light that fell from the little rose window over the doors.

The great linden tree was a black mass of shadow like a great bear crouched in the center of the village. A dog barked somewhere. He could feel the living village, the lives of the people all around him, in their homes, eating, sleeping, loving, breathing, gaining strength for the next day and the next.

Whatever he must do to make this safe, he must do. He had never felt such a weight, such a sense of duty. He thought of Florian, and he wondered what he would be like, now, after all these years, and whether he would still be a friend or be much changed. And he was afraid he would fail. These were unknown waters.

And it was upon this Witter, this strange man, this outsider, that all depended.

Witter

Inside the church, Witter was smiling. Nothing in this world really made sense, and this was a perfect example of the absurdity that drove human beings along their bumpy path to oblivion. He and Father Michael were drinking the rich red and earthy sacristy wine and trading Latin phrases in a minor contest of wits and skill. A glow was on, not only of wine but the teasing of intellect.

The wine improved intellect by removing the pesky impediment of critical faculties, thought Witter, smiling and drinking.

They laughed together. The conversation in Latin seemed a test not only of skills but also of insights, and Witter quickly realized he had underestimated this Father Michael.

"Your Latin is excellent," said the priest.

"And yours," said Witter. "I return the flattery."

"But I am trained," said the priest. "And you?"

"This is very good wine," said Witter.

"That is a weak evasion. Why?"

"Modesty," said Witter. "I am a meek and modest man."

"Where did you learn?" pressed the priest.

"On my own," Witter lied. "In a world of printing, you can master almost any knowledge, once you have learned to read. Professors are on their way out. Any man can learn anything now."

"That is good and bad. Good in possibility of learning, bad in translation of meaning, perhaps."

"Perhaps. But who has captured all meaning? Does not meaning grow, as each participates in knowledge?"

"Indeed, yet should each man know, uniquely?"

Then Lud returned. And the conversation in Latin ended. Lud's face was more constricted than ever.

"You are coming with me," Lud said. "You, Witter."

"Me?" *Impossible...*

And when Lud told Witter why he would be going to England, Witter was dumbstruck. Quickly his thoughts raced, first with denial, then with dread. Noticing Lud and the priest staring at him, Witter realized that this was real.

"A learned man, with languages," said the priest. "He will serve well."

They were serious.

"You are going with me," said Lud. "I do not like you, I do not like this. But you are going, and by God, you shall help me and make the best of it. You have traveled. You have languages. You know the ways of foreign places. Do not deny it. I see it plain. You must help me."

Witter was dumbfounded, at first.

To travel all the way to England, with this beast of a man, this half-tamed, half-read rustic battler Lud?

Then he saw it as an almost divine intervention in his behalf. He should have seen it from the first. It was almost as if he had planned the whole thing and prayed to Yahweh for it to come to pass.

Insane as it was on the face of it, such a trip presented him with one permanent advantage—he would at last possess proper traveling papers. He had not possessed real identity papers since Córdoba. Now he would have papers that identified him as Witter von Giebel. A gentile identity to protect him in all travels to come.

"Yes, I will go," he said. "I will do my best."

"Can you ride?"

"Can I ride?"

"A horse. I have never seen you ride."

"Horses are dear and I am poor," Witter said. Yes, he had ridden a horse, a finer horse than any here would ever see, a horse long taken by soldiers who destroyed his family, and all that now seemed lifetimes ago.

Said Father Michael, "The roads are dangerous, even if you join a trader's wagon train. Too many bad people out there these days, disgraced knights become brigands, thugs and rogues, God knows what else. Take the river barges, all the way to the coast, and then cross the channel at Buèges. A good barge is so much safer and easier."

"No money for hiring room on a barge," said Lud.

"But why not?" said the priest.

Lud flared, saying sadly, "You have helped me with the tallies these last years, you know better than I how bad things are. The roads it must be. No money for barges."

"I cannot ride a horse all those miles," Witter said.

It hit him hard, that if he did this, he would not see Kristina again for many weeks or months—perhaps never again. Anything could happen to him out there, or to her while he was away. The realization struck him through, and his breathing almost stopped.

"Your ass will shape to the saddle," said Lud. "I will help you along. Our horses, our money and daggers and papers, are all we will have to count on. And each other."

"Papers, of what authority?"

"Safe passages, on writs from the bishop, if he will do as Lady Anna writes him to do."

Father Michael said, "Such safe passages are not guarantees of anything. They may mean something only if taken by a favorable bishopric, or may be worse than none at all, if issued with the seal of a bishop hated in that place, wherever it may be."

Witter took a long deep breath, to say what he had to say now.

"There is one more thing that is important," said Witter.

"What thing?"

"You must respect me."

"I must what?"

"You must not treat me rudely. You must travel with me as an equal. We are not man and servant in this."

Lud glared, and Witter realized the man was actually embarrassed. "Servant? I am not one who ever would want or need a servant, but you must be a good reliable man."

Witter pressed on; it was now or never, and all this had to be said and agreed upon, or the whole thing would be an absolute disaster for them both.

"And you must trust me, and do whatever I say must be done—whatever customs we must observe—when it must be done, wherever we pass through those foreign lands. You will not know the words I am saying to foreigners. You must be willing to trust me in all ways and all things, or we will never reach England together. Am I understood?"

Lud cleared his throat. Witter watched him struggle with all of this.

Finally, Lud nodded. "Understood," he said. "And if you act in any way against our purposes, for whatever reason, there will be no place on earth or in hell where I shall not find you."

"Threatening me is a bad way to begin."

"It is no threat, Witter. And your death will not be a quick one. Now, am I understood?"

Witter looked at the scarred face, staring into the young eyes that seemed not to belong there, looking out at him from such a terrible mask.

"Understood."

"Then take my hand and we shall pretend to be comrades, until we are." Lud's right hand came forward, and Witter felt rough fingers as strong as iron tighten upon his hand and squeeze. And from Lud's strange eyes came conviction reaching out to Witter.

"Make your good-byes to your friends," said Lud.

If he saw Kristina, he feared the things he might say, might gush, might even frighten her. The Jew professing his love. Impossible. But he must.

No, it was best in writing.

Witter thought of the sacristy study where the priest's little desk held pen and ink and paper. There were feelings he must express, and then, like one condemned, he would go with Lud.

LUD

Lud was leaving soon, and there was one last thing here to do. He came down the stone steps and turned left at the bottom toward Kaspar's cell. He carried a lantern into the darkness.

Sig, Kaspar's father, followed behind, holding a clean woolen cloak. Old Vogler the gatekeeper, and Golz, his key bearer, had accompanied them with the keys, but now stopped and waited on the steps just above.

"It was Huber, not my Kaspar," Sig kept saying. "Huber persuaded my boy and used him to spite us all."

Huber had fled the village, and now it was known that Huber—drunk and angry at his fall from the stewardship—had helped Kaspar write the heresy letter and send it by a traveling peddler to the bishopric magistrate in Wurzburg.

"Kaspar was willing," said Lud.

"My good son was drunk, out of his right mind."

Golz said, "Poor Kaspar, he is never himself now. Please, Lud, do forgive him."

"Yes," said Sig, "yes, forgive him. I have always supported you as steward. You know that."

"The battle changed us all," said Golz.

Lud, standing on the stone steps in the lantern's glow, remembered this same Little Golz, who saw Hermo beheaded in the storm, who carried Hermo's head about in the mud, and was mocked by Max on the march, and who defended Kristina to the villagers, telling them she was brave. Lud looked at Golz, remembering all this, and realized what a good man he was. He hated this mess with

Kaspar, who was not worth the hair on the head of Golz, and yet they all begged forgiveness for Kaspar.

Bad luck was hunting him yet again.

Lud was thinking, *Nothing I ever do is right…*

First, there had been a clamor for punishment of Kaspar, for sending the letter without village consent. And after things had settled down, many villagers said Kaspar should be released, and that Lud had no right as steward to imprison anyone. Sig was the village miller, and everyone depended upon him, and he had wealth, for a villager. So Lud had considered his two choices. He could take Kaspar out in the dead of night and disappear him the ancient villein way: slit, shovel, and silence, the "three S's" of village farm life. Or, he could let Kaspar go. Sig had not threatened, but had more wisely blustered and begged and bribed.

"You shall have free milling for life, Lud, and Kaspar will realize how he owes you so much, I swear it."

Lud was leaving to go all the way to England, and disappearing Kaspar might cause a mess if anything went wrong. It was best to release him to Sig.

"He will be a good boy," said Sig, over and over.

"He is a man, not a boy."

"Yes, but he served the ram's head and valiantly lost his leg. His girl quit him. He can no longer dance. He has never been the same."

"Any fool can push a pike. So what if he has been to war? None is ever the same. Others went and do not behave like angry brats. You shall be responsible for him while I am away. And I want no free milling, Sig. Take better care of your son."

"I will, yes, of course, trust me."

"No more letters. He endangered the whole village."

"You have my word, and my gratitude for protecting him. I know there was much anger. But I have smoothed it out all I could. It was the reading that did it."

"There will be no more of that here. No more classes. No more broadsheets. No more troubles. When Florian returns as heir, we will return to the old ways that were always solid."

"Now that Huber is gone," said Sig.

"If Kaspar is disloyal again, it is on you."

"I take full responsibility for him, Lud, please."

"When I unlock this cell, this is between you and me, not me and Kaspar."

"For God's sake, please, unlock it at once."

Lud rocked the big key in the rusty tumblers until they clicked, and with a tug, he opened the cell. A stench poured out. Lud had allowed Kaspar to have ale. That was a mistake. He had drunk it all.

The big jug lay on its side empty. Lud choked and grunted in disgust. Behind him, Sig cried out. Kaspar was passed out in his own vomit in the cell floor.

Sig rushed in past Lud; he knelt and cradled his unconscious son, wrapped him in the new cloak, weeping, and carried him out. The good leg hung askew and the stump was bent sideways. Head lolling, Kaspar looked like a broken stick doll. Sig was sobbing miserably, kissing the filthy bearded face of his son.

"Kaspar, oh my dear son, Kaspar…"

Lud turned away and ran up the stone stairs ahead of them, hurrying now, leaving them behind as if escaping a fire.

Konrad

It was after the morning Matins prayers and the boys singing like birds and angels and the monks chanting, and before the morning wine.

Konrad had visited Mahmed in his chambers and found him dull and listless. His body, unexercised, looked flaccid and sallow. He wore his woolen robe, and his long hair and beard looked unwashed.

"You must bathe when you expect me," said Konrad.

"I do not bathe, for I no longer pray. But now I can drink wine. I have become a good man of Wurzburg."

"You stink of self-pity."

"I despair of my own lying," said Mahmed.

"Then be truthful when we meet."

"Truthful?" Mahmed grinned, but not in joy, and made an odd sound as if in pain. "Your Basil shows me the broadsheets, and there I read lies, purportedly said by me. He does it to gloat, to injure my soul, I am certain."

"Your words are reshaped but a little, for brevity and clarity, by my monks. You earn your life by assisting your host. That is only righteous."

Mahmed sat forward with a shocking earnestness; the suddenness of his motion startled Konrad.

"Do you know that I am trapped by Islam? Not only by you? That I am bound by my law, by Sharia, to assist you?"

"I know no law called Sharia."

"It is the good. The will of God. What we must try to be. As the beatitudes are to Christians, as the commandments are to Hebrews, so is the Sharia to me and to mine."

"This Sharia sounds interesting. I will have Basil come up to transcribe some of this Sharia."

"Will you print truth if you know it?" Mahmed's eyes were rimmed in red, and Konrad realized the man had been weeping recently. "If I say black, you print white. If I say yes, you print no. How can I pray? How can I speak?"

"I thought you said you no longer pray to your false God, Muhammad."

"Allah, not Muhammad." Mahmed wrung his hands together. "The Qur'an says, "There is no compulsion in religion. Sharia is our law. It is my personal relationship with God. It obliges me to be loyal to Wurzburg, where I reside."

"Loyal to Wurzburg? You? How can that be?"

Mahmed looked out at the sky through the wide casement of his window, which framed the river a hundred feet below. Birds were flying south against a fall wind.

Konrad said, "Look at me when we speak."

Mahmed turned back, and bowed in apology.

"Prophet Muhammad wrote the Medina Charter. Would you print it for your people? Muslims are held to Sharia, which instructs me to obey you. The same with Jews who obey the law of the Torah. And Christians who must obey the law of Christ, and is not that to love? To love all? Even your enemy? And does that not include me?"

"You are not my enemy," said Konrad.

"No, in truth, I am not even that."

Mahmed hung his head and turned away and covered his face in his hands, shuddering in shame. It was horrible, to be near such weakness. Konrad had come to think of Mahmed as the bishop's curious exotic pet. Now the feeling suddenly became one of even more contempt.

Konrad always knew when it was time to leave. He felt only disgust for this weeper. You could only get so much out of him at any one time. And Lorenz would not hear of having him put to the iron.

Later that day, Konrad instructed Basil to make some use of Mahmed's weakened and confused condition.

"Print something sensational, exposing the evil compulsions of Islam. Turn it one way or another. Add to that his claim about Jews. And how the Muslim tries to destroy the fighting will of Christians."

"Evil eye, that is popular at the moment."

"Say he has the evil eye then."

"The evil eye used in war, and to seduce virgins."

"Excellent. With drawings, the more salacious and terrifying, the better. Also we need heroes. Someone piercing the evil eye with a dagger."

"The people will devour these."

"And, Basil..."

"Yes, my lord?"

"Mahmed says you have been showing him the broadsheets. Is that so?"

"Indeed I have. The bishop may be critical, but cannot say we have not been honest with the Turk."

"Excellent. You are clever."

Basil bowed humbly. "I would rather be wise, but clever must do. Anything to unite our flock, anything to give them one singular mind, I shall do."

Now, in early afternoon, Konrad walked with Lorenz through the enormous stone vaults of the cathedral, where the stations of the cross had recently been enhanced with gilt carvings of angels on high. The angels wept pearl teardrops. Their eyes glittered with sorrow. Konrad could only imagine the expense. Lorenz was explaining their sacred purpose.

"Magnificent," said Konrad.

"Yes, Riemenschneider has outdone himself."

Konrad sniffed. "In becoming wealthy, indeed he has. Now it is said he is to be elected head of the city guilds."

"Riemenschneider is a good man of the church, gifted by God. Look at the colors, the exquisite mastery of form, the sorrow and the elegant wonder of it."

Konrad saw the merit in the work. Of course the artist was gifted. But Konrad had paid for a portrait from the man and the result had revealed his weak chin, not the jawline he had so clearly instructed Reimenschneider to paint. The painting was closeted, useless; worse than useless, mocking.

So Konrad said, "He is arrogant, and immoral in political thought. They say he even will admit Jews to the city council, if he wins a seat. Or buys one."

Lorenz turned to face him, with a scolding smile. "Jews bring good business. Many popes have defended the rights of Jews. Clement and many others. You always forget that Jesus and all the apostles were Jews."

"Luke was a Syrian gentile, I believe," said Konrad.

"Yes, that is so."

"You see, I am learned, a little, and art is false, all of it. More false, those images imagined by the artist, than the printings of Veritas Press."

Lorenz sucked his teeth with an expression of disappointment. Then his narrow face softened to the patient teaching expression, wishing to help Konrad understand. Konrad hated that, but smiled.

"Holy art, dear Konrad, the artist enriches us all with higher vision. The next Lenten season will inspire our people more than ever. They cannot make pilgrimages to Jerusalem, but they can come here and see the route of Christ's passion."

"No more crusades?" said Konrad.

"Indeed, and praise God for that."

"I think it is a pity, your grace. To crush the Turk, once and for all, that is a worthy piece of history to make any man's name."

"History is for men, not God."

Konrad thought carefully before pressing deeper. "A fight should be done right and for all time. But our wars quailed, never went far enough. Conquest would mean we would never again spend funds to fight them at the borders. Nor would we need new statues to show the way to Golgotha, since we would have our soldiers there and pilgrims."

"Christ preached against war, Konrad." Lorenz clucked scoldingly. "I sometimes send men to war, but reluctantly. You adore it but do not fight. You know, we are both princes in the league, under Maximilian, and so we are brothers in the Church and state, both. But we are so different, you and I. Yet so close."

"And with such relish do you show the suffering of Christ here. And you do relish that."

"As bishop I must reach a balance of control and freedom. The people must realize the cost of their salvation, so that they are grateful."

Konrad smiled. "Grateful and compliant. I concur."

Lorenz flared, as if stung. "Are you ever sincere? Ever truly in earnest? Or are you always mocking something or someone?"

"I am always sincere," Konrad said. "The stations of the cross do more than show, they inspire. Did you know, of the fourteen, only eight stations have direct meaning and source in Gospels? Is adding six more stations the sincerity you speak of, my dear bishop?"

Konrad had waited to fire this shot into the bishop's conceit. Lorenz sucked his teeth and regarded him with a curious and subtle smile before speaking.

"In popular faith, Konrad. We give legend credence through others due to popularity. Jesus falling three times under the weight of the cross? Not scriptural. Veronica's veil? His meeting with Mary? Not scriptural. Nor Jesus lying perished across Mary's lap. Yet the sacred suffering is truth."

"Really, you are an education in popularity, your grace."

"So why do we do this? Because, dear Konrad, belief is what we inspire. Faith is truth."

"Truth is the good." Konrad had waited for this rationalization, and now pressed his advantage. "Popular faith, yes, and that is the mission of Veritas Press, to mold the mind of the people as one. Nine of our finest monks labor to publicize our truths. To preserve the popular faith and keep it strong. Can you not agree upon that one central concept? That truth is the good?"

Lorenz turned and looked straight at him, and he reached out and took both of Konrad's hands. Konrad felt the cool fingers that were as slight and gentle as a boy's or a woman's. He did not pull away as was his impulse, and he looked into Lorenz's calm eyes, noting his narrow face and wet lips, and Konrad tried his best to smile with the love of a friend.

"Konrad," said Lorenz, "Truth is truth, truth unchanged. I agree that we need one another, and as allies and dear friends, but hear me. I tell you that your so-called publicists are too extreme in your stories, some of them preposterous, more strange every year."

"Truth is often very strange. For the common folk to understand truly, it needs shaping."

Lorenz was becoming red in the face.

"Hear me. When he tells you a truth, Mahmed is trying to bring understanding, but then you twist his words into something very bizarre and frightening. He is quite off his chess game now. And hardly touches his meals. But he drinks all the wine brought up to him and asks for more."

"This very morning, he insulted me, saying, 'I do not bathe, for I no longer pray. I drink now. I have become a good man of Wurzburg.'"

Lorenz laughed a little. "Yes, but look, is it not good, at least, that he no longer prays to his heathen God? Perhaps we can make him repent and even save his soul?"

Said Konrad, "Save his body first. Move him to chambers with no window. He gazes out too fondly at the fall below him."

"Poor man, no doubt he longs for his home."

Konrad felt a rise of his gorge; he wanted to shake Lorenz sometimes, for his stupid softness. How could one with so much power, with such duty to the security of the people, say such things? He tried to respond without anger, but it was impossible.

"Poor man?" Konrad could not hold back. "The Muhammadan lied about ransom and is fortunate to wear his head still upon his shoulders, and eat our food, and be kept like a prince. Next you will bring him a girl."

Lorenz sucked his teeth, making that detestable scolding sound, and said, "You use him badly."

"The unbeliever must earn his keep somehow. Even if only a figure of public scorn."

Konrad felt the bishop's fingers slide away.

"Konrad, you are too harsh. Mahmed is human. Not a beast. Not a creature to rouse hatred in our people."

"He is your war trophy, proof of our good in war."

"Lamentably so."

"You cannot raise taxes without blaming the need for war. You cannot keep the merchants and guilds paying their rightful share without enforcing authority."

"But to invent such tales?"

Konrad tried to think how best to convince this man, once and for all. Lorenz could be so dense. He wanted to be firm, yet sweet at the same time. He wanted to be loved—that was the key to Lorenz.

"Dear bishop. Hear me. I love our people. I love our good Church. But our people have short memories. Once they learn to read, they do read the Bible, no matter how terrible our punishments. And they begin to think for themselves—all kinds of thoughts—even that the rich should not be rich, and the poor should not be poor. They would remake the entire world to suit themselves. We must lure them to our truth. The stranger our stories, the more popular. The more popular, the more power to persuade, to protect the souls and the security of our home, our flock."

"Yes, yes." Lorenz took a pleading tone. "But, when we agreed to let you have your press, I was to approve everything, if you recall."

"You said yourself that you read them. Basil assures me that he sends everything to your offices first, but that you rarely comment."

"I have been remiss, but am commenting now," Lorenz said. "By showing the people how Jesus overcame his suffering, you see, we are exampled to be strengthened, to repress our own desires and ambitions, to spend our days praying and contemplating. Do you take my meaning?"

"You are wise beyond me," said Konrad. "But, is it not so when you add six stations to the suffering of Christ? Are not eight stations enough for his torment? You add six more not even in Scriptures?

But I understand. It is the same with Veritas Press. We stretch things if we must, in our constant battle for the good of the people."

"You twist all my meanings. I always beat you in chess, but never in words."

Konrad did not reply, having learned long ago that no answer was preferable to a weak answer. If he waited, the subject would soon change back to monuments and art and things of noble beauty, and the expense they incurred, and the necessary means to raise funds. There was nothing the bishop could do legally now to change anything.

They passed outside through the naves and under the arch of the twin towers, into a gray fall day. The leaves were down and blowing across the courtyard. Konrad wrapped his cloak about him, careful that the crest of von Thungen remained visible in front, over his heart.

Lorenz turned and looked at him.

"I know you and many others think me weak and vain."

Konrad was taken aback, for those were his exact thoughts at the moment. "Do I seem so judgmental?"

Said Lorenz, "Today I will prove to you that I do what I must, for the law, when it is required. Yesterday I judged a man. Today he is to be executed, and as his judge I must bear witness. Will you bear it with me?"

"What was his crime?"

"A heretic, preaching in the marketplace, against our church. Reading the Scriptures openly. Attempting to lead our people astray. Saying our authority is not valid before God. That each is one's own authority."

"Nothing forgives such a crime," said Konrad.

"I am glad that you agree."

Konrad pressed it further. Lorenz was too soft to do much punishment. "The people will expect a severe justice. You must set an example, to help them behave as they should, to protect them."

"And so I did, and sentenced the man to be quartered."

Quartered...

Konrad recoiled, felt an ugly thrill at the word itself, at the obscenity he knew that would come. Perhaps to be forced to witness it was a test by Lorenz, of their comparative manhood. And Konrad felt he had provoked Lorenz into a proof of moral courage, and he therefore resolved not to flinch. He wished he had not pressed so hard, nor agreed to come. But now it was too late, for to decline now would reveal deep weakness of character.

Now he saw that Lorenz was closely observing him.

"You thought me weak?" said Lorenz. "Your color has drained considerably, dear Konrad."

"Your justice will be a tonic for me and for all the people," Konrad said. This is what it would be someday to rule, he thought. To show strength where there was weakness. That was as good as truth itself.

Kristina

They prepared for a half-moon night when they could travel without lanterns. The first thin snow was on the ground. As night fell, they prayed for success and for safety, and put on all their warmest things, and prayed again. When they came out of their hut, the night snow was all blue with the rising moon. Everyone in the village was inside their own homes. Chimneys trailed smoked eastward. Then Kristina and the others heard a horse and wagon coming.

"Linhoff is coming with a wagon," said Grit.

Kristina looked at her. "Linhoff?"

Said Dolf, "How does he know?"

Grit said, "He came to me himself. Asking if he could have lessons of reading, with Witter gone. And I told him we would no longer be teaching, but there was other work we would do, to help write and print our beliefs."

"You trusted him?" said Symon.

"Shall we keep the good work selfishly to ourselves? You must put your trust in God," said Grit. "Yes, I trust him. And we need his wagon."

"It is Linhoff," said a voice from the approaching wagon.

Now Kristina saw two more walking with the small wagon. Ambrosius was leading the horse. And Max was walking on the other side. Then Jakop came along behind with a rope looped over his shoulders. She thought of them marching with pikes, hardly more than boys, on that road of war—Jakop, who had killed Ott; Ambrosius, who desired literacy and played hurdy-gurdy; Max, the jester, who now rarely even smiled; Linhoff the leader—and now they looked to her like men. To Kristina, they had come to help do something that was ordained by grace, by the heart, not by order of the state.

"We wish to come, to help," said Linhoff.

"Yes," said Max. "If they tell us we cannot learn to read, we shall write."

"Whatever I can do," said Ambrosius. "You brought knowledge to us, and we cannot stop now. We want to help bring your press back here."

"This is madness," said Dolf. "Is there anyone left who does not know of this?"

"Only us," said Linhoff.

"Trust in God," said Grit. "Did you bring the rope?"

"Just so," Linhoff said.

"I have the rope," said Jakop.

"None knows the paths like we do," said Linhoff. "Playing here as boys, we know every inch."

"Thank you," said Kristina to each, "and bless you."

In the silver light they made their way on the road, with the wheels of the wagon and the horse hoofs crunching, all their breaths steaming, and to Kristina their steps sounded impossibly loud, but there was no one out, it seemed.

Again, in her mind, she read and reread the letter Witter had slipped to her, without a word, with only his eyes lingering upon hers, when he had left.

No one has known me as you do. I have known no one as I know you. We have not touched yet you have touched me more deeply than I ever believed possible, and I go to try to do what I must, to protect all that I now must try to protect. If you will only wait for me and pray I may return. Surely there is one God with many names, who knows our hearts, our fear and our hope and our good and our bad. His will be done. More than your brother, Witter.

She knew it by heart. It went so much farther than she had expected, so much deeper, and she tried not to obsess on her own feelings. It shocked her that he felt this way for her.

More than your brother...

They went deeper into the forest and then moved with more caution, more difficulty, for the shadows of the trees were so black and impenetrable, and any breeze made false shapes of men and dogs coming at them.

It was bitterly cold. On the path, the clear metallic moonlight was harsh like a touch of steel upon the eyes. Kristina blinked, yet kept watching the impenetrable darkness of the trees, her vision wavering like a black curtain in the shimmering moonlight.

Said Grit's voice, "We turn back west at the fork, and then the road winds along the creek, is that not right? The creek joins the other at the big oak? That is where we shall find the press, sunken there?"

There was muttering from Symon, but Dolf agreed with Grit, and Kristina remembered it the same way also. But remembering the way brought all the other memories.

Stumbling and sliding over the frozen snow, moving beside the horse and wagon and the dark shapes of the men and Grit, Kristina felt the pull of the past, dragging her along.

She remembered it all so vividly that it seemed like last week, not years before, when they had left Wurzburg and carted the awkward heavy pieces of the old press, reaching the river and crossing by ferry, chased by magistrates, dragging the press from the muddy river bank, hurrying through the night, the trees, the dogs coming, and sinking the press in the confluence of creeks under the great oak. Then Berthold, falling, bolted. She and Witter running, caught by the dog she later killed. Pox in the village—so much death and pain. It all seemed like a nightmare that she had left far behind her and was now reentering. And the deeper they went into the old trees, the more she felt the unnerving sense of being watched.

She prayed and then prayer brought bright thoughts. There was brightness in remembering her child being born, in the teaching she had done, in the good days that became weeks and months and years.

"There," said Grit.

Everyone stopped.

Grit said, "There, see the great old tree, the two creeks?"

"All frozen," said Jakop.

"I brought an axe," said Linhoff.

"What good?" said Dolf. "Who goes in that water under the ice to fish in the cold mud?"

"A man tied to a rope," said Max.

"Which man?" said Dolf.

"Get wet," said Symon. "You die out here."

"I will do it," Grit said. She reached into the bed of the wagon and pulled out the rope.

"No," said Linhoff, taking the rope from her. He pulled off his big cloak, and looped the rope around his tunic.

Dolf took the axe and broke the ice along the frost-rimmed, frozen mud of the bank.

"What am I looking for?" said Linhoff, snugging the knot around his waist, up into his armpits.

Grit said, "There are three main sections. The carriage assembly and the impression assembly and the main frame."

Linhoff winced involuntarily as he lowered himself into the edge of the water, going down and down and down until he plunged and disappeared.

First Linhoff came up, spewing, coughing, with a tree limb. He plunged down again. Then he did not come up for too long and they hauled on the rope, all of them, hard, and up came Linhoff with the rope tied onto part of the press. Kristina saw that it was a wheel of old cart, covered with mucky slime and algae. They hauled it out and threw it aside.

"Damn," Linhoff said, seeing it was a wheel.

Before they could stop him Linhoff was down in the water again and he was pulling up, emerging, and had the impression assembly. Then he brought up the carriage assembly. They were thick with river slime.

"That is enough," said Kristina, "you are frozen."

"I will go," said Max. But he did not go.

"You said three sections, we have only two," said Ambrosius.

Said Symon, "We can build a main frame from wood. Those two are the ones we cannot build."

"Strip," Kristina said to Linhoff. She helped pull the wet clothing from him and wrapped him in his dry cloak. "Up, on the back of the horse. His back is warm."

"Wait," said Grit. "The type. The box of type. We can do nothing without the type."

Now Linhoff was shivering uncontrollably. He turned toward the water but Kristina pulled him back and the young man collapsed onto his knees, shaking.

Kristina looked searchingly at Max and Ambrosius.

"I will go into the water," said Max. But as before, he waited and watched and did not go.

"Can we come back for the type when it warms?" said Ambrosius. He was shivering though he had not gone near the creek.

"I will get the type," Kristina said. She tied her skirt and threw off her woolen shawl.

That was when Linhoff lurched back up onto his feet, and he shoved her away, and, staggering, he plunged back into the black icy water.

"My God," said Grit, "my God."

Half an hour later they were moving back down the road. Grit had insisted Linhoff ride the warm back of the horse. He was half frozen, dripping, shivering, teeth chattering. Linhoff's hands were tightly clenched from the cold and no longer worked. They steadied him on the horse. Kristina rubbed Linhoff's leg and arm on one side of the horse, and Grit rubbed his leg and arm on the other side.

The press pieces rocked gently, dripping on the cart behind the horse. The box that had carried the movable type lay on the wagon, half open, dripping. It had come open in the river when they pulled it up and all the type was lost. Linhoff had nearly wept.

"What good is the press now?" said Dolf.

"We will think of something," said Grit. "Have faith."

Konrad

Together, Lorenz and Konrad went down to the square. It had snowed in the night but the street laborers had cleared the main byways. Flanked by attendant monks and a civil guard of armed retainers, they sat on the high bench and observed.

The day was beautiful, not gloomy and gray, and he thought it was perfect weather, a crisp fall day with birds migrating, the tree leaves all colors, and the sunlight sparkling on the great spires of the cathedral.

The condemned, a small bald man with wide shoulders, wrapped and burdened in chains, was brought in a tumbrel with four horses tethered behind. His eyes were wide and white as two boiled eggs. Seeing him, the crowd seethed and cried out, and Konrad caught a stench of all the mawkers, taunters, and filth-throwers. The executioner monk stood well away, emotionless upon a high stool.

"You see, I can be strong," said Lorenz.

"What was his crime again?" said konrad.

"Bless me, I have forgotten," Lorenz said. "But justice is not high art, is it?"

Konrad considered before speaking. Yes, this was art. All persuasion, in every form, was an art.

He said, "Vile, but art nonetheless. The art of persuasion. To persuade the many through the example of one. Just as a good broadsheet can do."

Snowmelt dripped from the roofs. The street gutters ran with a dirty gray discharge. Many in the crowd were subject to drips and wore their cloak hoods up, looking like a horde of executioners themselves.

The charges were read by a monk and then a prayer said, and the condemned cried out to the mob, something about God's will be done and this world being only a portal to paradise. Or suchlike. Konrad could not hear it all.

Then the executioner gave an order, and the magistrates' man chopped off the condemned man's right hand and threw it onto a smoldering brazier. Molten lead was poured onto the stump of his wrist. Many in the crowd laughed at his shrieks. But Konrad also noted a large number out there who appeared sorrowful, resentful, anguished.

"The stations of the cross inspire hope and faith," said Lorenz, taking Konrad unaware.

"The stations of the cross?"

"Yes, you must realize that the souls of our people must be lifted from the mud of such spectacles as this before us today. Sacred art is the highest achievement of man, while serving God."

"My press achieves that end and at a profit."

Konrad looked out upon the mob and wondered whether God could exist in those bestial minds, those savage hearts, or if it all was a sham. Somehow, it was even worse than men like beasts in war. But those who showed intelligence and even compassion, he knew, they were the dangerous ones. They became leaders, persuaders, controllers. If only there were an easy way to round them up and break them for the use of the state.

"If that man were one of us," said Konrad, "those animals would be just as enthusiastic, or even more."

"You do not love our people?"

"I adore them. That is why they must be kept in their herd, with one mind. As I said before, persuasion is art."

"Stop making your points, Konrad, it is that poor wretch who today pays the price. Have some respect."

"I do deeply respect that mob, your grace, with my most sincere dread of them."

As the punishment went on, Konrad shuddered at their enthusiasms for this horror. And he watched the face of the bishop go sour with pity and disdain.

"The Holy Blood Altar at Rothenburg," said Lorenz, "if only we had one like that here."

"I have seen it. Their people behave no better for it."

"That is untrue, Konrad. I am told many sweet visions are seen at that altar. We must begin a new fund."

There was a roar from the crowd.

The condemned howled, and then made long, whimpering cries. He was seared with smoking pincers from the brazier. The waiting horses screamed, too, leaping, their hooves slipping on the wet slick pavers, as they were held ready by their grooms. Finally, came the main show that some in the wild crowd lusted to see. Others were openly weeping now. Some were bent over and seemed to be praying. None of them could be trusted.

Konrad stared out at those faces and despised them all.

Ropes were tied to each arm and leg of the condemned man. A horse was tied on the end of each rope. A groom was with each horse. A magistrate directed each groom, and a monk directed the magistrate. Signals were given. The horses first pulled in short tugs. The victim screamed and the crack of dislocated joints sent wild cries from the mob. But still the body was in one piece. Still, the man made sounds of suffering.

"Badly done," said Lorenz, and waved one arm angrily.

Konrad laughed. "Badly done? It is badly in nature."

"You know what I mean."

"Here is a riddle. If it is called quartering, why are there five pieces left at the end of it? Two legs, two arms, one torso?"

"Stop, Konrad, please."

The horses surged in four directions and new screams, more sad than before, more exhausted, came from the condemned, the horses leaping with arms and legs tied on. The man was strong and the executioner made joint cuts with a small axe, and on signal the horses surged again; and finally, the victim suddenly came apart.

Three horses stepped away, free. But one leg was still attached to the torso and the horse raced away, bolting into the crowd with the obscene thing like a monster bouncing on the chain behind him. The crowd rioted, many screaming, some clearly shouting in outrage, leaping away in all directions as the horse charged through them with the thing bouncing behind.

"The riddle is solved," said Konrad.

"No respect whatever," said Lorenz. "There are injured people down there. The horse has done much damage."

"God forgive him," said Konrad.

Konrad looked at the bishop with wonder. There were actually tears in the bishop's eyes now. Was this man truly a tool of the creator? He could send men to war, he could have this wretch so tormented, and yet he could weep?

"Judge not that ye be not judged, and yet you, a Christian, are a judge. And so you judged that man to suffer what he suffered. Was it not just?"

"And do you judge me?" Lorenz sucked his teeth. "A bishop acts as duty demands, Konrad."

"The same with my press. The same with my duty. Our life is rife with ironies. But ironies of necessity."

Below in the square they were dragging the remains to a bonfire. Konrad thought that Lorenz might vomit.

"Let us to the Marienberg. I need wine."

An hour later, they sat at an oaken table that was dark with centuries of wine stains from discouraged monks getting drunk, and now Lorenz was describing his visit to the court of Maximilian, from whence he had recently returned.

Konrad had been to Vienna many times, but listened as if every word spoken by Lorenz was truly magical.

Lorenz sucked his teeth, saying, "The Hofmusikkapelle was fabulous. Such boys singing, voices simply like angels, filling the Hofberg. I tell you, the glory of this emperor will endure. He has a new portrait of the empress, Mary of Burgundy, all their family. Splendid. And the organ, the organ! If only we had half such an organ here!"

"The emperor is brave and always tries new things, new ideas," said Konrad guardedly.

He knew that Maximilian approved of reading for the masses, and it worked for Konrad, as long as people were reading what he himself approved for them. Lorenz had said this to his face more than once.

"Oh, I almost forgot, your godson shall be returning," said Lorenz.

He said it as an aside, almost indifferently.

"Oh? I have several godsons," said Konrad.

"Yes, you are generous and do play the field. Many nobles do. If one godson does well, and others do poorly, you can still be proud. I refer to Florian Geyer. Florian is being sent home from studies in England."

"Florian is returning? Why?"

"His mother wants him home, as heir, I think. It was all the rage a few years ago to send noble sons abroad for study, to improve their chances at court. But England, England. There is an interesting choice."

"Myself, I always urged a monastic setting for Florian's education, here in our own good empire. But Dietrich insisted, and so England it was."

Konrad seethed yet pretended to be calm. Many years ago, he had arranged Florian's mail by diplomatic horse, and had read most of the letters before passing them along to Anna, Florian's mother. That was before the pox, and his dreams of her corrupted, and the comfort of her sleeping robe gift was ended. With all that, he still thought of her sometimes, the way she had been as a girl. Of years late, often he had not bothered to unseal and read Florian's letters, and now he wondered what they had contained. More, he wondered why he had not been asked to assist with Florian's return, nor even informed of Florian's return. He felt slighted. And suspicious. And the pain of old hurts came lingering back to make it worse.

Lorenz said, "A good father wishing to broaden his son. Perhaps for court, for diplomacy?"

"Dietrich wanted his son to learn to think, he always said. I argued against England."

"But English Henry is ally to our Maximilian and faithful to our church. They burn more than you would burn, if you were bishop. I do read some of your printings from your press, you know."

"Really? I am flattered."

"If you knew my true reaction, perhaps flattery would not be the right word."

"How is it different, your grace, when the Church adds stations to the cross, and I add stories of good and evil? Are we not both guiding the people to the inner truth?"

"The ways we define truth, Konrad, seem quite apart. At any rate, I signed safe passages for two Giebel men that his mother sent to bring young Florian back home."

Konrad had to force himself not to reveal too much interest. He waited a moment before speaking. The wait was but a few seconds, but felt like long minutes.

Finally, he asked, "Two? From Giebel? Who were they?

"A steward and his man. The steward was pockmarked, had a rude country demeanor, was a bit odd. His man seemed of a higher training somehow, something about his manner."

Konrad knew the man, the pock-faced dueler, the villein Dietrich had made steward. Lud, that was his name. Konrad had lost fifty gold marks in that contest. Of the other man, he had no idea. If they had papers only a day or two old they would be on the road toward France, still, by horse. Perhaps they could be intercepted. Or perhaps it was better to let them bring Florian home. He himself would need to reflect upon this and decide quickly. The fact that Lorenz was so pleased to have had these little secret doings irritated Konrad. But then there was always usefulness in the tricks of another.

"So," he said, "two country clods asked for safe passage papers and you gave them, just like that?"

Lorenz sucked his teeth. "With a letter from Anna Geyer. In her own hand, no less. Reading is becoming quite endemic, and that is a fascinating development for all."

"We have argued this too many times. Where will we be, when anybody can think anything they want? Reading brings temptation to those who do not know how to think."

"Is not that the point?"

"If I say that quartered wretch had bats fly from his mouth, and if my monks write it up and print it, the unwashed will all believe it as fact. That is the power of printing. That power cannot be denied, and the people must be served."

Lorenz looked appalled, amused, shaking his head.

"My dear Konrad, do not think so small of yourself."

"Tease all you want. He worshipped Satan if I say he did. It is truth if I make it truth. Those who can read will tell those who cannot. Those who were there and saw the execution will revisit their minds and realize they saw it, too. They will brag of seeing the bats fly out when he screamed loudest. Some will swear they saw the bats possess the horse and make it charge into the mob. Fools will come to blows over who saw what first."

"And that is good, your Veritas Press?"

"Indeed. That is its power. To create belief. Within a day at most, all Wurzburg will believe it is truth."

All? I think not. Only all who do not know how to think."

"Truth is a commodity to be bought and sold. Like barley. Created and hatched like geese, from the eggs of ideas."

"To think, I say. To read and learn for oneself. Your printing efforts pervert that process, but for how long? Many will learn to think, in time. As Florian's father desired for his own son. To learn how to think."

"Your wish to be loved is too great."

"You are wrong. Love can never be too great."

Konrad laughed; he felt a true and deep scorn. Florian would be a youth, hardly more than a boy. Seventeen, maybe. The age of strutting and boasting and fighting over girls. And truth? Laughable! What would such a youth know of truth? Truth was power. With power Konrad could make truth into anything he wanted. And he could take such a youth and mold him, too.

Konrad thought upon all this. But he did not say it. Instead, he selected something far less revealing of his own mind, of his own plans for Florian.

"England," he said lightly, "is full of windy notions."

"Their young Henry is ally with our Charles, and France walks on tiptoes between us, so all is well, and let us be grateful for that."

"Which way do they travel, land or sea?"

"The river routes along the safe, old Hanseatic League trade routes, they said, to Cologne and then Bruges for the channel crossing. The Ottomans presently rule the Mediterranean, so a river travel would be safest. Tradesmen use the road but so do brigands and bankrupt knights. They take the safe river routes by barge. Safe passage and good hopes."

"Too much foreign thought to educate a son."

"Perhaps Florian will not think so himself."

"Dietrich had strange ambitions for his heir. I myself have not been to England, and would not wish to go. We have fine scholars here. And who knows what ideas are taught in England these days?"

"They have their wise men. Good universities. Florian is at a place called Oxford, and if I am not mistaken, Erasmus teaches there, and others of esteem in learning and thought."

"Erasmus? Who is that?"

"Are you serious? With printing, thoughts move apace. You should read more, my dear Konrad. There are scholars and thinkers who delve in truth. You own a press and yet you do not stay current?"

"I read." Konrad sniffed, to let Lorenz know he had stepped too hard. "But more, I create ideas."

"Do not take offense. But listen here. It will be most interesting to meet young Florian and to spend a few hours discovering what he has learned there, so far from us."

"Indeed," said Konrad, indeed. "No one was closer to his father than I was, nor a more devoted cousin to his mother."

"Is that why your monks and magistrates wanted the Geyer estate under your protection?"

"You know everything, Lorenz."

"What a burden that would be. Only God knows what we are. I am sure such was only your sincerest wish to help them stay on the true path to God."

"You say it better than my poor words could ever do. And let me add that the funds I have pledged to dedicate to your works of holy art, such can only be given if I have them to give."

"In the end, you never fail to twist the simplest things into a knot," said Lorenz.

"How would you keep them untangled, your grace?"

"I will tell you something I heard as a boy: when you cannot use hawks, you must hunt with owls."

"That could mean almost anything."

"It is how I have maintained good order, with no risings, no revolts. For the good of all my people. Someday, perhaps, you will find what it means, for you."

Then they parted for the day.

Konrad went up alone to the antechamber off his suite of rooms. After his bath, his groom had rubbed him, and his mind seethed with distress, anger, confusion.

Hawks and owls my ass...

For the truth was, Konrad was in dire need of funds again. The silver miners in Saxony were threatening to strike unless better drainage was put in the silver pits, and his shares had dropped. The printing press was his best revenue source, but his relatives had ruinous debts that he had signed for, and many were being called. There were no Jews to blame and seize, for the cowardly Jews had stopped lending to those they feared. And his uncle had sent word from Wittenberg that their enormous investment in a Philosopher's Stone had not yet transmuted gold from base metals, but a breakthrough was imminent, and more funds were needed urgently.

God was testing him. That much was clear. And God always had a fatherly reason, if one could only tease it out through prayer...

And he thought, *God sends me this godson when I can most use him. Is this not proof that I am blessed, that I am approved, that I am doing the right work of God?*

He prayed that God might be moved by grace to answer him in prayer and to inspire him.

The elegant icon of Saint Boniface, saint of all Germans, looked down upon him from the wall opposite the carved stone fireplace. His eyes were full of pity or disdain—Konrad could never be sure which.

His velvet prayer pillow was snug under his knees and the velvet railing under his arms, and the fire kept just so by the prayer servant. All perfect for deep meditation with the Creator. His thoughts went out like open arms...

What must I do? What must be done?

The thoughts soon came numerous and fast.

At first he conceived a wild desperate plan—to send his own men to the barge port at Bruges and catch the two Giebel men and disappear them there. A monk and a magistrate could go on to England and bring Florian, his godson, back. Not back to Giebel, but back to Konrad.

Lord, direct me to Thy divine will...

Then, as he prayed, Konrad heard a sacred voice tell him this plan was faulty. He realized it was foolish and faulty. An angel's voice spoke caution to him...

No one can be trusted. There are no trusted men. You can hardly trust yourself. You would be blackmailed and have to have those men killed, and then the killers could blackmail you in their turn...

Besides all that, Florian would find out sooner or later that his mother's wishes had been otherwise. Not to mention also that Bishop Lorenz von Bibra was himself involved, issuing safe passages. It was the hasty plan of an idiot. God was like a patient teacher, leading him forward.

It was well he had prayed on this. Prayer always helped him think things through so much more clearly.

To help clear his mind, he went out upon the night streets, as sometimes he did, with two monks and two nuns and found young prostitutes and brought them, willing or not, to the Sacred Heart convent. Upon saving these girls, he proceeded to the abbey of the mendicant monks, who fed the poor and harbored the demented, and he gave them coin that their work might continue. On such a night, Konrad was blessed and praised many times, and cursed only a few.

As he walked through the night streets, with the monks and nuns about him, Konrad prayed, and then he slowly began to realize the truth. And it was a harsh thing to confront…the truth.

He was a foolish man. He wished to have faith in God but ambition was in the way, and the pressures of family; always the need for money. His one success was the printing press. His one voice was delivered to the people through that press.

Konrad felt a rising elation.

It was suddenly so clear, so vividly right, what he must do. He owed Dietrich his loyalty. He had once loved Anna so dearly, before she had the pox.

No matter what, Florian was his godson. He was callow, probably, a weak youth too softened by books, but with some learning from England, and malleable for shaping.

He would honor his solemn promises to Dietrich, whom he had loved, and who was dead. He would welcome the son, Florian, back. Sweep that green lad off his feet, lavish clothes and servants upon him, find him a mistress to school his lust. Groom Florian for the Vienna court. Even find Florian a noble betrothal, do everything to honor Dietrich that was possible, and win Florian over with all his heart.

He would use Florian's experiences in England—whatever they were—in broadsheets, damning heresy and radical new ideas.

He would mold Florian to strive for the good of the people. Florian would become the voice of youth, of the true Holy Mother Church, and of the state.

The people needed examples. Burnings and quarterings were good to caution the people. Wars were good, too, to enforce patriotism, to challenge any who opposed, to denounce them. But also good examples were necessary, heroic figures to imitate and follow. And to obey.

Konrad felt a deep, sweet centering of purpose.

Thank you God, for revealing to your devout and faithful servant the true way…

Late that night, he was kneeling again at the prayer bar. His knees ached on the prayer pillow and his shoulders were cramped, but his mind simmered with certainty.

Konrad found true joy. He wept a little before rising from the prayer bar. Mother Mary was smiling at him with encouragement.

In his hot, scented bath, near dawn, God inspired him to do his sacred duty. He must post spies so that he would know when the two commoners returned with Florian through Wurzburg. As godfather, he owed this trust, both to God and to Dietrich, that he would never allow his godson to be taken back to Giebel.

Witter

So now he was Witter von Giebel.

Fate had taken him another turn, and his odds of survival had multiplied. But he was paying the price—his old self-loathing came boiling back.

Now I am a good German, my father, you would be so proud of your son...

When Lud had come to say his farewells to Lady Anna at the castle, Witter managed to slip his folded note to Kristina, sealed in wax with the priest's little Franciscan seal from the sacristy desk.

"Take this to Bishop Lorenz and he must see it and read it himself," said Lady Anna. "Do not leave until you have his safe passage, with his seal. Avoid Konrad and his monks. Forget you were once a villein. You travel in my name, and Florian's."

Witter saw her letter, and that it was in Kristina's beautiful floral hand. In her letter to the bishop, Lady Anna had not given Witter the estate name, only the village name. But that was good enough, for now he possessed a document for travel that, for the first time, proved a non-Jewish identity. It was worth far more than the coins he had lost that night on the runaway ferry, nearly drowning in the river. That gold was trivial compared to the value of this identity he now possessed—a safe passage for Witter von Giebel, signed by the Wurzburg bishop Lorenz von Bibra, no less.

Then it was done and time to go.

Lud insisted they leave the village by night. There was a moon and light enough for the road. Lud wanted no witnesses. No village send-off.

By dawn they reached the river and then the bridge into Wurzburg. At the cathedral, Lady Anna's letter had brought an instant response from the monks, and they waited a full hour for the bishop himself to come for Matins from the Fortress Marienberg and give them a few moments.

"Say nothing," Lud had instructed. "Whatever the bishop says, it is I who must respond. Keep your lips tight."

Witter stood back and lowered his head. He felt paralyzed by even five minutes of attention from the bishop himself, who asked many questions of Lud regarding the lady, her condition, and the estate. The bishop even apologized for the false accusation of heretics and for the actions of the monks and magistrates at the harvest sharing. He seemed to have had a full report from someone.

And when Lud told the bishop they were traveling by hired barge up the safe river route, Witter kept his mouth shut. The lie was so big that Witter was appalled and afraid. But Lud said it flatly, and the bishop blessed their travel.

The whole time, Witter expected them to be put in chains and into a cell. It seemed impossible that he could stand with impunity before a bishop. But it was so. Then they were sent on their way with safe passage papers. The city was excited about a quartering to take place the next day, and ale was flowing in the stalls.

Lud was anxious to get away and got them quickly out of the city.

"There may be those with grudges against me here," he said. "Or some that may remember you as well."

"Why did you lie and say we take the river route?"

"You did well to keep your mouth shut. Continue to keep it shut, Witter."

They crossed out of the city and took the river bridge past the magistrates already sneaking drafts of ale, and went north on the main trade road.

The farther Wurzburg was behind him the more Witter felt fortunate. And then, far out on the road, passing trade wagons out into the open farming plains, passing from the lands of one estate through another and another, there was something else he at first could not isolate. He was sure it was the fear of the travel. Then he wondered, was he homesick? It could not be that.

A gentle horse rocked under him. The bones of his butt felt the hard, hot muscle of the mare that had foaled several times but was strong. She had been selected for Witter by Waldo, the groom and stableman. A soft-padded saddle was under him, a gift from Waldo meant for women. But he rode stiffly, in little unnerving jerks, and watched Lud riding his big horse as if part of the beast itself, shoulders loose, head lazy and easy. Behind Lud's mount trailed a packhorse that shambled along under its bundles of their food and provisions.

His new papers did not change the fact that he must always find a place away from the sight of anyone else, especially Lud, when he needed to piss. Sometimes he had to hold his water so long he felt like he would burst, and the release, when it came, was like a flood of fire, then bliss.

There was a great silence between them, and finally, Lud said, "I lied to the bishop because we can trust no one."

"But he gave us safe passage."

"To be used only if we must, by river barge, not by land roads. I lied because I am an ignorant man, and do not know who is good and who is bad. I lied because the monks who came to tax the estate belong to Konrad, who serves the bishop. They are both princes, Swabian princes, who are no more than a gang of warlords."

"But Lorenz does not join Wurzburg to the league," said Witter.

"No, every soldier knows that Lorenz keeps his hands clean with the church matters and that Konrad does all the dirty work of repression for the state. Very convenient. Both are rulers, and I trust nothing about them."

Witter said, "I see."

"You see nothing. I also lied to save face of my Lady Anna, who has not the wealth to send us on the river. The bishop would have insisted we take his coin for the river hire barge, and much face would be lost."

"You give them so much crop shares for tax, should not they give some back?"

"As I said, you see nothing."

"I do see that our safe passage is worthless."

"If these roads were good enough for Dietrich to take little Florian to the coast, they are good enough for us now."

Together, several times a day, they consulted the map.

They used the same Hanseatic Trade Route map that Dietrich had used years before when he had taken Florian to England. It was scribed on tightly rolled vellum and watermarked by travel and old rains. But the route was clear.

The old Roman roads with their rounded cobbles were submerged partly under dirt blown from nearby fields for ages. They were ancient roads that obeyed the rivers and mountain passes, north by northwest, then west. The map of roads showed how Lud and Witter must pass west up the Main River out of Franconia, across the frontier, and skirt eastern France through the Savoy at Grenoble, the Burgundy, and the Champagne. Then leaving Dijon, the Seine would lead them up past Troyes, Paris, and Rouen, and then from Normandy they would take passage across the channel to Portsmouth.

"The roads take us along the rivers we could be traveling by hire barge," Witter said once.

"Maybe I will sell you and buy river passage," Lud said back. "How would that be?"

"I am not worth that much," Witter said.

"For the last time, shut your mouth about the river."

Lud kept the map close against his body inside his tunic; when they unrolled it to consult a crossroads or river way, the sharp animal smell of Lud's sweat came wafting off the vellum. Yet there was true comfort in this savage companionship. The roads were dangerous.

Witter had never in his life traveled with a man who knew tricks of caution such as riding wide around crossroads, watching for fallen trees ahead. Twice they had stopped. Once, Lud pointed out a campfire of rogues, and they rode wide around it. The other time a tree had been felled in the road and they crossed a field on the far side, galloping when men began yelling behind. Witter found himself laughing. Before he had been like a rabbit, sneaking here and there. Never had he traveled with a man at arms.

The horse rocked under him. Once he woke with Lud poking him in the ribs.

"Night is for sleep, not day."

The road passed a series of villages filled with villagers who might as well have been from other countries.

When they took water or bought a meal, it was always the same: "*Beware the next village, they are not good people.*" And then in the next village, "*You are fortunate to have passed through that last village unharmed, they are not like us.*"

Passing the villages, out here, Witter thought of his life back in Giebel. How he knew the seasons by the particular fruits or vegetables that came ripe and were often left in a full basket on their stoop. How there was the sowing and the lambing and the calving, and then the harvest times of reaping and of slaughter.

He thought how it was life as told in Ecclesiastes, universal and enduring, a time for every season. And he thought how the life in the Scriptures was like this, the life of the earth. Not of cities where he had spent most of his day. Life as lived toiling and eating bread made by the sweat of the brow. He thought of the young single women there, who watched him when he passed, gave him little gifts, and smiled. And how, no matter how he ached as a man, he avoided them, and so earned the respect of their brothers or fathers. He knew he was almost revered, somewhat like a priest: sexless, devoted, teaching literacy from the love of his heart. Of course, it was not from love but from expediency. And yet he was amazed at how it had all happened.

Is it possible that I miss Giebel?

It was impossible, but true. He was already homesick for Kristina, and the passing villages reminded him so of the place he had spent the first good years of his adult life. Yes, Kristina was back there. And out here with Lud, he felt less lonely than if he had been alone. Even with Lud, with his unfortunate face and his stoic loyalty.

Then he knew what it was. It came in his father's voice, and the voice was happy and gentle and pleased:

In Giebel you earned back your pride and you found in yourself the love for a woman...

Now he was heading back toward the south border of Switzerland and then into France, two of the countries he had fled through years before, as a Jew. Now he was not a Jew. Now he was returning as a man with papers and a bodyguard and a mission from nobility—as ludicrous as it was true.

God's whims were not to be questioned, but they were difficult to keep up with. And he prayed for God's blessing in his time of danger...

Barukh atah Adonai Eloheinu melekh ha'olam, ha'gomeyl lahayavim tovot, sheg'malani kol tov...

Only prayer held him to who he was, what he needed to believe he was. And so on horseback, he prayed against his shame, beseeching forgiveness for his new identity, even though it was no more false than the others...

Blessed are You, Lord, our God, King of the Universe, Who bestows good things on the unworthy, and has bestowed on me every goodness...

It had rained twice the first day but now was clearing, and a wind was up from the west. The last leaves were being torn from the naked trees and the straw blew out of the empty fields. Mud in the road made a sucking sound under the passing horses. He wore an oilskin rain cloak and was quite miserable. Twice he had suggested that they stop at an inn, but Lud insisted they push on.

"We can sleep on the ground if we have not come to another inn by dark."

"Why do we not stay in abbeys or inns every night?"

"Lady Anna is not made of gold, that is why."

"So we travel the rough way, like villeins on the run?"

"Look, man, and listen. There is no money for this fine little journey to fetch Florian. Boat passage for the channel, and a bit more, is all the lady could provide us. If you have coin for inns and feasts, well then, let us enjoy it."

"I have none," said Witter, belatedly.

"We are men and we will go as men go. We will reach the frontier with France in a few days, if we do not foolishly delay because of a little drizzle that is hardly rain."

"France," said Witter. "Do you speak French?"

"The only words of French I know are those shouted in battle, some Frenchman cursing me, and those cried out by a Frenchman with a piece of steel in him. Once in France, we rely completely upon you."

Witter became obsessed. Never before had he had a companion who was deadly in arms. It occurred to him like a heady wine that he was dangerous now.

He could, for the first time, have someone killed on a whim. He could defend himself without fear, without knowing anything of fighting. He was free in a way he had never been. Yes, life was too bizarre.

They next day on the horse, he rode beside Lud. His butt was throbbing with every lurch of the saddle.

"You are stupid, and my tool," he said in French, *Vous sont stupides, et vous êtes mon outil*; and Lud frowned at him and asked what he said, and Witter replied that he said, "You ride well, I hope to learn."

"Loosen your ass and drop your shoulders," said Lud. "Let the horse do the work. She will follow my mount. Relax in the saddle and stop fighting her."

If he told Lud that some Frenchman had cursed them and was going to cut their throats, Lud would not know different. Lud would just act. He would certainly kill. And this fact was unnerving in its possibilities for both good and for evil. Witter realized how careful he needed to be in translating anything anyone said.

For two nights they camped under the stars.

The third day, clouds came just before night. Out on a main road, Witter was miserable, hunched over the neck of the mare. They pushed on through a heavy thunderstorm. Lud would not stop. At a crossroads, the faint yellow lantern lights of an inn showed in the gloom. Witter's mare was hard to control in the flashes of lightning and the booms of thunder. She reared and he fell in the mud, hard. Lud rode and caught her.

"The horses need a stable," was all Lud said.

At this point he would do anything to get off the horse. His butt burned like fire and he could feel a boil rising. He rode standing up in the stirrups until his legs cramped and he was forced to sit and suffer.

Lud banged on the inn door with the butt of his dagger, demanding a room for the night. But when the peep door opened in the top of the big door and a pair of eyes peered out and saw Lud, the eyes went wide and the door was slammed shut.

"Let me try," said Witter, drenched and chilled to the bone.

Witter rapped politely and the peep door opened again. Witter said polite words, courteous phrasings of greeting, in the false polite manner of a noble, and the door opened to him, with profuse apologies.

Upstairs in the room later, drying out in front of a fire, and enjoying hot beef stew and red wine, Lud said, "From here on, you are master and I your man."

"How so?" said Witter. He had wanted to propose something like this but had not dared. It surprised him that Lud saw it and was not too proud to do what would work best. "How am I your master? I cannot ride well nor fight. And you have the map."

"You know exactly what I mean," said Lud.

Lud unrolled the vellum map and studied it.

"You have courtesies and language. I have no niceties for this. Tomorrow we cross the frontier into France. I told you before, the only men of France I ever met were those in my first war. I know nothing of their language or French ways, only the old soldier's joke that they make love with their faces. So to them, you are the noble steward, I your man."

"Very well," said Witter, deeply pleased and relieved.

Lud looked at him. "But always remember, I am steward. You serve the estate. And I am on you like a hawk on a hare. If we are met on the road by rogues, or any others of harm, you let me fight and you ride hard away."

"Ride away where?"

"Hear me. You do not become involved in my fight. If I am killed, you ride hard away. You proceed alone and try your best what must be done."

With that, Lud pressed the vellum map into Witter's hands. "Here. Take it."

"But I would not proceed alone?"

"You will, by God. Swear it."

"You have my word."

"I said swear it. Swear it by God."

Lud leaned forward until their eyes were inches apart and Witter saw into the liquid orbs, saw sincerity and purposefulness that distilled into loyalty. This man believed in who he was and what he was. This man had purpose and belief in what he must do. Witter was astonished at the revelation and amazed at the sudden admiration he felt for a man he had so feared and despised.

And Witter said, "I do swear it."

He took the map from Lud's hands. Then Lud passed him the leather wallet.

"The safe passage. Lady Anna's letter to Florian. Take them as well. If we part, all is on you."

So Witter took them.

If we part, he lied to himself, *I will try to make myself forget Kristina and take these papers and make for the French coast and try to buy or steal passage down through Gibraltar into the Mediterranean and on past Italy to Istanbul…*

But he knew it was not true.

He loved Kristina and he would do whatever he must to protect the estate that protected her, bring the heir Florian, and get back to her, to take her away somewhere, if she would go. If she would love him, that would be the rest of his life, being one with her.

And for the first time in years, perhaps the first time in all his existence, Witter had a reason, beyond fear, for what he was doing.

Kristina

The snow had stopped. It was almost dawn when they trod through the slushy mud and finally arrived back on the outskirts of Giebel. They hid the cart behind the smithy, in the wagon shed behind the charcoal shed where Linhoff had gotten the cart to begin with. Kristina looked up once and saw Jakop watching her. He looked away quickly, but helped her when she dragged the empty type box.

"Let me," Jakop said. "Do not ruin your hands."

She looked at her hands. They looked like claws, half frozen and red; tools for work. She wondered at what Jakop had said. Then she realized how the others must see her—Lady Anna's handmaid, a reader and teacher and harper. And they were laborers, illiterate until now.

Max took the shuddering horse to the stable and Waldo came out and looked at them in the cold night, and Kristina realized that he knew all about this.

"How many know?" whispered Grit.

Kristina shook her head in response.

Kristina and Grit took Linhoff to the fire in their hearth in Ruth's house, and they dipped rags in the warm water bucket and bathed him.

"This alone was worth it all," said Linhoff.

"Enough," said Grit, winking at Kristina. "He is enjoying this far too much for decency's sake."

"If only I had not lost the type pieces," said Linhoff, dropping his head low, shaking it.

Grit said, "May God inspire us through His grace."

"Grit," said Linhoff. "What kind of name is that?"

"Marguerite," said Grit, with sad disdain. There was a harsh judgment in her voice. So rare for her.

"Much nicer," said Linhoff.

Grit sneered. "Marguerite is a name fit for a young fool, dissolute and reckless, shallow and cruel and vain."

Kristina watched Grit's face and saw Linhoff looking at Grit. It was a strange moment that Kristina could not fathom. It was as if the young man were falling in love with Grit, and Grit felt something, too, that deeply disturbed her with such impossibility. Kristina saw latent beauty in Grit's face that seemed to glow for a moment, like the embers in a hearth that looked gray and dead, until a draft of air from a suddenly opened door blew into them, making them flare. She could, for that moment, see the beauty of the stage, the actress that Grit had once been.

"Dry yourself, boy," said Grit hoarsely, sounding overly stern.

Grit threw a drying towel over Linhoff's head and got up and turned away and busied herself washing up.

Then, later, they all sat around a little fire in the center firepit of the floor, and together they broke breakfast bread: Grit, Kristina, Dolf, Symon, Linhoff, Max, Ambrosius, and Jakop. They chewed wearily, thoughtfully, and no one spoke at first.

"How do we make printing?" said Max.

Said Grit, "We find a place to work where none will know what they need not know, for it puts them in danger. Second, we build a new frame and clean and fix the press assemblies. We can easily make ink, but paper we cannot make here, and it is dear in price."

"How do we make type?" said Dolf.

"If only Witter were here," Grit said.

"The most important thing," said Kristina, "is what we write to print, and why, and where we give it out."

"Yes," said Grit.

"It must be truth," said Kristina.

Linhoff said, "It must tell the people why things are the way they are, why so much injustice, and that is truth."

Ambrosius said, "And why the rich make wars the poor must fight. And how they take our grain unfairly."

"If they cannot read they cannot know," said Max.

"If they knew," said Ambrosius, "they would rage up."

In the faces of the young men, Kristina saw excitement, and there was anger in their eager smiles.

"It must be the truth of love," said Kristina, "not of hate."

"This we can all argue later," said Dolf. "If that press is found, we are cooked. Where can we take it to be safe?"

"Dolf is right," said Grit.

Max said, "I know a good place. The old stone barn way out beyond the graves, in the woods far past the orchards."

"It is falling down, covered with briers," said Linhoff. "And I think it was never a barn."

Said Jakop, "Some say it was an ancient church."

"Ghosts," said Max. "That is why nobody goes out there. But we can fix it up. And the press too."

"Others will want to help, too," said Ambrosius.

"For now this is our secret," said Dolf. "I agreed to this but it must be kept low and quiet."

Kristina looked at Grit, her sister Grit, the only one here who could fully understand. "We have come so far."

Grit took her hands and rubbed them.

"Our little group, poor Berthold, poor Ott," said Grit. "And Frieda. I wonder what happened to poor pretty Frieda?"

Kristina remembered the last time she had seen Frieda, leaping off the ferry that terrifying night, Frieda running away down the riverbank, her swirl of blonde hair disappearing into the dark, with the old ferry keeper coming from his hut and shouting at them, with the magistrates and dogs coming.

Said Grit, "Perhaps God has other work for Frieda. Perhaps she is still in Wurzburg."

Said Dolf, "God's will be done. I myself have prayed for her a hundred times since."

"Who is this pretty Frieda?" said Linhoff.

"You remember Frieda, in the wagon," said Jakop.

"Jakop should remember her," Max said. "He is the one who piked her man."

"I did," protested Jakop, "but he was coming at me, it was a mistake, and then I said I would take her for my wife, to fix it up, but Lud said no."

There was an awkward silence. Kristina felt her stomach tighten at those memories and at now being with these men who had killed in war. Yet all were children of God.

Finally, Linhoff said, "More credit to Jakop's offer to marry, if the girl were plain."

"I wish I had not piked him," said Jakop. "Often, I see his face, his eyes wide at me. He could not believe it was happening, nor could I."

"That is war," said Linhoff. "War is killing. If another wills your death, how is it wrong to will their death?"

"War is glory, I thought," said Max.

Ambrosius said, "I would much like to write a broadsheet telling how false it all is, how they make boys want to go fight strangers, far away from home, and for what? For the riches of fat men in cities."

The young men traded sour looks of agreement.

"What fools we were to take that coin," said Max. "But our elders seemed to praise it when we marched."

"Every person must guard his own soul," said Grit.

"In the Scriptures I have read this," said Linhoff. "When I was a child I spake as a child, but now l am grown."

"And I will put behind me childish things," said Grit. "You say killing is right if others kill. How can wrong make right?"

"When you are there you have no choice," said Max.

"Then do not go," said Dolf. "Do not let them force you to go."

"No one forced us," said Linhoff. "That is why I help, and must be involved in the writing and the printing," said Linhoff.

"Brothers and Sisters, it is well we have a press again," said Grit. "We have not come all this way together to not do what we came to do, or to perish trying to do it."

Kristina said nothing; she was thinking of Peter. He was with Arl tonight, just for the night. She missed her little boy terribly. She ached to see him when she returned to the castle.

And it was as if Grit had read her mind.

For later, when they were alone and drying, after bathing from a bucket of warmed water, Grit took her hands, looked into her face, and spoke to her.

"You, Kristina, you have a child, and you should not have gone with us for the press. I have seen this new fear in you, since you have had your child. There is no shame. It is right, for you are a mother and a good one."

Kristina pulled her hands away. It was just before Kristina was to return to her duties with Lady Anna, and she thought of how she had felt safe in the presence of the castle, and how wrong that was.

She said, "I have been a coward. My fear has always been with me, even when I carried my baby inside me. Fear like poison."

But Grit stopped her. "No, my sister. Fear is normal. God gave us fear to keep us alive. You should not be with us when we print and risk what we shall risk when we go to Wurzburg to give out our broadsheets."

"We risk their lives as well."

"I fear the way Jakop looks at you," said Grit.

"Jakop? Me?"

"He watches your every turn, when you do not see."

"The way Linhoff watches you?" said Kristina.

"Yes. Old as I am, yes. It is a problem."

"Jakop," said Kristina. "You must be mistaken."

"I know when a man wants something," said Grit. "Once it was the curse of my life, of my very soul, and, oh, how I traded upon their lust, to my own destruction."

Dolf and Symon came into the house. They had brought wood to stoke up the little fire.

Said Dolf, "Linhoff said something to me that I cannot put from my mind."

"What, Brother?" said Grit, with dread in her voice.

"He and others have read from the Scriptures. Who has Bibles, I do not know. But he said that the rich do not sweat for their bread, and that is sin."

"Judge not that ye be not judged," said Grit.

Said Dolf, "Linhoff said it with deep bitterness. That God created a fair world but men have made it unfair, in their sin. And that wrong must be overturned."

Said Symon, "It is best not to attack the rich."

"The rich make rules," said Dolf.

"Their rules are false idols," said Grit.

"God's law is the rule," said Symon.

"To bring down the rich? Is that what Linhoff and his brothers desire?" said Grit.

"I do not know," said Dolf. "But teaching them to read brings out things unforeseen."

Grit said, "Love is our commandment, love for all, rich and poor alike. The rich, too, must be shown the true way. All are children of God."

Said Dolf, "Even if we can build up the press to work again, what will we do without type?"

"God will find us a way," said Grit.

There was a long silence, and then Kristina felt the need to take their hands, one by one.

To join life with them...

"I am one with you all," said Kristina. Their hands were warm in hers. "For if I do not fight for our beliefs, for my voice, to make this a better world, I do not deserve my child at all."

Then one by one, each of the others had their say.

While the others spoke, Kristina thought of Witter, of his letter, of the day he had fought the dog, and several times a day she prayed for him in her heart. Now she missed him terribly. He would know exactly what to do to make it all work. He would take charge and command and it would be done right.

Where are you now, Witter, where?

And it struck her that she was not worried about Lud. Yet she knew how deeply she did care.

Was it because Lud seemed permanent? Carved from stone? Capable of anything?

She just knew Lud would be back. She missed his strength, but she knew he would be back. Witter was like smoke, ephemeral and temporal and somehow so fragile. Her feelings for the two of them were all tangled.

"Without type," said Grit, "our press has no voice."

"Wood," said Kristina. She pulled her hands away.

It had struck her like the sting of a wasp, this revelation.

"Wood?" said Linhoff.

Kristina picked up a broken piece of firewood. She shoved the end into the packed earth, hard, and looked up at the impression, like a scrawled letter.

"Wood. We carve the type from blocks of wood."

In the earth she scrawled a single word—

cruelty…

And then with the stick she scratched it to oblivion.

Witter

As a boy Witter had once begged his father to send him to England for study, for many of his friends said Oxford was a place of such freedom that students hired their own professors, and were their own law and could not be prosecuted by the town. But Judah had patiently explained that the English universities at Oxford and Cambridge were backward compared to Córdoba, mere bastions of the papacy based in Christian dogma. And that debates there might even include whether Jews possessed souls or were to be treated as wild beasts. And yet, Witter had heard, from poor Werner Heck, that the great Erasmus himself lectured at Oxford. That new arguments of tolerance flowered there out of the muck of ancient wrongs.

The old vellum map was marked *Ox*, in red at their point of destination. And its inked lines and terrain roundels and snaking rivers showed they were still far from the channel coast. Already, the days were colder as they passed French towns one by one and the rivers, too. And there was so little difference in these French towns and in the lands behind Witter and Lud.

Only the language differed, and to Witter's educated ear the words were the words, the meanings their meanings, all the same. Thanks to his wanderings, he understood. There was an imprint of old fears there, too, in the understanding of many tongues, from the years of leaving one place after another, always fearful of discovery and persecution.

His boil had burst and he had cleaned himself squatting by a cold roadside stream as best he could, with dead river rushes and icy water. His misery abated only a little, and then there were more hours standing up so his butt would not bump in the torturing saddle.

One night was spent in a poor abbey where the mendicant brothers, sworn to vows of poverty and self-denial, were preparing Scripture readings and a barley gruel. Witter and Lud were welcomed almost as brothers. Much of the gruel was set aside in a copper pot for some reason. After the silent meal, the abbot told Witter that this was an abbey that gave charity to the insane.

Quietly austere, the abbot insisted upon taking them to visit the sufferers of madness, in their cells and restraints, and the barley gruel was dipped into wooden bowls and served to those who either devoured it or ignored it. No spoons were given, lest the insane harm themselves or others, the abbot explained. Each was served with grace and courtesy.

"You know all their names," said Witter.

"We are all one spiritual family," said the abbot.

"Is madness born or earned?" Lud asked Witter to ask the abbot. So Witter asked.

"Only God knows," came the abbot's answer.

On a whim, Witter asked something. It was a question long on his mind, with no good answer—other than the frightful and obvious one, that God was indifferent, or perhaps worse, a sadist.

"Why does God make them so?" he asked.

"To bring love from our hearts of stone," said the abbot.

And that night Witter found no sleep. It was such a beautiful answer. Or a stupid one. To punish one group to stimulate love in another group? Such thoughts vexed him even more deeply than usual here, among the mad folk and the sweet folk who cherished them. He lay on his straw pallet wondering, how could such wonderful people of mercy sometimes give themselves to such terrible cruelties? Burning some, while nurturing and protecting others?

Wind tore at Witter and Lud the next day, and they said little. Witter watched Lud and was ever more curious.

Lud was always on guard, but because of that, there had been no trouble on the road. Lud was clever at behaving as a servant, diffident, silent, but always observant. His eyes never stopped watching.

Witter knew that he himself could say anything, either in French to the common folk at the inns and markets they passed, or in Latin to tradesmen they happened on occasion to meet, or clergy at some rustic abbey for the night. Several strangers had asked openly why a man of even modest means would keep such a servant with such an unfortunate face. And Witter began answering that Lud was the brother of his wife, who had begged work for him, and some of the strangers blessed Witter for his pains in giving Lud charity.

Lud tended the horses with a skill and tenderness that astonished Witter.

"You seem to love them more than men," he said.

"Their lives are on our account," said Lud.

"Mine is no Bucephalus."

"What is that?"

"Alexander's great steed," said Witter. "Never mind."

"I do mind. Show the beast respect. If God were of a different mind, my horse Ox here would be riding my back, and not me upon his. I need his goodwill."

"Is Ox your favorite horse?"

"He is my only horse. Given me in battle by Dietrich, when my own good Jax was slain."

"Did you know that Dietrich named your horse the same name as the place where Florian studies?"

"Ox?"

"Ox is how Oxford is marked on the map. He named your horse not after a beast of the field, but after his son's university."

A dozen nights out, they rode along the river and Witter enviously watched a big barge go by, safe and sound, like a wooden castle with the river water its perpetual moat. People idled on the foredeck. Boatmen pushed long rods and guided the enormous rudder. It was still a good month before the rivers would begin to freeze.

There had been a light snow and the days were darker and shorter. A villein's house outside a village was cheap and Witter had convinced Lud they should spend a pittance to eat and sleep in warmth.

The room they shared was actually a stall in the barn, but the straw was fresh and shutters closed out the cold. A milk cow and a donkey made snuffling sounds now and then, somewhere in the dark. Witter's and Lud's horses had munched hay and Witter heard one pissing off in the dark.

Lud laid on one pallet and Witter on another. Moonlight filtered down through splits in the thatch roof and walls. Sometimes the logs and roof creaked.

"Why are you doing this?" came Lud's voice.

"Why are you?" Witter answered back.

"I do whatever I must to protect Giebel and my people," said Lud. "But they are not your people. Your people brought troubles to us."

"I am sorry for that."

"Do you do this for Kristina? Her man is dead…three, four years. Is she going to be your woman? Is she why you do this?"

"If only that were so," Witter caught himself saying. "I have seen you watch her sometimes."

Lud sat up. "If there is such a thing as a soul, hers is beautiful. It makes me want to protect her. I do not know why."

"Love is why she does everything. She says she is trying to reach God through love. Not the love of a man."

"Has she put a fire in you?"

"Do you want her?" said Witter back.

"That is the wrong question. She could never want a man like me. But I would kill to protect her, and I am glad she came to Giebel, even if she brought danger from outside."

"Do you think we will make it to England?"

"Pray for us. Maybe someone is listening."

"Pray?"

"Pray to Jesus. I hear you muttering prayers sometimes when we are on the road. Even though you are not a priest. Are you not trying to speak to Jesus?"

"I pray in my heart," said Witter. "I try."

"While you have His attention sometimes, Witter, inquire why some are killed and some are not, why some get pox and some do not, why some starve and some grow fat, why some are burned and some are judges, and why some love and some hate. Of those things I would like to know the reasons."

"So would I," said Witter. His boil was rising again and his ass ached again.

Said Lud, "Why does one boy live by the sweat of his brow and dig in the dirt to feed a lord, while another boy is sent to England to learn laws to rule others and live as a lord?"

Witter said, "My father always said that only a fool blames God for the choices of men."

"But did not this same God create all evil things? Wars? Rapine? The pox?"

"The attempt to reconcile God with the problem of evil has always been a difficult one."

He thought of his father Judah, bent forward praying in his *tallith*, the humble prayer shawl; of Judah's love for the work of Moses ben Maimon, who some called Maimonides; his *Mishneh Torah*; and how often his father insisted that such reason and the law would save them. *It is better and more satisfactory to acquit a thousand guilty persons than to put a single innocent one to death…*

Lud said, "He sounds wise, your father."

"Wise? Yes, he was very wise."

"Was?"

"Dead. Long ago, dead." Witter looked into the flames.

"In battle?" said Lud.

Witter thought of Judah's struggles with those who feared his knowledge, how Judah sought to reason with his judges, how he tried to rally his people to resist through sane arguments of law and from sheer decency, and how he lost everything, the lives of those he loved, his own life, everything but his faith and his righteousness.

"Yes, in battle," Witter said finally. "You could say that. A kind of battle." *But with words, with faith, not with swords. The enemy had the swords, and the fire...*

The blue glow of the moon mantled Lud's head and shoulders.

"Dietrich wanted me to learn. But reading has not comforted me. Just the opposite."

"Learning provokes doubt," said Witter.

"Yes. That is it. I am more restless than ever. All that I read points me to injustices and new questions, things better left unturned, like worms in a plowed field."

"Ignorance is easier in some ways, harder in others."

"But you and yours read and are burned sometimes for your labors, trying to help others to read. Why?"

"Why do they teach reading?"

"Why do you think it is worth the risk?"

"Their faith is stronger than mine."

"Reading has upset many in the village. Many are less content. They begin to question the way of things. Why one has and another has not. Is that what you want?"

Witter shook his head. He had no answer for this and was bone-tired, and he feared where this talk was headed. If a man awakened the beast and taught him discontent, would the beast not rise up and devour that man? He looked up and saw a sliver of moon through a hole in the thatch, like a dazzling eye of God peeking down at him, as one would peek at something unclean found under a rock.

"I need sleep," said Witter. He needed escape from himself, from the throbbing in his left ass cheek that ached with every beat of his heart. He closed his eyes. But Lud spoke again.

"Tell me one more thing, if you can."

Witter opened his eyes reluctantly, and turned, yawning. Lud was staring at him, his face a mask that seemed to float on the fiery gloom of hell.

Said Lud, "Why do you always hide your tool?"

"Hide my what?" Witter felt alarmed.

"Why cover it whenever you crap or pass water? When you dress? When you sleep? Or when you cleaned your ass the other day at the stream?"

Witter's yawn caught and pulled back; his heart jumped. Could Lud have seen that he was circumcised? Had Kristina told Lud he was a Jew? Of course not, she never would. He had to say something to change the subject.

Fumbling with his thoughts, Witter tried a joke, a risky return: "Why do you wish to see it? Are you so lonely?"

Not good. Lud's voice did not sound amused.

"If your tool is short, or if man-love is to your taste, or if you consort with yourself, Witter, I do not give a damn. Only that you get us to England, that you will fight if need be."

"I did not mean to mock."

"You had best take me seriously in all things. It is my business to notice everything about a man. So many lives that are dear to me depend upon it."

Witter reclined, and silently he waited. The dark seemed to hum in his ears. His ass throbbed. Anything he said would be wrong. And if Lud got up and came over and stripped him, there would be nothing he could do to stop him. And then Lud would know that he was a Jew.

Witter's right hand edged downward, along his legging, and he felt the thin iron haft of his little dagger under the cloth. Lud's terrible face crinkled in a faint smile.

"You have a dagger," said Lud.

"Yes." He might as well tell the truth. His hand pulled away from his leg.

Lud said, "I did not ask, I know you have it."

"I mean no harm to anyone."

"No? That is a pity. A dagger is made for harm, and more reliable than a prayer. Can you use it well?"

"Not well." He was glad he had not lied.

"It is no hope to you then, perhaps worse than not having one. You do not threaten with a dagger. It is for making a conclusion. By surprise if possible."

"I see," said Witter.

"Do you? Can you kill a man? I thought your kind believes only in brotherly love. The law of Christ?"

"I killed a magistrate's dog once," Witter said.

"A dog can take your face off in the time a wasp would sting you. You were lucky, if he was big."

"He was huge. But that was a lie. Kristina killed the dog. But with my dagger."

The very name *Kristina*, spoken, sent warmth through him that was inexpressible. He hoped that Lud could not see it, nor hear a quaver in his voice.

Lud's eyes sharpened. "There is more honor in that girl's little finger than in two like you, or me. And yet she killed, when she had to, to save your ass."

"A dog." Witter felt ashamed that he had never killed, and it angered him that he should feel shame for honoring the lives of others. Or had it been pure cowardice posturing as goodness? "Kristina killed a dog, not a man."

"And a dog is less than a man?"

"It depends upon the man."

"Well said."

Witter was surprised that Lud had said anything good toward him. And then he was surprised by the little sense of pleasure this gave him.

"She has pure will," Witter said.

"And you do not."

"No. I do not," said Witter.

"Neither do I. There is no genius in killing. When we have time, a few dagger tricks are easy to teach you, otherwise there is no good in carrying it."

"That would be good," said Witter.

"Killing is never good. Only necessary."

"Never? Never a feeling of satisfaction?"

"Yes, there is that. The relief of fear. And sometimes setting wrong right. But being judge and executioner both can make men mad, after the deed."

"But not you," said Witter.

"Do you think I am not mad?"

"I do not know."

"Nor I."

Lud turned away on his pallet.

Witter waited, but Lud said no more.

He laid back and stared up at the splinters of moon glow, the blue light dancing among the cracks in the old thatch ceiling. Cracks that became faces, if he watched long enough—he saw his father, his mother. He saw Kristina.

Witter lay there, staring, feeling a strange mixed sensation. He felt oddly safe, feeling threatened yet protected by such a savage man as Lud. And he was deeply confused, disturbed that it was so, comforted by this kind of man he had always feared, a killer and a brute upon whom his life now depended.

There is more honor in that girl's little finger than in two like you, or me. And yet she killed, when she had to, to save your ass…

He thought he had not loved his life very much. But he knew that Kristina had made him love it more. He had not wanted to love it more. How many times before meeting Kristina had he considered ending it? To show his life the contempt it deserved? By taking control, control of the one thing he could control, the time of his death…

Witter thought that even if Lud did see that Witter was circumcised, Lud would not care.

He does not care what I am, heretic nor man-lover nor perhaps even Jew, so long as I am loyal to his purpose…

Then he heard something—a sound like a hoarse whisper. He stared into the moonlit room and listened hard.

He would never be certain of what happened next.

He saw shapes moving, crouched—one, no, two.

Then he heard curses. He held his breath, hoping this was a nightmare yet knowing it was real.

All at once a dozen things happened. He heard the ox bellow, and maybe it was the donkey that brayed and kicked. The horses snorted and there was a jingling of harness and something huge collided with something else. A human screamed, or something that sounded part human. There were growls and things slamming.

Something big and hot and noisy fell crushingly on Witter. It blocked the moon glow. He tried to scream but his breath was gone. Witter jerked and twisted but was trapped. He gagged for breath. A stupendous fear swallowed him. Something bestial flailed and was bleeding and gargling, and he felt its hair in his face and its hands grabbing at him.

Kristina

Another winter was coming fast on sharp rising winds. The cocks were crowing later, the songbirds had gone, the fields were gleaned twice for after-harvest grain, and the woods were stripped by children of any last berries and nuts. Every able villager was hard at work laying by foodstuffs or fuel, and it was time for the winter wood to be laid by.

In the spring the men had used felling axes to drop hardwood trees, chosen not only for long-burning fuel but also to widen paths or to enlarge a planting field. They had left the branches on to speed the drying out of the wood. Now their felling axes chopped off the dead brown limbs, and with mauls and iron wedges ringing, they split the logs down. With other children, Peter wore long woolens and helped drag the cut limbs. Fat pine sapwood was splintered for kindling. Oxen pulled the big wood wagons. Giebel worked together in the gather. The castle had first dry wood choice and Merkel second, to make charcoal for his forge. Kristina had not seen such concert of spirit even in her time with the nuns in the convent, or with the hard-working brethren at Kunwald. It was good to be a part of something so righteous, an effort so united and unspoken.

Lud told her that other estate villeins gathered fallen branches or cut peat for cook-fires. Centuries ago many forests had been cleared for planting fields. Dietrich's liberal policy had carried over, of his villeins having access to the precious trees. Lud, as steward, made sure this was so, and lady Anna did not dispute the will of her dead husband.

"A good year for cutting," said Lud. "Not one leg or arm crushed by deadfall, nor anything chopped off."

For the castle kitchen, the best seasoned-out split wood was carted to the dry-roof woodshed. Lura and Leta sorted it by length and size and Kristina helped stack it for the sleeping room hearths as well as the oven.

The fires she built in the stone hearths were reassuring, for Kristina dreaded the verge of longer nights and the sun fading, as if God were turning from mankind in a final disgust. On the cold winds came a sourceless longing that troubled her deeply. She prayed for certainty. Sometimes at night in the brethren hut she held Peter asleep on her lap while the others slept, and she pretended the silent tears were stung from her eyes by the smouldering hearth wood.

Color faded from daylight. The tiny blue forget-me-nots planted about Berthold's grave withered and twisted into brown tendrils that Kristina removed each year at this time. His grave itself sank slightly deeper each year, so that the softer rectangle was clearly seen in the grass. Always, she took little Peter with her on the long walk through the gray and brown fields and orchards and down the road of the great forest where trees were concealing their life force deep within the earth.

Walking in the cold pale sunlight, holding tight Peter's little squirming hand, she wiped away her wind-whipped hair and fought all these wrong feelings. She told happy stories of his father...

"Your father was the wisest man I ever knew, the kindest, the sweetest of all men. He believed in peace and love no matter how dangerous it was to say so. He prayed for the souls of those who harmed others, whatever side they were on."

She told the half-true stories, bright-voiced, never knowing if her child understood, watching him fidget, pulling, wanting to wander about. Yet she always tried to help him realize the sacrifices that had been made, from duty and from love. It was always easy to tell Peter the story of salvation, for no matter what horrors on earth might befall any faithful believer, the end was always the same happy ending, up in heaven.

"This is where your dear father's body lies, but his soul is with our Christ in the eternal brightness of heaven."

Then she imagined the child being normal, even bright, and asking of his father:

If father was good, why did they kill him?

"Because they feared him."

If good, why did they fear him?

"Because he preached the love of all men."

And they did not wish to be loved?

"They did not wish... for others to be loved."

But her child broke from her hand and ran around her in circles, giggling and teasing her, and she thought, maybe God was merciful and wise to let Peter be ignorant of so much pain. The thought was so wrong. Shame flooded her.

Then a sharp pain stung her left leg.

She jerked around. Peter was biting her. His eyes were full of impish glee. She cried out and he ran. She sprinted after him. He was giggling when she caught him up and spun him up into her arms, squeezing him so hard that he squealed with delight, and then something dark released her and she was laughing and laughing and laughing.

Drifters were on the road now—homeless families and sometimes men, some on horse but most afoot, wearing old war clothes and torn tunics. Kristina and Grit were not the only ones who helped the unfortunate.

"In hard times," Arl said, "Giebel has never turned away someone truly in need. Our fathers and mothers taught us this, an ancient way of charity, and perhaps a wise way to deal with the desperate. And my father always said, never make one feel like a beggar. With the bread give them a bit of work to do, to not damage their pride and their souls. But never have we seen so many. Everything is coming unraveled, it seems, everywhere."

So the well water was shared and there were small gifts of bread or a piece of dried fruit, especially for the ragged children of such unfortunate folk, most of whom had lost their work or land and some their minds. Kristina did what she could, and she and Grit prayed for them together.

But there was little rest and little time to brood upon the fate of the drifters, or even of Lud and Witter, except in the deep of night sometimes, when worries robbed sleep. She prayed for them both and she tried to tease out her feelings for each and could not make herself known to herself. The cold deepened and bit though her cloak.

Keeping the castle clean and the sooty ashy wood fires hot during the day, and the food served and the linens changed and the curtains closed at night was all a relentless cycle of hard work, but there was much harder work ahead.

Said Lady Anna, "If there may be too little food, there certainly can be enough heat, for wood is one thing we have in abundance."

With Lud gone with Witter to fetch Florian, Anna had again assumed command of the estate. And the lady did it with energy unlike ever before.

Under iron-gray skies, many were chopping away at deadfalls along the forest, like an army of ants, breaking great trees down into cartloads. There was talk of man-killing ice storms and terrible winters lasting too long, and in a kind of determined dread, the axes and splitting wedges rang all day. Others dug for lumps of black coal in the ancient pit by the river, where it was said the ghosts of Romans wandered by night. Having heat was one thing they must be certain of.

Even Father Michael was seen with a splitting maul, his black robe whirling in the winter wind. He flailed away, doing little good, until men stopped to show him the good angles for striking the wood and how to hit the wood at the yielding seams. Then even more unexpected, the priest helped Dolf and Symon when they were carrying wood to the huts of the widows and infirm.

Gangs of ragged children played warrior, dodging their chores, indifferent to the cold. With their pet mongrels at their heels, they were rounded up by parents and older youths, trapped at their makeshift forts in the brush piles and made to help carry the wood and the filthy black lumps of coal.

Peter was with them, Arl said, playing war with sharp sticks for swords and pikes, and this distressed Kristina terribly.

How far her child had come from his namesake, the blessed apostle Saint Peter, who had fought with his sword to save Christ—and Christ had forbidden it. How far from her dream of her child becoming a new light in the dark world. The world seemed to have swallowed him up. Its vortex of murder bled down to the very children who played murder games. And no matter how many times she stopped him, he would always return to the same games.

The children sneaked and watched the slaughter in the barns and animal sheds, she knew. Creatures who would not be bred next year were killed, slaughtered, chopped into parts for smoking and grinding and stewing. Some children even helped chop up the creatures. At such times she tried to find Peter and bring him home, but often she could not.

Kristina smelled the animals' deaths on the smoky air and steeled herself to it all as best she could. People with blood on their hands and faces worked hard to lay by winter stores. She heard that Waldo traded two of the oldest stable horses to the Wurzburg butchers for grain to help last through the winter. But Waldo refused to sell the oldest, which was now spavined and lame, but had been Dietrich's warhorse. The village mongrel dogs begged for scraps, and several of the horses disappeared.

"They borrow from one another and have debt and are hungry and killing too many animals," said Lura. "Trying to make up for the shortage of grain. But next year there will be a shortage of animals as well."

Said Arl, who traded her weaving cloth with other villages, "Others have worse luck. Here the folk have always been free to hunt the woods and gather herbs and fish the stream, and to harvest before working for the estate fields, but it is very different elsewhere, and want elsewhere is worse than here."

"Dietrich was a good man," said Lura.

"Praise Lady Anna," said Father Michael that week in church, as he began Mass, and Kristina saw him looking straight at Lady Anna, in her box in front of the sanctuary. Although she was veiled as ever, Kristina was close by, attending the lady, and she saw her shoulders move and her head tilt back with good reaction.

Said Father Michael, "Honor the noble lady for her good in honoring her late and noble husband's word. Our dear lady knows that the villeins have need of sustenance; therefore she continues the largesse of her dear husband, allowing free use of forests and private fields. We know Dietrich basks in your glory even now as we raise our hearts to Thee. And praise God, and beg the Blessed Mother's mercy upon us and all others in need. May we each find the truth and may it set us all free, from the sin of ignorance, for God has given us our wit, our courage, our words, all the tools needed for our souls to find our own true way. Bless our brave and generous Dietrich, for wanting all to read."

Kristina sat with the veiled Lady Anna. She wondered whether Anna would become angry, having wished that reading and learning would stop, considering it a grave endangerment. But Anna never mentioned the priest's words nor railed against him, perhaps because the good words toward Dietrich and herself would then be lost. Then the lady's chin dropped to her breast and her shoulders quivered and she wept quietly.

Father Michael said, "Find the truth, Dietrich said, that was the essence of it, on his deathbed those long years ago. Learn and find the truth for yourselves. I was not there, no. I cowered in the sacristy, hiding from you, my flock, fearing the pox that ravaged you so. But you shall not find me hiding any longer. You shall not find me drunk, pretending to pray. And I beg of you all to forgive me, and help me serve each and all of you, and to receive your blessings. I belong to you all."

Inside the church, the world was briefly shut out, but outside, the race against winter hunger went on.

Arl let little Peter play with the ends of yarn as she weaved at her loom, her shuttlecock clicking away.

When she could, Kristina came and sang rhyme to Peter, as her mother had done with her, giving reading lessons disguised as silly storytelling…

"*A Black Cow Did Eye Four Geese,*

A, B, C, D, E, F, G,

Hay In Jay, Kinder Pray…

H, I, J, K…"

Yet Peter was not repeating or learning the rhymes, but was sneaking away to play with the gang of other children.

"You are seven now and you must speak. You must learn," she tried to tell her son, sitting him on her lap.

"When he is ready," said Arl, "he will.

"Peter, listen to mother. I named you for the apostle of Christ, who lay down his sword and did not slay the magistrates who arrested our Saviour."

"How can he understand such?" said Arl. "Let him play."

Said Kristina, "Peter, war is not God's way."

"Too many words for him," said Arl. "You are too impatient. He imitates the others."

"His father Berthold was so brilliant," Kristina said. And she thought how Berthold, on their wedding night, had warned against bringing new innocent lives into this evil world.

"Peter is Peter," said Arl.

Kristina's child gave a big smile and put his arms around her neck and kissed her with his rosy, wet face.

"Peter," said Peter.

He smelled of earth and woodlands. Kristina beamed back at him, wiping his filthy brown hair from his face. Tonight no matter what, she would bring him for a bath.

"Christ made Peter lay down his sword," said Kristina again. "For fighting is not the good way."

"Me not cry," the boy said, and made a stabbing motion with his fist.

"I told you he is learning to speak," said Arl. "Do you not wish him to learn his own free way?"

"Little Boy that Jesus Love,
come and dwell
like peaceful dove..."

"Fight good," Peter said proudly, laughing.

At her loom, Arl tried to stifle a laugh as she watched Kristina attempt to teach the child her own way.

"Fighting bad," said Kristina, as sweetly as she could.

Peter made a growl like a war cry and stabbed the air with both fists, madly. Kristina put him down, because she had wanted, without thinking, to slap him.

Arl turned her face away and Kristina heard Arl trying to stifle her giggling.

Peter whirled around twice and ran away.

Kristina's heart felt as if it were caving in upon itself. What hell had she brought her child into? How could she have pledged ten years to this place? What dire trap was this for both of them? She saw Arl watching her.

"When God is ready," said Arl, "Peter will learn. He is as God wills, as God has made him. And is he not a blessed child to let nothing hurt him?"

Something in Kristina went dark and wrong.

She glared at Arl. "You grieve your twins, but war took them from you. Hermo and Fridel went to be heroes. What if you had taught them peace instead?"

Once words are gone they can never be brought back.

Kristina felt as if she had stabbed Arl, and then stabbed herself. Arl's hands dropped from the loom shuttlecock and she stood away from the loom, staggering, as if Kristina had hit her a hard blow.

Arl began to crumble and then she broke and wept. Kristina felt terrible and went to hold her, but Arl pushed her away.

"Get out," said Arl.

"Please, forgive me, it was just fear for my child..."

But Arl wept, inconsolable, threatening Kristina with weaving spikes, waving them and raging.

"You judge me, yet act so pious. My Hermo was loved. Fridel was sweet as a lamb. Do you hear me? My twins were loved. By me and by Jesus, too. Not sent to play with strangers like your child. I pity little Peter. You hypocrite. You do not own heaven. Get away from me."

It was the worst day in her life since Berthold had been murdered by the magistrates. And it would take a long time to heal and repair.

Later, Grit said, "You can do a hundred good acts, or a thousand, but one rash wrong undoes them all."

The roads were deep mud, and the seasons could be marked by the last road peddlers who were passing through in their covered wagons, trying for a last rush of sales before winter locked up the world.

The peddler that everyone called Old Klaus passed through Giebel with his mule-drawn cart. Under the naked linden tree he sold out all of his books and broadsheets in less than an hour. He was not old but they called him Old Klaus because he had a bent back from birth. He sold ribbons and fringe and thread and the latest broadsheets, so the village all came out for his goods. But most of all they came out for his gossip.

Kristina heard of all this later, grimly from Lura, when Lady Anna asked her to report what was being said.

"Old Klaus was along the Swiss border far south, he said. There are many changes in many places. People are learning to read. There seems much discontent with rulers and such. Some are even changing how they live."

"In what way?" said Lady Anna, her tone dark.

"Old Klaus said many are reading the Bible translations and are angry about living so poorly. Some Swiss folk there have rebelled against the rule of the cities and bishops. Some Swiss villeins have rebelled against the lower nobility, calling themselves brothers and sisters, all."

Lady Anna stomped about, seething.

"What imbeciles. It proves that learning to read, without common sense, is dangerous. Unsound notions can deceive weak minds. The Swiss poor are like all poor, fools leading fools. Without nobility they will starve. And what lofty gain do they imagine violence will bring, when their cretinous heads decorate pikes?"

"Old Klaus said they are not all violent. Some want only peace. A whole new way entirely. But I should not tell it."

"Tell it all. What kind of way?"

"Well, he said it, not I. He said that, in a village by Lake Zurich, all villeins renounced their estate lord and were rebaptized and broke the locks off all their storehouses and chests and doors and share all, as the first Christians are said to share, according to the Gospels, they claim."

"Share? All? What is all?"

Lura answered fearfully, "Old Klaus said he was not sure but some say even maidens are shared, and wives, and all goods held free and common, no more villeins, none high nor low, nor would they serve their lord nor fight in armies, claiming war is murderous evil, though surely their lords shall have them all arrested, in time."

"Even from such trash as the Swiss, that is evil, incredible, and vile," said Lady Anna.

Lura had warned Kristina, in detail, of the rumors and of the rage of Lady Anna upon hearing it all. Kristina had felt joy at the news that others had renounced killing, that brotherly love was embraced somewhere, but she had dreaded the reaction of Lady Anna to such news.

It was later, when Kristina was brushing out Lady Anna's long hair and plucking out the gray, that the lady demanded to know the truth, without varnish.

Lady Anna had several of the most salacious broadsheets in hand, as if they were absolute evidence.

And she was furious. There would be no harp playing or reading together that day.

"What say you, Kristina, to such libertine doings? Women would never share their men. That smacks of the evil desires of men, not women."

Kristina looked at the broadsheets. The worst lies, the most outrageous, were from Veritas Press in Wurzburg. And they were so well written, so skillfully shaped.

"It is a sin in itself for such fine minds to be wasted," she said. "These publicists shaping tales for simpletons, to sell hatred in these broadsheets. Would such sell, without lurid carnal lust to bait fools? Besides, there would be inevitable failure of such false brotherhood."

"Men are weak and strong, both, Kristina. Weak-willed when they lust, yet strong in their desires. Beware."

"Fellowship does not mean that lust is a virtue. Sharing of love, yes. The flesh, no. Of kindness and charity and goods, yes. Of the love of all as brothers and sisters."

"Look at you. You own nothing whatsoever of your own, hardly even the clothes on your back. Everything you get you share and give away. Even to the poverty of your own sweet child."

"I have my soul, I hope," said Kristina, hurt and wary. Lady Anna's mood could turn like a snake, unpredictably.

"As hope we all," agreed Lady Anna. "But take care how you influence others here, for they are my wards. I protect the morals and lives and the souls of each and every one of them. And this estate is no commune. You have served near seven of the ten years you pledged. I admit I have grown fond of you. But never mistake my duty to my people."

Kristina argued no more.

There was deep hurt in the thought that she neglected little Peter. She fought not to reveal how deeply she felt that hurt. It struck her all the more deeply, for she feared it was true.

"Lady, please, I need more time away, my child Peter is becoming aggressive with other children. He fights. I can no longer leave him with Arl."

"You seem distressed when you should be proud. What good is a boy who will not stand up for himself?"

"I must spend more time with him."

"You have more private time than Lura or Leta; plenty for your child. Are you not spending it with him? What could be more important?"

What could be more important...

And the quiet anger in Lady Anna's words made Kristina know that she was blamed for all literacy in Giebel.

Despite all that, when she prayed, she felt an imperative, an urgency, to dispel such lies as those printed in the broadsheets.

When she told Grit, Grit said, "If there are seeds of truth in the peddler's stories that a village of Swiss villeins rejects war and embraces brotherly love, praise God. I will not speak to the salacious lies. But hear me, child, my sweet sister, it is even more important than ever to explain good fellowship without discrimination, as commanded by Christ in the book of Acts. But that is not the worst danger."

"We cannot keep a secret here," said Kristina, "when so many read now, so many know how we think, and when we print our thoughts, all doubt shall be gone."

Grit looked in her eyes. "Child, the sooner our little press can be working, the sooner our own truth can be shared in the minds of the people. But that is not what I mean when I say the worst danger."

"What danger could be worse than lies?"

"Guard yourself that any imagine us loose and easy. We must clear the air of such trash in all ways possible. Men are like dogs and they ever hunt out the vulnerable. With such tales of shared virgins and wives and such, God knows how their thoughts will turn upon us now."

"Lady Anna warned the same thing."

"And she surely blames us, not men. From now on, you do not walk alone, ever. We walk together wherever we go, and Dolf or Symon must walk with us."

At first, the work went on as it had, without conflict.

There was winter baking to be done in the castle. Because the bishopric tax shares this year had been heavier than ever before, the villeins had been left with less grain than ever before to last until the next harvest. The bygone winter months had eaten up the meager grain stores of many villagers, and others had wasted some of their stores in brewing ale.

Then, Lady Anna surprised them all. She had been reading, with Kristina's help, *Utopia*, by Thomas More, a volume from Dietrich's library—

"Consider any year that has been so unfruitful that many thousands have died of hunger; and yet if at the end of that year a survey was made of the granaries of all the rich men that have hoarded up the corn, it would be found that there was enough among them to have prevented all that consumption of men that perished in misery; and that if it had been distributed among them, none would have felt the terrible effects of that scarcity; so easy a thing would it be to supply all the necessities of life, if that blessed thing called money, which is pretended to be invented for procuring them, was not really the only thing that obstructed their being procured!"

Lady Anna informed Kristina, "Father Michael and I have prayed long on this, and God has persuaded me. I shall make Geyer grain available for the baking of bread loaves to give to needy families—those with old, infirm, and children, who would suffer from hunger. You shall assist Lura and Leta in the baking. A good hot tripe stew would help the infirm, also use dried apples for pies for gifts. You see, I am of reasonably charitable good faith, and not made of stone. The grain of the estate is not inexhaustible, so take care in the provisioning that we do not ourselves starve."

So, in apron and kitchen sleeves, her hair tied with string, Kristina helped Lura and Leta in the castle kitchen. Flour hung lazily in the steamy air, and the wooden cooking implements clattering. The women banked hot oak wood in the great hearth, which baked cellared carrots and onions and smoked meat stew, while yeasty kneaded bread was set to rise in clay bowls.

Kristina sang with a happy heart, feeling good and blessed to be able to help prepare food for those who hungered. Peter played underfoot and she feared he would be hurt or scalded. He seemed fascinated by the cook knives and she pried one from his little fists and he bawled in anger.

"Where is my good boy?" said Arl.

She had entered without Kristina seeing her. Kristina turned and felt shame and sorrow for her rash words of weeks before.

Peter ran to Arl and leapt into her arms.

"May I keep him, just for today?" said Arl.

It was the forgiveness that Kristina had prayed for.

"Bless you," said Kristina. With her eyes she tried to beg forgiveness, but Arl only smiled back. It was as if nothing had happened.

"I would keep him for all days," said Arl.

The other women looked at her and she felt perhaps they were judging her for not loving her child enough, judging her for judging the boy, who could hardly speak, much less begin to learn to read. Their judging came as a great shock to her. And she realized that she thought herself purer than they, and this disarmed and shamed her.

Arl took Peter bouncing away.

"Arl knows how to forgive," said Leta to Lura, as if Kristina were not there.

Lura said, "Kristina is human like the rest of us."

And Kristina realized that they knew all about what had happened at the loom; how she had spoken wrongly and cruelly to Arl of her dead twin sons. No secrets here, none.

"I tried to apologize to her," said Kristina.

"Enough chatter," said Lura.

When Leta and Lura cut up the animals and animal parts to make into meals, Kristina did not participate, always finding another task of hard work to do. This did not go unnoticed.

"You do not eat meat?" said Lura. "I see you avoid preparing meat, and pick it from your stew when you think no one is watching.

That is passing odd, since all others wish for more meat, and do not remove it."

"It has been years," she evaded, yet truthfully, not wishing to fully explain. " I lost the habit."

"Your religion?"

"No, because of the war."

"What happened?"

"I saw…something."

"What would change your appetite?"

"I saw inside a man, killed, his chest wide open. And I saw how…a man is laid out inside, just as a deer, just as a pig, all the same on the inside."

"The same? Just the same?"

"Yes, exactly." The chest Kristina had seen inside of had been Ruth's son, Matthes, split open by the blow of some weapon. Whenever she saw slaughtered beasts, or their rendered flesh, she fought against that memory.

"The liver, the kidneys, all their tripe the same?" Lura shook her head in disbelief.

Leta came listening, frowning, wiping her hands.

"Yes, all the same," answered Kristina.

Said Leta, astonished, "The heart and lungs, the stomach? All the same shape, all in the same placement, human and animal? Their hearts made the same?"

"Yes. I have not eaten meat since that day."

"That was when you were taken by Lud and Dietrich? You tended our wounded in the wagon?"

"We did what little we could."

Said Leta, "I wager that dead one, the one you saw into his insides, he was Turk or Jew, not a Christian. With innards as animal as hog or ox or deer."

"God made men all the same," said Kristina.

"How do you know so much how God made men?" said Leta.

"The Scriptures tell me so."

"Yes," said Lura, "I too have read that, in Genesis."

Said Leta, "If reading brings me even more doubt, I am not sure I wish to keep learning. The heart of Turk and Jew the same as a Christian? What next?"

They got back to work and worked silently for a long time. They loaded the split oak wood into the firebox of the great clay-lined brick oven, for Lady Anna forbade the use of coal here for baking, for it could stain the flavor, turning it vile and smelly.

Leta spoke, then, as if in regret of her earlier words.

"Many in the village bless you all for helping their boys. They cheered their boys off to war, proudly, and now most rue that day."

"It is a miracle," Kristina said, "to have a child. But the world can have its way with any of us."

"May I ask a question of you?" said Lura.

"Of course, anything." Kristina prepared for a question of faith, religion, personal history.

"Whenever stew is served," said Lura, "and God knows it is not always with meat, may I have your meat?"

They all laughed together. Lura was joking, only partly. She did want the meat, Kristina knew. It was a way of asking forgiveness for prying into a memory so ugly.

For hours they would work silently.

Lura could eye the oven bricks and from their glow judge whether they were hot enough to bake bread or the pies. Making pies took all afternoon. In a silent sisterhood of cookery, they sat at a long table cutting up the dried apples and shelling walnuts and pecans. Then the lids went on the pots, and the pots went into the hearth, and they sat and enjoyed licking the wooden spoons and sweating in the good heat of work—their bodies all scented with the rich aromas of food.

After any great effort of cooking or washing or sewing—or oven hauling ash—there were always the solemn tasks of cleaning up and the scrubbing of everything, and looking forward to a granted time of rest before returning to Lady Anna. Such were Kristina's free times. Lura and Leta, she knew, used them for an exhausted respite of sleep. After cooking, often they ate the scrapings as a stew.

"Take my bits of meat," said Kristina to Lura.

Lura looked at them. "That looks like a piece of lung. Or liver. I wish I had not asked about that."

But then, suddenly, Leta reached over and scooped them up and gobbled them down. "God made all. And who are we to waste the deaths of those creatures by not eating?"

"They were wasted when killed," said Lura. "But you are right. Food is not plentiful. We must lay by all we can. How we can. Do we not feed animals our good grass and grain? What say you to that, Kristina?"

"The grain feed would sustain many more of us, than would taking the life of the dumb creature."

"Is she not perfectly strange?" said Lura.

Said Leta, "None stranger."

"Nor would I change her," said Lura. "There may come a time of hunger when no dog is seen alive. But it will not be her that kills it."

That was a compliment that Kristina treasured.

Forgoing the free time for sleep, Kristina tried to spend some with little Peter, but most of her freedom she gave to the effort to spread the Word she believed she was sent to broadcast among all people she was able to reach.

That meant restoring the printing press.

Beyond the orchards in the old uncut woods, her brothers and sisters had chopped the briers away from the ancient stone edifice (whether church or barn was unknown), and cleaned it out inside, and stuffed the cracks with straw, and re-thatched the roof, replacing some of the beams that had rotted.

They worked against the cold, wrapped in cloaks and wearing all the cloth their bodies could carry yet still let them work with mobility. Only Dolf complained, and often, of his frozen hands and aching back. Symon kept frowning at him.

Grit rubbed Dolf's back and teased him, saying, "Do not tempt our maker. Would you be warmer on a stack of wood in Wurzburg Square?"

Dolf rolled his milk-eye at Grit in disbelief, and then he laughed so loud it made Kristina's ears ring.

Kristina brought hot bread and a pot of stew each time, and they wolfed it down with a quick prayer. The small hearth in their little house where they slept was not large enough to bake bread, only to heat soup and fry griddle cakes on stones, so any food prepared at the castle was devoured with great relish. The flavor of egg in the bread would sometimes make them moan with pleasure.

Kristina only brought the food when the young men were not there. There was hardly enough for a few.

"Is this gluttony?" asked Grit. "To eat without sharing with those others who help do this good work?"

"Gluttony is excess," said Symon. "We have little."

"Hunger is not gluttony," Dolf agreed. "They have family food in the village."

"Bless you for this bounty," said Grit, praying.

Kristina brought the extra food each time she could, for the work on the barn was cold, and she saw how gaunt were the faces of her brothers and sisters.

And, always, Peter weighed in her thoughts. When she could, she visited Arl's weavery, and stole time for her little son, and felt guilt she was not always with him.

His slowness was not better and he did not clean himself well, sometimes not at all, and Arl did not like letting him play with other children who teased and abused him. The gang of children worked hard, but only when their parents could catch them. As part of their mob, Peter was learning to hide from adults. The little mongrels, mostly harmless, still frightened Kristina.

Arl loved Peter, and Peter loved Arl, that was clear. But Kristina felt jealous when Peter hugged Arl's neck when Kristina wanted to sit with him on her lap and try to talk together. His face snotty and dirty and happy, she kept a cloth to wipe him whenever she was near.

Mostly, Peter ran wild with other village children and their dogs, sneaking away, though Arl tried to stop him. She told herself her child was a free spirit, the way God had made him. And she felt badly that so much fell upon Arl.

"Do not fret," said Arl. "When Peter is older and more mature perhaps he will learn to read and write and you would then read the Gospels together. Be patient."

Read together, as she had with her own mother a lifetime, ago, it seemed. A wonderful dream of a beautiful time. But within herself she was not convinced.

You are not a good mother, her inner voice said sometimes, and she would try harder, but she was always tired now. Serving Lady Anna, working on the press, helping the sick and infirm and the old, there was so little time left even for sleep. Nothing she did made her feel worthy.

And too often she found herself praying for courage. She prayed that her will came from righteousness, and not from her anger at the burnings of the family she had so loved. And she wrestled with the same dread and hope she had felt when she left Kunvald years ago, crossing a new threshold from which there was no going back. And yet she was a mother now, and the old doubts came hunting her. Even the once-beautiful thought of Kunvald was bitter now, as a sweet cake burned is bitter.

Only with Grit alone did she feel she could honestly share her doubts. On a frosty night, they stole time to bathe together in the stone tub of the castle bath, after the water had been heated and used much earlier to bathe Lady Anna. And even in the luxuriant steam, with the rare fragrant soap, Kristina still thought of their mission, of her fear.

"If the press can be revived, if we publish and are caught, we face torture and death. Sometimes, I doubt why I do this."

Said Grit, "You have yourself said, that if we did not do it, if we did not take the truth and use it to liberate others, we lose our souls. That you know you must fight for a better world for your son and for all."

"But what if this is mere vanity. Is it merely my own conceit in my wish to please God? Am I better than the worst at Kunvald? No, I am not."

"Yes, I ask myself this same thing. Is it just my own cheap pride in my stubborn willingness to die? Am I playing on another stage, all over again, wanting to be the center of attention? Am I helping to lead others into danger for my own hubris? At those times, I pray."

"What answer comes?"

"That I hate what I once was. That I was not put here to ignore my duty to others; my duty to the truth. That was shown to me when I was a dissolute actress; a pretty toy sold to rich boys and old men; a plaything, wanton, hating everything about myself."

"You are still beautiful, Grit."

"Little sister, you are kind. Your young face is lovely, but your spirit even more, and that is why men watch you when you do not know."

"Watch me? None watch me."

She wanted to ask *who?* but did not, for something in her savored the idea, wrong as it was. She felt embarrassment in wanting to know. Grit reached and turned her around and scrubbed her back.

Grit, sounding happy, said behind her, "That is what I love about you, Kristina. You do not even know. Beauty of face and body is an affliction, a test, and for me it created despair. You do not have a ruined life to look back upon and to despise, but I do. Call it my vanity, call it my pride, I call it my salvation. Even if I burn, I will never be what I was before. So that makes it easy to do what I must, and to believe in it."

"What would happen to Peter, if I were destroyed? He is so slow. So vulnerable. And I am sure the fault is mine."

"How do you claim such fault?"

"When I carried him in my belly, and we ran from the dogs. Did he sense my fear of the dogs? It sounds silly and yet how can we know? Did my own fear harm him? Make him think as a dog thinks?"

"Oh, my dear dear friend." Grit's voice held only love and concern. "You fear dogs. All fear one thing or another. I fear wasps. Once men said my beauty stung like a wasp. Many believe what a pregnant woman sees can impress itself upon her unborn. Whether

Peter becomes lapdog or war-dog, that is up to you, how you raise him, as I have said before."

"He imitates other children, playing war."

"Children understand other children before they understand us. He must live in this world as they do. You cannot keep him locked away. And I tell you this: your faith is impressed upon him, too. And how can that be other than good?"

"My faith is not much good, weaker, often more than my fear. Berthold was strong."

"We put haloes around the dead, Kristina."

"I am more rabbit than I ever knew."

"You stand up when you must, that is enough."

Grit said nothing then; her eyes were red but not from the soap, not from the water.

It was when they were walking outside, hunched in shawl cloaks protecting them against the wind that blew across the snow-covered fields, their woolen boots crunching the snow with each footfall toward the old stone barn, past the winter-bare orchards, that Grit said, "I will always love you, little sister."

"And I you, Marguerite," said Kristina, using Grit's given name, not her nickname, for the first time in years.

Kristina could not be at the old barn as often as she yearned to be. Nighttime and when Lady Anna napped in the afternoons were the only safe times. But to do so took precious time from little Peter, who was growing fast, and becoming erratic, wild. He often had laughing fits and was grabbing everything. Arl kept him for Kristina in the weavery, and she could not lie to Arl, so she told her, in trust, what was being done with the old press.

She had expected Arl to scold and warn her that a mother could not afford to risk so much.

But Arl surprised her, saying, "Peter is like my own sweet child. There are many things I too would like to write and say to the world, about how I lost my two sons, and to caution other mothers who love their sons. In time, will you help me write such thoughts as I hold? As sister to sister? Mother to mother?"

"I will, and you shall," said Kristina.

And they embraced in a union beyond sisters, one that only mothers understand. It was different than with her love of sister for sister for Grit. None understood a mother like another mother, transcending all differences.

The old stone building was not large and the holes and partings in the stones were soon packed with straw.

Dolf and Symon worked to clean the water-damaged wood frame and iron of the rescued press. They had the carriage frame and impression assembly both laid out at one end of the stone floor. The fecund creek smell came from the damp wood as they toiled, scraping and brushing.

"We will need beams to cut for a new frame," said Dolf.

"The iron screw is pitted a little but with fine creek sand we can polish the run all right, I think," said Symon.

"Without type, we have nothing," said Grit.

Oak was too hard to carve into letters by hand, but Linhoff said that a branch of the linden tree had broken off in a storm. It had been dragged away behind a wall but not yet cut for fires, and linden wood was easy to shape with hand tools. He had saved it to make bricks for the smithy forge, but there was plentiful oak for that. It would serve wonderfully, as if a blessed gift of grace.

Kristina's mother might have said, *To shape truth of thought from the flesh of a tree, which was given life by the one who made us all, is that not beautiful?*

By the heat of a small hearth fire, they worked with spare saws and old files and chisels that Linhoff had sharpened and secreted away from Merkel's smithy.

"We made pike heads in the smithy," said Linhoff, "and I led pikemen in war, and now we make blocks for printing, as if now we make pikes of our thoughts."

"Thoughts for good, not for harm," said Grit.

Said Dolf, "Thoughts are punished just the same."

"Thoughts are weapons," said Linhoff. "Have rulers not harmed us with grand thoughts of war?"

Such arguments came now and then. In each was a core of agreement, yet in each a moral conflict, and this worried Kristina—that they were beginning something with these young men, something from which there would be no return, something that could veer in a wrong direction.

Linhoff brought charcoal from Merkel's forge, but it was much too coarse, even crushed down fine. After some failures, Kristina made what seemed usable ink with lampblack and vinegar, and with a cook knife she cut a quill pen from a goose feather. When the tree limb was sectioned, and the good heartwood was ready, they cut it into uniform blocks of the size that they thought close to what was used for printing. They made enough blocks for three sets of the alphabet, plus a score of extra vowels, and then a set of capital letters.

It took two full weeks of secret meetings at night for the blocks to be sawed and filed into squares uniformly. Then, with enormous care and patience, Kristina herself inked the gothic letters upon each block—outlines that could be carved away to make type.

"They do not look like letters of words we read," said Linhoff, confused.

"I have drawn them backward as best I could," Kristina explained.

Said Grit, "When they touch ink on paper the letters will be as you have seen them before."

"Paper," said Dolf.

"Yes," Grit said, "we must find paper."

And then came the tedious work of carving and chiseling and filing away the dross wood from the inked letter that was desired. As they worked, sitting on the stone floor, Kristina heard the young men talking among themselves.

“Do not slip the chisel or it will ruin the letter,” said Linhoff. “Be more patient.”

“Cut my thumb all to hell,” said Max, sucking his thumb.

“Strange,” said Linhoff, “the ancient tree being used for such a new purpose.”

“The linden will have a voice now,” said Max.

“But what will it say?” said Jakop.

Linhoff said, “What we have learned, so that others need not be so deceived.”

“What have we learned?” said Ambrosius.

“To question,” said Linhoff. “The Scriptures do not say that we must blindly obey, but that every man must think and do what is right. Is that not so, Grit?”

Kristina saw how aware Grit was of Linhoff regarding her with his question, of Linhoff’s eyes seeking hers.

“The law of God’s love first, over the cruel law of man,” said Grit, looking back down to the block she was carving.

“Love is good,” said Linhoff, in an odd, teasing way.

“What of those who cannot read?” said Ambrosius. “Can we make drawings that show what we mean?”

“Who can carve pictures? Not me,” said Linhoff.

Kristina thought of Witter and his skill in art, and she thought of Witter and Lud, out there far away now, somewhere. She prayed in her heart for their safe journey, and she missed them both very much, she realized.

“Those who cannot read have no say in things anyhow,” said Max. “They must learn as we did.”

“They are people,” said Jakop. He looked up at Kristina and she saw that he wanted to please her by saying this.

“We must agree what to say,” said Max.

Said Linhoff, “If people can be made to fight for others, they can be shown to fight for themselves.”

Grit stood, looking down at the young men. She turned, glaring at Linhoff, who watched her.

Said Grit, “We will not advocate violence.”

The young men looked up at Grit, and Kristina could see they were surprised that she spoke so stridently. With a jerk, Grit's chisel slipped, and she dropped her wooden block and sucked her thumb.

It was Linhoff who rushed to Grit, even before Kristina reached her, and Linhoff took Grit's hand in his own, and sucked the blood from her thumb. Quickly, Grit pulled her hand away. Kristina saw hurt in her eyes, and something else, more like fear. Blood dripped from her thumb but she ignored it. Linhoff touched Grit's shoulder and turned away and returned to his work.

"An eye for an eye," said Linhoff. "I have read this law in the book of God, the Bible."

"That was God before he sent his son," said Symon.

Kristina tore off a strip of wool weave from her hem to bind up Grit's thumb, but Grit had already taken up her chisel and was working again, cutting a letter from the face of her block.

"A tooth for a tooth," said Max. "All are equal before God. Is this not so?"

"Do bishops toil for shares?" said Ambrosius.

Kristina saw Jakop watching her, and Dolf, Symon, Ambrosius, Max, and Linhoff all waiting to see what would be said.

"As Christ did command," said Grit, staring down at her block, "we must love our enemies."

"Lady Anna is rich," said Max.

"Lady Anna is not rich," said Kristina. "Nor an enemy."

"That is not natural," said Linhoff. "Loving an enemy."

Kristina stood and faced them all.

"But we must try," said Kristina. "We must never act to harm others."

Grit looked up at her and Kristina saw how her face, tight upon itself, softened and warmed and smiled. But Linhoff's voice came low and harsh.

"Pray hard," said Linhoff. "For we must have paper."

And that night—on her pallet in the chilly dark, with the fire crackling low and the embers settling—Kristina did pray, long and hard, but not for paper. She prayed to God for Witter to bring wisdom to Lud, and for Lud to bring strength to Witter, and for them to become as brothers, and for them to be well, to not inflict evil upon themselves in their travels, and for them to come back safe and whole.

She prayed as a sister for them both, and as she prayed, she knew that prayer was false. She wanted to love Witter more. Witter was a Jew yet devout in his belief in God. Lud was agnostic at best, a hardened cynic, probably an atheist. He never feigned piety and was brutally honest.

Witter was the soul she could share, if he returned. Lud was a killer. But as she tried to pray, she realized she did not feel for either man as a sister feels for a brother. And this troubled her in her heart, and kept her awake for hours.

Lud

It was so typical of life—that the threat of organized bandits or disenfranchised knights, desperate men on the road, would pale before the simple, numbingly routine dangers, such as sleeping in some local villein farmer's stable where local rogues could break in to do murder and steal.

This was the fourth day on the rivers, the day they were to reach Calais, the coastal harbor where passage to Dover was hired. The river barge slid along smoothly, and when the sun came out in the bleak early winter sky, Lud watched the horses yawn and enjoy the hay on the flat deck where they were tethered. His sword, lashed in leather under the saddle skirt, had not been needed, and yet it was essential in Lud's sense of need. Again, it was his dagger that was his best little friend.

In the dark stable there had been three of them, and fortunately Lud had no sleep in him, fretting over England and how hard it might be to bring Florian away, if he resisted for any reason. He had lain awake trying to imagine Florian's face, when he had heard them.

Also, it was lucky that the thieves were simple rogues and half-drunk, because one stumbled on the saddles and that was when Lud got the blade up in that man's groin. There was so much shrieking then and wild thrashing about that Lud feared knifing Witter in the confusion, and so the fight was prolonged more than necessary, had Lud been alone. There were shouts and curses all around.

"Witter!"

"*Sanglante merde! Poignardé me boules!*"

"Lud! Here!"

"*Sainte Mère de Jésus!*"

"Witter!"

"*Allez allez!*"

Two ran and one died. And then there was the old potbellied farmer in a ragged nightshirt, crying and screaming over his dead son, and the magistrates confused and stomping about, and Witter pushing Lud back and taking over to make order from the mess; all of them jabbering in the foreign tongue.

"It turns out the dead one was already accused of horse-thieving, and they had offered our horses for sale in a tavern before even coming to kill us," said Witter. "The magistrates were sick of complaints about them."

In the morning's tumult, because the farmer's son had been killed, a French magistrate had tried to extract a bribe, bringing three of his deputies along, all armed. Just when Lud despaired of trying to fight their way out of this, Witter had strutted and posed and used the bishopric safe papers, and the four magistrates had seemed suddenly very impressed.

It was good news on a bad morning. Lud was eager to be gone. "Then let us be on the road before his kin ride after us looking for satisfaction. If they had been masterless knights, real fighting men, we would be dead."

"We must sell the horses to pay for river barge passage," insisted Witter. "Our fare is a florin each, and they want another florin for two horses."

"River? We are going by road to the coast," Lud said, flaring.

"Our bishopric safe passage, when I showed it to the magistrates, is for river barge travel, not road, and we must embark here. There is a barge with space leaving at noon for the coast."

"Damn," said Lud, and he produced two of his gold florins from his pouch of fifty. "Damn damn damn. You and your sore ass and your shy ways. Damn."

Witter took the gold pieces, astonished. "You had passage all along? You have gold?"

"Mine to do with as I wish. If we are forced to hire river travel we must have the horses in England, too."

"By insisting upon the roads, you risked our lives and your precious mission."

"Yes, you are right. I was wrong. Now shut your mouth about it, or I will shut it for you."

"Without me you would be worse than alone here," said Witter. It was only too true. Witter had lost his fear of Lud, and that was both good and bad.

Lud more and more realized he was totally dependent upon Witter's skill at the graces, and Witter's own good will in their purpose together— to reach this Oxford in England and find Florian and persuade him to come home with them to Giebel. It was a tall order, and must be done. And yet there needed to be a sense of equality somehow.

"What were they yelling, the French thieves?" he asked Witter, to turn the mood if he could.

Witter laughed. "Bloody shit! Holy mother of Jesus! He's knifed my balls!"

It was funny in a horrible way and they laughed together, in relief and in the cruel twist of attackers being attacked. It was the first time they had ever shared a laugh.

The river passage toward the coast was boring and uneventful. They slept in a grain bin of bags, with the horses tethered on the deck.

The first day out, Lud slipped his hand inside Witter's tunic and had his little dagger before Witter even realized what was happening. All his fear of Lud came rushing back.

"Not bad," Lud said, waving the old blade between their faces, making a feint to Witter's belly, he made Witter fall backward, in horror, onto bags of grain.

"What are you doing?"

Lud pulled him back up with his free hand, and put the dagger back into Witter's right hand. "What you have is a push blade. Nice, long, thin taper, better for thrusting than slashing, but this will do, if you will learn a couple of simple things."

"You love the fear of others," said Witter angrily. He gripped the haft of the dagger so hard his arm quivered. But it was Lud's unconcerned calmness that was most disturbing.

"Cut me, then," Lud said, so casually that Witter wanted to run away. "It will feel good. Cut me."

Something in Witter snapped; sudden rage liberated him from fear, and without the old crippling thoughts and dreads to stop him, his body moved.

Witter tried to kill Lud. He really tried. But when his arm came up, Lud seemed to read his mind. Lud never looked at the blade, only his eyes. How Lud twisted his wrist and got the blade away, Witter did not know, but now Lud had the little dagger.

"Now what?" said Witter, panting.

"Now I will tell you something. Be patient. Fear makes you hurry. Do not go for the deathblow. Never. Trip him. Confuse him. Slash over the eyes, the forehead, start with that. Blood flow is copious there and blinds the man and frightens him. Then you can cut him up all you want while he leaps about howling."

Their afternoon alone below deck was spent this way. Lud showed Witter some feints and made him practice them.

"Knife fighting is like dancing, the same steps," said Lud, and Witter felt it, realized it, finally beginning to feel the rhythm. "Have you never danced with a woman?"

No, not with a woman. But it was easy in another way, because he had danced with men long ago. Danced the hora. Danced the Sephardic dances, his friends and cousins and uncles and his father all circling and turning and moving together. So now, Witter danced with Lud until he could do this dance with the daggers.

Their arms parried and slid and elbows and knees banged and the blades moved like the heads of two snakes in the air between them. Lud's gaze was unnerving, hard to return, and he noticed that Witter's eyes were soft, not hard.

Said Lud, "Look afraid, deceive me with fear. Act frightened and foolish, even beg a little, then cut me when I become mocking and less careful."

They moved their legs inside each other's, sidestepping and tripping. There were easy ways to do the dance. It was simpler than any of the courtly dances Witter had learned in Córdoba as a boy eons ago.

Witter began to move confidently, more quickly, and knew when he could do it well enough, because Lud said, "That is good enough. If we practice more you will be cutting me."

It was a revelation to Witter that cutting a man was so simple. It was easier than learning a long poem. It was fearful, too, the seduction of the whole thing.

He knew himself well enough to know that he was innately a coward, a man of thought more than form, and that he would always dread a fight with knives. It had been unnerving, being that close to Lud, dancing that way with the knives. It was thrilling and horrible yet intoxicating all at the same time. He feared most what he might feel should he kill a man. If he felt a thrill, he would be lost to himself forever. He knew himself that well, also.

Now, the feel of the little blade under his tunic was no longer comforting, but a threat of a kind he had never known before. And yet it was liberating. And that was the seduction.

Is it the coward, said Judah one night while Witter slept, *who fears to take the life of another? Or is it the coward, who does not value life and therefore has no fear of taking it? It is the coward who fears for his own life and takes that of another, it is the coward who kills…*

Four nights later, under a full moon, the barge docked at the mouth of the river, and the sea could been seen far out, where oceangoing vessels came and went.

They disembarked the horses from the barge and lashed their baggage up behind the saddles.

"I must negotiate passage to Dover, across the British Sea. The North Sea runs to the Atlantic here, and the waters in the strait are rough," said Witter. "It is only ten leagues distance across but the season is late for crossing and it may be expensive."

"Everything is expensive with you," said Lud.

They mounted the horses and rode in the moonlight past unlit stone houses to the wharves where most ships were tied down for the winter. They rode uneasily at the docks and a wind was coming up.

By lantern light, on the wharf crowded with ships, Witter negotiated with a slightly pockmarked captain who had no teeth and a beard to his belly. The captain kept saying "*no no no no,*" and both of them jabbered away in French. Finally, they shook hands. The captain spit in his palm first.

"Four florins," Witter told Lud, wiping his palm on a post. "We leave with the tide."

Grudgingly, from his precious little purse, from the only gold he had ever owned, derived from a duel and given by Dietrich as a prize, Lud produced the extorted fare.

"For the good of the estate," he said.

But now Witter was even cockier. "My tunic is soaked with old blood. Before we embark, you shall buy me a new one for my pains. Also, my tights are torn with holes. A quick trim of hair and beard also are in order."

"What concern is your vanity to me?"

"If I am to be your master, I must look like one. Are masters not vain and shallow creatures?"

"Dietrich was not," said Lud.

"Well, I must appear to be," Witter said.

So in a fop shop on the square of the river town, Lud did buy Witter a readymade new velvet green winter tunic, begrudgingly, but necessarily, and with trimmed beard and hair, Witter looked almost noble, for it was rare how Witter could master the airs of a noble, the courtesies and suchlike, that were a mystery to Lud himself. When Witter spoke to others in their language, there was always respect from the strangers, and times enough, a needed compliance.

"You do this well," he said, grudgingly.

"We each do well, that which we know."

They hurried the horses up a wide ramp onto the crossing ship—a small, pointy-bowed scow—for the tide was beginning to run out and they must cross before nightfall.

Lud had never felt more alone.

The deck pitched and the craft wallowed deep into troughs of gray sea that hid the sky, then rode back up high, leaving Lud's stomach below. On the aft deck, the horses crapped themselves empty and kicked and tore at their halters and he hobbled them front and rear, slipping in their dung on the wet wood deck, and covered their heads with barley bags. Their cries were like children's.

Then he was deathly ill, hanging his head over one side, his morning gruel joining the foam. And he worried what would become of Giebel with no steward watching them all like a hawk. Like geese they were, staying in their flock together, but without being herded, they would run off together in any direction, on any whim. No telling what might be happening back there now.

"England!" Witter said.

Witter's hand pulled him around. Witter was pointing ahead, and Lud saw a white strip of rocky bluffs. There was a fog running and it swallowed the little craft and then England vanished and it began to rain, a little, then harder, and then a steady drenching storm so much like the one in which he had fought his last battle in war.

Witter said, "Looks like we shall winter here."

"What?" Lud could not have heard right.

"The winter storms close the channel crossings. I had to bribe him to take us this late. I shall need an extra florin to disembark us, he says, for the English harbor magistrates."

"No, we must get Florian, and leave as soon as possible."

Suddenly, he hated England. He hated the idea that Florian was there, somewhere, dissolved in a crowd of strangers. How would he be now after so many years? He was grown, no longer the child who had ridden on Lud's shoulders, and learned the dagger and the horse and the grapple.

Would Florian be a fop, arrogant and vain? Full of airs, disdainful, officious? Somehow the thought was more terrifying than disgusting. To have lost Dietrich, and now Florian, too?

Do not leap before you are stabbed, he thought, fighting himself for balance and calm.

But then, Lud saw the bluffs again, whitish rock like broken teeth blurred in the storm, much closer. And he was to be stuck here in this alien place of strange customs and unknown words until the winter storms abated and the channel crossings would resume with spring. Stuck here at Witter's mercy, everything hanging on Witter's goodwill now, with only his own little personal treasure to sustain them, until they could find and extract Florian and get him home.

Florian, where the hell are you, boy?

The sight of the white cliffs and the harbor ahead, visible now in the opening fog, made him want to run away, but there was nowhere to run. He thought of the temptation he had resisted and fought off—to take what remained of his fifty florins, buy armor, hire himself as mercenary, perhaps rise through the ranks in battle. To spend his life without needing anyone, among strangers, killing other strangers.

But Lud smiled bitterly at that notion; he knew himself too well. He loved Giebel and he loved Dietrich and he loved Kristina and he loved Florian, too.

And if a man does not love himself, that hole must be kept filled with the love of others.

Witter

So this was England. He knew this wet green place was an island nation long ago bereft of its Jews, its rulers having persecuted and banished them all, and yet Witter felt an uneasy and completely unreasonable exultation. His English was rusty but good enough to play the educated visitor from Swabia in southern Germany, a citizen with safe passage of the Holy Roman Empire.

Despite a history of cruelty, English tyranny was no worse than and little different from all other nations and rulers. And here was their destination, at last. Perhaps at Oxford there would be a spiritual and intellectual light of reason. Werner Heck had been to Oxford, twice, and sold books printed there, obtained from the Frankfurt Book Fair.

Witter remembered how poor Werner had once praised Oxford: *Where there is enlightenment, there is hope for tolerance, when young minds and old unite and break their shackles...*

Witter could nurture that one hope, and he clung to it now. A rising elation buoyed him.

Welcome to England, Witter, the only Jew in the entire land...soon you will see Oxford...

On the foggy wharf where gulls cried and fishermen dumped nets of strange creatures, the fish traders milled about, shouting, and Lud disembarked ahead of Witter, with the terrified horses, down a shaky ramp from the ship. Stepping onto solid land made him dizzy yet took away both his nausea and his fear of the sea.

Great sailing vessels were coming and going and the wharfs were piled with goods of every kind imaginable, crocks and bundles and carcasses and skins and feathers and metal bars, and everywhere were the netted piles of fish.

Witter had conferred with the captain, and now, on the dock, legs wobbly, he briefed Lud on the best means of travel.

"We can hire a barge, the captain told me, up into harbor to the River Thames, and pass on through London," Witter said as Lud saddled the horses.

"Oxford is less than twenty leagues northwest of London. We ride from Dover up the coast and around, on to Oxford. Dietrich's map shows the road around, and we have no spare coin for barge hires, nor time."

"The captain says that road is dangerous."

"Arguing is dangerous. We waste time."

"I am master, remember?"

"To others, yes. But do not press it too hard, Witter. Without me you would be already dead, or worse. And do not make me grudge you when this trip is done. Florian's letters to his mother tell of the sweating sickness here, sometimes even at court. Passing through the city is too dangerous."

No point in arguing with Lud. Back on the horse and the pain in the ass. But not even that could dampen Witter's feelings of hope, guarded as they were. The sweating sickness was another thing entirely.

On the busy trading street off the quay they mounted and rode out of the harbor, not through the big city called London, but around its towers and walls and seething swarms of people and animals, through the low bottoms covered with crowded tenements, and on out by the map, along the marshes of the River Thames. Smoke clouds drifting like sooty islands stung their eyes with the acrid stench of much coal. Their horses sneezed and snorted.

"The coal bites the lungs," said Lud. "Dietrich never liked to dig coal from the old pit at home, for Lady Anna feared Roman ghosts would walk in the smoke of it."

Said Witter, "Coal is an old evil for the poor, and will be forbidden to burn, surely, the way it chokes the breath of all."

"Nobody frets about the breath of the poor, other than to wish it extinguished," said Lud.

Dietrich's vellum map indeed showed, north and west ahead, where the Cherwell and Thames rivers met; and at a low point in the Thames where oxen forded, was Oxford, the name a legend. It was where, Witter imagined, young minds were struggling to be liberated, in great halls of learning that surely birthed tolerance. Oxford, the oldest university in the English-speaking world, much older than Wurzburg University, fabled as the home of pure thinkers, and now of Erasmus himself. Witter's mind felt as if wine were poured into it, a wine of such wondrous hope.

Then suddenly he could hear his father's voice: Judah thundered at him like the ram's-horn roar of the shofar:

Hope is the wine of fools! Tolerance, here? After the first crusade, over two centuries ago, all English Jews were banished, their fortunes seized on All Souls' Day by Edward I, fleeing for their lives to France, Germany, Flanders, Spain, only to be imprisoned, tortured, burned, fleeing yet again and again. Have you forgotten your history so easily?

Judah's voice subsided. Witter was weary of his own relentless pessimism. Now he needed to believe.

Below the riverbank, the river was vile with waste, sewage, pieces of animals, rotted wood, floating things snagged on fallen trees that rolled past like great sodden corpses from mythology. People in rags washed clothes on the bank as if the water were clear and pure. The people took the water away in buckets. They bathed in the foamy murk. Witter had seen this all before, many times, many places. But obviously, Lud had not.

"Any we drink," said Lud, "we boil first. Let us hope the fire itself does not fear that water."

"Yes, water must always be boiled in such foul places. It will be different at Oxford," said Witter. The unreasoning optimism grew in him like a warming fire.

"You have been there?" said Lud, his voice hard.

"I have read in books of Oxford. There is wisdom in medicine and science and they will drink clean water there."

"Wisdom, your red ass. I believe what I see. We will be lucky if we are not caught and eaten before we reach your wonderful Oxford."

"What do you know of it?"

"A place named for oxen crossing," Lud said. "But I am only an ignorant man, unlike yourself. I expect nothing."

The stony side road bypassed London, moving away from the river for a time, and back again, and the smell of the city was smoky and sweetly foul. At first there were some big houses with gardens along the riverside, behind high stone walls, but then came less and less prosperity, and people in torn tights and ragged belted cloaks stared at them from hovels that made Giebel look like Wurzburg.

And Judah's admonitions came to Witter: *You exult in reaching England? My poor hopeful son, beware, beware…*

"Why do you look so happy?" said Lud, his lower face wrapped as usual, his eyes taking in everything they passed, alert, as if from any side, armed men would cut them down.

It was strange to Witter to think that Lud and his father, Judah, would agree upon anything, even in the abstract.

"Keep a sharp eye out for rogues. England is full of ravenous bastards and low types, all say so," said Lud.

"Oxford," said Witter. "Today we shall reach Oxford."

"And why does a foreign name stir you so? I see London pass behind us, another great city of rich and poor, stone and mud, want and troubles, and a river to ride along, but I see no cause for joy."

"Minds, brilliance, learning." He knew not what else to say, and it felt wrong to try to defend a place of such renown. What was it his father had so often said? *When you argue with a fool you are the fool….*

"Rein yourself in," said Lud, "We come to fetch Florian and be away quickly, that is all."

But Witter was full of the thrill of soon seeing Oxford.

Riding, his buttocks throbbing again, he considered how to broach this so Lud could understand. Lud spoke no more English than he did French or Latin, and Witter felt as if he rode with a dangerous and anxious beast on a chain, constantly advising Lud of what this man had said or that sign had meant.

"Lud, try to understand, think of it, a chance to meet Erasmus, that in itself is so marvelous."

"Enough. This is what I understand," Lud said. "You said yourself, the channel crossings will be impossible in a few days. We find Florian and we make him understand and we bring him back, willing or not, one way or another. We are not here to have selfish adventures nor bend over for writers of words. We must move fast, for I refuse to be forced to winter here."

Witter did not argue. He would have to see what happened and what the truth of Oxford was, in reality. Lud, he had no doubt whatever, would kill him if he did not need him, and if he were angered sufficiently.

Along the river marshes the land opened a little and the sun came out in broken clouds. The road, rutted by wagon wheels, went up and down through fields dotted with cattle and sheep and herders and herder cottages. Far off appeared a castle mansion, here and there, like a great tombstone atop a hill. They passed hay carts and trader wagons, and most were being pulled by hands—wretched people who looked up in fear and surprise at the passing horses. Those who did not seemed wretched were laughing and drunk.

Then on a rise, Witter saw the towers and walls.

"There," said Lud.

Witter saw a town laid out not unlike Wurzburg, with the walled wealth of cathedrals and towers rising in the center of a sprawl of huts and hovels that poured out across the fields. He did not know why his heart sank.

Lud halted his horse and unrolled the map in the sun. Witter urged his horse alongside to see.

"What does it say?" said Lud.

Witter read the red-lined markings: "*Horsemull Street and Queen's Lane and High Street, Queen's College.*"

"We have four, maybe five hours of daylight," said Lud, and nudged his mount, riding away.

Witter tried to follow, kneeing the flanks of his horse, making it lurch more violently under him on the ruts of the rough road.

Standing to keep his butt off the saddle, he saw the Oxford spires and towers and walls, closer and larger, and then heard the bells, and then, approaching the wide main street, he saw what he thought was a parade of some kind, a massing of men in robes, and then he realized that hundreds of men were fighting.

Lud

Lud rode slowly, watchfully, along the outer walls of what he now saw was a square-mile stone maze of old masonry pinnacles, struts, arches, spires, wide ways and alleys, and all the rest of a great nightmare nest of busy old stonework. The bottom level swarmed with noisy men and sounded like hives of spilled bees. His horse was anxious and he held the reins in close. At an open gate he stopped his horse and through the stone arch he stared at the full spectacle of hundreds of young and old men in fine robes all going at each other, but not with swords.

There was nothing more dangerous than a fight when you did not know who was fighting, or what was the object of the dispute. But this was a very odd kind of fight. Men with red faces were throwing paving stones and pummeling one another with fists and staffs and jerking hair and beards. Some were beating others with books or strangling them with their scarves. He felt his face scars stretch and his jaw spread open in a big grin.

Off his horse, Lud looped the reins around a tending post and climbed a near wall to try to see what was what. It was impossible that this was the Oxford that Witter was so praising, the Oxford where Dietrich had sent his beloved Florian to form his mind, the Oxford that was so costly, the Oxford of scholars. He would have laughed if he did not feel so annoyed at this delay in finding Florian. Witter scrambled to keep up with him.

Atop the wall, Lud looked down upon it all and saw magistrates with their chain cuffs around their shoulders, arms crossed, leaning against a far wall and laughing at the whole thing. That meant it was something personal and not a legal matter, and that much was good. He had to reach down and help pull Witter onto the wall.

Many were shouting; two groups were trying to drown out each other—the small group and all the rest against them. Lud did not understand the shouted English words until he asked Witter, and Witter—with a strange smile, almost a reverence of delight—told him.

"All have rights!" some shouted together. It was the small group, and some had broadsheets being torn from their hands and thrown or shredded by all the others.

"Might makes right!" the much larger group shouted back, drowning out the small group, ripping the broadsheets away.

Lud's eyes scanned the mob and he saw it surge like fish schooling, fighting, back and forth below him. One thing was plain, there were not many down there who knew well how to fight. They were young fops mostly and they threw cat punches like women, with much shoving and spitting and elbows and knees. They wore good gowns and almost none were threadbare. They must be merchants or professors or students or all.

He felt himself begin to laugh at them.

And then his eye, scanning their faces, saw a face that wiped his grin away.

It was *Dietrich*—his face was young and yet there was no other face like it in this world—*Dietrich.*

Men were swarming him like rats, ripping a few last broadsheets from his hands, papers that went flying away, and they were pounding him backward, deeper into the crowd. He was using good grappling moves and a good punch technique, hurting them, and he stood out for all that in this clumsy mob of fools and thinkers, but three were too many, and they were beating him down from the sides and from behind.

"All have rights!" the young man yelled in their faces.

Dietrich...unmistakably.

He knew that it was Florian, whom he sought and had not seen in many years. But in his heart it was as if Dietrich had been reborn in the flower of youth and was alone in a fight, outnumbered.

Lud leapt down into the churning bodies and shoved his way through like a man plunging along a logjammed river. This was no fight for daggers or to do grave injury. It was more difficult, for Lud knew that to maim or kill here would cause him to be arrested, and perhaps cause harm to Florian, were their connection known.

So it was a unique problem. It is easier to cut one's way through a mob, or to break a man than restrain him, for a cut or broken man will cringe, fall, or flee, but only one man can be restrained at a time, and in a fight with many, to restrain one opens others to attack. Therefore, Lud saw the only possible solution:

He would grab Florian and run.

He continued to push in among the crowd, and with a great grappling lunge, he had Florian by the waist. He wrestled Florian away from his attackers, and Florian began howling. Lud hoisted the young man aloft in one great jerk, up on his shoulders, and hustled him out of the melee.

But Florian was kicking and twisting violently and his fists were smashing down at Lud's face.

"Lud! I am Lud! You are Florian, son of Dietrich and Anna. It is I, Lud!"

Florian's face twisted around, inches from Lud's.

"Who speaks such Low German to me? Lud?"

In the breech of an alley Lud put Florian down and they stood together panting, staring in mutual disbelief at one another, and Florian pulled the scarf down from Lud's lower face and laughed in joy. Lud felt the air of day on his lower face, felt his mask of scars exposed.

"Lud? It cannot be!" There was no horror in the face so like that of Dietrich, no fear nor disgust in the brilliant young eyes that recognized him. "Lud!"

And Florian kissed Lud's scarred face; the first time lips had kissed him honestly in ten years.

Witter

Witter left his horse tied with Lud's horse and hurried headlong toward the shouting and screaming chaos that filled a square among the towers of learning.

He stopped and regarded it all. One group obviously was handing out broadsheets and the much larger group was attacking to destroy whatever was printed there. Some fought, some shouted, some were laughing and throwing garbage on the mob.

Witter looked up and saw balconies where older men in black robes stood looking down like crows, waving their arms with regret and a dignified distaste, not mockery. They were obviously professors, shouting—

"Stop, desist, we implore you!"

Dodging blows, ducking and shifting in the swarming clumsy crowd, Witter saw Lud hoist a struggling young man upon his shoulders, bearing him clear out of the fight in the square. Then they were hugging and hurrying away.

It had to be Florian. Lud would not waste time on any other, that was certain.

He followed them through alleys to streets away from the fight and caught up with them outside a plain stone building.

"Lud!" he shouted, and they turned and saw him.

Minutes later they were up a flight of stone stairs in a great common room with straw on the floors and no glass in the windows. He realized it was a dormitory. At the far end was a little smoky fire in a small hearth and students crowded around it. The most remarkable thing that he saw was a small printing press in one corner.

Lud and Florian were jabbering away in German like two lost souls finding one another. It was country German, full of slang, and Florian's friends just stared in wonder, obviously unable to comprehend a single word. Lud's scarred face was unwrapped but no one here seemed to care. A few had milder scars of their own.

Witter mingled among them, full of curiosity, and they took him for another student, apparently. Like Florian, they were all bruised and beaten but excited and recounting their battle, bragging as all students brag, ennobling themselves. But Witter liked them at once, for all their zest in life...

"Florian was giving it to them," one said.

Another said, "Florian, where did you learn such punches and grapplings?"

"My good Lud here, who helped raise me like a wild thing to fight and to hunt, before my studies and courtesies began. Lud is like my older brother; no, closer still."

Florian put an arm around Lud and pulled him closer. Witter could see the shy pleasure Lud took in this, like a child with a treat that might be taken away at any moment. He looked embarrassed but pleased beyond words.

Florian said, "They shall not defeat us by blows, when we have thoughts that overcome all resistance."

A student said, "They shout 'might makes right,' but a new day with rights for all is coming."

"For all have rights," said another.

"All have rights!" they thundered together.

Finally, Witter caught Lud's eye.

"Florian," said Lud, "here is Witter, another from Giebel, traveling with me as guide, languages and such."

Now they all turned and stared at Witter.

"Welcome, Brother," said Florian. He gripped Witter by the arms and pulled him in with remarkable strength, showing both vitality of body and of purpose. There was a marvelous exuberance about this young man, and Witter saw how his fellow students admired this quality, and harked to whatever Florian had to say. Florian so quickly introduced Witter around, that Witter hardly remembered any of the students' names.

Said Florian, "The fight was set off by a little broadsheet we printed, on our little hired press, for we all share the cost of paper and ink, with what little we have, inspired by a lecture of our great Professor Erasmus."

"Erasmus?" said Witter. The name thrilled him.

"The sons of nobles were incensed by his great words and called him a bastard. That is, the ones who even read it before ripping it apart."

In English, another student said, "Erasmus was born out of wedlock and is not ashamed of it, and nothing diminishes the greatness of his thoughts."

Said another, in Latin, "Simply what the Scriptures say, for all who can read, that God created all and all are equal under God."

Florian said, "Well said, my good Tyndale, when you translate your Bible someday, as you claim you will, make it all right. In their evil conceits, they believe themselves ordained by God to rule over others."

"I shall use the very language of the plowman," said the student called Tyndale, "and not the flowery tongue of the philistines, who think they own the world and that everyone in it should kiss their kingly arses."

Said Florian, "They feast on wine and capons in heated rooms and we eat tripe and gruel, but our appetite feeds upon truth, not lies."

Witter marveled at how these students traded languages about like a game of cards, how quick they were with dueling thoughts. He wished suddenly with all his heart he could live among such quick minds, to challenge one another, to break through the bonds of smallness, of hatred, of injustice. That was what a university of ideas meant.

The intellectual joy was intoxicating. He thought how, with Florian and Lud at his side, he would not be alone; he would be guarded, assumed gentile, even introduced as an equal...and this winter could be spent learning, and he could sit at the feet of great men, and perhaps in time, though he was not a student, even be accepted in his identity as Witter von Giebel, comrade and attendant to Florian, the heir. If the channel crossing were too dangerous, could staying here through winter not be possible? His hopes rose up.

Intruding, ambushing him here, his father's voice came and tried to reach him:

Are you so ashamed, my son? Is this world so dear to you that you pretend to be who you are not, even now?

And he fought back:

Would you even deny me hope, Father?

Now he watched Lud and Florian trying to get to know one another, smiling so warmly, watching each other like a father and son, or like an older brother fondly with younger, reunited after many years. They spoke privately in the country German slang that Witter knew was so intimate among regional men, and he knew that only he, of all others in the hall, understood them. Lud's mask of a face glowed with love, and was not hideous, for the first time in Witter's memory of the man.

"You are so like my father," said Florian to Lud.

"You are the one like your father," Lud said. "You are a grown man when I expected a callow youth."

"And Lud is Lud, as unchanged as a rock."

"We have no time now, let us talk on the road back to London."

"Back to London?" said Florian.

"Tell him," Lud said to Witter. "Say it best."

Witter said, "Your father, you know, is dead, and you the heir are needed at the estate now. The situation is dire, and your mother has sent for you most urgently."

"Dire? But my studies in law," protested Florian, "are yet unfinished. I cannot leave Oxford for at least another year."

Witter turned his head, realizing that a priest had entered. He had come so unobtrusively that at first no one noticed. He stood watching and listening without flourish, simply, modestly. But all who saw him turned with enormous respect.

The students went silent, and all bowed. This obviously embarrassed the priest deeply.

"Erasmus," murmured Florian.

Witter was thunderstuck at the spoken name.

So this is the great Erasmus…

In the gray light from the glassless window casements, Erasmus was somehow Moses-like, Witter thought. He moved erect but without pride, lean and sere, his robe black and unadorned, his hair graying and his lean face austere; but his eyes drew the gaze of others, his awareness rich and intense with great depths. Witter was simply astonished.

Near Witter, Florian stared, his mouth fell open, and he went to one knee. Lud was obviously surprised at Florian's reaction. So was Erasmus.

"Please, up," said Erasmus. "I feel responsible. Hardly did I recognize the stir my words, mild as they were, should make."

"Erasmus," said Witter, in deep admiration, "Erasmus."

"Call me Desiderius, please, not so formal, I am but a priest. One whose words in lecture caused riot."

"What was your lecture?" asked Witter.

"*Sileni Alcibiadis,*" said Florian.

"Marvelous," said Witter.

"You have read it?" Erasmus said, surprised.

And Witter felt a thrill, able to quote a passage, to prove himself here: "*Anyone who looks closely at the inward nature and essence will find that nobody is further from true wisdom than those people with their grand titles, learned bonnets, splendid sashes and bejeweled rings, who profess to be wisdom's peak.*"

"Exactly so," said Florian, with obvious delight.

Witter felt a rush of pride, alloyed by a pang of self-reproach for exposing his foolish vanity.

"Where did you study?" asked Erasmus, his deep eyes regarding Witter with unnerving intensity. There was that glow of spiritual intensity that one felt more than saw.

"Here and there," evaded Witter. "I have read your work in Dutch and Latin, both. It is such a brilliant promise of hope for tolerance."

Lud stood and said, "We have no time for this fawning, we must embark away. The longer here, the more exposed to sweats and pox and fools with daggers."

"No sweats nor pox here in over a year," said Florian. "But many fools with daggers, most quite clumsy indeed."

There was laughter.

The others all ignored Lud.

Erasmus bent and gently, with one forefinger, touched Florian's bruises along his forehead, wiping his hair from the hurts. The priest shook his head in seeming regret.

"*Sileni* means what is beautiful of inner man may be unseen in the outer man. What we saw today was both: ugly with intolerance, beautiful with the fight for truth. Yet I would never have pain or injury caused in behalf of my thoughts nor beliefs."

Florian said, "We must fight for the rights of all. They would have rights only for those of might and wealth and title. Christ said all are equal in his eyes."

"Truth," said Erasmus, "truth is like water through the fingers. It is belief that holds truth. But one man's belief is another man's enemy. Still, in the writings of young men there is hope for truth. And tolerance is truth."

Tolerance is truth...again, like something his father would have said.

"What writings of young men?" said Witter.

Now the students gathered around the master.

Answered Erasmus, "Many. Some writers are students here, some are priests, others elsewhere: my own dear friend Thomas More and his *Utopia*, imagining a world of pure tolerance engendering plenty, where all beliefs may worship, free of persecution. And William Grocyn. John Colet. Johann Froben. In your Saxony city of Wittenberg a young priest is making quite a noise. Luther is his name. There are others, in your country, too, like Muntzer of Mainz. Their broadsheets are already abroad in your country, and Luther's sell in many places above all others."

"Even yours?" said Florian.

"Yes," Erasmus said, feigning irritation, so that all the students laughed. "Young Luther is quite the noisy upstart. But I tell you, seriously now, with literacy, a great sound is waking the souls of men. Write well, each of you, and continue to add your voices to theirs."

Witter was spellbound. Erasmus was so like his father, Judah, in calm thought and depth of reason, all given in a simple sense of kindness, without the least pomposity.

Tolerance is truth…

Witter felt his heart leap, yet he did not trust it. Too often before had he hoped and found the hope a trap.

"Tolerance for all beliefs?" he asked.

"For all beliefs," said Erasmus. "Free of persecution."

Florian said, "Tolerance is not truth unless one fights to make it so."

"To kill is an act of tolerance?" said Erasmus. "Tolerance means the love of all."

Many of the students laughed at the wise turn the professor gave the thought. Witter felt an irresistible impulse to speak. He tried to hold it back.

"The love of all?" he heard himself saying. "Surely not even the Turk or Jew?" Witter felt dizzy as if he had stepped out on a high ledge over a great height. He spoke with a sour disdain, to protect himself, and heard some of the students hiss and moan at the words *Turk* and *Jew*.

"Surely there are limits," a student said.

"First, one must be human," said another.

Some even laughed at this. It was as Witter had feared, and his heart sank with fear and anger. Yet there was hope, still, in what came next. For, Erasmus did not laugh.

"I suggest you also read Maimonides, and Hillel, and broaden your sense of morality," said Erasmus. "Read Abu Hamid al-Ghazali as well, for he greatly influenced the thoughts of our revered Thomas Aquinas."

The students stared in absolute astonishment.

"A Turk?" they jeered.

Said Erasmus, "The wise all counsel love. Our sacred Christ was a Jew and commands us to love unconditionally. All men are brothers. It is simple. Love commands tolerance. And Christ's command to love is the essence of truth. Ignorance is the ally of Satan."

The students traded wary, uncertain looks. Witter felt a thrill, and saw their minds stretched beyond their known limits. And was this not the purpose of learning to think?

"All men are brothers?" said Witter, craving more.

"They were not brothers who attacked us," said Florian.

"Dung-holes all of them," said Lud. He shook his head and paced beside Florian.

Some of the students cheered Lud's words.

"Fists are not arguments," said Erasmus, and his gaze gently scolded the students, Witter saw.

"What if they bring swords next time?" said Florian.

"We too have swords," a student said.

"Swords," said Erasmus, "are a failure of ideas. And worse, a denial of love. I must go. I only came by to ask you to spare yourselves this fighting. The concept of tolerance is made illogical by violent reaction."

Erasmus turned to go, with a sweep of his heavy robe.

Florian gripped the hands of Lud. "You see, old friend, that I must stay and continue to learn how to effect justice in this twisted old world."

Lud now had a disgusted look on his scarred face, and he addressed Erasmus without the slightest air of groveling.

"Erasmus?" said Lud.

Erasmus was leaving, but paused, turning.

"You wrote *Handbook of a Christian Knight*?"

"I did," said Erasmus, answering Lud in perfect German. "You have read it?"

Lud turned and tapped Florian's chest. "Please inform this young man Florian, who so worships you, of the part where you describe the duty of a knight to those under him who are in need."

Said Erasmus, "That duty extends to all people who dwell in the darkness of ignorance. No matter what the dangers to those who bring the light."

"Not the duty to self," said Lud. "I speak of the duty learned even as a child. I speak of the home, the estate, of food and shelter and safety."

Florian looked humiliated before Erasmus, his revered master. "I can speak for myself, Lud."

Then Witter's last hopes for a winter in Oxford came crashing down.

"We bring a letter," said Lud. "From your mother, in her own hand."

"In her own hand? My mother does not write."

"She does now. And when you have read it, you will understand your duty."

Konrad

It was a cold, gray afternoon of very light blowing snow, and the city was all lit for Candlemas, to prepare for Holy Innocents' Day.

It was too cold to ride Seiger, for the icy roads might crack his beautiful hooves. Last month he had caught a groom jerking Seiger by the nostrils and the groom had hung upside down until he passed out and his nostrils ran blood. Since then, Konrad had sent one of his bodyguards to randomly visit Seiger. This morning, in the heated stable, Konrad rubbed down Seiger's sensuous flanks and the horse sought his endearments and the apple slices he fed the horse from his own clenched teeth.

Today, when the horse took the slices, their lips touched. It was always surprising that the velvety nose had bristles. A groom once warned him a horse could bite off a nose. But this only made Konrad trust Seiger more than ever.

If there were anyone who doubts the existence of the Almighty, thought Konrad, *let them behold the loving perfection of this powerful creature…*

Later, kneeling in the great cathedral, deep in prayer, Konrad felt secure, steadfast with God. He breathed in deeply the reassuring pungency of incense.

Covertly, enviously, he watched Lorenz at the altar, celebrating solemn pontifical Mass. With the monks chanting and then the boys singing, Lorenz appeared.

Lorenz was no longer the unremarkable-looking man of ordinary life. He was transformed now and magnified by his astonishing accoutrements—his mitre, the tall headdress with gold ribbon lappets falling down his shoulders like a halo. On his hand that held the pectoral cross, the episcopal ring flashed in a beam of slanting sunlight from the great stained glass window, and his sloping shoulders were draped in the pontifical dalmatic, the white silk tunic, spotless, with long sleeves fringed in gold.

Most amazing, Konrad thought, was Lorenz's crosier, the shepherd's crook staff of office, in gold but crafted to appear as formed from wood, as John the Baptist might have carried. Lorenz wore purple and gilt liturgical gloves, as if his bare palm might taint the sacred staff.

Yet, even now, watching Lorenz with envy in his majestic rituals, Konrad knew he, too, was chosen, a cornerstone.

His frail physique was no accident of birth. He was being tested, he knew. The constriction of breath that came in times of great stress—that, too, was designed to make him strong, to tame his cowardice for great works ahead. His destiny had brought him an ever-greater closeness to God, and with it, God's grace, bringing many revelations that proved a superiority to all those below who needed the proof of beautiful mystery in the church.

"The people require continual support in their faith," Lorenz often said, and Konrad agreed.

But not the same way. The people had too little faith, so little intelligence. They needed to be driven and trained and herded. They needed a hard whip hand lest they stray too far. Konrad was certain of this as surely as the sun rose each day.

Once Konrad had asked Lorenz, "Is that what you once meant, by hawks and owls?"

"Perhaps you will understand me someday," Lorenz had said, with that inscrutable smile that was so infuriating.

There would be the tedious singings and mystery plays and fruit puddings and humble tripe pies and all the candles and Nativity figurines and the great Mass, all a magnificent show for the ignorant, so that they knew how well they were led on the true path. Veritas Press was producing a special series of woodcuts for the illiterate, images showing the birth of Christ; and with a special twist inspired by a dream Konrad had, there would also be woodcuts of evil-looking Turks and Pharisees lurking about the manger. No doubt, it was divine guidance.

When he took his meetings with Basil at Veritas Press. it was thrilling to conjure up stories with the monk publicists all in one room, all of them amazed at the quickness of Konrad's thoughts, all admiring his ideas, his daring concepts for broadsheets. He assigned two guards to follow him at a distance like shadows. At Veritas they stood near the doors and the monks were suitably unnerved and impressed by them. Power influenced everyone, no matter how well they pretended to be immune. God himself was the ultimate power, and all monks threw themselves at those eternal feet.

Meeting Basil at Veritas kept the hideous little monk away from the grand town mansion, where nobles and artistic and other influential friends gathered in a permanent salon of wine and music.

In the fine upstairs office that had been Werner Heck's, Basil weekly reported to Konrad.

"No river barge was taken either from Wurzburg, nor even as far as from Mainz, by papers of safe passage," reported Basil. "But they must return, if they do return, back through Wurzburg. The bishop asks to see this young Florian upon his return."

"I know, I know. Lorenz is eager to know all about Oxford and suchlike. I must see Florian first, that his meeting with the bishop be shaped correctly."

"I understand."

So Konrad fretted about Florian, but saw that waiting was his only recourse. He had prayed on this and the answer had been that either the two from Giebel would not make it all the way to England and back, or if they succeeded, then young Florian would be delivered back here, into his hands, to shape and mold into a fine instrument for God and the good.

More often now, Konrad visited Lorenz at the Marienberg. Sometimes he used the guest chambers in the favored tower with the river view, instead of spending the night in his town mansion, which was so close to the town square that the cathedral bells tolling the hours annoyed him no end, though it would be impious to admit it. And he wished to learn more of Florian.

Visiting the great fortress always gave one a deeply reassuring sense of state permanence. Also, good story ideas were always to be had from the Muhammadan hostage pining away there.

As Konrad had suggested to Lorenz, the supply of wine had been cut off, and Mahmed was no longer drunk and sour during visits, but anxious and restless. One could get him to say almost anything if he was allowed out on the ramparts for a few minutes of daylight. Of course, this was done only with strong guards to prevent him from leaping.

Konrad entered with his bodyguard just behind, and saw Mahmed standing in a heavy robe at his casement. The casement was high and two iron bars were affixed like a cross, in sign of the crucifixion. Mahmed's long hair was like a wild woman's, uncut, as was his shaggy beard. He had lost weight and his dark eyes sagged in his skull.

"You enjoy the view and the bells," said Konrad.

"Have you seen the Hagia Sophia in Istanbul?"

"No," said Konrad. "I would hardly wish to see the cathedral of Constantinople that was perverted into a mosque for unbelievers."

"All men believe something. Perhaps it is all the same thing with different names?"

"Only one is true."

"No need to be impolite, my prince. Your cathedral glitters like a jewel box of stars, so very beautiful. It is from the time of Herod, having all children less than two years old slain, is it not?"

"I believe that is so," said Konrad.

"An unlucky time for children. And yet the celebration of the birth of one child, your Christ Jesus."

It always amazed Konrad how much Mahmed, a disbeliever stubbornly destined for the eternal fires of hell, knew about the one true religion of Christ.

"That is what I want to discuss with you. You shall demonstrate chess, with ten picked opponents of the town. You shall play them all at one time in turn."

"Chess? In public? To what purpose?"

"Are you afraid our people will tear you apart? If that becomes our wish, to put on that kind of show, we shall simply quarter you. Many have demanded it."

"Quarter? Quarter me?"

Konrad enjoyed seeing the blood fall from Mahmed's dark face, leaving it ashen and pale. How hard he had worked in years past to break down that shield of indifference. Now Konrad saw the true coward beneath the proud outward face. God had at last revealed this truth and Konrad gave a little inward prayer of thanks. He heard his guard at the door give a low chuckle, no doubt enjoying the Turk's fear as well.

"Look how you blanch. And I heard you were brave in war. A deadly murderer of Christians. Rest easy, we will have guards for your chess games."

"I eat my bread on another's table."

"Meaning what?" Konrad sensed another evasion.

"I must deserve my bread."

"With God's help, you understand at last."

"But, why chess?"

"I am surprised you must ask why. It is obvious. To demonstrate to all that intellect without faith is folly."

"Of course, that is true."

"Indeed it is. The people will see that, even with your intensity and skill of mind, your heathen soul is lost, and therefore the true path to heaven is not reading and learning. Unless you wish to denounce your Allah and convert? We can make much of that also, if you decide to seek the love of the one true God."

"If, as you say, we cannot have one God with many names, and if God has made us in His image, perhaps we should regard one another as true brothers."

"I do not see your logic."

"God is love, Christ said."

"Blasphemy only denounces a killer like you, Mahmed."

Mahmed leaned closer upon the rampart. "I see…witness the Turk, winning at chess though damned. Behold such a fiend and do not bother to learn to read nor think. Why do you not trust your own people? Must they believe lies and be blind to follow?"

Konrad felt a sting of anger at the presumption of this Turk, to challenge anything, for any reason. God was testing Konrad's resolve, he realized.

"It is not necessary that you see, Mahmed, nor agree, nor even understand, only that you obey. Otherwise, there is no point in your life, is there? I see you staring out there as if you might dare to jump. Will not your soul fall to hell, if you destroy yourself?'

"There are many ways of self-destruction, it seems. You know that has not been supplied."

"After the chess, if you have won all ten games, wine will reward you, but if you only defeat nine, I am afraid you must ask your Allah for wine. And now, back inside, so Basil can make note of your thoughts about the Nativity."

"The Turk's thoughts of the birth of Christ?"

"Exactly."

"Christ is a Muslim, a Jew sent to lead the Jews, and a sacred prophet in Islam, deeply revered for his message of love and forgiveness."

Konrad turned and paced, to control himself. He felt his blood surge and pound in his skull. He wished at this very moment he had Mahmed chained to the floor in the deep chamber of the ecclesiastical court, where Werner Heck had been chained, with all the good pressures allowed to seek truth. Instead, he controlled his voice.

"Our Saviour is not a Muslim. He is the Son of God."

Mahmed's answer came quickly: "Then why do you not obey his command of love?'

"And why do you drink wine? Is it not forbidden?"

"*Si non caste, tamen caute,*" said Mahmed.

Konrad knew that it was a common saying in old Latin, and it annoyed him that he could not place it.

Then Mahmed sneered and Konrad saw him look again, out over the space below the high ramparts, where the wind now whipped across the river and the bridge and where Wurzburg stood beyond, all aglow.

At Mahmed's motion the guards moved closer. Mahmed suddenly turned away from the wall, and went back into the walkway through the stone arches. The guards came closely behind.

A week later—with the tiresome smiling rituals of Christmas over at last, and all the bribery gifts given to the city poor—Konrad was at Veritas, and Basil reported to him in the publishing office, the two of them alone. Konrad repeated the Latin phrase he had not quite caught.

"What did Mahmed say?" Konrad asked Basil. "It was Latin, of course, but his accent is so poor."

"*If you cannot be truthful, be cautious,*" said Basil.

"So he mocks our mercy and taunts us."

Konrad went into the antehall, where a fire was roaring in a great fireplace, and warmed himself. Basil followed.

"Basil, what if we converted him?"

"Your grace, I should not judge his mind, no more than a wild wolf's. But his eyes do burn with hatred."

"Mahmed would hardly make good kindling for a fire, but he would be a wonderful convert. His confession of faith in Christ in Veritas Press would sell far and wide."

Basil clasped his hands together, as if beseeching. "I have tried and tried, your grace. The wine only softened his mind, not his heart. I am convinced that only with torture would the Turk convert."

"Lorenz will never hear of it."

"Our bishop is soft and liberal, I fear."

"Watch your tongue," said Konrad. Of course it was true; but walls had ears, and the most dangerous words were those that he believed himself.

Basil came closer, whispering now. "And yet, all men are called to heaven, your grace. Even some who are so holy, like our splendid

Bishop Lorenz, are sometimes welcomed back sooner than others, for his eternal reward in the bosom of our sweet Lord."

"Speak of that no more, do you hear?" said Konrad.

Basil blinked with a feigned innocence. "Of what, your grace?"

"I know not what. Never mind."

The thought of poisoning Lorenz had crossed his thoughts a dozen times but blackmail was always a fear, and Konrad had enough fear in his life as it was. His creditors in Munchen and Wittenberg were calling on his estates, politely for now, and his stewards had driven them off with a warning, but no doubt they would press and press until embarrassment became necessity. The artisan and craft guilds demanded a seat on the city council of burghers and resisted more taxes. The miners in three mines were demanding better conditions and pay. People were learning to read and becoming haughty and resistant to authority.

God had lain this all upon his shoulders. There must be a great holy purpose to it all. Rome ever increased the taxes that must be paid by the cities and the states, but this payment to the work of the True Church was a sacred duty. His fate seemed tied to that of Christ Himself.

Only the profits of Veritas Press were keeping him in decent fashion. As bishop he would be wealthy and invulnerable and could start a new army for war, anytime he wished, and reap enormous bribes and profits from the arms and grain and livestock dealers. That would drive the silver prices sky-high and the mine shares would reap enormous dividends. But Lorenz was healthy, and Konrad feared the loss of his own immortal soul. Even the thought of murder was as guilty as the act itself, Christ had said, very plainly.

He dismissed Basil, with a guilty disgust and a bit of fear. He relied too much upon the little monk now.

"Leave me," said Konrad. "And make certain the chess match is well publicized. None may report nor print the story except our Veritas Press. Make it exciting. Hold it in the great wing of the Justice Hall."

"We shall guard the Turk, your grace, that his throat is not cut by one of our devoted readers."

With the success of Veritas Press, Basil was becoming bolder. Perhaps when Florian came back, Konrad thought, he would set the youth to assisting Basil, to report on all of Basil's movements. The thought brightened him. An hour later he was back in his town mansion, avoiding the salon of guests, mostly hangers-on today, none of real influence, only leeches he could hardly afford to feed and entertain. And yet it was all necessary for a show of wealth that was ever more necessary to maintain credit—the less real money he possessed, the greater the need to prove the opposite.

In his fine upstairs chambers, he sent for wine and prepared for a bath. During his steam and rub, it all seemed to fit wonderfully together. His asthma never bothered him here. The constrictions never came when he was so relaxed, musing upon means by which to increase his usefulness to God's holy purposes.

Florian would become like a dutiful son, hanging upon his every word, relishing the lessons of life that Konrad would so generously impart. Florian could write beginner articles for Veritas, starting off with simple things like outrages of foreign heresy, English court sex follies, and other certain good sellers. It would be good shaping for the young man, green as he must be, and moldable as newly dug clay. He could give the youth his ermine cape, for it was out of fashion and time for a new longer one.

And, of course, the Geyer estates would be under his protection, and Florian, the heir, would be deeply grateful.

And at last, he would have bested Dietrich. He slept well and deep on that surety, warm in the downy depths of his great bed, cozy with warming bricks underneath, while a snowstorm that same night froze two dozen to death along the river shanties.

It was when he presented himself at the Marienberg Fortress the very next day that his dream was shattered.

"Look, Konrad. Look who has arrived."

Lorenz was breathless. With him was a young man in a filthy traveling cloak, sodden with road dirt and the smell of horse and rain.

Staring in disbelief and wonder, Konrad knew instantly who it was. For the young man had the face of Dietrich.

"Florian," said Lorenz. "This is your godfather, Konrad."

"Prince Konrad," said Florian, boldly, and embraced him with arms strong and unafraid.

"He needs bathing," said Lorenz, ringing a wall bell for the attendants.

"Yes," said Florian, "forgive me, your grace. My good comrades, Lud and Witter, wait in the cold outside, and we have traveled many days in bad weather and now just arrived back in Wurzburg."

Konrad felt amused; Florian was so like Dietrich, his father, to care for low-rankers when in the presence of two princes, one a bishop. And Konrad saw that the bishop loved that very flaw in the young man.

"We must hear all," Konrad said. "All your adventures."

"In time," said Florian. "I stopped to pay my respects on our way to the estate. There is much strangeness in the city."

"First a bath," said Lorenz.

Lud

Lud had achieved his most important goal—to not winter in England, and bring Florian back at once. The sooner they were home the more secure the estate would be with the heir in place. And the sooner he would see Kristina again.

Despite the late season, crossing the strait to return had been easier than the first crossing. One of Florian's student friends was the first son of a sea captain and passage over to the mainland had been fast and safe and free, and on a larger ship than before.

Then the road had gone well. Florian rejected Witter's belief in river barges. No longer was Witter playing master, and Lud his man. Florian led them home. He was young but fully a man, in all ways, and he was sure of himself and also capable, a good combination in men—especially men who were heirs and lords of estates, with so many lives depending upon their good nature and intelligence.

Lud felt true, if hidden, joy. It was almost as if he really had Dietrich back. So many of Florian's traits, even some of his habits of speech, were like his father's.

There was ice in some of the river eddies, and Florian insisted the horses were faster. Florian's horse, though majestic when Dietrich had left Florian at Oxford a decade or more before, was getting old but still could travel faster than Witter wanted to move. And Lud had used his gold florins when the weather brought down ice and wind on them, and a villein's hut or abbey was needed to get through the night.

Lud wanted to be close again with Florian, and they were, in the sense of brothers together, but not close in mind. They would never again be what they were so long ago—Florian the boy eager to learn the ways of fist and blade, and Lud the master of those physical things. Florian had grown far beyond the limits of Lud's knowledge.

What made this distance feel even worse was that Witter engaged Florian in long talks on the road. And soon the two would be off in flights of ideas that made Lud feel a stranger.

Riding behind them, or ahead of them, he heard their talks and debates—spirited arguments in languages Lud did not know and pretended not to hear, of writings and philosophies that Lud had never heard of, much less dreamed existed. When they did speak in German, he recognized arguments about tyranny and evil.

Finally, on a long stretch of open road, he interrupted them. It was the old, desperate question with which he had struggled, both in peace and in war. He had argued it with Witter but perhaps Florian could give a good answer.

"Look here," said Lud, riding up between their horses. "How can God be good if God created evil?"

"That again?" said Witter.

Lud would not let it go. "Our priest has taught me to read. But this harried me long before and I cannot wash it from my doubts. That God toys with us. Created us to play with."

Florian laughed a little, and it hurt Lud.

"Evil is the absence of good," said Witter. "Maimonides said this in his *Guide for the Perplexed.* Of course, he was a Jew, and others have surely said better."

"Yes," said Florian, "I have not read the Jew Maimonides, but I think Aquinas, too, makes good arguments to reconcile God with evil."

Said Witter, "Man creates evil by omission of good, not God. At least the optimists believe so."

They were fencing, not giving good answers.

"But," said Lud, "did not God create all, even the void that came first, even that which is absent, before that which came after? As day cannot exist without night, is not God the sum of all? Why make Satan? Why make hell? Why make fear?"

They both laughed but Lud did not see the humor.

"What on earth have you been reading?" said Florian.

"Some of the Bible. The *Handbook of a Christian Knight.* But long before I could read I struggled with things that made no sense. Reading, I hoped, would quench doubt instead of adding fuel."

Said Florian, "None is better with a dagger than Lud, and we must sharpen his thoughts equally."

"What, then," Lud pressed on, "if this world were not created by God? Since God you argue cannot create evil, yet so much evil exists in this world, who did create this world? Are we amusing someone or something? Are we little more than entertainment?"

Lud saw Witter twist on his horse and stare at him with a long look, a deep look of thought containing surprise. But Florian was shaking his head and obviously trying not to laugh. He reached over and slapped Lud's arm.

"Lud," said Florian, "I love you, and you are master of many things, but philosophy is not one of them."

"Here is the thing. I know I am not wise. But how can I discover my own nature if my mind has nothing but itself to discover itself with?"

"Do you believe in God?"

"I only know what I have been told or have read. The problem of evil vexes me deeply."

Said Florian, "For each man, one by one, there is nothing without God. Such confusion is why the princes and bishops rule so absolutely."

And so, still dissatisfied, Lud shut up.

Witter and Florian returned to their bantering.

Lud was silent, angry; their answers felt shallow. Like thin soup on a hungry day. But Lud could not frame the why of his doubt. So he said no more and let them rave on, back and forth. As if annoyed and wanting to exclude him, like an obnoxious child, they often spoke in Latin when he was near.

It had begun snowing in flurries and the water in ponds and creeks was riming and growing sheet ice.

On horse or eating in camp around big fires—for deadfalls from the big storms were still plentiful here—Lud marveled at how Florian was drawn to Witter's knowledge, and how much knowledge Witter indeed did seem to have. Guarding his feelings, Lud realized that he felt a deepening jealousy of Witter, with every such day that passed. And yet he felt closer to Witter than to Florian, for Witter actually did listen to him.

Best to reveal nothing, when unsure.

Kept thoughts, safe thoughts, Dietrich always said.

And then Lud finally decided to accept his fate, as usual, and his bad luck—that Florian responded more to new thoughts now than to their old comradeship. He felt sorely the gulf between villein and master. Doubly so because Florian tried to pretend they were equals.

So he focused upon his mission: *Get the heir back to the estate, and make things solid again…*

In half the days it had taken to reach England, they found themselves riding into the outskirts of Wurzburg, along the Main River, and in an iron-gray frosty dusk, the shapes of the skyline began to harden in the soft light.

Under Lud, Ox snorted, smelling the city, and tried to urge ahead, to move faster the way horses moved when wanting their stall and their hay. Soon, the cathedral glowed like a floating fairy, a mass of candlelight glittering in its spires. And now the singing could be heard, rising and falling, boys' voices a mile away. That made Lud smile. He felt the scar tissue of his hard face soften a little.

Lud knew it had to be Candlemas.

Then, as they rode closer, the great spiky-towered bulk of the Marienberg Fortress arose from the Wurzburg horizon, like a horned monster awaking from the earth and rising to shake off its winter ice. Lud shuddered and not from cold. They came along into the first of the fortress's great shadows.

"Home of the Wurzburg bishops," said Florian. "For eight hundred years. How would you take it, Lud?"

"Take it? That?"

"You are a soldier. How would you take it?"

"With plenty of salt," said Lud, "then ale."

"I am in earnest. How would you set an assault?"

Lud looked up at the great rectangles of mountainous stone and the cresting towers at the corners that gave crossbow and arquebus angles on both sides.

Thinking aloud from his horse, he said, "Concentric walls, steep approaches. Big guns might breach those walls if you were a rich soldier. If poor, miners might undermine them. Either way, a host of good men would die to exploit the breach."

"Too much trouble," smiled Florian. "I believe I shall use the gate, rather than miners or cannon." And he laughed his little dismissive laugh again, which Lud so disliked.

"What gate? Why?"

"Because I am stopping there."

Florian turned his horse toward the fortress, on to a wide gravel land along the riverbank.

Turning his own horse, Lud said, "Why not straight through Wurzburg and home by night?"

"No, first I must see the bishop," said Florian.

"Why must you?" said Witter, and Lud saw his alarm, and how hard Witter tried to conceal it.

Florian looked up at the towers of the Marienberg.

"It was Lorenz von Bibra who wrote you safe passage, and in my mother's letter she said that he insists that I see him on the way home, and that I not tarry should Prince Konrad see me, nor should I seek him out. The bishop has instructions for me."

Kristina

When Florian returned to Giebel and presented himself to Lady Anna, there was shock all around—how much he looked like his father, Dietrich. Kristina, attending the lady, was as struck by this resemblance as the others, including Lady Anna herself.

Seeing Witter and Lud behind the heir, Kristina had to lower her eyes to control her emotions. She had a wild urge to fling herself at them. But which she would have embraced first, she did not know. She praised God, praying, standing there, and she began to weep silently with joy.

"Mother," Florian said, and swept Lady Anna like a child up into his wide arms.

"I am so disfigured," said Lady Anna. Now Kristina heard the lady sob behind her veil, overwhelmed. She tried to wriggle free from her son's powerful arms but he would not release her.

"You are my beautiful mother."

"Do not lift my veil, I beg of you, no."

"Yes." And he lifted it and looked into her sobbing face and kissed her eyes and then her lips.

Of course Florian was young, but he was made like his father, Dietrich, the same posture and bearing, the same half-smile as if to private thoughts, the same strong face. Most remarkable was the sense of wisdom and strength his presence brought, for it seemed that Dietrich was, in his son, still living.

Kristina raised her eyes and sought out Witter and Lud, standing behind Florian, as together they hung back in the shadows of the entry alcove.

"Must everyone share our joy?" said Lady Anna.

"I invited them," said Florian, when his mother protested. "We are comrades."

"Yes, of course. Yes, you are right. Please, come in and sit, please come, both."

Kristina saw that Lud seemed shy and embarrassed, but Witter was the opposite, glad to sit and behave as an equal.

"I welcome all who have helped my son," said Lady Anna, "and we may as well have our priest, Michael, and feast all together."

The next hour blurred in Kristina's awareness. She caught glimpses of Lud and Witter stealing glances at her. She was here to serve and so she did. But the girlish pleasure she took in their awareness of her made her embarrassed with herself. She knew what Grit would say, yet still she felt such an irresistibly intense joy.

Father Michael came, breathless and excited.

"Florian, I am burning to hear of your adventures," said Father Michael. "Witter says you know Erasmus?"

"One of my masters," said Florian. "So brilliant and yet humble as the dust. His light will help lead man from this infernal darkness of hatred and intolerance, I swear it."

Kristina, serving wine in the goblets, wondered at this. It was almost something Berthold might have said. Florian's eyes glanced up at her and followed her face to her throat and her bosom, and he nodded politely with a smile of thanks. She noted to avoid him whenever possible. Yet she was drawn to his young, brilliant energy.

They feasted with as much bounty as the kitchen could muster up, and a ham and capons were roasted with nuts and berries, and there was plenty of wine. The long room was gold with myriad candlelight from every side. Kristina well knew what a sacrifice Lady Anna was making for the return feast of her son. The stubs of all these candles would need to last through months to come. The wine could have been sold but a new cask had been opened. The hog that had been slaughtered would have been bred next spring.

Florian told of Erasmus and other professors and other students, and of the divided sense of brotherhood that was sweeping the university, setting nobles against commoners, lords against servants.

Father Michael was enrapt, hungry to hear more.

"Christ did command for us to share all," said Father Michael, "to love one another."

Clearly to show which side he was on, Florian stood and took a serving tray from the hands of Lura.

Lady Anna stared through her veil as Florian invited Kristina and Lura to sit and dine.

"Join us. Do sit, if you please, ladies."

"Someone must serve," said Lady Anna. "They shall eat later as is our custom. They shall not want."

"Why later?" Florian insisted. "Let us all be as one."

"Florian, behave, you embarrass my maids."

"Please," said Lura, "I do not wish to sit."

"Do join us, I beg of you," said Florian.

"Do, sit," said Lady Anna, finally. "Humor him."

So, with traded looks of uncertainty, Kristina and Lura sat; and Florian got up and served two plates and placed the plates before Kristina and Lura. Then he sat back at his own plate, his eyes sparkling with his own private delight.

"We humor my son," said Lady Anna, "only for tonight, out of our overflowing joy upon his return. And because he reminds us so well of his great departed father."

Kristina and Lura picked at their food and watched the others, like two dolls at a child's table.

"Did you receive my letters these past years?" inquired Lady Anna of her son.

"I did, Mother," said Florian.

"Yet you stayed there, so far away, knowing your father dead and our situation here quite uncertain? With things so bad that I was compelled to send for you?"

"My father commanded me to receive my education. He made this plain in his letters and to you, Mother."

"Thank God you are safely here."

"Your letter that was carried to me personally by Lud left me no option. Especially the way Lud put it to me. I did not know there was such need. Such uncertainty. No, I could not refuse. Even though my studies in law are yet incomplete."

"Now you are master here."

"In title, mother. But I will attend Bishop Lorenz."

"You? Lorenz? How?"

"He has invited me to join his bishopric as his personal attendant in law and administration and travels."

"What does that mean? Personal attendant?"

"He wishes me to assist him in travels, and as confidant, hopefully."

"Travels where?"

"We shall soon see. I return to Wurzburg in three days."

"But you only just arrived home. Three days?"

"The bishop wishes to begin travel at once. I believe he wishes to shape me up, form me, and train me. Konrad will be livid, for that is his duty. But I know not to trust him, thanks to your letter."

"Then you realize our situation."

"More than you do, I fear. The world is changing fast, my dearest sheltered mother. I mean to be at the forefront of what is coming. That is the best way to protect the estate. And I must earn my place in the new world to come."

"What world is coming?" said Father Michael.

Florian nodded at Witter. "You tell him."

Witter said, "Freedom. Every man his own lord. That is what they were fighting over at Oxford. And you read it more and more in the little broadsheets from all over. People are learning to read for themselves."

Kristina saw Lud staring at his plate, obviously not wishing to be dragged into any of this.

Said Florian, "Every man able to read. Every man his own priest. All have rights, Mother. They just do not know it yet. Like these two ladies here. Can they read? No. Can you read, Mother? No. Why has the priest not taught you? Because he wants to control the mind of all."

"You are rude to our guest the priest," said Lady Anna. "And I can read. Yes, I can. And so can these maids of mine, both can read."

Florian stopped eating in mid-chew. "Really?"

"Yes," said Lady Anna. "Kristina here has taught me to read, and write as well."

"The priest did not write your letters for you?"

Said Lady Anna, "I wrote them with Kristina's guidance. But I wrote them in my own hand."

Now Florian looked at Kristina. Kristina felt the intensity of his awareness, his eyes searching hers with genuine interest. Yet there was more than that, and she blinked and did not know where to look.

"Kristina, that is your name? How is this, that you can read, yet you serve?"

She glanced at Witter and Lud and they were both looking straight at her. Her eyes escaped to Florian.

"There is honor in serving, sir. All serve. Even the bishop serves God, and he must serve the people."

"Well said. But please do not 'sir' me."

"She indeed shall 'sir' you," said Lady Anna, "as is proper. Serving does not reduce her."

"Ceremony dampens honesty," said Florian. "Kristina, tell me how did you learn to read?'

"My mother and father taught me when I was but small. And others have taught me more since."

"Where are your parents? I would enjoy learned friends. I have much enjoyed Witter here, in our many talks on the road, for he is extremely intelligent and well read, though apparently he serves under Lud, even. Has your family all moved here?"

"No. They are…dead."

"Dead? I am so sorry. Of plague?"

"Her parents were burned," said Lady Anna. "Long ago. For reading the Scriptures, and other books."

Kristina felt nauseated. She wanted to get up and hurry from the table. She sat stiffly, enduringly.

Florian, rather than change the ugly subject, pursued it.

"Dear God. Burned? Of this I would know more."

"Sir, please," said Lura, "let her be."

"It is the truth that makes us free," said Florian.

Said Lady Anna, "But not at the table. Now let us not speak of dreadful things, for this is the return of my son, and the heir."

"Let the truth come out," said Florian. "Let us share her injustice and know what she has suffered."

There was a silence. Kristina saw Florian watching her, waiting for her to reveal the horrors she could not, and it was unnerving. She begged God to make this stop.

But it was Lud, not God, who stood and spoke to Florian now.

"Florian, let it be. We are all tired. You have made your points well enough for now."

"Lud, I am no longer the boy you taught to fight and hunt. I am the heir. Mind your tongue."

"So," said Lud, "now suddenly we are not equals as you so made claims, just a while ago here? What has changed? Do we not all possess equal say in what goes? Or only when it suits your pride?"

Kristina saw Witter and Father Michael both visibly shrink back. The long candlelit room was as tense as a flash before thunder. Lud had never been challenged in anyone's memory here. And Lud never said anything he was not ready to back up instantly.

Witter stepped away from Lud.

Florian's face, staring at Lud, turned red, and it seemed he would scream in rage; instead, suddenly he threw his head back and bellowed laughter, exactly the way Kristina remembered Dietrich doing.

Florian went to Lud's chair, and Lud was already up, in a stance poised for anything.

"By God, you have bested me to perfection, Lud. What a prize you are, and just what I need from time to time. Father was wise to make you steward. When I heard it I was stunned. But you are the best, as ever."

Florian threw his arms around Lud and they hugged like grapplers, each crushing down harder, until they broke apart with twin explosions of breath.

Then Florian turned to Lady Anna.

"Mother, dear, am I your inconstant prodigal?"

"Do not tease. Not now. You are my son. All depends upon you now. All."

"I am going to serve a great bishop, and will make my way up in that world, and send money home, and letters."

"Send books," said Lady Anna.

"This man Witter comes with me," Florian said. "I have asked and he has agreed. I need a man of learning and languages at my side who understands certain things."

Kristina looked at Witter, surprised. Witter looked back at her and she felt him searching her face. She did not know what to express, and looked away.

"Your night is not over, Florian," said Lud. "Giebel has its own surprise also, for your return."

Lud

"How long since you danced here?" he asked Florian.

"Nothing on my account, please," Florian protested.

"You are the excuse, not the fun," said Lud.

Florian laughed his hearty laugh.

"Witter? Father Michael?"

"All who wish to come," said Lud. "Any not too good to dance with the girls and tillers and smiths. This is feasting villein-style, with all the wild revelry of good honest abandon. Unless you fear to let yourself go."

"My God, real village girls," said Florian. "How I have missed them. Let me at them."

"You go ahead," said Witter.

"You are coming," sad Lud. He grabbed Witter's arm and pulled him along, knowing Witter might take the chance to go see Kristina first.

"For me, back to my church," said Father Michael.

The villagers had heard of Florian's return and another feast was done the same night. But this one was very different, far from the attempted formalities and order of Lady Anna's welcome feast.

It was held in the barn of Sig's mill, the floor swept out for dancing, and lit by lanterns hung on the high beams. No heat was needed, for that would come from the barrels of ale and the music and the bodies of all the dancers. The violin was sawed by Sig himself and the hurdy-gurdy cranked by Ambrosius and the ale brought by everyone, and a long table at one side was heavy with meats and breads and even sweets.

And Lud was glad. It had been far too long since Giebel had let itself go wild. The smells of bodies and food and ale and the roar of music and laughter was water to a man dying of thirst. Lud drank it in greedily.

The cries of wild, lascivious dancing and booming music thundered from the barn. They entered and Lud saw sunburned girls flinging their skirts high, the white flash of thigh making him ache, first in his chest, then lower, until it was stiff to walk. The boys were skillful and proud, lifting and twirling their girls in the old high-step way that had always been wilder and more daring than the dances of city folk. There was plenty of ale in the big kegs and all brought their cups.

Now and then a boy would pull his girl from the crowd and they would disappear somewhere back through the stacked bales of hay at the rear stalls. Old men danced with their laughing withered ladies and little boys danced with girls not yet old enough for men, yet showing the first bloom of their coming ripeness.

Like all good barn dances before this one, the air rang vibrant and wild with joy. The people melted into one. Grudges were forgiven and men got drunk and danced and laughed. Yet, there was a kind of panic to it all, Lud felt, as if all felt some great change were coming, and each must take all the joy possible from this fling and all its precious moments. The fiddle wailed and hurdy-gurdy sawed, creating the sense of frenzied animals chasing faster and faster.

Lud took it all in and felt heady and hot even before his first clay jug of ale, which he downed in one long chugging rush, his face wrap unwound, his head thrown back. When he looked again he saw Florian dancing.

In her long, colorful, ornately woven heavy skirt and winter blouse, Greta, the pretty daughter of Arl, sister of the dead twins Hermo and Fridel, had caught Florian and now they opened the center of the packed earthen floor. Greta's beauty glowed tonight, and dancing with Florian set her ablaze. And Florian was feasting suddenly on the whole carnate frenzy of his people. He was the heir and he was joining with them as one of them and they all roared in time with the violin and hurdy-gurdy. The wild steps of Florian and Greta became wilder and more daring, their bodies brushing together and pressing and colliding.

The chanters stomped their feet and cheered in time. Lud realized he had forgotten to rewrap his scarred face after the first jug, and thought, *what the hell, I am what I am. Let them take me as I am.* He downed another jug of ale in one draft, as if trying to quench the inchoate flame that blazed in his groin as he watched Greta flinging her beauty at Florian headlong.

Then he saw Kristina.

There she was, far back at the barn door, peering in like a little child stealing a look as the parents held a gaiety. In a half dozen steps Lud skirted that side of the crowd, moving along the barn wall, and before Kristina could run away he had her by the hand, pulling her into the dance.

"No, please, I do not dance."

"No?" He whirled her round and she came flying under his arms and into his chest the way the other boys were twirling their girls. They whirled past Witter, and Lud saw Witter's face all dismayed and Witter turning and backing away through the crowd.

Kristina cried out in startled delight like a child. Lud whirled her more strongly and felt her girlish shape against him. She recoiled back, her eyes wide with shock, and he whirled her round and round and kicked his own heels high. She began giggling and he was laughing with her. The music caught up with them and people began clapping as he whirled and whirled her, and they staggered together dizzily and leaned together, the two of them against a rough barn wall, both panting heavily. He was close and he felt such joy, and that made her afraid.

"I...must...go..." she gasped.

"You liked it," he said. "Admit you liked it."

Then Kristina fled from him, as if the barn were burning.

He thought about going after her. He knew he had much to drink and this warned him not to catch her, for he might do more than he meant to do. And then something else happened that changed it all.

He heard noise that was not happy. Somewhere out on the floor, someone was shouting, louder than the music and chantings. Lud turned and looked over the heads of the crowd and he saw someone limping and jerking about on the dance floor. Lud pushed his way through the people.

Kaspar...

Trying to dance the way he once did. But now with one leg and a crutch for the missing leg. There was a collective moan as they all saw who it was and what he was doing.

"Greta! Greta! You were mine! I was always the best dancer! You promised to wed! You lied! You whore!"

Kaspar swung the crutch and fell. The crutch would have slammed into Greta's legs, but Florian put out a quick leg to deflect it from the startled girl.

Sig's violin screeched to a halt and Sig hurried clumsily through the crowd, pushing toward his son.

Florian released Greta and he and others tried to help Kaspar upright, but Kaspar shoved them away, yelling. He was drunk, that was plain. He had been crying, his face red and swollen. Kaspar was mad with rage.

Sig reached Kaspar, and Kaspar spit full in his father's face. Sig was on his knees sobbing, face in hands. Kaspar saw this and laughed bitterly.

Through the crowd, Lud moved toward Kaspar. He felt angry and disgusted and sad altogether. Kaspar began snarling, saying forbidden things now, things that could never be taken back.

"You girls think twice about the boys kicking high and you lifting your skirts! They laid with girls in the whore wagon on our march! Yes they did! Look now at their faces and see the truth! Girls forced, girls taken from farms, girls like you, for coin to fill the rich bastards who made that war! And the priests, too, they blessed it!"

"Shut your filthy mouth," said Linhoff.

"All that was years ago," said Max.

The mob around them became very hushed now. This news was shameful and caustic. Throats had been cut for much less. Kaspar kept yelling, encouraged by the sudden shock on all the faces.

"Your denials tell the truth, you know it."

"Those girls were just Muhammadan sluts," said Max.

"Shut your filthy hole, Max!" shouted Linhoff.

Lud wanted to do something, but everything he thought of would only make things worse. The people were all staring at the boys, one then another, as if they had just sold all their souls to Satan.

Kaspar laughed crazily. "Yes, by God, they gave their levy coin to the monks for prisoner Muslim girls, they laid with unbelievers!"

"Not true!" shouted Max.

"They were Bohemian girls, Slovakian girls!" shouted Ambrosius.

"How do you know?" yelled Kaspar, triumphant. "And did you not pay? Were they not tied down?"

"Please, son, do not do this," said Sig, horrified.

"Truth is wanted here, Father. Is not truth what you taught me? And them that ran are here, too! Yes, by God, they ran! You with the hurdy-gurdy, you Ambrosius, tell how you did run! Get that grin off, fool! You did run! And the heretics were in our wagon and sewed my leg up, so I lost it! Yes, they spoke evil words and spells, they did!"

A silence filled the old grain barn louder than the music and shouting before, and Lud could hear himself breathing. Kaspar got up and fell down again.

Lud knelt beside Kaspar and gripped his arm firmly, feeling the pulse racing in the hairy flesh.

"Kaspar, this is not what you want."

"Tell them, Lud, tell Florian they ran. Tell Greta that I stood and was a man. Tell her how I lost my good dancing leg."

"I am your friend and I ask you to be quiet now."

Lud moved to lift Kaspar, to carry him somewhere he could set him down to sleep it off, and that was when Lud felt the scrape of a blade like a hot iron raking his ribs.

There was a collective gasp as Lud leapt back, holding his side where the tunic was sliced, blood between his fingers—but not much. Just that quickly Florian had Kaspar from behind, in a head-lock. A little dagger dropped from Kaspar's hand. Kaspar's eyes bulged and he struggled for breath.

"No!" begged Greta. "Let him go, please!"

Florian released Kaspar, and then Sig and Merkel and their friends, a dozen men, all helped; as if bearing a dead man, they took up Kaspar, and he wriggled and sobbed as they bore him grimly away.

And that was the end of Florian's welcome feast.

Now Florian lifted his arms, and all regarded him.

"Dear friends, I am weary from the road, yet full of delight and love. Tomorrow I go to Wurzburg to attend Bishop Lorenz von Bibra in his duties of state. I thank you for this generous welcome home for me, and I am deeply grateful for your support of our steward, Lud, and your loyalty to my mother and to the estate which belongs not only to the Geyers, but to us all, to each man and woman and child who lives and crafts and shares and toils on this land."

Lud saw the shock in the villagers' faces as Florian's words sank in. Lud himself was astonished at the thoughts, unlike anything ever spoken in his memory, even beyond those of Dietrich.

"Dear friends, I congratulate those of you who strive to learn to read. To those belongs the future. We long for the day when all men are brothers. Until that day comes, may God bless you all."

These words silenced everyone. They all stared at Florian. Lud realized that Florian had just encouraged literacy, whereas his mother had condemned it. Florian was heir, and lord now, and he had just urged all to learn to read. He had even regarded them as equals in his way of speech.

Then Florian bowed farewell, and in the stunned silence, Lud saw the disappointment was most bitter in the girls' faces as they watched Florian take his leave.

The next morning, in a heavy cold fog, Lud came out, feeling weak, sick where the blade had cut his side. He saw Kristina come out to speak closely with Witter, and Grit and Symon and Dolf as well. He could see that Witter was loved, or at least respected.

Kristina touched Witter's face in a way that Lud would have killed to have known. He looked away.

But Kristina came next to him. She said, "They say you were cut last night."

"Why did you run from the dance?"

"I felt…dizzy." She was clearly embarrassed, and blinked, her face turning red. "Where were you cut?"

She fingered his side, through the heavy cloth, and when she found the wound where he had bound himself with winding cloth, it stung like fire and he winced. She was so close that he could smell her breath's sweetness and he wanted to bury his face in her long hair and kiss the velvet base of her throat. It was fool's madness, thinking of her this way, when there was less chance of having her than getting ice in hell.

"There," she said.

"It hardly broke the skin of my ribs."

"Please, may I see?"

"It is nothing."

He shoved her hands away. The thought of her fingers on his bare skin was too much to deal with now, with a ride ahead that was important business.

"I meant no harm," she said. And he was glad she confused his lust for simple bother.

But he thought of her all the way up the road.

For the next hours, Lud rode halfway to Wurzburg with Florian and Witter. Then they said good-bye at the edge of the forest, where the towers of the Fortress Marienberg and the cathedrals of the city could be seen over the roll of land.

"You have done well as steward, old friend," said Florian. "I will serve and send money home and make my way in that world, until I can return with security for the life that all deserve. A new world is coming."

"How can there be order in that new world, if all have a voice? Whose voice will be heard?"

"You must have faith in the mind of man, Lud."

"Good-bye," said Witter to Lud. "I will bring books for you when I return. You have been a good friend."

"Is Kristina yours?" said Lud.

"What?" Witter stared.

"You heard me. Does she want you?"

"You have asked me this before, Lud."

"That was then, this is now."

"She wants love," said Witter. "But not mine. I think she wants more than any man can give."

Lud reached and took Witter's hand. Then let Witter go, and rode close to Florian and embraced him so hard the young man was pulled half from his saddle.

"Cut first, ask later," Lud said. "Watch all, trust none."

Florian smiled. "Just what you told me when I left with my father all those years ago. I never forgot."

"All more true than ever. If ever you need Lud, I am your man, always. As I was with Dietrich, so am I with his son."

"Read," said Florian, and gripped his wrist. "My old friend, read and find that truth that so eludes you."

Then Florian released him. Lud watched the two ride away into the fog, with a last wave from Witter. When he finally lost sight of their melting shadows in the gray mist, he turned his horse back toward Giebel.

With each torsion of the horse's stride, he felt the slight twist of his body on the saddle, and his side ached and he could feel his pulse in the cut. He had wrapped his chest with rag under his tunic, and that was that. There was even a satisfaction in the throbbing, for the pain meant he had tried to help Kaspar, for whom he felt responsible. To remark on the cut openly was to add to Kaspar's troubles, and for Sig, Kaspar's father, he felt pity.

But he knew that there would be deeper troubles now, after the vicious insults Kaspar had said about the other boys. Who whored and who ran. The gossips would already be buzzing, and if the truth were not bad enough, lies would pile upon lies, and there did hatred fester and grow. The fact that the words were true made the damage far worse.

Bad luck would always be his closest comrade. But there was strength in expecting nothing more.

And as he rode home in the clearing fog, Florian's words troubled Lud, and echoed like a prophecy…

We long for the day when all men are brothers…

Where had he first heard these words? Not only in Oxford. Not only from Erasmus, Dietrich, nor Florian…

Then he smiled and it was a brilliant and bitter smile—he saw a great ironic circle of thought attempting to join itself and become complete as a snake bites its tail—for he now remembered that those words had come to him first from Kristina, long ago, and not from some great leader, not even from Dietrich. He had overhead Kristina in the wagon speaking quietly with the Turk hostage. A young woman prisoner of war longing for all men— even her enemies, even her captors, men who might violate her, murder her—for all to be one with her as brothers…

Witter

For the first time, Witter felt he was on a mission beyond that of simple physical survival. It was frightening and yet exhilarating.

A dawn fog had broken up and the sun was bleak like tarnished silver, breaking through the stark naked trees.

Witter rode just behind Florian and admired the younger man's easy style of riding: graceful and effortless, hardly touching the reins, guiding with his thighs and keeping watch on the passing woods. There seemed a sense of purpose to every gesture, no matter how small.

Riding a horse was almost a pleasure now for Witter. His ass cheek had healed of its saddle sore, and his legs had toughened, and the horse rolled powerfully and easily under him. The animal and its harness were symbols of wealth, and he enjoyed the respect a horse gave a traveler on the road.

The towers of Wurzburg appeared first in the risen sun, and then the river bridge and the city itself.

It was as if he had been dealt a hand of cards at a gaming table, a once-in-a-lifetime winning hand, here with Florian, with the Giebel identity; not a Jew to be loathed, but a gentile of learning and languages valued and trusted, able to move in the shadow of a young noble who had been sent for by the bishop. It was heady stuff. He had fear but the intoxication of Oxford and the sense of comradeship with Florian were like wine after a deathly drought of emptiness. And it seemed somehow that he had a purpose now, something unknown, a destiny yet unrevealed.

If he could be of influence, any influence whatsoever, his mission would be worth his fear of what it might cost. That was how

Kristina lived and it was a good feeling. It was as if some old gaping wound inside him was at last beginning to knit closed and to heal. If he could do this well, perhaps he would return to Kristina as a man she could admire and even love. Of his letter she had said nothing. He hoped that meant something good, not bad.

His desire for Kristina was as foolish and as strong as ever, and perhaps he could return to her in a way that she would value. He knew himself well enough to know that, because he felt her too good for him, he believed she could not possibly want him, and he loved her for that alone. Such was his inverted self-esteem. But he knew if she would leave with him he would take her anywhere.

What were they doing, trying to save the world? The world did not want to be saved. The world wanted to fling itself into the abyss of lust and greed. Was not that all too abundantly obvious? Even Father Michael saw it.

When he learned of Kristina and Grit trying to cut letters by hand from blocks of wood, he smiled with pity and in wonder at their stubbornness to be heard by the world. He admired them for trying.

Florian's words broke his thought.

"We must be patient with our beliefs, in Wurzburg, and say nothing of this among the clerks and monks and soldiers of Lorenz and Konrad and the magistrate. Wipe the front of your mind clear of the rights of all men, and realize that we shall be in the bosom of tyranny, for it is there we must learn and grow, and find our way to the greater goals."

"I am relieved that you realize this," said Witter.

"For you, best you are my man attending me in languages, but otherwise unread, no more than a servant. When alone, we are as brothers and equal in our discussions of what we observe and think."

"Understood, my lord." He gave a twist of sarcasm, and Florian did not miss it, yet was not offended.

"Save your barbs, Witter, my new friend, for care of how we seem to others. It disgraces me that a fellow man calls me his lord. You are the most learned man I have met outside Oxford. I need your honesty and your counsel. And for that you have my gratitude, no matter how vain or shallow I may seem among the others."

They were not out of the deeps of the great winter-naked woods, when two men on horse rode out and blocked their way. Witter looked to turn his horse back, in quick fear, and saw that three more men on foot blocked their way behind. Two carried crossbows.

"Be calm," said Florian. "Stay here and do not speak, let me approach them."

The two on horse rode slowly up to them, and now Witter saw they wore tunics and mail. Neither wore a helmet, and one had long blonde hair and the other's hair was close-cropped. They were hard men but not sneering—more weary and hungry, as if drained of all emotion.

Florian rode without haste, directly, halfway up to meet them. Then he stopped his horse and calmly waited, showing no distress or fear. The ambushers moved their horses to Florian and circled him once, and Florian did nothing. Then they talked. Witter saw them all begin to relax and lean on their saddles, and then they traded twists of smoked venison and chewed while they talked.

Witter felt the mass of the horse, its weight shifting, its breath a steam cloud, and he sat feeling perfectly naked and saw with relief that the armed men behind on foot did not yet approach. Finally, Florian returned. The men on horse waved to those on foot and all went back into the tree shadows and soon disappeared.

"The two on horse are knights," said Florian.

"Knights? Like your father?"

"Poorer, even. There are many levels of knights. Some like monks, living from war to war, holding no land or too little on which to live. Those knew my father. That is why we pass unmolested. One remembered me as a child. The other once served with Lud also."

"Why did they stop us?"

"Why, to rob us." Florian laughed.

"Rob us? But you said they are knights."

Florian's face darkened. "These are strange days, Witter. Men do what they must to feed their families. Someday I will help them.

I know not how, but I swear things must change. Men of honor are too rare."

"Thieves are honorable?"

"Men who are good for nothing but war can either become magistrates or thieves," said Florian. "Which has the greater honor? And who made them good for nothing but war?"

Witter did not truly know the answer, and realized it was better to say nothing. Sometimes Florian seemed more like an old man than a bearded youth. At other times his judgments seemed rash and frighteningly optimistic.

Witter, as he had a thousand times in his life before, considered an escape. He could simply ride away. He had papers, but little coin. And winter was coming on hard. So he did nothing. He followed, and endured his own fear.

He thought of the ancient Jubilee in Israel, when every fifty years all slaves were freed, and everyone started over. And yet, every time he felt the urge to flee, to start over, wherever he went or did not go, he always ended up the same way. Following, fearing, regretting. And now was no different.

He clenched his teeth under his closed lips as they rode along the high riverbank. On the lower bank across the river, the city spires pierced the smoke of winter fires. They came up the paved way that approached the great iron gates. Presenting themselves at the great Fortress Marienberg, entering the enormous shadows of its towers, filled Witter with overwhelming anxiety. And yet, Florian seemed utterly confident, as if they were walking in an open field. Witter stayed as close as possible to the young man.

When Witter, in his anxiety, wanted to speak, Florian pressed a finger to silence his lips. His horse released a great clot of dung, plopping noisily to the stone pavers, as if sensing Witter's near-panic.

The guards sent for a monk and Florian spoke to him briefly, and that was that. Guards bowed and took their horses, and Witter saw that Florian was well respected.

"I speak," said Florian, "not you. Inside these walls we are no longer equals."

"Now I shall call you lord?" said Witter. "Will it not disgrace you, as you so recently said?"

"I need your eyes and ears now, not your mouth. Play your part and I shall play mine. Listen and remember all."

Witter almost panicked and ran but forced himself to act indifferently as they entered the great alcove. The gate closed behind them and the guards with helmet and pike stood watch. And then it was too late to do anything but go through with what he had thought an adventure, and now felt was a trial of courage and self-control.

Monks brought them silently, with hand gestures only, up three flights of stone stairs deep into a tower and then into a waiting room with no windows and a gilt-trimmed double oak door hinged in brass. They sat on a bench that was as polished as glass.

And now they were inside the bishop's study chamber.

Witter sat back in the shadows, trying to be as invisible as possible. The stone of the chamber sent the monks' voices clearly to his ears, and he perceived their dim faces in the light that slanted from the casement beside them.

When the bishop entered, behind a monk that might have also been a guard, Florian and Witter quickly stood.

Lorenz von Bibra was hardly a mighty figure to command fear and awe. He wore a night robe embroidered with the cross and a nightcap of woven wool. His face was small and red and he sucked his teeth. When the bishop moved, he was bent forward. He came to Florian and took the young man's large hands in his own bony ones, sucked his front teeth, and smiled.

"My prince," said Florian, kneeling, "my bishop."

The bishop pulled Florian back to his feet.

"Face me, my son. Your father Dietrich was a great knight, highly honored for his valor and his intelligence. He was a dear friend of mine. It grieves me that he is gone from us. His candor was always a touchstone of honesty."

"I am confused, your grace."

"How so, my son?"

"You say you value candor, so I will speak truly."

"Please do no other."

"My prince, my bishop, you honor my dead father, yet neither you nor Prince Konrad attended his funeral."

"You speak too harshly. There was pox everywhere."

"My father served you well as a loyal knight of the Wurzburg Bishopric. And he served prince Konrad well as a loyal knight to fight to defend our southern German lands."

"We prefer Holy Roman Empire, not Germany," said the bishop. He was frowning now.

Witter was shocked by Florian's plain manner, even to the bishop. It was neither smooth nor politic nor wise, and Witter shuddered inside, waiting for the bishop to react.

"Your father would have warned you that candor without respect has severe limits, Florian."

Florian bent forward, humbly, and apologized.

"I present myself at your service, and to the empire. Forgive me, your grace, it is my habit to speak plainly from being at university, where I studied law."

"But you speak honestly. I value that. You do not flatter. I am smothered by flatterers and falsehoods."

Lorenz relaxed again, and smiled, and again sucked his front teeth with the tip of his tongue, and it gave a boyish candor to his lofty role as bishop.

Witter felt relief, and a burning need to urinate. It was mad that he was here. Yet he was fixed by some urge to know, some great curiosity utterly compelling, absorbing him as he witnessed with fascination this discussion between the great bishop and a young lord.

His fascination soon vanished and turned again to fear, when the bishop decided to acknowledge him.

Said Lorenz, "Your man back there, what is his name?"

"Witter. A learned man, guide and linguist."

"He is admitted only by my fondness for you. But look, you, there. I instruct you to listen well, as will my monk. Do you realize that to relate our words could mean your death?"

Witter choked and could make no words from his constricted throat.

Florian spoke for him, and said, "He does."

"Very well. Men should understand consequences."

Witter nodded and that seemed enough. He forced himself to breathe and he strained not to pee himself. He had wanted to be at the heart of things and now he was trapped inside them. But Florian was insanely at ease.

The bishop moved closer to the hearth fire, warming himself, and gestured for Florian to join him there. Witter stayed right where he was.

"Freedom of thought," said Florian to the bishop, "was encouraged by my masters."

Said Lorenz, "Law and freedom of thought, those are strange bedfellows indeed. Erasmus himself was one of your masters, I hear? Is it true?"

"Yes, your grace, and other great minds; so many."

Witter realized that a monk sat deep in the shadows behind Lorenz, busily scribing, as if every word said were gold to be distilled from the tinkling air. Florian wanted him to remember every word spoken, and Witter was very good at that. It was his curse, in fact, to be able to forget nothing.

Said Lorenz to Florian, "We have much unrest. We tax, yes, and we are taxed. Rome expects us to pay an ever-increasing tax to the Holy Church. That is first of all, before anything else. That money must constantly be found, despite all our problems of city guilds, the estates, many impoverished knights, the miners, and always our borders and trade routes, dear God, ever plagued by bandits and skirmishes with the Ottomans."

Florian spoke with enormous respect. "Yes, but you are both bishop and prince. You protect the affairs of Church and Prince Konrad the affairs of state. Which is a greater duty? I ask it humbly."

"We both defend the Church." Lorenz shook his head with a slow gravity. "You know that the league protects all of the southern lands of the Holy Roman Empire. Prince Konrad and I, as princes of Swabia and members of the league, we assert ourselves against outside threats. Konrad has the army and the magistrates. He no doubt shall become bishop after me."

"May God grant you many more good years."

"They will not be easy ones. We have seen the failure of village levies in war, so mercenaries must be used from now on, as Prince Konrad wisely advises. He is right. Leave war to professionals. But they are costly and taxes must be raised. No, not easy years, I fear. If I were to join Wurzburg to the Swabian League, I would be bound by the will of the league to make wars. Yet we would also be under the protection of the league."

"You have much weight to carry, your grace. The people may not share your enthusiasm for raising armies, and paying their cost. Especially now that many are reading."

"I do not punish reading, only reading of Bibles, for the common man needs guidance relating the meaning in the Scriptures, lest he lose his immortal soul from wrong conclusions."

"And Prince Konrad?"

"Konrad does his best with his press to convince the people, and we hold fairs and festivals and parades. Fine young nobles like yourself will someday lead, and then you will understand our troubles much better."

"I am here to serve. Command me, your grace."

"As I have said, I fear from their unrest that the threat from our own people seems to be growing. You will have much work to do as my assistant. You will help be my eyes and ears."

"Perhaps our people should solve their own unrest."

"And by what alchemy could that be achieved?"

"If each had say in the outcome, perhaps."

Lorenz regarded Florian for such a long time that Witter felt anxious. Then Lorenz said, "What is the greatest source of social disorder, in your estimation, Florian?"

"Do you wish me to speak plainly, your grace?"

"It insults me to waste my time with answers that mirror my own questions. If you are any value to me, it is in intelligent candor. If you cannot speak plainly, your mind is useless. I shall repeat the question. In your estimation, where lies the greatest source of disorder among the people?"

"Inequality, your grace."

"Inequality? Of what? Morality? Faith?"

"Over the centuries, the accumulation of commoner debt has given all land and wealth to the lords. Yet the lords must pay tax to the Church and emperor. The question of wealth is not only a moral one, but also a question of disorder. Without equality there can never be lasting stability."

Witter was stunned. This kind of declaration was the very thing that Florian had warned against, and Florian himself was saying it. Whether by impulse or design, it was impossible to tell. But there was no mistaking the conviction in Florian's voice. Witter bit his lip, waiting for the bishop's response.

Said Lorenz, with keen interest, sucking his teeth, "There is always inequality of God-given gifts, is there not? Does not God give power in that way, by birth?"

"God gives a mind to each and that is a sacred trust, to help open all minds to God's truths."

"And your solution?" said Lorenz.

"That all learn to read. That all learn to write. That all learn to share their thoughts. That all become one shared mind, one agreement of brothers. You esteem my father. In his letters to me he expressed this wish many times."

Lorenz leaned back and smiled and sucked his teeth.

"Never speak such things in the company of Prince Konrad, I advise you, my son."

"What is his power?"

"In effect, Konrad assists me, preparing for his role one day as bishop. He and his monks enforce ecclesiastical law under my rule, and I am focused more upon the secular law. Yes, the two often collide, but they join in the rule of power over the people. My power."

"Then you as bishop rule Konrad as well."

"It is complex, but yes. We are both princes of the Swabian league also. With his press, his influence has grown. Many lords agree with Konrad's views that literacy breeds discontent and discontent must ever be crushed. Konrad and I do not agree with your brotherly visions."

"If I have overextended myself..."

"I told you to speak honestly. You are young and the young are exuberant and they see the future better, for the future belongs to them, not to the old who are leaving this world. As you serve me, keep those thoughts between us, and do not challenge Konrad, ever."

"I am here to serve, your grace."

"As am I. As are we all. And we begin at once. We have many long days ahead."

Witter was to spend the next months in a whirlwind of formalities and courtesies that he had not imagined possible in his adult life. He was issued a bishopric pass to go freely in and out of the Marienberg. It was a large bronze coin with the bishopric cross on one side and the arched fortress gate on the obverse. With the pass coin, and the safe travel identity he now possessed, Witter felt safer than he had in a decade.

The power of tyranny, at your disposal...

And though he mocked himself for it, he enjoyed its comforts. And the freedom to go as he pleased was delicious and exciting. The fortress stables kept his horse groomed and ready, wearing a fine new saddle. Twice on the first day out in the city he had encountered magistrates and produced the bishopric pass coin, just to watch their dim eyes widen with awe.

"Pass on, sir, with all respects. Take care among the gutter trash of the city. If ever you need us, we are ever ready to bash a head or two."

Now on his horse he explored places he had never dared in the years with Werner Heck. In stone byways shadowed by great towers, the city was rotten with an underbelly of cruelty and suffering. He saw the hanging grounds and the beginning of a quartering and several duels, mostly between drunks, and the row of steaming taverns and bawdy houses where painted girls sang on a small stage outside, to lure in men who had money to choose one for upstairs.

The narrow streets were adrift with the jetsam of human failure, and people begged and sold whatever they had, including themselves, and children ran in packs like little wild dogs, stealing and fighting and sometimes rolling drunk in the filthy gutters. Above all this went the wagons of tradesmen, and above them the gilt carriages and fine horses of the wealthy and the powerful. He had seen it before but never from a place of surety, from a fine horse, in fine clothes, with a Marienberg pass coin in his waistcoat.

At the fortress and at bishopric gatherings, Florian was busy meeting and greeting and learning. Witter followed in Florian's shadow, rarely speaking, and never to anyone but Florian, when asked. His eyes and ears were wide open and he took it all in like a dog on a hunt with his master. He watched how well Florian navigated these dangerous and rarified waters, and learned to match his own motions and steps to Florian's. No one recognized the lowly printer he had been; he was a lord's man now, an invisible low-ranker. Nobody of rank actually looked at him.

The strangest time in his recent life was now. He could not avoid attending Mass with Florian—the first Mass since he had renounced his faith so long ago.

He feared it would all come tumbling back, almost too strange to bear, and it did.

Kneeling and crossing himself, Witter relived that nightmarish day, many years past, when he had avoided being burned alive. He had renounced his faith to become a *converso* by attending Mass in the Córdoba cathedral. He had kissed the stones before the altar, prostrating himself before the crowds and before the wretched figure of Christ dying miserably nailed to wooden beams.

Judah wept, rent his garment...Witter could hear his father's sorrow, could feel his anguish...

Now, Witter knelt to save his life. He listened to the Latin and saw the icons and stained glass and watched Bishop Lorenz in his robes. The icon of the Blessed Virgin resembled Kristina somehow, and especially the sweetly shaped lips. That was the only time he felt anything good. The rest was the living nightmare.

His faith was ashes in his mouth. First, pretending to be of the state-church that had immolated all whom he loved. Fleeing across Europe in search of sanctuary. Never finding it. And now this. Pretending to be an Anabaptist had only made it worse.

Since that day, he had begun to think again of escape. He thought of the Ottoman lands. He needed to know if the rumors were actually true—that the great Ottoman seer and ruler Suleiman welcomed Jews, saying that the European kings were fools for chasing away and murdering their most prosperous and hard-working citizens, to the greater profit and growth of the Ottoman Empire.

Rumors were rumors, nothing more. But he wanted to see the Turk. He found it impossible. No one could get anywhere close to that tower. It was for political prisoners and renegade clerics, and the Marienberg guards kept it sealed. Witter watched for any chance to meet this Ottoman prisoner outside his tower, but it did not come. He framed imaginary conversations with the Turk, by which he might learn of safe passage to Istanbul, but each scenario gave him away, and with horror he realized that such questions led to the conclusion that he might be a Jew.

Their quarters were a chamber in the far tower, above the servant quarters, and Florian had a large room and Witter a very small adjoining one, meant to be a guest study for Florian. Food and wine and firewood were abundant, attended to by bishopric servants in green livery. A tailor was in permanent residence and Florian sent Witter for a full set of waistcoat, tunic, and greatcoat, with new tights of the woven kind, all in the deep ochre of the Geyer estate.

And it was incredibly odd, to be fitted for expensive items of apparel (which identified him as a service member of the elite), while at the same time memorizing the passageways through the fortress for means of escape, should he be found out. Then there were the ramparts from which one could jump, if necessary.

Witter kept his face blank. If they could see into his mind, past his eyes, all would be lost. Let them think him a dull man, one without resources.

Suicide was always a last out. Last because, if he killed himself he'd be sent straight to hell, his father had warned him. But it was hell here or hell there, and hell here was certain. And maybe hell hereafter was a tale for simpletons to obey the church-state, and to frighten children. Maybe God was not that vicious after all. And if the Creator were so vindictive, so needy of human adoration, would you want to spend eternity with him? And how could a man ever hope for heaven, anyway, as cowardly as he was? If his noble father and sweet mother and sister, who were burned for their faith, were in heaven, how did a craven such as himself possibly deserve to join with them there? And then there was the possibility that eternity was a myth we played upon ourselves to alloy our fear of death and nothingness.

So he played his role and kept his watch.

Prince Konrad invited Florian to visit his Veritas Press, and lavished gifts upon him, of a jeweled dagger and sash, and a velvet cape threaded in silver. Witter saw how this embarrassed Florian, and for Witter, the visit to Werner Heck's building, now Veritas Press, was deeply depressing and frightening. It all added to his dizziness, the sense he was farther from himself than ever before.

He thought of the good times there with Werner and how Kristina and her brothers and sisters had arrived and joined the work, and now that seemed like wonderful golden days of another life entirely. Now the press churned out cartoons of devils and warriors, heroes and villains, broadsheets that demonized Jews and Turks and celebrated war and the Church as if God blessed bigotry and mass murder; it was propaganda for the masses who could only half-read or not read at all.

Each night when they retired, Florian wanted to review the discoveries of the day, and often Witter was compelled to recall them word by word, as was his role. Some nights they reviewed broadsheets gathered from the market square.

More and more there were reformist ideas from other cities. And Witter heard much discontent among the city men, about taxes and unfair levies. Reading stalls were increasing weekly.

Access to the broadsheets and pamphlets from all over Europe were now within his daily grasp.

And there was a growing excitement over this best-selling reformer priest, a professor of theology at Wittenberg, named Martin Luther. Erasmus and Luther were competing for who would be the best-selling author in Europe.

Witter perused Luther's ideas in the stalls, put forth as sermons to Christians. Luther's thoughts mostly railed against the Church's peddling indulgences to buy one's way out of sin.

It was even rumored that Bishop Lorenz would soon forbid the sale of indulgences. Lorenz was building for himself quite a reputation as a forward thinker. Lorenz was also criticized for being soft on the Jews, Witter heard, but people were soft on Jews for one reason only, to extract revenues. And when revenues did not come fast enough, they burned Jews and took all they had into the treasury.

Then, he found Luther's opinion on Jews:

Jews are blood-relations of our Lord; if it were proper to boast of flesh and blood, Jews are more close to Christ than we. I beg, therefore, my dear Papist, if you become tired of abusing me as a heretic, that you begin to revile me as a Jew...

Witter felt a brief and foolish rush of hope. But then, Luther went on to say that he expected all Jews to convert to Christianity, and Witter thought of how he had converted, by threat of fire, and he saw no difference here, except that Luther had not the power to send people to the stake. At least so far Luther was only a professor writing highly popular broadsheets. He had made his name tacking some arguments to a cathedral door, and calling the pope "Anti-Christ" for selling indulgences. A genius for publicity. Lucky for Luther, too, that the Church so overreacted, damning and excommunicating him, bringing wide fame and helping sell anything he scribbled.

Florian looked forward to each day's catch of the latest broadsheets, and they spent much of Florian's stipend from the bishopric on such materials.

He had once thought that the reading craze would peak and pass, but the hunger for new ideas was like a fever running through the people. And it excited Florian even more than it did Witter.

"Here is our hope, Witter. Here is our future. These sparks of awareness will someday flame into a bonfire that will burn this world clean of all evils."

"What sort of bonfire?" he asked, warily, with dread. "Will the fuel be ideas, or will it be people?"

"We cannot yet know its shape, but the mind of the people is taking birth. The more they learn to read, the more they yearn to know, and the more they know, the more will they demand to be changed."

Witter had heard such words before, from the denouncements of the Inquisition, yet he knew Florian meant them for good. But he also knew that fire meant pain, and Florian's desire to change the world was a dangerous conceit, and a fearful light that shadowed him. So he sought to soften Florian's nature.

"There are two kinds of change," said Witter. "That of violence and that of peace. Christ proposed love as basis for change. Your father desired that, I am sure."

"Lud told me you are pacifists, you and those who came with you. He told me also of your courage, to help wounded in war."

"I was not yet with them then. Kristina and the others helped your wounded, not I. I met them in Wurzburg."

Florian smiled. "Yes, because you are all printers. You worked for the condemned Werner Heck. I know also of the old press they brought from Wurzburg and are trying to repair."

So Lud knew it all. Witter should have known.

Witter had also been told of the press in the old barn, confided by Grit. His help was needed. Grit had begged him to try to obtain metal type, if he could, without alarm. But the fact that Florian knew this too was a bad shock.

"If they print and give out broadsheets, the Wurzburg magistrate could be led straight to us," he told Florian.

Said Florian, "Do not fear nor be surprised. I know all of that, and if they print their truth let them. I welcome reading in my estate. You know that I do. But do not mistake my equanimity for weakness. When the time comes, when all men are ready to live as brothers, if a great price must be paid, I will fight, and kill if I must, but only when history ripens and the people are ready."

Witter took these words with horror as one takes a poisonous medicine. Life here was stranger and stranger. Florian, he knew, held radical beliefs of change, and yet Florian played the game so well. The game of advancing himself, of earning the bishop's admiration, of playing the role of young man rising for a place perhaps even at court.

"The emperor is coming," said Florian one day, breathlessly. And Witter wondered: *Are you excited to kill him or to flatter him?*

In early spring when the roads thawed but were not yet mud, the aging emperor Maximilian von Hapsburg came in a long carriage train of courtiers and mounted guard for a full week's visit with the bishop. All Wurzburg came out to cheer, for free ale flowed and criminals were pardoned.

"All the ruling princes of the league attend," Florian told him. "Bishop Lorenz has not joined the league, despite Konrad's wish that Wurzburg would do so. So they are the only two princes not members of the league. There are nine princes of Swabia and there are dukes attending the emperor, and many Hapsburgs as well. I will be mingling behind Lorenz and you shall attend and shadow me and absorb all. Swabia is all of southern Germany, and you may overhear useful things for me."

"I am confused, Florian. What can you wish to gain?"

"We shall see."

That night, at the ball, following the great High Mass in Wurzburg cathedral, Prince Georg Truchsess von Waldburg presented his mother and his radiant younger unmarried sister, Barbara, and Witter saw how covertly but keenly Florian watched Barbara. Despite his general wariness, Witter was as enchanted by these glittering people almost as much as he hated them.

Before the feast was served, he and other servants of low-rankers were cordoned off to a waiting alcove to one side. There was a great deal of pomp and a few speeches, then drinking and toasts and cheers and laughing and eating and then the music began.

In the gold light of the vast hall with a feast at one end and the dance at the other, with musicians and chandelier candles numerous as stars in the milky way, Witter caught glimpses of Florian dancing with the elegant young Barbara, and she was willowy next to his strong frame. Many watched them dance, and he heard Konrad comment to Lorenz that they bloomed like two flowers together.

"Witter, I am so lucky," Florian said that next dawn. "I had not seen her in many years, my betrothed, Barbara. And she has now grown into such a beauty."

"She is indeed lovely," Witter said, but something heavier freighted his mind. "When the princes were cloistered together, no attendants were permitted."

"Good reason, too."

"Can you share it?"

Florian mused. "They debate the best way to raise revenues, but the great thorn in their sides is the flood of broadsheets demanding reform for the commoners. And a subversive pacifism is becoming covertly popular among certain regions, among these secret cults of Christian reformists. New bounties must be offered to root out these heretics—else how can villeins be formed in ranks and ordered to march and kill, if not for Christ and country?"

"I see."

"Do you? Konrad brags of his monks writing broadsheets damning all heretics and pacifists; creating wilder and wilder stories to inflame the ignorant public mind. The emperor seems pleased. Konrad trots his Turk out—a hostage my father took. I have heard of this Turk, Mahmed, but Lorenz has not let me meet him. Konrad has him exhibited, plumed like a devil in peacock feathers, and entertains the emperor with a rapid chess game, this Mahmed against Wurzburg champions."

"At those times is he available?" said Witter. "To confer with the public, I mean?"

"Perhaps, when he is in a chess game," Florian shrugged. "I suppose, with his opponent. But many in the public would love to put a knife in him. Or much worse. There are plenty of guards."

Witter's mind raced at the possibility of playing a game of chess with the Turk. Yet that would expose him to many eyes, focused and watching such an event. It would be a terrible risk. Perhaps worth it. Yet what if the Turk called out against him, and repeated his questions? Such a risk was too mad.

"Why are you so interested in this Turk?" asked Florian.

"The young woman who tended his wounds for your father lives on your estate, that is all. I thought it fascinating. What happens following the chess match?"

"Nothing. The Turk is sent away, back to his tower at the Marienberg, and to the princes the emperor reveals his true purpose for his visit—a new army must be raised, with even more taxes. The assembly of city councilmen and the miners union will be furious. The estates will surely suffer. The emperor is going to send his army to Spain to fight the French, and revenue must be found."

"Another new war?" Witter almost laughed in disbelief. These people chased madness upon madness.

"More like a war that never ends. But it will drain poor desperate Swabia again, and worse, they will need to raise mercenary forces to control the cities and countryside."

"What will you do?" asked Witter. "Is there some advantage you seek?"

"For now, smile and seem merely eager to please. Lorenz looks troubled, at least. What can I do? I am only a young man in love."

So life was just that twisted upon itself, like a riddle.

He realized that Florian was being drawn into the courtly life. Like many young men, Witter thought, his strong ardor for new ways would be diminished by stronger urges—by the love of a woman, by necessity, by one compromise after another; and for many, he knew, marriage was the greatest compromise, and when children came, and promotions were desired, radicalism passed and men became their fathers.

It was in the early summer that Witter was on an errand to buy new broadsheets, and he stole an hour and made his way through Wurzburg to the walls of the Jewish Quarter.

He no longer felt the thread of who he was. His father Judah had not come to him unbidden in dreams or words in many months. Perhaps it was because his father condemned his son's desire for Kristina, a woman who was not a Jew.

The old weeping room in the alley, opposite the Jewish Quarter and synagogue, had been his place of honesty—the hidden place where there was only truth, and nothing false surrounding it.

He wanted to sit inside there and view the street through the peephole, and to feel, if he could, the man he had been before he had met Kristina and the others, before he had gone with Lud to Oxford and come here now with Florian to the bishopric. He wanted to be as he was before he had become excited about life again, before he had found love with Kristina. Even if she did not love him, he wanted her, and that was the pulse of life again rising in him like sap greening a tree.

But when he came to the rough old building he saw that it had been torn down. Seeing the building gone was like another piece of himself, degraded and abandoned and condemned. He slid down from the horse and took it all in.

Chanting came from the synagogue behind those gates across the alleyway.

Witter saw a young rabbi with an elder rabbi, both in the synagogue doorways, now turning, now staring at him. They wore yellow cloth stars sewn to their dark robes. He felt naked in their sight.

And yet he realized that in his good tailored dress they would take him for a man of influence, and they would fear him. He wanted to go kneel and beg their forgiveness. He knew their forgiveness had no bottom. He despised himself and knew he deserved nothing. Then they bowed gracefully to him questioningly, as if expecting him to speak.

And Witter mounted the horse clumsily, nearly falling off, and fled like a thief from their eyes.

His mind raced. He needed to report something to Florian when he returned to the fortress. The mood of the city. Were the city guilds meeting? Was some radical priest agitating? Who were the prime movers of disquiet in the city? What were the latest broadsheets saying?

The day was dying with a darkening chill; in windows, candles and lanterns were already being lit. It was time to get back. Best to at least buy some broadsheets to take back to Florian.

So Witter rode his horse steadily through the random backstreets of stalls and street food vendors and into the street parallel to the main square. His horse turned a last corner toward the square, and that was when he saw her.

He reined in and the horse stopped dead still in his tracks, and he was staring.

They came strolling toward him. Two men, both fops, had each side of her, both of her slender arms in theirs, and their hips pressed hers as they walked, and he could see her girlish body shaping the red velvet material.

Witter knew the men would take offense yet he could not break the spell of his staring. A white ermine cape framed her long, white throat, and her pretty face was heavily painted and her blonde curls arranged high on her head in the current fashion, her little breasts plumped up so impossibly tight that her nipples emerged like buds. A smile was on her little, round face, but it did not touch her eyes, which looked stunned and anguished.

"Is it you?" said Witter. He moved the horse into their way. Looking down at them, at her.

She stopped. Her rouged lips fell open, seeing him. The fops both stopped awkwardly, holding her arms, impatiently glaring at him. He saw they both wore gilt daggers, but pompously, for show. Her eyes, now obviously recognizing Witter, widened with something like horror. She tried to back away and pull her arms free, but the fops held on as if she were property just purchased.

"Frieda?" said Witter.

Lud

His side ached from Kaspar's blade, and he kept his chest bound tight with rags, as one binds a broken rib. It would have to do. Even in winter, a steward had tasks to oversee, or do himself, if others did not do them. People did what they must so that all things continued, flowed, moved ever forward together.

Long ago, after his first battle at the age of fourteen—when he had gone with the false pride of unseasoned youth, and had feared and killed and wept and then killed more—he had been ashamed of his anguish at all he had done, and Dietrich had consoled him:

All things flow into one...for all it is the same...

It had taken years for him to puzzle out the meaning. Like so many of Dietrich's teachings, it had become a way of believing, and a source of strength in hard times.

In a world like this one—where people killed or were killed, killed to eat, killed to obey, killed to protect, killed to take, killed from rage and killed from fear, and always someone was trying to kill another person first—a cut from a knife was just one flicker of pain. Each person was one thing in a river of struggle. Life was all one thing. And pain was a great part of that flow. And for all it was the same.

Like this little slice-cut in his chest—it was nothing. His chest wore as many scars now as the old black iron armor given him years ago by Dietrich, which now hung on a cross inside his hut. But he knew the wound was infected.

Firewood was needed constantly for church and for the infirm. Plenty had been cut and split, but hauling it was hard labor. Food for the hungry—that they needed the most. He needed Father Michael's help with the tally of stores, for the granary level in the stone silo was falling fast, and he knew there were thieves in the village when hunger came calling. He dreaded catching someone, and did not post a guard on watch as he knew he should have.

Even Huber would have done that, he knew.

When he neglected to post a granary watch, the elder men organized one. Sig and Merkel and the others. They did it without asking and without comment. And yet Lud could see their disdain for him in their faces.

"The granary watch is good," he said to Merkel.

"You are strong in many ways," was all that Merkel said, and it was a kind of forgiveness. "But beware of the softness of Kristina and the others, that it not weaken you in ways that harm us all."

The priest kept a small fire going in the sacristy, and every time Lud came there, with a cartload of split wood, Father Michael was reading by the fire, poring over a new stack of books, and praying. He had changed, and Lud wondered where it would all end. This priest did nothing halfway.

"Do not heat the church," said Father Michael. "It is too great a space. We will not have Mass till the cold breaks."

"What are all these new books?"

"Everything I ever meant to read before I no longer have the chance. Everything that might hold a clue to the meaning."

"The meaning of what?"

"The meaning. I cannot say what if I do not know what it is. What others have taught me has not served me well."

"That, I do understand."

"Do you?"

"I want to begin our lessons again."

Father Michael closed the book in his lap and looked at Lud for a long time, as if seeing through him.

"Look at me. I am no fit teacher," the priest said.

"I am no fit pupil. You teach me well enough."

"I cannot teach myself well. Reading does not illuminate the closed mind. Books do not break through the walls of a blind mind. I am struggling, Lud. Learning from me now is like a drowning man clinging to the point of a sword. It makes no sense."

"You make no sense. I wish to read, that is all."

"You read well enough. Go read. You have all of Dietrich's library. And broadsheets are everywhere now."

"But there are questions, and I must have answers. I need to know what the larger words mean."

"What questions most vex you?"

"If I killed, before knowing that Christ forbids killing, am I yet hellbound? And if I decide that I will not believe in hell, is my eternity to be nothing, emptiness?"

"You do not mention heaven."

"Heaven? If King David was beloved of God, and he slew so many, and lusted after Bathsheba, and sent her husband Uriah, a loyal captain, into the hottest forefront of battle to die, there is hope for anyone, even me. But I doubt heaven. It may be a story for children."

"Lud, I have spent my life buried inside the minds of other men, absorbed in their writings. And yet there is so little that needs knowing, in the end. Christ commanded us to love. All the other words are used by men to justify their hate. I cannot get past that anymore."

"Love and hate are how we are made."

"And we are forced therefore, to choose. For me, words seem so empty, unless they inspire actions. I am only now coming to this. And much because of you."

"Because of me?"

"You see, and you act. You do not think so long that you can weaken your resolve with words. You act."

"And damn me for all of that. I act? Even were I not so disfigured, Kristina would never have me, I know, for fighting is what I do best, what I know best. Is that what you admire?"

"So, this is about Kristina, is it?"

"She is part of it. I cannot draw down my own will. I am not lovable to her. She knows I have killed so many."

"Then do you wish to confess?'

"No. I wish to understand why God made me as I am."

"Lud, if you seek answers, I am the wrong place to search. I know less than nothing in certainty."

"Bishops and princes and the Church, they send armies to kill, and yet if you read, Christ says killing is wrong."

"Christ made that very plain."

"I want to continue our lessons, I said. Reading only confuses and angers me more deeply than ever before."

"I will give you one more lesson then."

Now the priest looked directly into Lud's eyes. Lud felt as if he were looking down into a well, at night, the glint of the sad, dark eyes like the reflection of stars floating on the icy, black well water. The priest's gaze lingered, then loitered, until Lud made a move to step backward, disconcerted.

Father Michael's hands stopped him by reaching up and taking Lud's face and cradling it, as tenderly as if cherishing a treasured object.

And the priest kissed him lightly yet fully on his lips.

Lud jerked back defensively, involuntarily, as if from a cut. His arms were up, shoving hard, and the priest fell backward away from him, the thin white hands flailing.

"God," said Lud. "Goddamn..."

Father Michael curled in a ball on the stones and wept into his sleeves, trying to hide his face. Lud stood there. Then he knelt and tried to turn Father Michael's face up to look at him.

"I love you as a brother," said Father Michael. "Can you not accept me so?"

Father Michael turned up his bony face and looked at Lud with sad, dark lingering eyes. His face was red and pained and his eyes were pouring, streaming, blinking.

"Why do you not take a woman?" Lud said.

"And you? Why do you not take a woman?" said the priest, accusingly, almost pleadingly then.

"Because I am hideous."

"No, Lud," the priest said. "Your face is a beautiful mask, beautiful with all the scars of suffering."

"You imagine that suffering is somehow beautiful?"

"Look at Christ, behold Him, dying for love of all."

Lud looked up at the wooden Jesus with the staring pearl eyes. He had never seen the thing up so closely before. Flowing tangles of hair and the deep-cut lines in the sharp face were made by the many swirling grooves of fine chiseling. The artist, some country artist, knew suffering all right.

This torment was strong and real—unbearable agony twisting the soul like a rope wound to breaking—not like the false soft grace of the girlish Christ in the great Wurzburg Cathedral. Only the pearl eyes seemed false, following him whichever way he moved, like a cheap trick of some festival magician. The rest was pure agony.

Lud shook his head. A knot had formed in his belly.

Why did this maker of miracles not use His power to free himself? To sear the souls of His tormentors? To fry their minds with holy fire? Why did He permit God His father to use him so cruelly, for the cheap sins of the trash of this world? Or was it all just a lie, to scare children and make men obey their lords?

"Fool," Lud said, and he could not have told anyone at this moment whether he was calling the Christ a fool, or the priest a fool, or himself.

"Brother," said Father Michael, still on the floor.

Lud turned away; left him like that.

If he stayed, he might have begun kicking him, and if he did, he knew he would kick him to death. He would kick the man until the unwelcome stirring low and deep in his belly was gone.

Quickly now, Lud turned from the staring weird eyes of the dying wooden Jesus, and he shook his head in wonder that the world, and his own being, still held surprises.

Lud came back two hours later, having walked the night alone with a growing pity for the priest, and with something else far less understood. As he was shaking off the cold, he did not see the priest at once.

Lud smelled wine. Jesus still stared.

The sacristy fire was burning so brightly that sparks and flames were leaping and spilling onto the hearth. Then he saw why. The hearth was full of burning books.

"Michael?"

He heard a groaning spitting sound and he turned and saw the priest wriggling at the end of a rope. An overturned stool was under his feet. His hands were above his head hanging onto the rope, pulling hard, his face was purple and his tongue out, and the rope was around his neck.

Whipping his dagger out, Lud cut him down.

The priest fell on Lud and they both lay in a heap, the priest gasping, clawing at the rope around his throat. Lud helped free it. The knot was amateurish.

Lud felt fire in his side. The priest's fall had ripped apart the binding and opened the cut. He swayed, dizzy and nauseated, and had to lean against a post, fighting to clear his vision.

He saw Father Michael, on his hands and knees, retching and gagging. "Why…why did you stop me?"

The waves of pain subsided and Lud felt a swarming pity that was now becoming disgust and then anger. The priest, his face twisted in pain, looked up at Lud, beseeching.

"Damned priest. You are a fine ass. Why did you wait for me to come back to begin hanging yourself? I know why. You wanted me to stop you."

"No. No. It is finished."

"It is finished? You think using Christ's words on the cross makes this righteous?"

The priest rolled onto his back and lay there.

Lud pushed away from the post. The burning books made the room sweating hot. The sour smell of spilled wine made Lud gag. He looked at the fire and saw there were no books left to save. Sooty flecks of pages floated and danced in the orange, smoky firelight of the sacristy.

"I have no purpose," said the priest.

"Then make one."

"I am repellent and have no worth."

"Then find some, damn you. The people are sick at heart, they are hungry, they are scared."

"Leave me be," said the priest. He sat up and put his arms around his knees. "I am not worthy of the bread I eat. Let others have it."

Lud knelt with him and looked into his face. The priest had been crying so much his eyes were swollen almost shut, and the pressure of the rope had broken surface veins like those in the leaf of a tree, except they were red, turning purple.

"Listen, priest, at least give the people hope. Hope is your work, is that not so? Words of hope are what you peddle? Food for hungry souls?"

"As soon as you go I shall stand on the stool again."

"You spoiled, weak, selfish bastard."

Lud stood up and gripped the priest by the hair over his ear and jerked him upright. Father Michael squealed and began to cry like a little boy. He twisted and kicked and rubbed his rope-burned throat.

"You are lucky the rope did not break your neck nor burst the big veins there. As it is you look like a raspberry."

"Leave me alone. Ignorant man."

He shook the priest by the shoulders, hard.

"But then of course your knot was a silly one and you gripped the rope and held yourself up, and you were lucky I was on time for my lesson, as you expected I would be. If anyone had stopped me on the way here you would still be dangling, for your arms are too weak to hold out long."

"You think I staged it all?"

"I know you did. Half of you wanted it but the other half did not. Is this taking action? Is this what you meant?"

"Leave me be, please."

Lud slapped him, openhanded, so as not to break bones in his face. The priest's head recoiled and he stopped his snuffling and stared back with wide-open eyes.

"Now, priest, you listen to me and listen well. You discovered that killing yourself is not what you want. Find a way to use what you know. You say God is love? Go work to prove it. You want to make the world right? Go make it so, by any means you must. You want to take action? No one is stopping you. If you do not try you have already failed."

"How can I do any of that, if I do not care? How can I do anything, if I do not even love myself?"

"I do not know how. I have never been able to even like myself. Loving others has to be enough. But listen, you do know what is in all those books you burned. Go find a way to prove what you are. Find a way to do what you want others to do. Sell your life dear, if you must die. Let the actions be inflicted upon your enemies, whoever they may be, not on yourself."

"I have always envied and admired your physical courage. Me, I do not have the courage even to die." Father Michael hid his face in his hands and crouched, sobbing. "I do not want to die. But I do not know how to live."

Lud had to look away. An impulse to kick the priest came and went. He tried one more thing.

"Would you not go straight to hell, if you were now dead by your own hand?"

"I am in hell already," said the priest.

"Listen to me. This is not real suffering that you value so. Go out and find some real honest suffering, if you must."

Lud had no more words in him. He went to the wine jug and slapped it off the low table and it broke and gushed bloodlike across the stones.

And he left the priest like that.

It galled him that such a learned man could ever admire him for anything at all. And it discouraged him, too, that a man of such education could be so weak, that books had not made him stronger. Nor had books unwound his confusion.

Staggering out into the cold night, he felt blood, hot and wet, making an itchy trickle down his side. With each stride, Lud felt a sharp pain from the wound, and the blood was seeping through his under-tunic. He knew it was wide open.

Damn, damn damn damn...

There were candles in frosted windows. The great wraithlike shadow of the naked linden tree held the ground in the middle of the square. Its myriad branches shook and their icicles sang in the whistling wind. Passing under the black arms branching out like hands, Lud looked up where he had climbed as a boy.

Looking back at the gray shape of the church, he wondered if the priest had already hanged himself again. One could not change another man's destiny any more than he could change his own bad luck.

Lud ground his teeth and gripped the wound in his side; he bent low in the night wind, and was drunk with pain now, staggering back to his hut, alone.

He fell to his knees and sank away.

When he woke, the sun was still not up. He was numb, almost frozen, and his legs did not work. He looked up and saw the mothering linden tree beseeching him. Or was it mocking him? He knew every branch, had climbed them all as a boy. Then he knew it did not care. He sensed its quiet gravity rooted deep into one place, and its indifference to things that crawled upon the land.

Dimly he realized he was exposed to the cold, dry wind on hard ground, in the village square, the village sleeping all around him, and if he slept again he would lay here and die, and that was not acceptable.

So then by sheer force of will, he reached forward with his arms, digging his numb fingers like claws into the frozen ground, and dragging himself little by little the endless distance toward his hut.

Kristina

Another winter was letting up. The mottled skies were staying clearer and clearer, and there was more gold in the purple of the rising and setting of the sun. Sometimes the warm air blew in from the south now, as it always did in early March.

Lud's wound, the cut on his ribs by Kaspar, had made him feverish for three days. Kristina had visited his hut and cleaned the wound with vinegar, and tended him twice a day for a fortnight. The priest had found Lud unconscious and had run to her for help.

He lay in his bed of straw, but he sat up each time when she knocked and entered. Quietly and dignified, he covered himself with his faded old sleeping robe. He turned his face away when she opened the robe and she waved her cupped palm up to her face and sniffed the wound odor. In the second week the sour smell was gone and the healing smell was strong. He took the sting of the vinegar better and better as the wound sealed itself.

She found herself thinking too much about him. And she missed Witter as well—his sharp wit, his intelligence, his knowledge. And his fondness for her.

Tending Lud, Kristina said little and he said little, yet their eyes often seemed to speak somehow. She had to remind herself that he had killed and was willing to kill again. She realized how much she had come, by degrees over these years, to admire him. Lud asked so little for himself of anyone, as if he expected nothing from life but to serve others. In some very real and practical ways he did serve more than she or her brothers and sisters did. And Lud was strong in spirit. She resisted admiring him more than she already did.

But his mercy for Kaspar was irresistible and added to all the other things that drew her to him.

Sig came often and begged Lud to be well and to forgive Kaspar, and Lud only asked that Sig read to him from his books. Arl came with a new wool blanket, and Lura with good hot food, and others came, and Kristina realized how these people had grown to care for Lud.

If they had feared him before, it was different now—his mercy to Kaspar, his tolerance for others, his fairness to all, and his amazing lack of personal greed as steward—all these things had endeared Lud to the villagers of Giebel.

In the second week, Kristina was alone with Lud in his hut, and he was better, watching her while she bathed the wound and redressed it with freshly boiled linen.

He stopped her hand, taking it by the wrist.

"Is it Witter or is it me?" he said.

She stared at him.

"I know Witter is handsome," he said.

"Witter? Yes, I suppose. But what is that to you?"

"Is it not my face that horrifies you?"

"I do not understand," she said, but she did understand. The harshness of his tone shocked her. She looked at his face, his scarred face shadowed by the oil lamp glow. His lips were trembling. She saw hurt in his eyes. Not the hurt of his wound, but something deeper. Something accusing her.

"Your feet hardly touch the earth," he said, "for you are avoiding this world. What makes you so afraid?"

"I do not understand," she said. "Please let me go."

His eyes sought hers and she blinked, frightened. He would not release her wrist. He looked at her hard.

"You do not eat meat, you give away any possession given you, you share food. You give and give. Is it because there is an empty place inside you? And you try to fill it with love of many, instead of love of one?"

"I love Christ."

"Your constant excuse for everything. As any ordinary nun would say back. Yet you are not a nun, and like all nuns, you are a woman, and human, with human feelings."

She was indeed afraid, and yet something else in her stirred, and it was not fear. "Please, release my hand, you are hurting me."

"I know what you are doing, Kristina."

"Doing? I am helping you, that is all."

"I know about the press. The old stone barn. I know what you are going to try to do. Is Witter preparing a place for you all in Wurzburg?"

"Witter serves Florian, not us."

"Everything Witter does, he does for you. You mean to write and print your beliefs and to put them out in the Wurzburg market, I know that. You care nothing for your sweet life."

"My life is a gift from God and I cherish it."

"And your child?" he said.

"That is between me and God." She resented that he would dare use Peter against her to attack her faith.

But he kept on, and said, "What if Florian learned of all this and told Konrad?"

She had thought on this and had a ready answer.

"Has Florian Geyer not urged us to learn and think and read and to speak our minds truly now?"

"What if others told? You think secrets can be kept here by anyone? You risk yourselves bravely, but you risk all others here. Is that good? Is that holy? Is that wise?"

"Will you stop us?" she said.

"Do you want me to?"

"No," she lied.

Part of her wished that he would stop them. If he stopped them, the danger would pass and she would have tried her best. But she sensed her own lie. Her own betrayal of her trust. And she felt ashamed.

"When I led troops on a march, I made them stop and take water. They obeyed, for they thirsted. The only need in these lands is food in the bellies of all, and heat in their huts. For that any would fight."

"To fight is to murder. We want no fight."

"I am only steward. But I will stop any who brings danger here, if it comes. Or I will die trying to stop them. And many others will die. Is that what you want?"

"You know we wish no harm to others, ever. We want souls to be free, to know, to choose their own truth."

"You want souls? You seek this truth everyone speaks of so much? You mean your own truth. To believe as you do. Pray to your god. Ask what is right."

"My god is God. Yours and mine, and He hears all."

"Not all. Any time I tried He never listened nor answered back. He did not listen when he took my wife and little ones. When He left me to live cursed with this face no woman could ever love."

Kristina shook her head. "You live, and you have much good in you. And it is not your face I fear."

Lud pulled her wrist and jerked her closer, inches from his hard face, and she saw the red veins in the white of his eyes, so close, and the soft warm center of his black pupils.

"What then do you fear?" he said.

"What you are. What you are willing to do."

"And what of you? Everybody here likes you, yet you are willing to put them at risk. Ask this God of yours what is right, I say, and be sure you do not share death and pain with others, in your need to do this foolish thing with the printing press."

"Better to risk death in this life, where death comes to all anyway, than to risk being lost for all eternity."

She felt no fear of him, only the hurt in her wrist, gripped by his hand like a vise of metal. His hand relaxed a little. She pulled and he released her.

"Listen to me," he said. "There is a great storm coming in this land. If the people rise up against their masters, many will die. I have seen it before. The weak rise up and the strong crush them back down."

"We work for peace, not war."

"You work to control others. Just like everybody else."

"That is not so."

Lud was up now, and she stood not daring to move while he paced the small straw floor in a circle around her. He held his side with one hand.

"I fear for you," Lud said. "I see you shouting 'Burn me! Burn me!'"

"Do you think I love this world so much?"

"You should respect your life more. It is a gift not to be taken lightly or tossed away for pride. You need to love in this world where you were born. This may be the only world there is. You need someone to love. One who loves you and will protect you."

"We are all brothers and sisters."

"You know what I mean."

In one motion, Lud took her hand again and he sat on his narrow bed and he pulled and then she was sitting beside him. She wanted to run and to stay, both.

Then she knew he wanted to kiss her. He was strong and she felt secure close to him, as if he could keep from her all that was evil and fearful in this world. She knew he loved her, now she knew. And when she realized that she wanted him to kiss her—looking into his eyes with his scars meaning nothing now—she knew she would let him do it.

"Please," she said, and felt his hand release her wrist.

They watched one another. He lifted both his hands and took her face into his open palms, gently now, and his face came close and she closed her eyes and felt his coarse beard and then his thin lips and his kiss. It was sweet and gentle at first, then he moaned and pressed her sudden and hard.

She twisted her face away and his hands released her.

"I felt that you wanted me to kiss you," he said. "And I wanted to kiss you. Is my face so evil? So unnatural?"

Her hands went to his face and her fingers traced the pox scars, the fibrous mounds that connected one upon another down his jaw into his hairline. He flinched from her touch as if he himself were repulsed.

"I am too ugly to love," he said. "Do not mock me."

"I see only fairness and strength and courage. Those are such comely things."

"And what do you feel?" said Lud.

She did not know what more to say.

She pulled backward and stood and saw him watching her. He shook his head. She stepped back again, afraid now. But he made no move toward her. Nor did he rise this time from his bed.

"Look how you reel back in disgust," he said.

"It is not that..."

"Do not come again." He got up and threw the hut door open.

She ducked out through the doorway like an arrowed deer, out into the sunlight, where the normal world went on as if nothing had changed.

She wanted to tell Grit of Lud's kiss, but she knew Grit might think only that Lud had heard the communal sex rumors. Finally, she did tell Grit.

She could have never guessed what Grit's question would be. It was nothing about gossip or morality.

"Did you like his kiss?" asked Grit.

She told Grit how she did not want to see Lud as a good man and she summoned the memory of Lud in the battle years ago, when she had first seen him, in the storm where men hacked other men to pieces just as the Giebel folk now with bloody faces and hands cut apart the animals in the winter slaughter.

She told Grit how it had all changed, when she saw Lud standing alone against the Wurzburg magistrates and the monk on his horse. She saw him working as hard as anyone else and taking nothing for himself. She felt his strength when he wanted to kiss her. She felt her own strange unexpected love for him, like warmth spreading through her body.

"Once I thought him like a monster. But now I see him a wholly different way. Yet I do not want to."

"Beauty is strange. Some people we see, at first, like Frieda, so lovely, then the more you know them the less lovely they seem. Others are always the same ugliness. But not Lud. The longer you know Lud the more handsome he seems. It is the spirit that comes through the outer appearance, in time. Do you now find him goodly to see? Is there a good feeling when he comes near, or when you approach him?"

"Yes. I feel safe. Protected. Respected."

"Does he love you and you him?"

"My feelings are so mixed. I do not know his. Only that he wants me. That I do know."

"Do you love him?"

"It is a feeling I have never had before."

"Yet you are troubled. What of Witter?"

"Witter?"

"He is a good man. None more cunning nor more learned. He seems your type. You know he loves and wants you. Anyone can see they both want you."

"Lud is a man of war and death and killing. But now I know he loves me. And good Witter. Witter is…"

She could not say, *a Jew.*

Would Witter not want a Jewess, a woman born of his blood and his faith, with whom to share his faith and raise his children so? Was it not like-to-like as in the Scriptures, each after their own kind?

"Witter is what?" said Grit.

"A good man," Kristina finally said.

"I see you drawn to Lud, little sister. Because he is strong and he takes away fear of others. Yet you deny him because he is the enemy of brotherly love. There is your conflict. But listen to me now. Lud does not toy. He is no fool of lust. He is a steadfast man, and his feelings are true, and you must not lead him falsely."

"I did not lead him." She wondered if that were true.

"We women do not know how men watch us. What they think when they watch us. Never let Lud kiss you again, unless you will give him all of yourself. Do you hear me?"

"How can I give love to a man who kills others? How can I let him be with me, and be a father to little Peter? My child already is too drawn to violent play. I have prayed and prayed but no good answer comes. Anyway, he told me to not come back again to tend his wound."

"There is your proof of a good man," said Grit.

Kristina knew now she wanted Lud and it was a selfish desire, out of her weakness, she felt, for it was all wrong, yet she felt dizzy with it. She held onto Grit.

Said Grit, "With our press, we must say who we are and what we wish for the world, and we must set the record straight about ourselves in all ways, and remove suspicion that can make women despise us and men seek to be alone with us. Be careful with Lud. He is outwardly a hard man and that often is the disguise of deep and sincere emotions. There is much danger in rejected men. Especially those rare ones who are solid and truly in love, and cannot forget. And you have not known love much, have you?"

Kristina felt Grit stroke her hair, like mother to daughter more than sister to sister.

"Grit, what will become of us?"

As Grit held Kristina her eyes turned inward, as if seeing something far off, something both sad and horrible all at the same time.

"We must print our faith, that our beliefs will reach others, and perhaps our faith will last when we are gone, if go we must. Only God knows that."

In the old stone barn, the air smoky with the fire that heated them from the broken hearth, the little blocks had been carved, the lampblack gathered, and the oil ink mixed. The new foundation bed for the carriage assembly of the press finally stood ready.

The icy roof of the old stone barn thawed and began leaking, water dripping inside, plopping into clay jugs and basins, and they cut new thatch and broke off the ice and repaired the roof. The fire was kept low, for the chimney was broken. But there was nothing the young men could not do, it seemed. And as yet, there had been no overt attempt by any to touch Kristina or Grit, nor did any of them even suggest anything unwelcome.

Temporarily, even the paper problem seemed solved by Linhoff. He said, "Many broadsheets have nothing on their obverse. Why not use the blank side to print our messages and articles? We can mark an X across the broadsheet's old side."

"No," Grit said. "Leave the message on the other side. That way we can hand them out with the old message face up. It can help us hide them."

Kristina saw the genius of it: "Yes, and whatever the old broadsheets say, let us dispute it on the other side, with Scriptures and good arguments of God's love."

"Perfect," said Max. "Giving us time to hand them out and get away before the true message is read."

"Is it too cowardly?" said Symon.

Said Dolf, "We will print some special ones just for you, Brother, to make sure you are taken by magistrates."

There was some jostling and jesting at Symon's expense. And much agreement for Grit's strategy, as it made the whole prospect seem much safer.

Lots were cast for who would write the first broadsheet, and Grit had won. To Kristina, it seemed a reward for her leadership.

Grit spent days writing her piece. Kristina set the type herself. An old broadsheet was placed into the press, with its blank side to the inked print blocks.

In a sudden excited frenzy, they prayed, set the type quickly, and rolled on the sooty ink Kristina had concocted. And then Dolf held the carriage steady and Symon turned the screw and ran the creaking press plate down upon the paper, pressing it onto the inked blocks.

When the screw was brought back up, Grit carefully pulled the printed paper away. Kristina and the others eagerly leaned over Grit's arms to read what it said. And Kristina heard herself reading it aloud—

"Why do 'Christian' nations rebuke the command of our Saviour, Jesus Christ, and make murderous war? Why, if Christians profess to be a religion of peace and unity, are armies raised at great cost, funds which could feed the poor, and educate the poor? Is it because if the poor could read, they would know that our Lord Jesus forbids such killing?"

Kristina paused, for the next words were everything—she felt they could heal the whole world:

"Love thy enemy. That is His command. Beware of losing your immortal souls forever to perdition, if ye raise a hand against another. Heed the words of Christ, not of kings and bishops and lords of war!"

They all took turns reading it. The young men who had been to war were stirred up to a frenzy.

"Are we only to blame for war?" said Linhoff. "It seems one-sided. The Turk should at least be equally damned."

Said Max, "More damned, since the Turk does not believe in Christ as holy."

"I have seen the Turks' slaughter of us," Ambrosius said. "What of their murders, their unbelief, their evil?"

"All who do murder do evil," said Grit.

"I repent of murder, done by accident," said Jakop. "But what good man would not defend his family by killing their enemies?"

"I have killed in battle," said Linhoff. "Many have killed. Are you saying we must go to hell? Is that what we have worked so long to say here?"

"Where you go for eternity," said Grit, "is between you and God. None are priests here, yet we each are our own priests."

Said Linhoff, "If a Turk walked in here with a sword, meaning to kill you, Grit, should I not try my best to kill him first? Would I be wrong?"

"Turks?" said Grit. "The Turks are very far from here, but Wurzburg is not so far."

Said Ambrosius, "What if magistrates came back from Wurzburg to arrest and torture and burn you? Would you stop me from raising my hand against them?"

"As Christ did to Peter, I would," said Grit. "I would not have your sin of murder on my account, never."

Linhoff laughed sourly. "Ambrosius kill a magistrate? If you tied the man down, maybe he would dare."

"Killing always is wrong," said Kristina

"So you say Lud is going to hell?" said Max.

"Lud?" said Kristina.

"Yes, Lud," said Max. "Has he not killed many? If it is as you say, that killing is always wrong, all who kill will burn in eternal fire?""

Kristina felt a rush of emotion, and realized it was her desire to defend Lud. The thought of Lud in hell chilled her heart, made her want to hold him close. Realizing this, she felt her face flush hot with blood, and she blinked.

"I judge no one," she evaded. "Who is worthy to judge another?"

Said a voice at the door, "And yet you would judge these brave young men for wishing to stop evil."

Kristina heard the voice and whirled around to look.

The others all turned and talking stopped.

It was Father Michael. His arms were full of a bundle wrapped in cloth.

Everyone stared at him.

Said the priest, "God gave the Promised Land to the Israelites, and they slew the inhabitants thereof with His blessing."

Kristina stared at the priest in wonder. He was beaming, as if in the grip of a serene rapture.

"Father," said Linhoff hastily, "we are just cleaning out this old barn, I mean…"

"That is not true," said the priest. "I have watched you coming and going across the fields. Now I know."

"What will you do?" said Grit.

Kristina saw the young men staring at the priest, and for a moment she feared for him, for what they might do to him, for fear of his authority with the Church.

Said Linhoff, "You cannot speak of this. You cannot send a message to Wurzburg nor to anyone."

"Be not afraid," said Father Michael.

"What do you want?" asked Grit.

Father Michael said, "I know what you are doing, and I am here to help you do God's work."

Whispered Max, "Father Michael has lost his mind."

"Is he drunk?" whispered Linhoff.

But Kristina saw it was not the drunkenness of wine or ale. He was intoxicated with himself. The priest's eyes and face were clear. Clear for the first time since she had met him. Clear and bright. And frightening, for all that.

Said the priest, "I know you have no paper. I have brought you sacristy paper."

Said Kristina, "May God bless you."

"Wonderful," said Grit.

Father Michael put his precious stack of paper down on the press tray and then he faced them and lifted his arms, high, as if to lead them in prayer.

Instead, he pulled a small volume from the inside of his robe. He opened it with deep respect and care.

"You do blessed work. Look what Erasmus himself has published in his *Novum Instrumentum,* his Latin translation of the Greek New Testament."

"He speaks of us?" said Grit.

"He speaks of each person taking action, on behalf of their own discovered truth. Let me read just a certain passage, of Erasmus' own comments, to you all..."

"Those who are deprived of their possessions and driven from their hearths and homes, those who mourn and are persecuted, may be called blessed; that in their case death is but the transition to immortality. Whoever, constrained by the spirit of Christ, preaches, urges, enforces, invites and encourages such doctrines, is, I say, a true theologian, even though he be only a digger of the soil or a weaver of linen; and whoever, through his walk and conversation, testifies to the truth of such doctrines, is a great doctor."

The priest gently closed the book.

"You, you," said the priest, "you and you and you."

He looked around at them. Kristina realized the deep implications of this. That even Erasmus, the great papal scholar, was acknowledging the right of each to learn and to think and to decide what was right from wrong.

"Do you understand?" asked Father Michael.

"Such words hurt my head," said Jakop.

Grit spoke up. "Erasmus is saying what is plain to any who read the Scriptures. That any law that forces men to act against their consciences is wrong, that men must read for themselves and think for themselves."

"But, give unto Caesar what is Caesar's," said Max. "That is what Christ Himself said."

Said Grit, "The state and its ministers always twist those words. You tell me now—indeed, what truly belongs to Caesar? His life? No, that is on loan from God, it is God's property and can vanish at any moment. Does Caesar own his own flesh? No, his flesh, like ours, is made from the dust. Are we property of Caesar? No, we belong to God and are bound first by the laws of God."

Kristina felt such a deep loving admiration for Grit, as Grit spoke with such simple dazzling clarity. It was as if Grit knew how to speak from Kristina's own heart—truly and unafraid.

And the others all were visibly moved to thought.

"I have never considered it just that way," said Father Michael. "But Christ was speaking in riddles, to evade the trickery of the priests' questions, was he not?"

Said Grit, "Christ was mocking Caesar, in my deepest belief. For Christ said love thy enemy, and Caesar says slay thy enemy."

"Believe as you will," said Father Michael. "I have seen what I must do. We must liberate the people, we must lead them to the light. Whatever powers that have reduced the people, they are evil and must be abolished."

"Abolished how?" said Linhoff.

"You speak of violence," said Grit.

The priest's next words chilled Kristina.

"I am leaving. I will join the true priests, like Muntzer, if I can find him. It is said that the land will burn with the flames of truth."

Said Grit, "You are drunk, that is certain, but not on ale or wine. Something far more dangerous."

"Do you hear what you are saying?" said Kristina.

Father Michael went back to the door. Kristina stared at him. He had never looked so happy before, she realized. He turned once more and touched his chest in farewell.

"I am free at last. No more will I live embittered by the entrapments of the Church that has turned its back on the people. There is only one way to cleanse this land. Take arms and throw off your yokes! Strike down the evil ones and walk with our lord God. Now, who will go with me?"

Kristina looked around, hoping the young men would not go, and they traded glances and did not move.

"Pray for me," said Father Michael.

Then he turned and walked out and was gone.

Kristina ran out the door, into the sunlight, and caught him.

"What has happened to you? What has changed you so?"

He looked at her from clear eyes that seemed all too bright. He was thrilled to some inward joy, and she thought of Berthold when they had embarked so long ago from Kunvald together. She expected the priest to say *a vision,* or *a dream,* or *an epiphany in prayer...*

"Lud," said the priest. "Lud showed me the way. That for each, there is a unique way to the truth.'"

She stood there in wonder. "Lud?"

"I was blind and he made me see. Lost in my own failure, and that was conceit, and I wished to end my life."

Kristina stared, not knowing what to say.

Said the priest, "Lud is a man who takes action, and he is my brother. All men are brothers."

"Yes, this is so, you are my brother," said Kristina.

Father Michael smiled blissfully into her eyes. His face looked clear of pain, boyish and determined.

"In all my studies, I never knew this before. Only action will justify my brotherhood with others."

"Then stay and work with us."

"That is not enough, not now, not for me."

Then Father Michael turned from her and went striding away across the field, with a skipping step, like a boy escaping a dolorous task and embarking upon a wild adventure.

The time was fast approaching to distribute the broadsheets. Their plan had been discussed, debated, voted on, and agreed on.

In the next days before the secret time to depart, Kristina spent much time at Arl's, on the weaving room floor, playing with Peter. She valued each precious day as if it were her last on earth. She watched Arl weave and envied her—how Arl had no compulsion to go risk her life, how Arl knew nothing of broadsheets nor burnings, how Arl wove her cloth and hummed and lived her life.

As the days came closer, Kristina dreaded the very idea of returning to Wurzburg, and worse, leaving Peter. On this journey to Wurzburg to hand out the broadsheets and risk all, even her life, and perhaps never return to her child, she prayed and begged for a way out.

She knew she might never see Peter again, and under that lay another deep pressure. She could not let the others take this risk all upon themselves. Leaving Peter was wrong, but she could not take him with them, and not going was wrong. The conflict tore at her.

Prayer did not answer this nor settle her soul nor quiet her mind. She remembered her mother and how her mother had left her, and she grieved all the more.

"What is wrong?" asked Arl, watching her.

"Nothing," Kristina said, and it was a lie.

"Your boy is a fine child," Arl said.

"Yes, I am blessed, thank you."

"Pray God he will not grow up to be a soldier."

"He will not."

Arl's fingers moved faster on the loom. "I thought Hermo would not go. Fridel wanted to go prove himself, but I thought Hermo would stay and make me a grandmother."

"I wish your boys were here with you now."

"Yes, oh yes. But when the men all become excited together, whatever it is, there is no stopping them."

The next day Kristina gathered her traveling things, her cloak and food bag, and knew this was wrong, and yet felt she must do it. She bathed Lady Anna and dressed her. And then Lady Anna wanted to hear the harp, so Kristina was forced to sit still and play, feeling too nervous to move.

Finally, the last day came when all was in readiness, and she was going.

She went to the barn as one condemned.

But, at the barn, everything changed. When they were ready to leave for Wurzburg, their prayers all said, all prepared, Grit argued with Kristina that she must not go with them.

"You are a mother with a child and you must stay here."

"I must do what we all do, together." She felt incredible relief, yet argued.

That was when Symon said, "The broadsheets. They are gone."

Dolf and Symon had discovered that the readied broadsheets were gone. Dolf and Symon looked relieved. They had been dragging ever since it was voted to hand out the broadsheets in Wurzburg. It had been a tie and then Symon had weakened and voted yes, to Dolf's chagrin.

They searched high and low. The sheets could not be found. Grit was beside herself with disappointment. Then Linhoff and the other boys came to the barn.

"Why the long faces?" said Linhoff.

"The broadsheets are gone," Kristina said.

She expected Linhoff to be shocked but he was not even surprised.

"I know," said Linhoff.

"You know what?" demanded Grit.

"It is done. Old Klaus came through, and he takes our words to the Wurzburg market."

"You gave him our broadsheets?" said Grit, in disbelief.

"He will see them to the market for distribution."

Grit was furious. "That is a cowardly way. What if he is taken? That will be on our souls, man."

Said Linhoff, "Old Klaus, crafty fellow, he will sell them for sure. Besides, he can hardly read. It is perfect. With the bishop's words on the front, he is safe, and he will profit."

"Did we do this for anyone to profit?" said Kristina, deeply upset. "To risk their life?"

She felt a terrible guilt, now, that she had so dreaded going to Wurzburg and used Peter as an excuse to beg God to forgive her. And she felt relief that compounded her guilt. It was a dizzying sense of life renewed, as if she had been untied from the stake.

"Better if Old Klaus sells them," said Max. "More seriously will they be valued and read."

"And if he is caught?" said Grit.

Kristina knew the answer. If Old Klaus were caught, he would lead the magistrates straight back to Giebel.

Witter

In the street off the main square, one of the hard young men with Frieda (he absolutely knew that it was her) showed a harder face than the other, and he wore a fashionably groomed beard running up thickly into his hairline. His wide cap and flowing hair hid his ears, and yet somehow Witter realized from the flatness that there were no ears to be hidden. Passersby gave him wide berth. One saluted him with a deep bow.

So they were not fops after all. They were soldiers out for sport, dressed in their best finery like wealthy students. But their faces were not the soft faces of amateur scholars.

"Sir," the earless man said, "you block our way. I do not know you. Do you have business with us?" It was said with a hard smile that held a challenge. "I am Captain Ulrich of the Fifth Landsknechts, at your service."

"Frieda?" said Witter, dumbly staring at her.

"My name is Paulina." Frieda threw her head back. "Sir, I do not know you. Have you heard me sing?"

"Sing?"

Witter realized that he was playing with fire. Was he out of his mind? The mercenary company was stationed out at the barracks end of the Marienberg and he hardly saw them unless they were on parade for some bishopric occasion, with drums and banners and a ceremonial firing of the cannons and muskets.

Said the hard one, "Our Paulina is the sweetheart of the Wurzburg orchestra theater, sir. She knows all the newest and most popular love songs."

The other laughed and said, "And many other good things."

He could not say, *You know who I am, Frieda.* And suddenly he realized that she and he both were at grave risk should they acknowledge one another and expose their former identities. Now he thought he smelled the odor of absinthe coming from them, sharp and pungent and with the bitterness of wormwood.

Said the hard one, "Your horse sports a Marienberg mark and stable saddle, sir. If it did not, I would take offense to your blockage of my way."

"Excuse me," Witter suddenly said, and turned his horse aside. He bowed and moved his horse away briskly, and he felt their eyes on his back.

At the corner, he stopped the horse.

Witter looked around. He had lost sight of Frieda but he knew it was her. Yet it was passing strange and sad. He thought of the shy, pouty, pretty girl, the little sister Anabaptist, so protected by Grit and Kristina. Of her jumping from the ferry at the river and disappearing at the last moment into the dark, back toward Wurzburg, that terrible night years ago when Werner Heck hanged himself on his chains from the bridge to give them a last chance to escape the crossbows of the magistrates.

In the square was a rally apparently of guildsmen, most in their city robes. Their speaker was a tall, gaunt man standing on a low wall and shaking his fists and ranting:

"Why does the city council refuse the vote to the guildsmen who pay such heavy taxes for them to spend? Is it because we guildsmen would expect our taxes to be spent wisely, equally for all who pay? Do the wealthy of the council fear equality? Why is there taxation without the vote? Should we withhold our taxes and our labor, until they understand that we too are men?"

The crowd cheered him and then there came the magistrates rushing the crowd with their dogs and clubs and chains. Witter did not even want to see the panic and the fight. As the bashing began, he turned the horse and rode away, back down another alley.

That night in the fortress, within the great stone walls, Witter lay on his pallet, trying to sleep.

It was not only social injustice and unrest that stirred him. It was Kristina. He missed her terribly. His loneliness was made worse by thinking of her, and so he tried not to. Lud was there at Giebel now, and he was not. Lud would have time to sway her, to woo her.

Far better not to think of her. Perhaps he would never see Kristina again. *She is not of your faith,* Judah would have said, *you are not of hers.*

It seemed like a century had passed since his family had been destroyed and he had fled. He tried to find something to hold on to. Sleep would not come, and he tried his best to pray, in hopes his father would come speak to him again…

Keep me from iniquity, disgrace, and sin…

May I not be overwhelmed by temptation or despair…

The words only mocked him. His mind turned and he thought of Frieda.

He saw Frieda's face. Its innocence had been stripped away. The beauty was there but not the sweetness of spirit. The groomed surface of her flesh was like an empty mask.

No doubt Frieda was consoling herself with wormwood wine and perhaps opium and the other common panaceas sold in the chemist shops. He had tried such things long ago and found them wanting, and worse, they were dulling of the instincts of survival, the very skills he honed constantly.

How Frieda had come to this pass, he could not know. She looked stunningly worse for wear, her freshness gone, devoured by the grind and lust of this city. But it was not a new story. And he resolved then and there to follow this opportunity, and to find where Frieda lived or performed or submitted, or however she survived.

The urge was as imbecilic and sentimental as it was somehow compelling. He meant to somehow bring Frieda back to Kristina, as a good sheepdog brings a lost lamb. Kristina would love him for doing that. And perhaps he would love himself a little for doing it.

Frieda's fall from grace, as he reflected sadly upon it, was like the city and the country itself. He watched this society losing its center, the tyranny and authority all slowly imploding, a collapse so gradual that it was nearly imperceptible, yet with a relentlessly growing momentum.

A most popular broadsheet, anonymous, was "When Adam Dug and Eve Spun, Where Was the Nobleman?" But he did not dare be caught with one.

Florian now spent his days with Bishop Lorenz, and now Witter was quartered alone in the original room. Florian had moved to the bishop's side of the Marienberg, to much better chambers. Still, at least twice a week, Florian visited Witter's quarters at night for a report on happenings and rumors in the city.

He reported it all as Florian had assigned him to do.

The city guilds were agitating, protesting for a vote in the city councils. And word spread of scattered small revolts on far-flung estates, where the villeins had abandoned the fields and seized certain properties, and of debt-ridden knights who had lost all and wandered the roads, some reduced to banditry.

"This all conforms to what I have myself observed in the shadow of Bishop Lorenz," said Florian. "Lorenz wishes to be only a man of God, one who does not wish to punish others for learning and bettering themselves. He leaves the dirty work to Konrad, the real power and the threat to all reform."

"Are they not both princes? Both serving the emperor?"

Said Florian, "Konrad has taken control of all the secular power. Lorenz leaves all matters of force now to Konrad. Konrad's response to agitation is to ever harm the people—to increase the number of magistrates and to begin training a larger army. I fear what might become of us all if Konrad ever becomes bishop. Keep your eyes and ears open and watch for open signs of revolt."

"What will you do in that case?'

"You shall know when I do it," said Florian.

Witter sensed that everything was about to change.

And it did, on a hot day the next week.

Witter had been riding, for riding had become more and more pleasant a pastime, a luxury now that it was so unnecessary. His buttocks were tough now. The saddle sores were small knots and hard as bark. He had been given a fine young mare at the Marienberg livery, for his older horse was war-broken and had been requisitioned for the bishopric Landsknechts training out in the field. The officers killed many horses in training.

Witter was trotting the frisky young mare down along the wide river quays where boatmen and dockworkers labored and filth rolled in the brown water. Destitutes lived there on whatever they could steal or beg or scavenge.

He saw a vast crowd shifting out of Wurzburg and pouring down along the river toward a much greater crowd.

Two thousand had gathered to hear a traveling priest from the troubled mining town of Zwickau, a priest people said was named Thomas Muntzer.

Witter had no idea who he was at first, and could hear him shouting, but he was too far away to make out the words.

Standing high above the heads of the mob, the priest was up on a pile of fallen trees, as if ready to be burned.

Muntzer wore a black robe and cleric's cap and had his waving arms lifted to heaven. He stood over the crowd, on a great fallen log, and his shouted words boomed over the excited crowd.

Riding up closer, Witter could now hear shouts even over the loud cracking of the hooves:

"Our world concocts a poisonous faith!"

Then, slowing the horse, he could hear Muntzer over the heads of the mob, clearly, though hundreds blocked the way:

"When Adam dug and Eve spun, where then was the nobleman?"

Now Witter realized the wildly popular anonymous broadsheet had been spread by Muntzer and his followers.

Witter's eyes scanned the faces and they were poor people, men and women of every age and kind, herds of children underfoot, swarming and feral. There were many guildsmen, some in good robes with embroidered signs of their guilds, some in the aprons and vests of their trades. There were painted women and labor women and ex-soldiers wearing rags that had once been tunics in war. He thought he saw a familiar face and was sure it was Huber, the drunk who had been steward at Giebel before Lud. Huber, screaming in agreement with the mob, echoing Muntzer's words, did not see Witter at all.

"You sweat and toil but you have no say, no vote, nothing for your taxes which they spend for war and ceremonies. Is that the way of God?"

The crowd roared; a nerve deeply touched.

It was not only laborers and guildsmen and the merely curious there. Witter saw priests, too, most of them rapt with Muntzer's statements, the stronger the better, and he thought one was Father Michael, but knew that could not be, not Father Michael, who was a greater coward than Witter believed himself to be. Yet it so looked like Michael.

He pushed his horse closer.

"Michael!" he shouted, his voice lost in the noise.

The priest did not see him. Father Michael was pushing his way closer and closer forward, toward Muntzer standing on his log.

Muntzer's voice gathered them all in.

"The present church is an old whore! What can the godless know of true faith, since they have never been saddened by unbelief? In many towns the miners have had enough. The villeins sicken of their unjust yoke! The weavers starve though they work through the nights! And again I say, when Adam dug and Eve spun, where was the rich man? Yes, the time of the harvest is surely here, dear brothers!"

Hearing Muntzer's words, Witter discreetly spread his rain cloak over the Marienberg mark on the flank of the horse, and across the bishopric saddle. But those around him paid him no mind. They were all spellbound by the radical priest and his clear and direct imperatives.

"The wealthy hide behind their great walls, but I say, beware, ye chaff, who everywhere screams that it is not yet your harvest time."

Three magistrate patrols came down the road from Wurzburg with chained dogs. They had obviously been sent to break this up and arrest the priest. Witter saw them halt when they crested a little rise and beheld the mass of the host there.

"Those who should preside most supremely over Christianity, since they are called princes, supremely prove their lack of faith in all their actions and plans. Yea, I would rather instruct heathens, Turks, and Jews speaking of God and giving an account of God's rule!"

The great crowd cheered and approved and Muntzer had to lift his arms to continue.

The word *Jews* sent a crackle down Witter's nape. He dared not hope that the world could be changing so. He had been deceived too many times before.

Some off duty soldiers were listening and laughing at this, and a horde from the crowd suddenly turned on them, charged them, ran them down and swarmed and beat them without mercy, nearly kicking them to death.

Witter backed his horse away. There would be hell to pay now. The magistrates would charge into the mob. But he was wrong. They just stared, they did not move.

A priest in the crowd saw this and pointed at the magistrates, saying, "Behold, wretches whose souls are sold, like dogs chained to dogs, and which are the men they will arrest today?"

Father Michael. Shouting and shaking his fist. Witter knew it was him, there was no doubt now. The crowd surged around the priest.

They roared at the magistrates as if baiting them to charge. The magistrates stood their ground, then one by one, they backed away from the angry mass.

Muntzer cried, "Ah, the traitors reveal themselves! Are they not common men, like us? Why do they serve our oppressors?"

It was incredible to see, but the once-feared magistrates were themselves afraid. Their dogs barked and strained but they jerked them back on chains, trying to stay together.

Witter felt a thrill. It was as sharp as a knife. It cut through all his soul. It was sweet, pure hatred.

Someone threw a stone and it hit a magistrate dog and the dog squealed like a stuck pig and jerked its handler off his feet. Witter laughed. He wished he could kill them all.

Suddenly, the crowd was laughing and many people began picking up stones, and in a hailstorm of missiles the magistrates began to run back down the road to Wurzburg. Their chains were flying like snakes about their shoulders, their dogs running with them happily as if it were a game. Above the crowd, Muntzer laughed and shouted.

"If you give yourself to evil," cried Muntzer, "you become evil!"

Witter had never seen anything like it in his life. The crowd cheered. They snarled and raged. All their years of pent-up fear was released in one great surge.

And then Witter heard himself cheering, too. Driven by a wild impulse, suddenly he drove his horse forward and ran down one fleeing magistrate and then another, tangled in their own chains, and the mob howled, cheering him on.

The men fell under him with screams, and he rode away from the mob with an exultation that was overpowering. He shouted and shouted to the sky, and bent over the horse's hot, pulsing neck, the hooves driving faster and faster, the road flying under him.

He had no idea who he had become.

Konrad

For days Konrad had suffered successive attacks of constriction. The fire would boil up and his throat would close, driving him to his knees, feeling like the devil's grip was upon his throat. It was an accident that he was visiting Mahmed, amusing himself with the helplessness of the disbeliever, offering Mahmed amnesty should he publicly renounce his evil faith—to be reported by Veritas Press—when an attack occurred. It bent him double, down to his knees.

"My lord," Basil cried, and tried to lay him out on the floor rug.

"No," said Mahmed, "sit him up, not down."

"Do not touch his grace!" cried Basil.

But Konrad himself, face red and breath stopped, desperately gripped Mahmed's assisting hand. It shamed Konrad to be assisted by his victim, the disbeliever. And yet when Mahmed pushed and sat him up, the relief was immediate, undeniable. The drool at the corners of his lips tasted bloody where he had bit his tongue.

"Never touch the prince!" cried Basil again.

And the bodyguard with them finally moved to intervene. But now Konrad waved them away.

Mahmed then did strange and remarkable things—holding his hands upon either side of Konrad's chest, saying, "Gently, there is nothing to harm you here, gently let the breath come, sit up relaxed, that is good, good to breathe easily, slowly, gently…"

When the attack was over, and Konrad could sit in a chair, Mahmed told him that his father had been a surgeon.

"I myself had no talent in healing, though they invested much training in me, for a third son. So I went into armed service. Have you had this affliction since boyhood, becoming much worse in your male ripening time?"

How could Mahmed know this? Konrad was amazed.

"Is there an evil spell upon me?"

"No spell. It is an affliction, often of the highborn."

Konrad reasoned that must be so. He was highborn. It was much more acceptable, nobler that it were so.

"Is there any cure?" he said.

"One quite famous case."

"Tell me."

"A renowned philosopher of medicine once treated a great ruler, al-Maliki, a sultan who suffered from melancholia as well as this constriction of breath. The sultan took such excellent advice and was cured."

"I suffer no melancholia," Konrad lied. "But tell me anyway, what was this advice?"

"We will not hear it!" pleaded Basil. "Who was this deceiving wizard, this pretend healer?"

Konrad silenced the monk with a glare. His breath was better and better, sitting up this way.

"Maimonides was his name," said Mahmed.

"A Jew!" cried Basil.

Basil tried to speak again but Konrad lifted a silencing hand. The fire of constriction had eased enough for him to breathe a little. He wanted to hear more, anything that would help.

Mahmed's counsel was simple but strange: honeyed drinks, fruit but no red meat, no strong drink, meditation in prayer, and riding his horse often in fresh air.

"All of these would help greatly to relieve the pressures that shut off your life's breath," said Mahmed.

Afterward, Basil warned, "Witchcraft. He put a spell of infernal demons upon you, your grace. We must bathe you in vinegar and the hottest bath you can endure, at once."

"No," Konrad said. Remembering only too well such a bath following one of his spells when he was a young boy. It was hell.

He would ride his horse and eat lightly and pray much more. Giving up red meat would be the worst. And no wine. But he resolved to try it.

When they were down from the tower, Basil said, "This Maimonides was a Jew. You cannot follow the lies of a Jew, your grace. The Jews migrate to the Ottomans, and there all the unbelievers commingle in utter evil together."

"Lorenz loves his damned Jews, and the double revenue they bring," said Konrad. "The pope himself has advisors in Rome who are Jews."

Basil was abashed and bowed and said no more.

Konrad felt a flush of equanimity. He was a worldly forward-looking prince and had transcended petty regionalism and narrowness, if it would ease the affliction that had hounded him, made him small, since boyhood. God must have sent him this unbeliever, to serve him in this way.

So, when Konrad was out of the city, on his yearly visit north to Karlstadt and his Thungen castle estate, he rode with a retinue of mounted Marienberg guards. Instead of riding in a protected carriage, he rode Sieger, and he wore the silver and gold armor, exposing himself to demonstrate his courage as was fitting for a prince.

It felt marvelous.

But at his estate, there was a week of enduring the usual misery of complaints.

Always the same flattery and wheedling; relatives seeking positions, loans, and hinting of bribes to be had; villeins dissatisfied with the steward's punishments and sharings-out.

With the prioress of his abbey, Konrad had prayed piously at the marble tomb of his dead wife, but it was at the modest grave of his old wet nurse that he had truly grieved and wept, and clawed the fresh earth with his ungloved hands.

No one could think him an unfeeling man. Nor was he. In fact, he well knew, he felt too deeply. His innate compassion was so sensitive that he was forced to chill it with constant leavenings of cold, pure reason, along with much prayer for strength.

On the return ride from Thungen, he let Sieger run for several miles. His guard retinue had much trouble staying with him.

Yes, this was what he needed. He felt strong, manly, as if Sieger's energy flowed up through him, too.

Then, back south to Wurzburg, there were so many beggars that the road guards had to sometimes drive them off. After passing through villages where sour faces watched without a single cheer, his road guards fed Sieger some common village grain that soured his belly, and Sieger passed gas constantly for hours.

Nearer Wurzburg, passing through the forests, he thought of stopping down by Giebel and seeing Anna for the first time in so many years, but the fear of horror that her face were so scarred changed his mind, as it always did.

Scatterings of worn-out men in old black iron armor were seen several times, and his road guards reported them as bankrupt knights become brigands, but they withdrew without incident into the trees. Konrad felt naked, thinking how a bolt might fly at him or strike Sieger unseen. The lavish armor chafed his skin and the sweat itched miserably.

Even more than an ambush, Konrad feared the look in the old knights' eyes—lost and strange—and, somehow, he realized that he felt more exposed to their minds than to a bolt, and wished to be inside the stone walls of the Marienberg. But he held his head high, not giving them any view of his weakness. And he suffered no constriction that day.

They were his children. Why did they not love him?

So upon his return to Wurzburg, Konrad was in no good mood. The city seethed with beggars, crime, suicides and want, and angry malcontents.

The news of the radical priest Muntzer preaching outside the city and the riot that drove away the magistrates awaited him.

"Our magistrates ran away?"

"We hold them under arrest for your judgment. But the mob was enormous. At every public assembly," said Basil, "the people clamor and gather to complain among themselves. Even at wedding feasts and pilgrimages and guild feasts and even church ales. Every chance they have, they foment together."

"Then we forbid assemblies."

"Which ones?"

"All."

"Will the Bishop Lorenz permit this?"

"The security of the city is in my hands."

"There will be great resentment."

"Good. Arrest the dissenters."

"How, your grace? They assemble in half the villages and in the woods outside estates. We have not the men to arrest them all. And we have deserters as it is."

"Make examples to terrify."

"The people grow numb to our many examples. They moan for those being executed. Their mood is dark, your grace."

"Basil, if you cannot do God's work, tell me so."

"Please do not mistake me, your grace. If I had them here in my fists I would tear them to bits and burn them all. We shall close the city gates at dark. Raise the bounty on seditionists and heretics. Let all see that we control them. Order is duty."

"Better. Much better."

He read Basil's reports and went to work restoring order. Wurzburg was like a child needing constant correction. But it was good to take charge.

First, to mollify Lorenz, he ordered a handout of bread, with Veritas praising his charity. An emergency tax on the city council paid for the handout, and the wealthy burghers of the council were incensed, but Konrad knew they were terrified and would yield, for every one of them was begging for guards to be posted at their mansions.

Next, Konrad had the magistrates publicly flogged, those who had run from the stoning of the mob. It was his own brilliant idea that each was branded on his forehead with the letter F for *feigling*—coward.

"Common men fear nothing more than being mocked for cowardice," Konrad told Basil. "They will go to war or duel, risk death, kill their own brother, do any mad thing to be thought brave. This will brace up all the others."

As a noble act of bishopric mercy, acknowledging former service, the magistrates' ankle cords were not cut before they were flogged at the city gates with only the rags on their backs. There were two crippled by a runaway horse, Basil said, and they lay in an ox-drawn tumbrel cart, half-dead. Their dogs were sold to the bear baiters for the pits. The two crippled ones were dumped off the bridge into the river. Veritas did not report the last two.

Recruiting was boosted by double bonuses. There was no shortage of starving ex-soldiers ready to take the bishopric coin and eat their fill and sleep warm, and war dogs were breeding in plenty.

The monk publicists, toiling under Basil's direction at Veritas Press, reported the Muntzer rally as a conjoining of traitors with Satan, where infants were sacrificed and eaten. The printing sold out in half an hour, and the city burghers were very afraid. But a good half of the broadsheets had been set afire in the bishopric market stall by persons not yet found.

Still, Veritas was an incredible success. Konrad knew the value of thought and belief. And the press had never been busier or more profitable than now.

Reported Basil, "It is amazing—the more unrest, the more broadsheet sales. People are hungry for all kinds of controversy. People feed upon hate as dogs feed on carcasses. They cannot seem to get enough of it."

Basil was learning well, but Konrad frequently found it necessary to instruct the monk.

"If your subject describes a Christian, he kills evil Muslims because he is a great hero of God. If he is Muslim, he kills innocent Christians because his religion is evil and such evil compels his evil acts."

"What of our own terrorists?" asked Basil. "There are Muntzers popping up in every corner it seems now."

"If he is a priest and denounces the Church, he is certainly possessed by demons, and he must be burned to save his immortal soul from eternal fire. Those who confess and repent will only be beheaded, not put to the purifying flames."

Lawlessness was indeed a situation becoming worse with every rightful attempt to control the people. Theft of military supplies, even weapons and horses, was a bad problem. Konrad had a double guard on the Marienberg stables and especially on his own stable at his town mansion, for Sieger's safety.

There was sabotage, too, wagon wheels with spokes cut out, cannons with spikes in the touchholes. Vandalism for no good purpose anyone could imagine, as if people throughout the land were slowly going insane.

"In all cities of the whole region," said Basil, "there is much agitation. Against church and noble alike. Renegade monks preach against the papacy and the Swabian League. City guilds are restless with taxes, demanding a vote equal to the city council regarding the dictates of nobles and princes. The low wish to become high, as roaches climb the walls even of great mansions."

"Armies must be raised," said Konrad. "We must be prepared for any uprising and crush it instantly. And recruit new magistrate patrols for the city. Hard men who are desperate for the coin and will do what must be done."

"We know that Lorenz does not wish to raise taxes again to raise armies, your grace. If we advocate too much for new armies in our broadsheets, the bishop may act against us. He fears rousing the mobs to even greater rage."

"Lorenz is so weak. Yet it is best not to force him. He believes men will change ever for the better, and that God blesses the natural progress of that change."

"Your grace, little fires can devour great forests if unchecked."

"Exactly so." Konrad considered the ruinous cost of outfitting armies for war. Waste that could be employed to build fine new castles. And then he thought of the bounty of victories, and the great wealth that came into treasuries from the vanquished, and the thrilling power that accrued. "The league will hire mercenaries and the bishop will comply with revenues as he always must."

"He will resist. He has forbidden Muntzer to be arrested even when he spoke against the Church. Now he has even invited Martin Luther here to visit."

"Yes, I know. Lorenz must be mad."

"Mad or not, our Lorenz is bishop. Your grace will be expected to also meet Luther, of course."

"More and more Lorenz encourages the reformers," said Konrad. "If this continues, Wurzburg will become an open nest of them."

"Help us, your grace," said Basil. "Help us who believe in the Holy Church as it has always been."

"I am doing all that I can do."

Konrad had prayed long upon this many times. And the answer always came back the same…

Lorenz believes God is flexible. That God is willing to change. Men change, not God…

Said Basil, "What of your godson, Florian Geyer? Can he be used? Perhaps as a city guild watchdog on some council? Or put him into Wurzburg University to spy upon the nests of radical students?"

He did not wish to think of Florian, and especially not of Anna, Florian's mother, who once had been his dream, and had been poxed, and now was reduced to a thought of property, and loss, and revulsion. But he could never openly admit any of this. For now, Florian was just another loose detail of life.

"No," said Konrad. "Florian follows Lorenz about like a lapdog all day. He is of no use to us. Not yet."

Konrad felt tired and gave a dismissive wave of his hand. He wanted to go out and be with Sieger. Riding Sieger was always an experience of unconditional love, pure of heart, and Konrad wanted to feel the power of Sieger, surging, thundering, strident beneath him. When he rode Sieger, too, strangely, just as Mahmed had said, the constrictions of asthma did not so afflict his breath. He recalled that Mahmed said that this had been a Muslim doctor's advice to a great sultan…or had it been a Jew's advice? No matter.

It seemed correct that he too would have benefited. Was it not an accepted fact that men of high rank were of more sensitive natures?

Basil's voice broke into his reflections.

At the chamber door, Basil said, "Do not forget, Martin Luther visits Lorenz tomorrow. You are expected to attend."

Konrad grimaced.

"That fat-headed reformer devil. Luther will do any trick to promote his book sales. May I bring poison?"

"Please, your grace, do not jest of such things, though no doubt you would be praised by the angels. However, it would be easy to kill him outside the city when he departs."

Konrad had prayed long upon this matter. There was as yet no sure sign from God that such a death was justified, or even wise.

"Luther travels under safe passage from Saxony, and the last thing we need is a war with other nobles. But, as you say, there could be a most regrettable accident on the road when he is departed far away from our protection. Who could have known? We could even praise and bury him here."

How he was perceived was everything.

That night, alone in his tower chamber, the body attendants dismissed, he ate a simple meal of roasted squab breasts and apple slices and grapes. A slice of coarse bread was grainy as sand and hurt his teeth, the sort of plain bread Christ himself might have broken to eat.

Musing, Konrad stared into a great hearth fire, pondering, praying, seeking…

God knew he was afflicted, prone to asthma, too soft, a man as secretly weak as he had been when he was a boy. To be strong did not come naturally. Where others punished almost with fervor, he did so sadly, not wishing to soil his mind with such ugliness. God helped him to overcome his weakness, and to be as strong as God's work demanded him to be.

If he was perceived as strong, he was strong.

As Saint Francis, one of his favorite saints, had proven, God forgave weakness and revealed to the faithful the best ways to find strength to do God's work. Konrad fought his own softness by being harder and more resolved than any man could deny. And that hid his softness well enough.

It was well that minds could not be read. And that knowledge was reserved for those with the right power to wield it, for the good of the whole.

But, what was it that Dietrich had said, all those years ago, about literacy?

I would share minds with all men, if we could…

He was wishing Luther dead, staring into the fire, when he realized that his breath was easy, the bile was not coming, the throat not constricting, and that he would not be punished by God for heeding the medical advice of the devil-worshipper, the evil peacock, Mahmed.

Lud

It was late summer and a hot, dry day. The high grass spears were tipped in yellow. Waldo rode beside Lud as they crossed field after field, passed through orchards where ripening apples could be grabbed under low boughs, and streams crossed to water the mounts.

For years, as steward, Lud had ridden Ox along the border of the estate, often with Waldo, and the circuit took all day in good weather.

Out here he could try to stop brooding upon Kristina.

When he rode past the ancient cemetery, Lud slowed the horse and paused, as he always did, to stare at the grave of Dietrich—and the same thoughts always came strongly to him there:

How could such a great spirit of a man be laid there, immobile for all time? How could such energy pass from this world and not go somewhere?

Then he rode on past the wall of trees where the old stone barn was overgrown by the encroaching woods, and Waldo pointed to it and Lud rode wide around. Waldo could not speak but he understood all that he heard. "Waldo, I know what they are doing in there and I do not know what to do about it. Dietrich would have permitted it. You know he encouraged reading, writing, and printing."

Waldo shook his head and signed a danger sign.

"I know, I know," said Lud. "But Dietrich is gone. I know not where, but he is not here. And hard times are here. So, for now, let them be."

They rode on through the bright, dry heat.

There were no fences, only landmarks. Without a routine of vigilance, the crops of neighboring estates would encroach, and their herds would be pastured on good Geyer grass, which needed to be ripe for Geyer cattle and sheep and goats when the herders moved the flocks and pasturing time came.

The estate was an ancient, magical place, of fog and old forest. He had explored it all as a wild boy of the woods, with the other wild children in his herd. The estate lay on the southern plain of the Main River, and millennia of topsoil had enriched it there. The fertile plain was farmed for three thousand years, it was said, and the old ones called the rich lands the *Ochsenfurter Gau.*

The horses passed a great oak and Waldo pointed to it and they both smiled. Once, Lud's gang had found a sunken place under the old tree among the roots. They had dug and dug and unearthed bones and the rusted shell of a helmet with a skull inside, and the bronze hilt of a sword.

"Boys play war and are scolded for not working," he said to Waldo. "Then they grow to men and play war, and are praised for it."

Waldo smiled and shook his head. He pointed to the dip in the ground. Lud remembered. The gang had invented and acted out rituals there, pledging loyalty to the old gods whose names they did not know. Now, most of them had become men, some older, too, like Sig, and Merkel, and Waldo, and some were long ago dead in war. He wondered what had happened to the bronze hilt. Merkel had fought him for it and was a much older and bigger boy and finally had won the fight, but Lud grinned, thinking of the bites he had inflicted and the blows he had ignored. He wondered if Merkel still had the old hilt, and the bite scars.

Waldo pointed ahead across a field.

"I see them," said Lud.

This was what Lud had come for today. In his and Waldo's saddlebags were cheese and fresh loaves of bread.

Just inside the trees at the edge of the field, the ragtag band of itinerate men—formerly men of war—were waiting. Lud's heart sank, seeing them so reduced. They were woods vagabonds now, but they had been fighting men and farmers and some were knights who had known Lud and Dietrich in better times.

Some time ago, Waldo had discovered them and reported, with hand signs, to Lud. Lud had considered what Dietrich would do. And he knew it would be the right thing.

Lud slowed his horse and saw the women and children fading back to hide behind the men. The men came forward, surly and wary. They looked starved, gaunt, not mean but weary—the look that tired men have when they will resort to anything necessary. Wisps of smoke came on the air with a scent of meat, and Lud now knew they were poaching just to survive.

Waldo rode forward and signed to them and Lud dismounted. He pulled the saddlebags of bread from Ox's rump.

Stiff words of greeting were exchanged.

Their lead man was tall and white-haired and wore a chest of old black iron armor. Lud realized that he was a knight. Some with him wore ragged gray tunics with a beast's head, maybe an ox head. Lud was not certain of the crest. And maybe the armor was stolen.

"I am Lud, steward of this estate, and we bring you bread, to welcome you, and ask you to respect our fields. The game in the woods is for all, that is our custom."

Waldo caught his eye. Lud saw what Waldo saw— crossbowmen in the trees, almost perfectly hidden.

The old man said, "I remember you. You served with Dietrich for the Swabian League many years ago, when we put down the Slovenian revolt to the south."

"I was little more than a boy. That was my first action."

"Alfred von Steinmetz, a knight, sir, and I rode with Dietrich, your father."

"Dietrich was my master, sir, not my father," said Lud.

"I thought I knew different, but no matter. We served well together. Is he well?"

"He is dead these several years, of pox."

"Dead. Another good one gone," said Steinmetz, looking sincerely disappointed. Then he brightened and said, "But at least he died at home? He and I always hoped for that."

"He did die at home."

"Your courtesy honors you." The old knight waved his hand at the wall of trees. "You have just saved your lives with your own fairness. We have crossbows in the trees, their eyes on you. Forgive us but we are alive only by unrelenting caution."

Said Lud, "We are alone and mean no harm. These are bad times for everyone."

"They are. The Swabian League forgets its old friends these days. I have lost my estate. Back taxes claimed against too many promises in bad times. These faithful villeins have left our land, with me. There are many such on the roads now. It is a sad sight to see other knights set adrift."

"They say soldiers and veteran men of war are wanted by the Wurzburg bishopric now. The guilds agitate for voting on the councils and other unrest is there."

"They starve the people to march their armies and parade. Would I serve those who have robbed my heritage?"

It puzzled Lud. "How did such scum as magistrates drive you fighting men off your land?"

"They tried first with magistrates, twice. We sent them yipping home. Then came men at arms, on horse. They caught us exposed at harvest time in our fields, and they drove our women and children out like sheep."

"The cowards," said Lud.

"So here we are now, as you see. They took everything."

"I grieve to hear of your troubles. We ourselves are sorely pressed by want, and the demands of the bishopric, and shall keep good watch."

The old knight waved an arm graciously, not unlike Dietrich would have, and Lud saw how he was mannered, a man once used to a higher station and much finer times.

"Will you take meat with us?'

"We must finish the circuit, as I am steward."

"And a fine one, while it lasts. I wish you better luck than mine. Let us pray for a new day."

"Prayer will not change the day," said Lud.

The old knight said, "They say hope makes a good breakfast but a bad dinner. The faithful never despair."

"Farewell, sir."

"Farewell, friend."

Lud remounted Ox, and he and Waldo rode off back toward Giebel, and his mind was stuck in one thought...

Dietrich was my master, sir, not my father...

I thought I knew different...we served well together...

Witter

Witter woke in a sweat not knowing where he was. Nor who he was. He woke disembodied, and only knew he had done something evil, so wrong that it had turned him inside out. This woke him with a twist of pain.

He was in the Marienberg. He was safe. His body was safe here. The fortress walled out the world of want and troubles. But inside him, that was what was wrong.

He woke and remembered laughing and riding his horse and then he remembered what he had done.

Philosophies, intellect, all the books he had read, all the languages that he knew, all his righteous indignation of the persecuted Jew, now they all meant nothing.

He was just another animal.

He had attacked men with his beast, his horse, he had ridden them down and laughed and the crowd had cheered and he had loved doing it. He loved their screams and the sense of their fear and nothing could ever change that now.

Help me, Father…

There was no answer; he was alone.

Father, please…that was not me…

In the dark chamber, alone, Witter bent over and clutched his face and wept.

But no pain came out of him, only tears.

The next day, he left the horse in the Marienberg stables, and he walked out of the fortress and down the long winding hill road, and across the bridge, and into the city. Soon, he stood in the alley that divided Wurzburg from its Jewish Quarter, and he stood at the double-door gate that was open for the day.

He thought of how it might feel again, inside a synagogue. Whether he would feel whole again somehow, whether the mystery still would accept him. How many times had he heard the chanted words. He tried to recall them now…to piece them back together in his mind…

Within these walls we sit surrounded by numberless generations.

Our ancestors built the synagogue as a visible sign of God's presence in their midst.

Throughout our long history, our endless wanderings, it has endured, a beacon of truth, love, and justice for humanity.

Its presence guided our ancestors to lives of righteousness, holding up to them a vision of their truest selves.

In our turn, come we into this sanctuary to affirm the sacredness of our lives.

May we enter this place in peace.

May holiness wrap around us as we cross the threshold.

He could see inside through the gates. There was a market square like a miniature one of the big square at the cathedral. There was a synagogue.

Weariness, doubt, the flaws within our hearts, the harshness of the week—let these drop away at the door. Let peace settle upon us…

Some bearded Jews came out and he saw them glancing nervously at him, and heard them speaking in Yiddish, obviously believing he could not possibly understand them. Hebrew was spoken in the temples and studied in the Torah and other sacred writings and learned essays. But in the street, Yiddish was overtaking Hebrew as the fashion among German Jews, for no gentile could understand any of it when rapidly spoken.

"What, another goy from the bishopric? He wears that cloth."

"So greedy. When will they leave us alone?"

"When we have no more to lend and they burn us instead of paying up."

"Wait, he is going through the gate."

Witter entered the inner world of the quarter and it was like heaven—the old familiar smells of the righteous food cooking, the calls of mothers to children in Hebrew, but some in Yiddish now, for the ancient language was becoming as corrupted as the land in which it struggled to survive.

A rabbi crossed the square and Witter followed him. People stared and some called to the rabbi and the rabbi was the one he had seen before, with long curls and beard and the long sallow face with rich dark eyes. The rabbi turned. Witter almost ran into him. The rabbi's eyes searched his and Witter was suddenly, unexpectedly, afraid.

"May I assist you, sir?"

"I want…" fumbled Witter.

"What is it you need?"

"To talk." Witter said this in Yiddish. The rabbi's eyes narrowed in surprise. And suspicion.

"To me?"

"Yes, please. At your synagogue."

"I am afraid that would be impossible." The rabbi smiled nervously. "But you are welcome at my home. It is quite near."

Witter followed the rabbi past many more staring people. When they passed together, people stopped talking, people stopped working, children stopped playing. The rabbi moved bent over, as if humbling himself to everyone they passed in the street.

Finally, they entered an alcove and climbed clay tile stairs and came out on a small terrace. Witter could see over the roofs of tile, and the cathedral spire and the Marienberg were shapes against the sun, throwing massive shadows everywhere.

A very beautiful young girl in modest clothing dropped her eyes when she saw them enter. Witter knew not to stare at her. But something about her face sent him reeling back in time, like everything else here seemed to do. Then he realized—she had deep lovely eyes like Bianca's, his betrothed, dead long ago. Witter stood there, stunned, and the voice of the rabbi brought him back.

"Will you sit and rest yourself in this humble place?"

They both sat in wicker chairs. The silent girl brought slices of apple. She bowed to her father and withdrew.

"Thank you," Witter said, wondering what to say.

"I do not lend money," said the rabbi. There was a sobering fear in his face. He struggled, it was obvious, for his rightful dignity. "I am Rabbi Levant. Ask anyone. I have nothing to lend. So, I do not lend money."

"Money?" said Witter, speaking now in Hebrew.

The Rabbi raised his brow and blinked in surprise.

"You speak Hebrew, yet you are dressed in Marienberg style and color. Did you not come to borrow money?"

"No."

"Then why are you here?"

"Why am I here?'

"Without guile, speak. What do you wish from me?"

Witter put his head in his hands and tried to think. Why was he truly here?

What words would say it? What was this all about? Then, he heard himself speak, almost without thinking.

"I almost killed two men, so that strangers would praise me. I do not know what is happening to me."

"Who were these men? Jews?"

"City men. It does not matter who they were. They were the kind of men I have long feared."

The rabbi stared. "What do you think is happening to you?"

"My truest self is gone, I have no peace."

"Many have no peace in these times."

"Please, listen. I am losing my soul," said Witter. "Perhaps it is already too late. Very likely, too late."

"You are losing your soul?"

"I no longer know who I am, Rabbi. Help me, please."

The rabbi shook his head and looked across the rooftops at the cathedral and pointed to the spires.

"Very well, sir, I will help you. You see there, your cathedral. Go and confess and the priests will take care of you. I cannot help you."

"But…I am a Jew."

There—Witter had said it. He expected the rabbi to open his arms and hug him and to weep with him as a prodigal son returned home. It had taken an enormous amount of courage, but he had said it.

"I am a Jew," he said again, to be sure he had said it.

The rabbi narrowed his eyes. "Who sent you? I told you, I do not lend money. I am a man of little means, devoted to study. And I must tell you: we are bled dry here. So many have come to borrow, because they know they can extort with fear and not pay. But you cannot drive blood from stones. Have a little mercy upon us."

"Please, believe me. You do not believe I am a Jew?" Witter said, this time in Yiddish. "Can you not see one of your own?"

"So you are a linguist. You are wasting your tricks upon a poor man, sir. I promise you, we do not break the law by accepting renegade Jews here. We obey your decrees to the letter."

"Why do you not leave?" said Witter.

"Leave? Would that be your answer?"

It has always been my answer, thought Witter.

"This is our home," said the rabbi.

"What of Jerusalem? The Ottomans welcome Jews, is that not so?"

"You insist upon this little test to trick and trap me and then testify against me, but why? You know well enough that the bishop has said if we leave we go naked, with nothing but our clothes. And we would never pass through those lands and live to see Jerusalem. If we are not of value, we die."

Now Witter became angry. He stood. He could not help himself. He looked about them and into the hallway and saw no one watching. The girl was nowhere about.

They were alone.

"See for yourself," said Witter.

He opened his tights and revealed his groin. Still, the rabbi was unconvinced.

"Very sly. Your parents had the good sense to do that for you, to reduce disease, and they must have been well educated. But it proves nothing to me."

Witter had not wanted to use his father's name, but now he felt he had no choice. He was here, and he needed to kneel and pray and be saved from the terrible man he was becoming. He needed to be told who he should be.

"My father was Judah of Córdoba. Perhaps you have read his works."

The rabbi jerked back and hissed between his set teeth.

"You are caught in your own lies. Judah of Córdoba was burned with all his family many years ago. You should have picked a lesser name for your story."

"I am his son. I was not burned."

Now the rabbi was even more visibly angry.

"You are Judah of Córdoba's son and you were not burned when all the righteous there were herded into the synagogue and all burned together. I see. And you live in the Marienberg and you wear the cloth of their power and their Christ, and you come here to taunt a poor man and frighten him for credit that you never intend to repay."

"No, please, I only wish to talk."

Witter went down to his knees and begged.

"I beseech you, Rabbi, open your heart, help me."

The rabbi shrank back, looking down at him in fear and rebuke, and yet, with a miserable kind of compassionate pity.

"Get up from there. You say you have lost your soul. Now I believe you. You have learned Hebrew from a book or a prisoner and you defame a great man."

"Why will you not believe me?"

"The only way you would not be burned would be to convert, and no son of that great scholar would do so. That is how I know you cannot be him. And I beg of you again, please leave. I have so little. But I will give you what little I have."

The rabbi was pulling a little meager coin purse from his cloak and Witter shoved him back. The rabbi fell backward, his knee striking the balcony stones, and he shouted in pain. His beautiful daughter came running out, her Bianca eyes twisted in fear for her father.

"Please," said Witter. "I am not a bad man!"

The rabbi threw himself in front of the girl protectively, as if Witter might attack her on the spot.

"Why must you despise us?" she cried, begging.

"Oh dear God," said Witter. "Oh my dear God."

"Rachael is only a child, please do not touch her," said the rabbi, and threw the purse of coin at him. "That is all I have, please take it!"

Witter ran.

He ran down the narrow stairs and fell once on the way down and tumbled and caught himself, and then he was out into the sun, past wide-eyed people, and he ran and ran.

In the alleyway outside the gates the horse waited nervously, and some children ran away, but not far.

Please my Father, I am going mad…

But there was no inner answer, no voice of Judah, only the sounds of human life all around.

Witter's horse kicked when Witter reached him and Witter, abashed and distracted, tried too abruptly to mount. He had forgotten to first free the reins from the iron ring in the wall. The watching children began laughing.

He was sobbing, Witter realized with horror. The horse reared and jerked back, tangling its reins, before Witter tore the reins free and rode away like his ass was on fire.

Konrad

At the Marienberg, a wind blew in the stone casements bearing damp river air and the faint stench of the city below, and heavy curtains were drawn. Konrad was a breakfast guest of the bishop. Florian was there close to Lorenz, as Konrad expected. Lorenz was in a high mood, expecting Luther's visit. Konrad's mood was exactly opposite.

"It is a mistake," insisted Konrad, "not arresting priests like Muntzer. We must make dire examples to warn the public. Inviting Luther is another bad idea, I say."

Lorenz sucked a semi-boiled egg from its shell, with noisy relish. Then he sucked his teeth and regarded Konrad evenly.

"You have control of the city. I have granted you my support in your secular duties, but mine is the Church. Martin Luther is a man of the future, and I will not have my mood spoiled with petty offensive debate."

"Petty? They rouse the scum and praise the rabble. I have forbidden public assemblies to preserve order."

Florian spoke, but quietly, "Your grace, public assembly is one of the most ancient and revered freedoms."

Konrad could hardly believe his ears.

"Did you say something?" said Konrad, with a cutting stare at Florian. He had heard perfectly well, and did not wish to correct the young man's impudence here at the bishop's table, where it would sting too deeply.

"Do not spoil breakfast with ugliness," said Lorenz. "Besides, when Muntzer preached, it was your magistrates who ran away."

"That will never happen again." Konrad felt chagrin at this truth. He turned his attention toward Florian. "Are you rested from your journey? Ready to start in on state business?"

"I have not been asked, your grace," said Florian.

"All in good time," said Lorenz. "Let us get our bearings first, and know who we are. Yes? In here, all is quiet and in order. Let us enjoy our peaceful time together."

Konrad carefully observed Florian while they ate dainty spiced meats and sweetbreads, which Florian picked at, his eyes cautious and watchful, especially of the bishop's every word and glance.

"So, young Florian, did our young Oxford sage enjoy the jousts in Britain? How do they compare to our good German men and horse?"

"Indeed, tell us all," said Lorenz.

Said Florian, "I do not spend the money of our estate in jousting, nor have I ever attended a joust, in all my memory. My father did not believe in jousting, either. Too much money is spent upon expensive horses and weapons and armor and fashion, money that is bled from the villeins. How can they not resent seeing a lord in livery when their child bawls from an empty belly?"

"I would rather hear of Erasmus," said Lorenz, "than a child bawling and such things."

Konrad saw an opening. "Florian, young man, you seem to adore your villeins almost as dearly as your father, my great friend, Dietrich, did. But he was sick of them. He told me he intended to make changes to the Geyer estate, bring strictness back, raise production of crops, and rebuild the castle."

"He never wrote me such, sir."

"I want to help you succeed. I promised Dietrich and I have promised God."

"And I sincerely thank you, as godson. And I know you would never speak other than pure truth."

"Here is the truth you must now heed. Throughout Swabia, all princes agree, and the estates are now demanding rent from their tenants, not shares, and this proves to work well to pay their taxes."

"Well for them," said Florian. "But I will never do this on the Geyer estate. It creates enormous resentment among the tenants. They are crushed under an enormous burden of debt, and when men lose hope, they become dangerous."

Konrad sat up and tried to command authority here. Such ideas were an outrage.

"Who is concerned about the feelings of villeins? They neither own the land nor have rights to it. We too are crushed under an enormous burden of debt. What do you suggest we do? Give up? Give the people to anarchy and ruin and surrender to Lucifer and the Turks?"

Lorenz cleared his throat and lifted his hands for calm.

"Have you heard of Jubilee?" he said softly.

Konrad remembered something vaguely. "Jubilee? Is that a feast, a Hebrew celebration of the Old Testament perhaps? I am not sure."

Lorenz sucked his teeth and smiled beatifically. It was the superior manner the bishop affected that Konrad despised the most.

"Every fifty years," said Lorenz, "all debt was forgiven. All mortgages absolved. And all were the same. All were equal and could start again afresh as equals. This would rid all debts and all pressures would end, and it is the way Christ would have guided us with his command of the beatitudes."

Konrad was appalled. He laughed.

"Dear bishop, are you jesting? If so, good; I am laughing. Please tell me you are in jest."

"Dear prince, I am in good earnest, with good will."

Konrad stood. He could not help himself. This was impossible. "Our powers would collapse, our nobility would cease, all would be in common, all would be common."

"And all the want and troubles of all Swabia would end with a stroke of a pen." Now Lorenz looked at Florian, who had yet not spoken. "What does our youngest noble here think of such a plan, I wonder?"

"Shall I speak freely?" said Florian.

"Would I ask otherwise?"

Said Florian, "My bishop, Jubilee is a brilliant possibility, and in its essence of forgiveness, so lovingly Christian. The people would revive."

Konrad had had enough.

"Jubilee is Jewish, not Christian."

"Our Christ was a Jew," said Lorenz.

"May God bless you both. But hear me. Florian, you are my godson, not a lapdog. What will you do on your estate? Give it all away to the tenants? We forgive the exuberance of the young, but that is dangerous talk from anyone. And dear Lorenz, you, my fellow prince, you are bishop, not Saint Lorenz. Or do you wish that on your tomb?"

Lorenz looked at Florian, and said, "Give him his answer, young sir. I want to hear your true mind."

Konrad glared through his smile, staring at Florian, trying to send him a message of minds, a threat.

"One nation," said Florian, "and all its inhabitants being brethren, one God, one law for everybody, rich or poor, such is my longing."

"That would be our end," said Konrad.

"Or our true beginning," said Lorenz. "All men walking in the same light, together, as one."

Konrad shook his head and made his excuses to leave.

When you argue with fools, you are the fool...

Konrad decided he must hold off on the commission, for now. If Florian was testing the waters, he was wiser and more cunning than his father, by ten lifetimes, using noble and radical sentiments to seem one thing while plotting to climb the ladder.

And that night, deep in prayer, God spoke, and Konrad realized he may have underestimated the young man, and that Florian may indeed have a very bright and useful future, if he could be well harnessed.

Send me a sign, to serve Thee best, O Lord...

And the sign did come, not long after that.

The very next week, at breakfast in Konrad's town mansion, Lorenz was abuzz with certain news.

"We shall have a visitor, a young monk, a professor of philosophy at Wittenberg University, whom I want to meet. He visits Wurzburg University, and I have been invited to meet him."

"A monk of what order?"

"Augustinian. We have read his broadsheets from Wittenberg. He is becoming somewhat popular. Listen well to us so that later you can help me discuss that which we recall. Your man and my monk recording. It should be interesting, for I have read Luther's broadsheets from Wittenberg. He is quite the forward thinker. Your thoughts are much congruent to his."

It galled Konrad that the city, not only Lorenz, was all abuzz with the celebrity reformer priest's visit. But Veritas Press announced it first.

Basil reported: "We did impress a very negative cant to the coming visit by an upstart cleric, a professor of theology, grabbing for fame by denouncing the Holy Mother Church that trained and educated him. But these broadsheets did not sell. Hardly a one."

Konrad moaned. "Shut out by the publicity of Martin Luther. We must learn from him."

It had been truly a slap in the face. Konrad vowed never to forgive the people for embracing such a vile upstart.

When Luther arrived in a modest carriage, with an armed cavalry escort of Saxony, the city turned out to cheer.

The meeting was the same day, in the greeting room of the cathedral, not the Marienberg Fortress, which was a sign of the way Lorenz wished to acknowledge Luther—religiously, not politically.

Konrad noted that Lorenz sat Florian at his right hand for the meeting, no doubt to impress their guest, a thick-faced young priest whose name Konrad associated with law.

"Is your father not advocating at law in Wittenberg?" asked Konrad.

"Indeed he is," said Luther.

Konrad saw an opening. "I am recalling a case there, of some great fortune in dispute by heirs and creditors, some greedy Jews who were found against by the court. The noble's defender had your name, Luther."

Luther took the attack in stride. He even smiled.

"I, too, studied law. At the University of Erfurt—a beer hall and whorehouse, more than a place of learning. My father had shares in copper mines and wanted to raise me above his station. Law seemed empty to me, the vain decisions of men, not the sacred trust of new ideas and faith, but I tried to honor my father's wishes."

"A good son will always do so," said Konrad, seeing a weak point to strike upon.

"There is reason," said Luther, "and there is intuition. One day I was riding home with two dear friends and a thunderstorm came with great lightning, and my friends were struck down, and I fell from my horse to my knees and begged God, I swore to Saint Ann, I promised to become a monk if I was spared. My father was furious, saying all his money had been wasted on my studies. But I knew my destiny then was with knowledge, with the Church, with the liberation of minds. Between reason and intuition of God, I shall and must choose intuition."

Squirmy fellow, thought Konrad, *harder to catch than an eel...*

"A true man of God," Lorenz said. "Liberate the mind and the soul must follow. That is the future."

Luther looked at Bishop Lorenz, and bowed gracefully. "I knew you would understand, your grace, for even in Wittenberg, so far away, we have heard of the wisdom of your court, to let men change as God wills change."

"Change is natural, as rivers flow," said Lorenz.

"Violent change?" said Konrad.

"Indeed not," said Luther. "God gives nobles their rank, and crowns their kings."

Florian said, "And men who learn to read, what of their struggle with so many new realizations?"

"God gives men minds for reasoning. That is good. But if villeins should ever take arms and rise in evil violence against the Holy

Church and the rightful law of the state, it is the sacred duty of the princes, to chase them down and destroy them without mercy, like wild beasts gone mad."

Konrad was surprised, and pleased.

Now I know you, he thought.

"What of Jews?" said Konrad, pressing further.

Luther shrugged. "If Jews convert, I wish them well, for they are Christians, they are good. If Jews do not convert, they must be rooted out of the body of the people like disease or vermin, and eradicated. They are too wealthy to be honest and too many good Christians are in debt to them."

"I would not judge them so harshly," said Lorenz. "They work hard and almost never violate the law."

"They keep their own secret language and only value property," Konrad said.

"Too harsh," said Lorenz.

Konrad looked at Luther for comment.

"In disbelief, your grace, the Jews do judge themselves," said Luther. "Theirs is a false and blasphemous intuition."

Konrad smiled despite himself. Lorenz looked disappointed. But Konrad now knew Luther was on the side of the state. Perhaps he was radical in church beliefs, no matter. He was a creature of the order of power.

Obviously, with things going bad everywhere, Luther was traveling from court to court to save his skin. To set the record straight as to his loyalty. Luther was ambitious and he supported the princes and all nobility.

Later that day, Konrad met Basil at Veritas.

"There will be no accidents to befall Luther."

"Why have you changed your mind? People read his broadsheets and they line the streets to cheer him. What of our duty to God?"

"It seems now he is worth to us more alive."

"But surely we planned it without flaw?"

"Never mind that. Luther is not the fool I expected him to be. He has made it clear he is on the right side of things."

"Praise the Blessed Mother. It is a miracle, surely."

"No miracle. He is a man with the fears of a man. Luther has made himself safe, joining our side, and we shall leave him go in peace to support us during the storm that is surely coming on."

Konrad knew God had His almighty hand in this. For following quickly upon Luther's visit, another marvelous thing happened.

Florian came to present himself at the town mansion, and without the usual polite chatter—he was so direct, so much like his father, Dietrich—asked for a commission in the Landsknechts. It was as if God had handed Florian to him as one buys a new pet dog to train for war.

Said Florian, "Your grace, with the emperor's army away in Spain, fighting the French king, Swabia is vulnerable. It is your recruitment of new companies to guard our home that has compelled me."

"Compelled you? How so, Florian?"

"During deep prayer," said Florian, "I remembered my loyalty to you, my godfather, as my father, your friend, would have wished. I searched my soul, wondering, how best for you to use me? Then I knew what I must ask. A commission as officer in your Landsknechts."

Florian looked quite sincere. Konrad was surprised, and he smiled in confusion at Florian's request. What trick was this? Had this youth hatched a plan to advance himself?

"Landsknechts?" probed Konrad carefully. "What of all your liberal talk of men as brothers and all such liberal screed? I thought you would go serve Lorenz as a man of the church."

"I realize, your grace, that I am not fit for holy work."

Konrad felt the excitement of unexpected gifts.

"Did Luther's visit discourage you?" he asked hopefully. "I was not much impressed."

"Indeed, he angles for influence, your grace. He was not the man I expected."

"Nor I," said Konrad. "So you want to learn to command my troops in the field, is that your desire?"

Florian took a respectful tone.

"Exactly, your grace. I have studied the theories of command and troop movements, and all the classic battles of history. It is my godfather whom I do wish most earnestly to serve. I am a knight, as was my father, and I carry his sword, and would begin as an officer of cavalry and rise from there."

Konrad felt a consuming glow of pride. He had Florian. He owned him now. This young man was bright and clever. He saw who would rule, perhaps sooner than later, and he was keen to come under Konrad's wing.

He stared hard at Florian. "It does make perfect sense. You need funds for your mother and estate, and a commission pays a good wage, and in war, a bonus for each field victory. And it is a step on the ladder that all young nobles wish to climb, especially low-rankers like Florian Geyer, son of Dietrich. Your father was highly respected, but he died a low-ranker all the same. That was his pride. His strange admiration of the lower classes, and the permissiveness at the Geyer estate, even letting the lower classes share the forests and fields."

"And yet, your grace, you have told me he changed?"

"Before his last campaign, yes, in the end he did change. He saw that nobles must lead, as God wills us to. Our burden is to bring order and light to the darkness of the commoners, and their resistance is proof of their abysmal ignorance. And I am glad to assist the son of your father, whom I dearly loved."

Florian had his eyes down and said nothing. Konrad sensed he had pushed too hard. Time to finish up. He was enjoying gloating but enough was enough.

"If I commission you in Landsknechts as an officer, Florian, you will be a professional, serving with mercenaries, and they are hard soldiers. You will need to learn fast, and when you give commands to your men, you will need toughness and no mercy in the order of discipline."

Said Florian, "To serve is all I ask, your grace. Landsknecht formations are the new way of fighting, formations of gun and pike. That is the future of war."

Konrad felt a warm satisfaction filling him like fine wine. The youth was sincere. He was yielding himself and ready to be used.

"You are my godson. I cannot refuse you."

"Use me as you will, your grace."

"Come and kneel and kiss my hand."

This was life felt deep and wide, to have the son of Dietrich and Anna bent down upon his knees. Florian came and knelt and kissed his hand, and Konrad felt he might almost swoon with pleasure.

Witter

Witter had been brought by a servant to Florian's quarters in the bishopric towers of Marienberg, and now he was helping Florian pack his traveling kit. There were many new clothes of expensive tailoring, gifts from Lorenz and Konrad both, and Florian tossed the old clothing aside for Witter to keep. Florian was raging in a quiet fierce voice almost too quiet to hear.

"He lies to me," said Florian. "Saying my father's conscience toward men was changed, before he could share it with me. Konrad is an evil man, Witter. The worst kind, an arrogant man with a sharp brain, and the belief that God directs his hand. I fear for the people."

Witter was astonished by this news of Florian's commission. His mind raced to find his own place in such news.

"Shall I travel with you as manservant?"

"No. Just listen to me, Witter."

Florian was angry, his face red, telling his story.

"Konrad tells me that I shall learn to lead men in battle, and make my name, and send money home to my mother. Work hard and rise. Show that I can be hard and loyal. It seems my low-ranker father, Dietrich, was Konrad's favorite cousin—if endearingly strange in his taste in books, and in people, but Konrad insists he and my father were close, very close, always."

Florian hacked and spit as if ejecting poison.

Witter was silent, careful when Florian was this way. So strangely like Lud. Men who were willing to act were never to be provoked when they were trying to control themselves.

"I knelt and kissed his hand so basely like some mewing cringer. Yes, the hand of one so eager to steal my heritage and my father's estate. I shall bide my time, I shall learn, and someday I shall amply repay Konrad's loathsome generosity."

Said Witter, "I saw your father in Heck's bookstore several times. He had excellent taste in reading. Once he was there with Lud, too, after they returned from the border war to the southeast."

"Things must change," said Florian, waving his arms as if wishing for a fight. "I swear it, things must change. My father sent me to be educated in philosophies of change. Of the rights of all men. And I am his son."

"So, do I now return to Giebel?" said Witter, thinking already of seeing Kristina again.

Florian stopped and blinked and looked at him.

"No, I will be issued everything else in arms, when I report to the officer's barracks, and then I shall be away in the field. You cannot return home no matter how you wish it. I have work for you here."

"Were you forced to do this?" asked Witter.

"Just the opposite. I angled for it. Having studied all orders and histories of battle, away at Ox, now real duty is what I need, to learn the line command of massed infantry and the movements of cavalry. There is a new way of war, the gunpowder way of foot soldiers, and much for me to learn. Someday I may need to use it well."

"To what purpose?"

Not answering Witter's question, Florian said, "I cannot take you with me to the Landsknechts, as I am training with cavalry for mass assaults and will be much in the field. Use my quarters at the Marienberg, and keep watch on the unrest in the city guilds and in the actions of Konrad, and send me letters through the Marienberg couriers, but do not express yourself too directly. Write as if Konrad were your hero. But give the gist. I will hear too many rumors in the field."

"May I not return to Giebel just each week or two?"

"No. Do as I said. Kristina can wait for you."

"Kristina is not mine to wait." Witter felt a flush of longing, and embarrassment.

"Pity, then," said Florian, hefting his sword and sash. "I saw how you watched her. I thought she was. But then, poor Lud looks at her the same. I leave you some of my signing bonus so you can buy a woman here if you must quench the fire. Find a tavern girl, not one of the street."

"That is not… something I do."

"Many say that," said Florian, with a grin that further embarrassed Witter. "But you must stay and send reports until I return."

"Reports of what, exactly?"

"Everything of change. High and low. To Konrad, I said, someday I would repay his generosity. And I shall. Oh yes, Witter, how well I shall repay it."

"I do not understand."

"You will, one day. Until then, I shall train hard as an officer and learn the arts of mass warfare. While I serve and learn, and earn, you shall observe here. Cleverly disguise your meanings, and communicate in letters to me everything that happens here."

So as footman, not on his horse, Witter attended Florian's departure. With other footmen he walked beside his master's mount until they reached the great Marienberg parade ground, then the officers rode away and left their footmen at the crowd barrier where half the city was gathered for the show.

Witter watched Florian ride out into quick formation with the other officers on horse, the hooves chopping up the groomed green turf. Their silvery armor flashed in the sun, and he thought of the poor knights who were sometimes seen on the road in their old black iron armor, rust-stained with rotting leather hinges.

Florian now wore a polished silver helmet with lifted visor, with the short red plume of a mid-level officer. Florian was outfitted in the Marienberg livery, to receive the Swabian League's commission from Prince Konrad. This was a military event and Witter marked that Bishop Lorenz, the renowned peacemaker, had not attended.

Witter stood and watched the commissioning ceremony. Bugles and fifes and drums kept an aggressive beat that encouraged a lighthearted sense of war. Nobles and clerics sat with Konrad up in the guarded grandstand, some of the ladies waving ribbons. Witter wondered how many of these celebrants had ever seen real war.

The cavalry on horse turned and moved in one perfect line and raised their sabers to salute Konrad. Footmen raised plumed pikes in salute.

Hundreds of red-uniformed men in black hats, four ranks wide, fired muskets in a single volley, with one officer on horse and his saber held high. The thunder echoed away into the sky. Strings of blue smoke billowed into a single monstrous cloud. Officers rode out from under the cloud and passed not far from Witter. He saw that one was Ulrich, the earless professional soldier, from the street with Frieda.

A great cannonade went off and Witter cheered with the rest. He hated all these people.

They were the violent ones who had driven the peaceful from their homes, burned them, tortured them; they were the ones who made all their own rules and took whatever they wanted, and did it all in utmost piety. They were the ones who hated yet who believed themselves blessed of God, righteous, and just. They were sleek and plump and fashionable, guarded by hard cruel men, and Witter hated their parade of might and their outrageous, pompous celebration of mass murder.

He imagined Samson pulling down the temple upon the tormenting Philistines, and he would have pulled down the sky upon all this parade, along with himself, if he had had the power. And he knew that his father would have wept with disappointment at so much hate poisoning Witter's soul, but Witter no longer heard Judah's voice these days.

Florian rode magnificently on a lively black gelding in his finery of war, the metal flashing, and Witter saw in his posture and lifted head pride and arrogance that could not be theater.

The humility of the self-seeking student was gone. Witter felt a shudder of loathing, now even for Florian.

He tried to remember why he had admired Florian, why Florian said he was doing this...

There is a new way of war, the gunpowder way of foot soldiers, and much for me to learn. Someday I may need to use it well...

Witter shrank back into the crowd that watched the cavalry parade and prance, and then, ahead of hundreds of marching musket infantry, Florian rode away to a command with the Fifth Landsknechts.

That had been a month before, and now on a bright and beautiful sunny day, the great Wurzburg cathedral bells tolled and word spread that Lorenz was dead, and that Prince Konrad von Thungen was now bishop.

Broadsheets from Veritas Press were given away free in the square and free ale flowed, by grace of the new Bishop Konrad. The broadsheets told of his love of the people and how a new age had come—one of prosperity and justice for all men true to the church-state.

Drunks muttered in the taverns about poison and some said it was the sweating sickness from England.

Citizens with city positions said they were glad to have Konrad now, instead of the weak Lorenz, that maybe the radical miners and farmers and students would be brought to hell. Fights broke out between the two sides, those with everything to lose and those with nothing to lose.

Witter wrote Florian of such things, and wrote with such sarcasm, such glowing praise of Konrad, that the opposite, the truth would be understood.

The greatest difference was announced in a Veritas broadsheet:

No more shall bishopric and state be separate powers of rule, no more shall Church and magistrate work apart. The old faulty way is done. Our new Church and state, conjoined under our Prince-Bishop Konrad, shall be one mighty power for the perseveration of God's good for all...

The impact was felt everywhere, and the change in the pressures of authority was immediate. The city guilds and the city councilmen protested the arrests of some of their representatives who petitioned for equal voting rights with the members of the Swabian

League. In the markets and alleys people sang street songs of equality over injustice.

Violence was in the air. It was like the time the stone had hit the dog and the crowd had rushed the magistrates. The people were taxed and indebted and hungry and jobless and angry; carriages of the wealthy had been stoned, harnesses cut; and things needed only the right spark to set them off.

Witter wrote all this in clever sarcasm to Florian, as if appalled at the lack of respect for the church and state.

He bundled broadsheets to send Florian, those from Veritas as well as from reformers. Some reformist sermons, especially of Muntzer, were seized and burned and their hawkers arrested. Witter saw arrests of broadsheet sellers who hawked ideas and stories opposed to those of Veritas Press. Veritas spread broadsheets warning that the evil Turks were watching and waiting to pounce if the people grew soft and weak. Witter sent everything relevant.

There was a new series featuring Mahmed, "the Evil Peacock," and his alleged confessions of Ottoman atrocities against Christians, followed by essays demanding new wars against the Turks, titled "Attack to Defend!"

The last traces, of the golden era of liberalism under Lorenz vanished. Reformers spoke and published at their own peril. Burnings and quarterings, mostly of heretics and political prisoners—those who gave out broadsheets or otherwise denounced the injustices of Konrad's bishopric rule—became a common public entertainment. It seemed that drownings, hangings, and beheadings were now routine for the common criminals. The number of magistrate patrols doubled, then tripled.

When Witter wrote of all this, disguising his meanings in letters to Florian, he often thought of the day of the commission parade, and he hoped that Florian had not changed his heart, his mind, his soul.

Witter was wary always, but he still came and went with the perfect impunity of a ward of the Marienberg. Wherever he went in the city, increasingly he was resented and even feared when he presented his pass coin for identification to a magistrate patrol, or when his Marienberg horse mark and saddle were seen.

Witter's world had completed its turn upside down. He played the role of the enemy he had always feared, and despite all that, he loved it. It was a wonderful time in his life, because he was free.

He went where he wished, when he wished.

Gathering up his courage one night, he went to the orchestra theater and took a private box. He sat and drank wine, and through the curtains he watched as a painted-up series of prancers and dancers hoofed their way through tired routines, some of them yawning. And then Frieda appeared.

She was announced by a fat, little man waving jeweled rings that dazzled on every finger: "The Enchanting Paulina!"

The crowd of sporting men came alive.

Spellbound, Witter watched Frieda perform on the little lantern-lit stage, dolled up in her frills and paint. Two pretty child novelty musicians, one girl with violin and another girl with lute, played the melodies. They played like marionettes in some tragic Greek farce, dancing in Hades.

Frieda knew all the popular French love songs, translated into German. No songs of protest were sung here, nor street songs. Only romantic songs with catchy melodies, of love and submission, all of them basically the same: a woman faithfully grieving for the loving arms of her dead husband, a fallen knight, a great hero...

Disdain, harshness without joy,
sad thoughts, deep sighs,
Great anguish locked in the weary heart...
Fierce bitterness borne secretly,
mournful expression or without joy,
dread which silences all hope,
are in me and never leave me;
And so I can neither be healed nor die..."

As Frieda sang, she danced coquettishly, and the sporting men and students cheered and jeered and shouted for her to bare her breasts.

Witter had wanted to be amused, but he felt incredibly sorry for her. He found himself indulging in a fantasy of taking her out the back way and rescuing her, riding her back to Giebel through the bridge and the forest, and of Kristina throwing her arms around him, loving him at last, respecting him at last, wanting him at last.

Then Frieda's songs were done and his whole ludicrous notion of rescue was like one of her sentimental ballads, or some fairy tale in some ridiculous broadsheet.

When the serving girl came with more wine, Witter sent for Frieda. A fat, little fop looked in at him and winked.

"We are honored to serve a bishopric man, good sir."

Frieda came with a tray of wine to present herself to his box. When she saw him, she blanched, and tried to back away, but he caught her and had to pull her by the hand to make her sit.

"Leave me alone," she said, "unless you pay. I have to give him the money."

At close range she looked bruised, yet still so pretty, with her brilliant blue eyes and blonde curls. Her face powder was streaked with beads of sweat from the stage lights and her song and dance routine. She looked at him fearfully, and yet there was a puzzling defiance about her.

"What has happened to you, Frieda? Tarted up for these louts? You are a fine, good, intelligent young woman."

"What has happened to you? In bishopric livery? Do not dare judge me. I know you. My time costs money. Pay me or go. I do not like you and never did."

So he gave her a coin. "Very well, here."

She put the coin through a slot in the wall, and pulled the box curtains shut. The noise was still all out there but now only the box lantern light illuminated them.

"What is your pleasure, Witter?"

Her little white hands lifted to her bosom and he realized she was opening her gown, her eyes steely as she looked at him the whole time, and he reached out to her hands to stop her. For a moment he felt her softness and jerked his hand back.

"Please do not. You embarrass us both."

"Then why are you here? To save me?"

"You make it sound ridiculous."

"You are quite ridiculous."

She laughed, making him feel like a fool. And yet it seemed that she laughed more at herself than at him. There were dark lines around her eyes for one so young, and he wondered what those eyes had seen.

"Then you came for my story, is that it, Witter? I know your kind. You want to feel superior and hear my sad little story? Then save me, put me in some room all to yourself, so you alone can have me whenever you want?"

"I do not want to use you, I swear it. What happened to you since that night when you jumped off the ferry and ran away from us?"

Frieda took up her goblet of wine and downed it all with her head thrown back. She nodded, swallowed, rolled her eyes, and, finally, began to tell her story; and as she told it, it poured out of her.

"God has cursed me. That is the truth. Men stare wherever I go. They call me beautiful. They want to touch me. They give me gifts. They offer me things. I ran from that ferry because you were all mad. And because I fear water so. I ran and I ran. For the next days I starved. But men in the streets kept calling to me, trying to talk me up, trying to fondle me, and many did. I prayed and I prayed, but merciful God—the same who let my Otty be killed—only sent me men wanting to be alone with me."

Frieda looked at the tray and took up Witter's goblet and drank it down, all of it.

"Not much good without the absinthe. But that is another story. One at a time. I sold my hair at a street stall and gorged myself on the one good meal that could buy. Then I had nothing more to sell. I starved two more days and I was fainting when a woman took me into her stall and then took me home and gave me ale and I woke with a man asleep with me. A filthy man. I saw my gown and got it and I ran from there. I wanted to die, and already I was hungry again. Where were you then, Witter? Where were any of you then?"

A serving maid interrupted with more wine.

"Absinthe," Frieda said to the girl, and she brought a small green flask and poured it into the wine. Frieda offered her goblet to Witter. He shook his head no.

"More for me," said Frieda. "God's love made liquid."

Witter knew the wormwood smell—he had first tried it years ago in Amsterdam, for escape, but it was the opposite of escape, and the next days had been the most unnerving of his life.

Frieda drank until it was gone. Her voice was more slurred now, and she trembled and smiled a little, and her trembling crooked smile made Witter inexplicably nauseated.

"God did not want me anymore. Only men did. I was abandoned. So I decided I would show Him. I was too afraid of the river to drown myself, so I was going to steal a cook knife from one of the market stalls, but when I went to the square, a man was being quartered, and his agony terrified me, so I could not force the knife into my skin. So now you understand."

Her eyes sought his, and he realized she needed him to understand something that he was actively resisting. He thought for something to say, some consoling words, but he kept seeing her former face, the once-clear eyes overlaid now with the hard eyes seeking his, and he felt too sickened.

Then she went on...

"My body was my curse. When I prayed I heard God laughing at me. And if you are fondled and bruised too many times, you begin to feel it less and less. So, the next lecher who spoke up to me, the little man with jeweled hands, I went with him and got a meal and learned to play the sweet thing. This is his orchestra theater, oh yes, the popular place, very popular. I sing for my supper. And I submit to base acts when I must. God has cursed me, he is a mean bastard, cruel, and deceitful. And he most certainly he is a man."

"God did not curse you, Frieda."

"Oh, I see, you know Him well. Have you read of what befell Kunvald? How Johannes and Rita were burned begging God to stop their pain? Once I dreamed of escaping back to Kunvald, but God has taken care of that for me, too."

"Let me help you somehow."

"Help by leaving. Your time is up. There is my sad story. Pathetic, because all the girls here have the same story, more or less. But lechers are worse fools, and we girls know that. Is a story all you came to buy tonight?"

"If only you had come with us on the ferry that night."

"Can you turn back time?"

Witter leaned away from her. Her eyes were hot and she seethed with loathing for him, he could see that. Her smile was bitter and she no longer looked pretty. There was madness in her face, and it frightened him.

"Come again if you dare," she said, "and I will tell who you really are, and I shall come laugh at the square when they brace you on the ladder and unreel your bowels and cut your tool off and quarter you."

After that night, Witter stuck to his mission of scouting events and reporting to Florian. Seeing Frieda had been like a nightmare. And he had caused it himself, out of this new hubris he had acquired in the city. With his Marienberg pass coin and his horse and his fine clothes, he had almost forgotten who he was.

Witter resolved to be more careful. He moved within his own cell of isolation. His father's voice was silent, still not speaking to him. And the world was becoming more dangerous with every week that passed.

More and more homeless came drifting through Wurzburg, and the bishop's magistrates formed special squads to round up the vagrants. Most were villeins who had fled their homes on the estates where there was not enough food. If a villein could last a year away from the estate without being caught and returned, he would be free, by law. So the magistrates made a tidy sum for the bishop by catching the fugitives, chaining them, and sending them back in chains to their estates for the bounty that the estates were bound to pay.

More big news was that the famed artist, Riemenschneider—who had sculpted the lavish marble tomb of Lorenz—was voted head of the city council. And it was widely known that the new bishop, Konrad, disliked Riemenschneider as much as the former bishop Lorenz had loved him. No more bishopric commissions came Riemenschneider's way. And the city council constantly petitioned Konrad for an equal vote in matters of taxes and levies, and was denied.

All this Witter dutifully reported by sealed letters to Florian, with the official mail carried by the Marienberg horse and supply couriers that came and went out to the training fields of the Landsknechts, as regular as clocks, from the fortress.

He had been doing this for three months when the next shattering news came to Wurzburg.

The emperor, Maximilian I, was dead of the sweating sickness. And his son, Maximilian II, known to hate Martin Luther and all liberal ideas, and to be a great friend of bishop Prince Konrad, was now emperor.

All of this bad news came flooding through Wurzburg. There was so much Witter could hardly keep up with it.

And then on a hot summer day in the square, he saw Old Klaus, the road peddler, hawking broadsheets in the square, and saw him arrested. The magistrates recognized Witter and let him look at the broadsheets from Old Klaus.

"I can read so this is my duty, sir, to weed out these that call for war and unrest against our good state," the magistrate captain said. "These peddlers get these papers for nothing from villages on the road and then make coins selling them here. We shall have him squealing in no time where he got them, you can be sure."

Witter flipped through the rumpled stack of broadsheets, many published by Veritas Press. When he turned them over, on the other side he saw all sizes and types of print, most crude and semi-literate. Then he came to one different from the rest. It was even cruder, printed with wood block letters obviously hand carved.

Its heading was "Christ Is Love, No Taxes for War!"

He read it and a chill ran through his spine, for he could almost hear Grit and Kristina speaking, and he knew this one came from Giebel. And yet it made him want to smile, seeing how they had used the hated Veritas Press paper to spread their own message, printed upon the blank sides.

A monk with the magistrate took it to read: "Rise Up, Christians, Take Arms and Throw Off the Yoke of Injustice!"

"I did not peddle those ones," said Old Klaus. "I can barely read and am a good patriot and former soldier, I am."

"He is right," said Witter to the monk and magistrates. "I saw another hawker handing those out. That bent fellow you have, he was just passing through the square. Look at the other side of the broadsheet, there is Veritas Press on that side."

"That is all I saw, good sirs," said Old Klaus.

"You wear Marienberg livery," said the monk.

"I serve the bishopric." Witter showed the monk and the confused magistrates the Marienberg pass coin. They bowed to it as they always did; not to him but to the cross of authority inscribed there on the metal piece.

"Our magistrates are fools," said the monk, in apology. "Only one out of twenty can read even a little, and a little knowledge is a dangerous thing."

The embarrassed magistrates released Old Klaus and the peddler stared at Witter, and Witter knew Old Klaus recognized him. Then Old Klaus went hurrying away.

"We cannot stop all such broadsheets and rallies," said the magistrate. "Times are changing and we do not have enough men to stop it all."

"Keep up the good work," said Witter, and rode away.

So it is coming...

Sooner or later there would be some kind of uprising, with all the horrific repression of one side or another.

He was riding back to the Marienberg through a gathering dusk, and remembered Mahmed's chess match. It had become an annual tradition that Konrad was carrying on, apparently. Witter had seen it posted in the bishopric stewardship office, outside on the notice boards there. And on impulse, he had scrawled his name, Witter Geyer, there on the list of other names. Twenty times since he wished he had not. But if he did not go now, it would perhaps be even worse than appearing there.

The square was busy with business of all kinds even at this afternoon hour. As if the world was never changing.

When he came to the festival stall he saw Mahmed in his peacock feathers looking as if he had aged a hundred years since last year's match. Dozens of spectators were crowded around the chess table and guards kept out the commoners who milled about outside the cordons. Witter waited more than an hour and was about to leave, when his name was called.

A guard led him through the press of people and then he sat across the little ornate chess table from Mahmed.

A monk announced, "Behold the Evil Peacock, as he threatens yet another good Christian, the sixth today. You see him much deflated from the time of Bishop Lorenz. In his wisdom, our Bishop Konrad has removed the Turk from his fine chamber and put him into a cell in the penal dungeon, as any other common killer or heretic deserves."

"Guest takes white," said Mahmed.

"*Inshallah,*" whispered Witter, so low he could not be certain Mahmed heard him. But he detected a flicker in the dark eyes, the face lowered but the eyes gazing suddenly up at him. And Mahmed said, "Indeed, God willing."

Witter opened with his queen's gambit, advancing the queen's pawn. Mahmed countered with a knight, and said, "Do not take God's name in vain."

"You cannot escape God," said Witter, moving another pawn in the Queen's gambit, "nor is there any other who can help or protect you."

Mahmed stared at him intensely.

"You have read this?"

"As it is written," said Witter.

He had read the Qur'an as a boy, along with the great books of all other major religions—those that had been translated—from the library of his father. And he knew that he was probably the only person in Wurzburg other than the Ottoman himself who knew that verse.

"When a servant thinks of me..." said Mahmed.

"I am near," said Witter, finishing the Qur'an verse.

Mahmed's eyes searched Witter's and Witter kept moving the pieces and said no more. Mahmed's game was as incisive as it was intuitive. Witter could think several moves ahead but it seemed to him that Mahmed saw the whole game, all. Within a dozen more moves Witter was forced to concede. The quickness of each loss was devastating.

"Brilliant," said Witter, with genuine admiration.

"Who are you?" said the Turk.

"That is a question all men struggle with. Call me Ibn Tufail. For like you, I was born as a blank slate."

His father had loved the works of Ibn Tufail, the famed Andalusian Islamic philosopher.

Mahmed blinked back at him, the deep dark eyes widening.

"You have read *Hayy Ibn Yaqzan*?"

Witter had said enough to rouse the curiosity of the Turk, and he dared say no more. People in the crowd were beginning to edge forward, seeing words being exchanged. He had used Ibn Tufail as bait for some future meeting, but how they would meet he knew not. The novel *Hayy Ibn Yaqzan* told a story of a feral child isolated on a desert island, his mind formed through experience alone. There was no original sin, only a wild soul, yet unmarked, to be formed by life itself.

A blank slate. A *tabula rasa.* Just as Witter was here, a blank slate imitating whatever was around him. Just as alien as Mahmed was, a stranger in a strange land. In that sense, they were brothers. Mahmed's eyes searched his. For a moment, suddenly, Witter did not feel alone.

The crier announced, "The Evil Peacock eviscerates another good Christian!"

"*Inshallah,*" Witter said, and left through the crowd.

"Wait," said Mahmed, "please..."

He looked back and saw Mahmed's eyes following him until the bodies of the crowd walled him away.

The rest of the day and into the night he could think of little else.

It had been liberating to sit with Mahmed and lock minds with him. And it was a desperate risk, worse than meeting Frieda, yet he had made contact with the Ottoman. He had no idea how or when he might meet him ever again. But he knew he would be remembered. Somehow, with no child of his own, with his family gone, with Kristina nowhere near, being remembered seemed very important now.

He had reached out to one as alien to this place as he was, and they had met minds, and none around them had seen anything other than a game of chess in which another Christian was humiliated by the Evil Peacock, the Turk whom all Wurzburg loved to hate.

A wild scheme was hatching in his brain. It was impossible and daring and no doubt suicidal. He would need to ponder it long and deeply, and gather more information, and he would need a remarkable and nearly impossible set of circumstances for it to have any chance to work.

Kristina

Linhoff and his comrades had argued bitterly for a broadsheet advocating armed revolution against all injustices, and Kristina resisted, but it was Grit who argued them down.

"Try honey before you try vinegar, my friends. What did your war bring you but pain and regret? Try our way now. And this time, we hand it out ourselves. We take it to Wurzburg. We shall take care, and not openly do it. We have learned from the past."

"I hope so," said Dolf.

Linhoff had given in and the others had grudgingly followed his lead. Kristina saw how he secretly watched Grit, that was too plain, and Linhoff wanted to take command of everything. It was as embarrassing for Grit as it was flattering.

"You warned me before, and now I worry for your safety," said Kristina.

"Something in me," said Grit, "reminds Linhoff of something he can never have. I know I am almost old enough to be his mother, but I do know how to handle men. Linhoff will find a willing girl, there are plenty who want him, right here in the village."

A full hard week was given to the printing, and they prayed and prepared for the journey to Wurzburg, to take their chances and hand out the broadsheets.

"This time we do it ourselves, as is right," said Grit.

"No choice," said Linhoff, "Old Klaus has not come this way since the last time."

Grit shook her head slowly. "We have used him many times. He has never failed to come for new broadsheets before now."

"I pray he was not taken," said Kristina.

"Yes," Dolf said.

Said Grit, "Do let us pray, for Old Klaus, and to beg for the sustain of our own steadfast faith."

The sun had been good, and the summer barley and rye—the grains of the lower classes—were up in the villeins strip sections, and in the estate sections the grapes blossomed and the wheat was coming well.

Kristina loved this time of year—the colors and the warm fragrances on the air and the birds and squirrels and rabbits and women with pregnant bellies from last winter's closeness in the snowbound huts. Crop and wildflowers were up and the fields blossomed everywhere. It was going to be a good, ripe year for all.

The children played in their gangs and Peter ran with them. The blackbirds and crows and pigeons all came in their great flocks to nest in the fruit trees. And Kristina prayed and grieved over what to do. Go with the others and risk death, or stay and be loyal to her child, who would be left behind in this world if she were to perish.

Lud was hardly speaking to her, and Witter was still gone and perhaps would never return.

Eight years had passed and there were still two full years in her bond pledge to serve Lady Anna. Yet her mother's love made her fear for her child ever stronger. She and her child were still safe here for now.

But all that was changing fast.

There was the afternoon when she came to the lady's chambers to brush out her hair for her bath, and what she saw stopped her cold.

Lady Anna had Peter on her lap. In his little hand was a fine little gilt toy dagger. Kristina was positively horrified.

"Only seven now, and so manly. Look how he pulls my veil down. He does not fear my face. Look how he kisses and hugs my neck. I shall dress him and teach him to read as you have taught me. He shall be my son when he is away from you. How can that hurt you or him? Let me be generous."

She did not know which way to turn. She could not leave Peter here. She could not take him with her. She could not abandon her brothers and sisters to go alone.

Dear Lord, help me, show me the true way...

Sometimes her mind ranged back, as if seeking answers yet unfound. Kristina remembered how she had been almost arrested, how Witter had saved her, how they had all run from the monk and his magistrates that day years ago.

In a dizzying rush now, here in this same L-shaped bedroom chamber, she remembered how Dietrich had died, his body tormented by pox, bathed in vinegar, his every breath a battle, and how he had commanded all to learn to read.

She thought how Lady Anna had almost died. Dietrich had died upon straw soaked in his blood, and apart from him, Lady Anna had suffered through and survived in her own straw, when there were no more linens left to comfort her.

"Now, Peter, show your mother," said Lady Anna.

"Show me?" said Kristina. Her mind returned to the present.

Peter laughed. He and Lady Anna traded smirks and Lady Anna winked and Kristina saw they had a secret. Kristina braced herself for whatever it might be. Through her child, the world was closing in upon her, its conflicts all converging.

Peter hopped off Lady Anna's lap and ran to the harp in the far corner, and Kristina moved to try to catch him, fearing he would smash the harp in his wildness.

"No," said Lady Anna, "let him have the harp."

Then, as if in balance to all she feared most, a miracle happened. God showed mercy, and more...

Peter stood behind the harp and waited, ready.

Lady Anna sang a little melody.

Peter played it exactly on the harp. His fingers plucked the strings, with an inerrant accuracy that Kristina knew comes only from a gift of God, at birth.

"Sing any melody," Lady Anna said to Kristina.

Her heart was pounding. She sang a hymn, the first measure of "God's Love the Greatest Gift to Man."

Peter smiled and played it exactly on the harp strings.

"Oh, thank you," said Kristina.

She rushed to embrace her boy and he squirmed free, wanting to show another time how clever he was with the harp.

"I did nothing," said Lady Anna. "He just went to the harp and imitated something I was humming. And we have proceeded from there. Our creator gives mercies, for often when one thing is taken, another is hidden there in its place. Peter has a genius, you see."

The next hour was one of the happiest of Kristina's life, singing with her boy playing the harp, as if they had trained together for years.

God had smiled.

Even at this darkest of time, God had smiled.

Then came the day of reckoning, when they must go to Wurzburg and do what they had come from Kunvald so many years ago to do. They had been remiss, but now it would be done.

It was early morning, and they were finishing up the last of the printing when Lud came to the barn.

Kristina turned, because she saw all the others looking up. Grit screamed.

"Get out of the way," said Lud.

There was an iron bar in Lud's hands, and he came toward them, lifting it.

All jumped back. But he went for the press, swinging the bar. It rang on the iron screw and the screw shattered and bits of iron flew everywhere.

Linhoff and Max and Ambrosius and Jakop all scrambled away into the corners, as far from Lud as they could go. Dolf and Symon ducked to the floor and cringed in place.

Kristina just stared, dumbfounded. Grit moved toward Lud, and Kristina grabbed Grit's arm and jerked her back, just in time, for Grit had moved into the path of the bar and the next swing of Lud's iron bar would have taken Grit's head off.

Lud swung the bar again and again and again until it was bent and the press looked worse than it had when they brought it out of the river. It lay in a heap of splinters of wood and broken iron. Lud then stood there, arms sagging and exhausted. Wood dust hung in the morning air.

Now he turned, panting, and looked around at them all.

"Is blood what you want?" he said.

No one spoke back to him. Kristina was numb with shock.

"If blood would wash the sins of this land away," said Lud, "I would kill until I was swimming in it. But the high will always crush the low. The princes stick together. That is how your precious God made this world."

"No one wants blood," Grit whispered.

"You argue and preach love and peace and all it will do is incite much killing."

"That is not what we want," said Kristina.

"Killing is what you get for showing wrongs."

"Lud, we will go. We will leave here."

"Kristina cannot leave, the rest can go. She has bond for two more years and must serve it out."

"We cannot leave her here if we go," said Grit.

"Listen to me," said Lud. "There is a new bishop in Wurzburg and a new emperor in Vienna, and they both hate the new ideas. Things can only bend so much until they break. The poor are hungry and their lords so freighted with debt that many estates are bankrupt. We have been lucky only because Florian sends Lady Anna his commission salary, and because here most share what little they have. But we cannot last forever. The roads are full of drifters and in city and country, both, the people are angry. With this press and your stupid pride you will get all of my good people here killed, and I cannot allow that."

Linhoff started to rise and speak, but Lud threw the bar at him and Linhoff had to slam himself sideways against a wall to dodge it. Then others covered their heads.

"Anyone else have anything to say to me?"

No one did. Lud turned and was gone.

Konrad

Wurzburg was joined to the Swabian League. Konrad had achieved his first and foremost goal upon becoming bishop.

And yet no forces were coming to fill out the Wurzburg ranks. Konrad consoled himself that all nine princes in Swabia—most of them bishops like himself—were busy putting down turmoil.

The Swabian couriers rode constantly with guards from city to city, through southern Germany. All Swabian nobles now faced exactly the same problems that Konrad confronted, and part of his day was now dedicated to trading messages with the other princes who composed the protective league. In case a revolt broke out, they would join forces, as they always had. Their combined strength could crush any rebellion, and history had proven so.

So, there was little time for rest. Less and less often was he able even to visit Sieger. He sorely missed the rides, and especially the times of breeding, when Sieger mounted a fine mare that was restrained by harness, and Konrad felt almost as if his soul joined the soul of the magnificent creation of God.

It fell to him to remedy all the softness of Lorenz.

Church and state were now fully one entity. Where before they had been uneasy bedfellows, Konrad combined all authority in the Wurzburg Bishopric under his control. Where before he had served a weak and permissive bishopric, as magistrate authority of the state, now he was the one and the only. One power.

Lead me, guide me, help me be not weak, but strong and zealous, unwearying, in your service...

No more would the weakness and permissiveness of Lorenz enfeeble the church-state. Konrad thought of hawks and owls, and if that were the choice, he would be the hawk.

As if the unstabilizing forces of social unrest and the debt crisis were not troubles enough, there had accumulated complaints from a few of the outlying abbeys—and even from the monasteries—of abuse of serving boys and other vulnerable acolytes by senior monks and clerics.

Konrad put this down at once, and with a vengeance. He made it dazzlingly clear that he was not permissive as others might have been, and never would allow such sinful and lewd exploitation of the powerless.

There were many arrests, all in one swift week.

It was no accident that he ordered his court arranged exactly as was the custom by Lorenz. Lorenz had been famed for his fair justice, and Konrad used this well, but with one difference: that the Church and state courts were now combined into one authority.

Konrad ordered Basil to chill the stone floor with open doors all night to the cold.

When the chilled stone of the court was crowded with muttering onlookers held back by magistrates, Konrad entered from a heated antechamber, in his grand judicial robes and gold chains. His breath fogged before his face as he took the high chair of justice. The whispering ceased.

The penitents were made to lie prostrate on the stone before the judicial throne. Their bodies quivered, teeth chattering. Those who had come to court not in heavy robes but in their best finery suffered the most.

To one shivering transgressor, a dandy in silk and brocade, begging and weeping on his knees before him, Konrad said, "Those weaker than us are like our children, and you have made your sacred vows vile, and for the next twenty years you shall not see the light of day. May God visit you and heal you. You have escaped beheading, but in the years to come you will wish it had been administered."

Veritas Press praised the equanimity of Konrad's justice, and his popularity went up for a short time.

But at night, from the lofty Marienberg towers, he gazed down into the smoky lights of the city canyons of masonry. He could see lights moving and shapes in the murk, and he could feel Satan on the prowl down there.

He had not been home to his own castle estate in months. He felt that if he left, there would be anarchy. So he stared down at the city he had been given by God to rule, and he thought of all the vain hopes and dark dreams down in the deeps below him, in the streets and rooms, of all the evils hidden among the swarm. Then, he thought on himself, too, how foolish were his own dreams as a child.

As a boy in his father's castle he had feared the men who served, the men who trained, the men who talked loud and coarse. And his father was the loudest of all.

To escape, he had wanted to become a priest, and his father said he was too much of the blood of his mother, and at age ten had sent him to live for a time at the monastery where he worked like a common child in the scullery, until he no longer wished to be priestly, and begged to be sent home.

He had learned that some priests were austere and as kind as saints, and others stank, and some were gluttons, and some groped, and some were sad, and a few were brilliant. Their unpredictable ways were frightening and the loneliness of sleep on a board in a stone room was terrifying beyond belief. His father had laughed at his confessed fears and (in open embarrassment) gave him to the tutors and the master-at-arms who all treated him with the same disdain thinly disguised as fond respect. His pimply face had repelled the girls, and he had loved Anna but she had taken Dietrich.

In the hottest months, the stench of the river came up on the shifting winds and passed into the Marienberg itself. It smelled of that monastery so long ago. And all those monks of his youth were now combined in one face, that of his most useful tool—Basil.

When Konrad smelled the river, he was reminded of all the human scum rising like the filth that mucked the river, and he wished there would be a flood to carry it all away. He longed for the freshness of his castle, far from this hive of sin and treachery, his great estate where he could ride all day with his retinue of huntsmen and guards and see only those villeins who toiled and bowed and served him.

Such a righteous weight is upon me now, help me be wise in my rooting out of the evils permitted by Lorenz, and may he now in eternity see his failings at your sacred hand...

He had taken the bishop's crown upon his head in the great cathedral where Lorenz earlier had been laid to rest inside the ruinously expensive marble tomb sculpted by Riemenschneider. The ceremonial chanting and hymns and praisings had droned on endlessly. He had kept his face suitably sorrowful.

Then at the moment of greatest solemnity, he strangely recalled how the first version of the tomb had an older face carved there, remarkably lifelike. Lorenz had ordered it re-carved for a more youthful appearance, as if eternity cared a whit. In mid-ceremony, thinking of that, Konrad had fought a terrible urge to laugh. With all of Wurzburg watching, with the priests chanting and intoning, he lowered his face and shuddered (and let them think that the effort of not laughing was that of not weeping in the glory of God, for his dead, most dear friend the Prince-Bishop Lorenz).

Life had come full circle and it was his turn.

Now he enjoyed a massive income.

Now his former creditors cringed.

Now he controlled the taxes and levies and all matters of trade and commercial licenses.

Now he commanded and could raise an army.

Now his best friend at court was the emperor.

Now he sat in the judging box at court.

He controlled everything except the minds of the people themselves. And to let them know who he was, Konrad tripled the number of death sentences. Basil complained that the crowds were thinning at executions, and that more variety was needed, for even at quarterings the reactions of the condemned had become too predictable.

The prisons filled with people under question, and many magistrates had to be given bonuses to act as tormentors. Too many gaolers were always drunk and some going mad, with suicides more frequent than ever. Veritas broadsheets warned and made it clear that demons were at work in all of this.

The Holy Mother Church wanted all renegade priests rounded up, but too often they were amid swarms of hundreds, even thousands, of their clannish followers, all the deluded trash that ever squandered good bread.

Sometimes, deep in the night, Konrad would steal away from the Marienberg, with only two picked bodyguards, and take a small carriage to the cathedral. There, alone, he would immerse himself in the enormity of silence that filled the great naves and seemed to hum high in the stone arches. His mind would clear of the clamor of the day, and that was when he could hear the voice of God, truly.

So much lies heavy upon my shoulders...give me the strength to protect the true kingdom of our Christ...

As ever, with silence and prayer, God spoke and the answers came in thoughts perfectly formed.

It was the weakness of Lorenz, his liberal permissiveness that had birthed so much want and so many troubles. The people needed a strong hand now for their own good. That was plain. The evidence was everywhere: people learning to read; people rejecting the good laws; people of low birth thinking themselves as good as the highborn and demanding equal rights. Had he not argued with Lorenz against all this? Had he not predicted just such a fatal outcome?

They would all feel his strength. The other Swabian princes would marvel at the results. His friend the emperor would praise him at court.

If the world saw him as weak, fear was the answer. Fear was everywhere and he would fight it with greater fear, as fire fought with fire.

He would bring the Landsknechts back home from their patrols and border disputes. He would decree martial law. He would begin a reign of terror so severe that none would dare oppose.

Basil was euphoric, and said, "This indeed is the most merciful way to restore order. A little more pain now, to save the soul of the patient."

"Examples must be made, first and foremost."

"We have our good list ready. Eyewitness accounts of enemies of the state and Church, and confessions verifying all arrests, with only the correct just pressures applied."

Konrad examined the list often, for new names were constantly being added.

The enemy list bore the names of all traitors on all estates and all merchants who complained or resisted their just taxes and levies; also troublemakers, and there were hundreds of those names. One was Lud, the pockmarked servant of Dietrich who had fought a duel years ago and cut up a good officer.

And then Konrad stared at the list…he thought he saw wrong, but there it was—Florian's name.

"Florian? My godson is on the list now? But he is in the field. What could he have done?"

"Forgive me, your holy grace," Basil said. "Reports come from Florian's commander in the field of Florian spreading extreme ideas among the other young officers, many of them knights like Florian himself. He has become popular, especially among the young knights."

So, it was even Florian, his own godson. This news came on a particularly bad day, when a dozen magistrates had deserted and refused to arrest a city gathering of unionist scum demanding a vote on the city council.

"Bring the young fool back. Send his man to fetch him. Do it now. I have a document in hand now that will crush this young upstart right down to size."

"The old debt claim, over three hundred years old? Surely such a claim is not even valid?"

"Exactly."

"And you will not protect him?"

"I shall own him. I shall bring him to heel now."

A tax warrant for an ancient debt against the Geyer estate had been submitted by Kollegiatstift Neumunster. It was a sign of the times, when every church and city were scrambling for funds and searching their old records. Konrad knew it was a ludicrous three hundred-fifty-year-old claim, and as bishop, he could easily reject it. But the claim had come fortuitously, by the grace of God, just when it was needed most. He saw it as a fine trap.

"Your grace," Basil warned, "should Florian not yield to the church tax, excommunication is mandatory."

"It will never go that far. Florian adores his betrothed, Barbara, and has far too much at risk in a brilliant future at court under my patronage."

Yes, Florian would come to heel.

He would use the tax to punish his godson, ostensibly for his radical ideas. He would shape and bend Florian to serve him and Wurzburg, and God. Dietrich had neglected this most sacred duty. Konrad would finish Florian's true education.

"A bishop who punishes his own godson," said Basil, "can only be seen as a fair man, and such a right man, being well respected, is also most certainly a feared man."

But that night when Konrad prayed, when he opened himself to his maker and to the Blessed Virgin, he faced the truth, that he was punishing the young man because he was hurt—Florian had spurned his role as godfather, his love of God, and his open arms.

And only God understood how it was an agony to be the one who held high the torch of truth so that the light might reach down into the very deeps of darkness and evil.

I will be exalted in the nations; I will be exalted in the earth…

He would bring young Florian safely into his sanctified embrace, like his own dear prodigal son.

Or destroy him.

Witter

At the Marienberg, the sour little senior monk, Basil, had called Witter to a meeting in the clerical offices of the fortress, instructing him to hand the message wallet to Florian personally.

"Your lord Florian is granted the honor of his own footman bearing him this personal communication from our prince-bishop. Bandits and rogue knights are abroad too often now. For your safety you shall have escort."

Witter had always known when to leave a place; this instinct—which he likened to the inexplicable sense of knowing when one is being watched—had saved him many times. A tiny voice in him screamed:

Time to go. Run, run away, go now…

But he resisted, would not listen. Not this time.

Fate had hounded and tormented him for so many years. But now it had turned and hitched him to a star, and that star was Florian Geyer, and Witter meant to make the most of it. So he served as footman to Florian Geyer.

"I entrust you with this," said the monk.

He was handed a fine red leather courier's wallet, clasped with a gold Wurzburg cross—a thing worth ten years of crop shares for a common villein—and he knew it contained the sealed letter from the bishop to Florian.

"Such an honor, holy father," said Witter to Basil, the monk. He meant it sarcastically, but did his best to sound sincere.

The monk frowned at him. "Do not address me as if I am the pope. It smacks almost of mockery."

"Forgive me, but you are such an important man."

The monk puffed up as expected. Sometimes lately, when he was in the presence of authority—especially a ludicrously officious person like this monk—Witter felt his face struggle to be still. Perhaps it was a sign of overconfidence. Once he had been terrified, yet now he fought a terrible urge to smirk, as when he had been a boy.

For now he was certain it must be some great promotion of Florian's rank. Everything in the monk's fretting manner hinted of some momentous change. Witter forced his face and hands to be still, listening.

"In the present unrest and troubles, we have lost several couriers recently. Know that to break the prince-bishop's personal seal is to be punished with greatest severity. As the road is so dangerous, you shall have the escort to serve your distinguished lord, the godson of our holy grace."

"Sir, I shall guard the message with my life."

"Indeed, you do, and never forget that."

Back in the bedchamber, alone and gathering his things to leave, Witter bellowed out a laugh. He felt a tremendous sense of hope. The laugh felt deep and defiant. Then came a sense of warning, a sense that he was indulging in bravado.

Florian was on the rise. In Florian's shadow, as his man, his confidant, there was no knowing how far he too would rise. And if Florian should gain even more office in his relationship to the bishop, there might even be a chance to travel abroad with diplomatic passes—even to Ottoman lands, where Jews were welcomed with open arms and he could at last escape Christians altogether.

"Pride is the mask of one's own faults," Witter remembered his father saying, when as a little boy he was too bright, too cocksure with his recitations, *"feel the meanings, not your delight in your skill of memory…"*

But it had been so long since he had felt anything good about himself.

Yes, it was daring, yes, dangerous. It was shallow and seductively thrilling. He had never played a role this long and it was dizzying yet exhilarating at the same time—a foolish feeling, he knew, yet could not resist indulging in it. And the fact he was on his way to see Florian made him anxious to go. The journey meant leaving the safety of the Marienberg, but shedding all its hatefulness, and there was always hope that Florian was being given some great advancement. Perhaps for a few days of celebration they might return to Giebel and he would see Kristina.

At the stable he ordered his horse up from the grooms and found his escort waiting impatiently.

"Volker, Captain of Cavalry, attached to Sixth Landsknechts," the officer said brusquely, as if acting as riding escort were far beneath him. "I am returning to my regiment. Never ride in front of me, sir."

It would be a grim journey, Witter soon realized. They rode out of the Marienberg gates together, Witter just behind.

Witter sized the man up obliquely. Captain Volker was a graying cavalryman with a stiff back and enormous mustache. Looking at the captain in his fancy embroidered maroon waistcoat with gold piping and his plumed cap, Witter instantly loathed him as he despised all such professional killers. And yet Witter was wary of his own sense of superiority, too, his hidden intellect and knowledge, riding beside this trained creature of war. His own secret pride was at work, and he knew he must guard against becoming overconfident.

The pavement stones steamed from a night rain. Their horses clattered across the great bridge where, every time he passed it or saw it, Witter thought of that night years ago. Of poor Werner Heck jumping to his death, to give them the extra moments they needed to pass downstream under the guarded bridge on the loose ferry.

The stones ended and the road was muddy with deep wagon ruts of standing water. Volker rode straight ahead as if the way were smooth and clear. The sun was up and hot for a fall day, as the horses clogged out into the muddy countryside.

Witter kept a covert watch on this officer riding with him, a killer by trade, a mercenary, a professional.

Reasoning it out, there were bad hints of treachery. The letter could have been carried by the captain himself, so Witter ostensibly served some other purpose, but he knew not what that could possibly be. He felt like a bad actor in a play, and felt the captain was always watching him. Suddenly, the captain rode up close. Witter caught a breath of the sickly sweet perfume the man was wearing.

"Give over the message wallet to my safekeeping."

Witter swallowed hard. "But I must not, sir."

"I said give it over." The captain's voice hardened. "Give it to me or I will be insulted. You are a soft fellow and do not want me to be offended, I can assure you."

Witter felt ashamed, and a fierce anger arose in him. Now he was indignant. He turned haughtily to the captain, giving him the correct attitude of a superior. That usually worked best for dull men who had spent their life in routines of obeying others.

"Sir, you are my escort only."

The captain broke out in a raucous laugh. "Just teasing, and testing a little. Good man."

Witter said nothing back, pretended to smile, with a comradely good nature. His heart hammered.

There was a false edge to this man, a feigned comradeship that set off Witter's survival sense. The man's poise in the saddle, his puffery of posture, the way he looked down his nose at some beggars in a village they passed through, the very angle of his cap covered with badges, all were warnings to keep silent.

Witter recalled some wisdom Grit had once said. *One could never be punished for something one did not say, and could never take back something once said.* So he tried to say nothing.

"Barley, devil take it all," the Captain said. "I worked my share as a boy. Makes me sick even to see it. Cut and shock it, and the awns burr into your hide. Soldiering freed me from those chains. Won my commission on a field of battle, I did, in the Slovenian peasant revolt fifteen years back. Nothing to lose, all to win."

The vast fields had been harvested and filthy beggars gleaned the rows with a feverish intensity, stirring little when the horses passed. Witter saw their desperation and his heart went out to them.

"I rode through here last month," said the captain. "There was a storm and the lazy bastards could not finish harvesting their lord's fields before their own were ruined by hail and wet. If they worked harder they would not now be on their filthy knees. Or if they were soldiers."

Witter thought of how much better the Giebel villagers looked. They always seemed to have enough. They were given crop shares most generously, were allowed to hunt the woods, and, when storms threatened, allowed to harvest first, before they reaped for the estate itself. But these people looked like some other race of beings; so weak that many were on their knees crawling for roots and grains.

He felt their miserable stares as an accusation, and it filled him with a sad recognition that he, with all his fear, was more fortunate than they. He thought of Kristina and Grit and all that they tried so hard to do. And he was here riding as comrades with this man of such contempt.

A few scavengers ran to the road, hands out, begging.

The officer sneered down at them from his fine horse.

"Villeins are all cowards. Their dirty faces stare, they glare behind your back, but they cringe to your face and they do fear the sword. Never turn your back to them. Their little snotters, too. Giving alms only teaches them to beg, you know. And to beg is to hate. To hate is to go to hell."

Witter tried to say nothing back, his mind full of barbs. He clamped his lips and looked up at the sky, then at the road far ahead. He hoped the man now would ride on in silence, but like so many dim and officious people, the officer loved talking about himself.

"My life has been served to defend those of rank, such as our bishop. I am no knight, like your young master, but a good soldier. More Turks I have cut down than the hairs on your head. Sacked their towns, put the fear of the true God into them, taught their women and children, too. That is the selfless life of a man of war. No time for soft men these days. Your Florian Geyer has learned much of tactics, and could become quite a good officer with the line."

Witter felt a cold and squirming sensation in his belly. Was this bastard toying with him? Witter's own temper was rising, hot and bitter.

"Could?" Witter said with a big, false smile. "Is my master not a good officer?"

"Your lord Geyer has become quite popular, but mostly with many of the disaffected officers. Especially the younger ones who often have suffered an excess of education. Too many ideas confuse a man and dull his vital instincts."

Witter wanted to laugh at this dangerous idiot; he tried to frame some response that was evasive, yet mild.

"My master does his duty and serves loyally."

"Even though you are far beneath me, I am plainspoken. Speak as man to man. No one is testing you. None had said otherwise of your young Sir Florian Geyer. He is much admired as a knight and as a serving officer. He fights well, as he said his father taught him. Indeed, he has won two smart duels with equal rankers."

"I had no idea."

Witter had never seen that side of Florian, and he both admired it now and feared it. If Florian threw his life away, Witter would be far out on a limb alone. All the trials of bringing the heir back would be for nothing, and Kristina and the others would again be in harm's way, vulnerable, unprotected.

"Your master backs his ideas. All officers and the men, too, they respect that. However, it is also his ideas that some find unsound, for an officer knight who also happens to be godson to our bishop. Tell me, has he shared his ideas of reform with you?"

A warning went off. "Reform, sir? What is reform?"

"You know very well what I mean, so do not anger me by denying it. You are the servant of a would-be reformer, knight though he is, learned though he is."

Witter said nothing. He felt the greasy weight of hatred in his belly, wanting to ride away from this man.

"Me, I like Lieutenant Geyer," said Captain Volker. "Many officers do like him. But we cannot tolerate discord. First this hypocrite monk Luther sets poor against rich."

"Luther, I believe, is a priest, a doctor of theology, not a monk." As soon as he spoke he wished he had said nothing. The officer glared at him.

"To hell with credentials! Luther is a devil. All the while making himself large, while lining his pockets by siding with the nobles. Since then all the villeins have agitated for reforms. One local stirring and then another, every year. All throughout Swabia and spreading everywhere."

"Terrible," said Witter, "just terrible."

The captain raved on, "And Luther's followers. Like this radical priest Muntzer preaches equality for all classes, as if a mongrel nation is what God wants. Now Muntzer has the silver miners and weavers all stirred up. I heard him preach to a mob once. He is a devil and will surely one day get all the villeins to rise up and they all will be killed."

"Pray God it shall never happen," said Witter.

The officer leaned closer from his mount. "What if I speak plainly now. Just between two men. Do the reformers speak truth? Do we not desperately need a change in this land?"

Witter's instinct was to lie, to evade, and it did not fail him now. "How can anyone hope to spend eternity with our Blessed Virgin, without serving her?"

The captain snorted. "No need to be careful with me, man. Speak your true mind."

"I do, I do. Only the Mother Church can save us."

"The Church? Ha. Their stories are for little children and imbeciles. The state is the Church is the state. Have you heard that the villeins of the Abbey of Marchthal refused labor? Yes, and at St. Blasien too, then those in Steinheim, over near Memmingen, they now refuse taxes and all right duties of labor. What do they want? They demand a say. Many also in the cities, the guildsmen, the artisans, they can now read, and they even want to vote in the city council to determine their own fate. Can you imagine what will happen to them?"

They would be free, thought Witter.

But he searched his mind for something suitably ludicrous. "Villeins voting as equal to nobles chosen by God? You might as well let pigs ride horses."

Captain Volker stared at Witter for a moment, then threw his head back and roared, laughing.

Said Witter, with deep piety, "I am certain that when my master learns of these outrages he will be as appalled as indeed I am."

"He would be a fool to work for such changes."

"Indeed, sir, but he would not, I am sure."

"So you keep saying. So many knights these days are reduced to banditry on the road. Your master is fortunate to have such a guardian as Prince Konrad."

The captain said little more. Witter felt his eyes on him often. He forced himself to sit up straight and not keep looking over at the man.

The land began to rise and they came out of the lowland farming plain and the harvested fields up into a forested valley where, from far away, explosions could soon be heard, rolling like thunder.

"The noise scare you?" said the officer.

"It was not thunder. Was it guns?"

"Landsknechts. The field firing range. They practice the new way of war," said the captain.

They passed a picket line where pikemen saluted.

Then the woods opened and the road came to the perimeter of a great field. Massed lines of Landsknechts maneuvered. They were foot soldiers with muskets, firing mass volleys from troop formations several ranks deep. Maneuvering beside them were swordsmen with spears that seemed to be guarding the musketry flanks from attack.

Then Witter's eye picked out Florian astride a horse.

Said Volkman, "There is your master. He has become a dashing good line officer. Ride behind me, and slowly now."

They moved slowly along the perimeter.

In silver helmet and breastplate, red-plumed to signify his command role, Florian was riding up and down the rear of the musketry line, waving a saber, shouting and commanding. Sergeants followed him on foot and yelled at the men Florian pointed out.

Witter realized that it was a reloading practice, for speed, to see how many volleys could be fired per minute. One rank fired, then withdrew to reload as the next rank stepped forward and fired. The forward ranks constantly rotated back in this manner, so that the front rank was always firing.

Across the field were stacked bales of hay. Each volley sent hay flying into the air so that hay bits floated everywhere like yellow snow. But the laggards in reloading were dropping their ramrods or their lead balls or stumbling in the boot ruts in the sod of their field. It was comical and fearsome and vile, and Witter felt his gorge rise with loathing. So much expense for killing, when children were starving in the fields.

"That is might, young man," said the captain.

"Magnificent," Witter said thickly.

"You know, at first I suspected you as a damn reformer or such. Florian is protected by his rank with the bishop, but that would not go for one low as you. To tell you the truth, you even look a bit of the Jew to me."

Witter stared at this strange man for a moment of sheer frozen panic. Then the captain laughed, exposing yellow teeth, and slapped Witter's arm.

"A joke! Ha! You should have seen your face. A Jew! That is a good one on you! Ha! But no offense."

"None taken, sir." Witter took a deep breath and bowed low. "I have been called many things, but never *that*."

He felt even more desperate, and the old self-loathing came squirming up in his gut.

He thought of how brave his father had been, and yet with such a son. He hoped Judah could not see him now.

So weak, and such a fool…

And yet it was Judah himself, his brilliant father, who had chained him with such an unbreakable respect for life, respect that brought him such seeming cowardice, and for a heady moment

Witter savored a fantasy of plunging his little dagger up under the chin of this captain, the way Lud had taught him, to watch the hard, stupid eyes bug in surprise. But it would never be, Witter knew, and he felt cheap for having the evil and silly thought. His one act of honesty had been running down the two magistrates on the horse, with the mob cheering him on, and he had rued and mourned that day ever since.

Those who are merciful to the cruel are cruel to the merciful. But his father, Judah, believed in mercy for all, above every other act of man. It was the same with Kristina and Grit. Mercy for anyone, everyone. Even at the cost of their own agony and death.

Jarring him from thought, another volley thundered from the ranks of muskets. Witter jumped involuntarily.

Then, doubling his alarm, the captain slapped Witter's arm again.

"Observe, man, and remember this. For you are witnessing a great force for good order of the state. Those are the ranks that will decimate any revolt, should so many fools gather to end their lives together. All those bales of hay would be meat and bone and blood."

"Wonderful," said Witter, "heroic, grand."

"Heroic? Officers might be heroic. Do you see their flaw?"

"Flaw?"

"Of course you cannot. City man. I tell you, with a single squadron of cavalry I could rout them from flank and rear, run the guarding swordsmen down and drive them all and roll the muskets up like a rug."

"But you say they are the future."

"Indeed, against revolts they are. Those guns are crude ranks, but effective. All villeins and miners and city trash who think to rise equal to their betters will get the bad end of that. But they can never replace good officer cavalry."

"It must require great courage," said Witter.

"Not courage, the sheer joy of it." The officer smiled, showing his yellow teeth. "Joy that soft men such as you shall never know. I leave you here. Move your horse behind the trees lest a stray ball find you. Many of the new dolts jerk this way and that when they fire. We will break them of that. Wait here and I shall instruct your master."

The captain rode off in his perfectly arrogant style.

Witter, trembling, moved his horse behind the trees. They kept firing. Now and then a buzzing whizzed by like tearing cloth in the air. The horse pawed and snorted.

In this strange place that was his life, Witter thought again now, as he often did, of Maimonides trying to explain away evil. How there were three causes: by nature upon you, by other people upon you, and by you upon yourself.

God was not responsible, Maimonides claimed. The need to love God was too great to admit any implication of evil.

Witter sat alone on the skittish horse, waiting, and his eyes began to water from the stinging clouds of gunpowder that drifted across the fields. A ball tore through the branches overhead and leaves drifted down.

No, Witter thought. *You, God, You. You created all, including all of this that now surrounds me.*

Leaning out, he could see the captain riding.

The old officer, sitting high in his saddle like a king, made the perimeter, avoiding the gunfire, and finally came to Florian.

All from you. Even the captain. Even the lead balls cutting the air. From you. You, the great mystery...

Witter saw them out there like deadly little boys playing war, saluting and leaning together from their horses, and then Florian saluted again and suddenly rode away, riding hard behind the ranks, around the perimeter of the open field, avoiding the mass firing.

Soon, Florian came, breathless, surprised to see Witter. His brown horse was lathered and snorting and tried to touch noses with Witter's mount.

"They sent me," said Witter, before Florian could speak.

"Why are you here? It must be damned important."

Witter produced the leather wallet and handed it over.

"It must be. The bishop's monk sent me with this. Surely it is another advancement."

Florian opened the wallet and pulled out the thick folded parchment letter, breaking the wax signet seal, and he had not read much when his face began turning red.

"Advancement, you say?"

Witter stood back, astonished at Florian's anger.

"Damn him," said Florian. "He summons me back with this calumny? With this blackmail?"

Witter could not hold his tongue. "What does it say?"

Florian held the letter out at arm's length like something foul and rotten. Witter could see the flourishes of pen and the great gold wax seal of the bishopric.

"Instead of a courier, they sent you with that damned tool of a moron captain. He surely picked your brain all the way, did he not?"

"He did. I mean no. He tried."

"My opinions are neither wrong nor hidden. Yet they seek to damn me for them."

"Damn you?"

Not answering, Florian turned his mount and began to ride away. Surprised, Witter pulled his reins around and kneed his horse, chasing after Florian. Another volley from the lines of Landsknechts came rolling, and the horse jumped and ran harder.

They rode on out of camp past the picket lines where the musketeers and footmen with pikes saluted and stared.

It took a full half hour to catch Florian on the road, and only because Florian finally reined in. Witter was exhausted and badly shaken.

"Where do we go?" he asked.

"Home."

"Not Wurzburg? To Giebel?"

"Yes. Home, I said."

"Can you not tell me what was in the bishop's letter?"

"A false debt I must pay or be excommunicated."

"But...there is no money."

"Konrad well knows there is no money. In lieu of payment I must sign a mortgage upon the Geyer estate to him, and serve him personally, to crush any revolt in the city and thereabouts, and to beg for his counsel to correct the grievous errors of my thinking. I have been reported to harbor seditious sentiments. I am resigning my commission. I will not bend to this."

Florian shook the crackling parchment and it fluttered wildly, frightening both horses.

"What will you do?" said Witter, unable not to ask it.

"Konrad thinks to bend me to my knees before him, to break me to saddle? It provokes exactly the opposite from any man of honor. And I am my father's son."

They were hardly on the road for an hour when the horsemen caught them.

Florian heard them first and whirled his mount to face them. Witter wanted to ride hard away but Florian said, "Hold, man. You cannot outride cavalry officers. Hold and face them."

Florian was right. Two cavalry officers. Witter recognized Captain Volker, his escort from Wurzburg, but not the other at first.

Then as they came within slowing distance, pulling up their mounts, Witter recognized the man as the one from the street, the one with no ears, the scars hidden in his hair and his beard. The one with Frieda.

What was his name? Was it Ulrich?

"Volker and Ulrich," said Florian, low. "Not good."

"Geyer!" shouted Volker.

"Do you miss me already, friends?" Florian smiled and Witter was astonished that he could pretend so easily.

Volker shook his head. "You are a good young officer spoiled by bad opinions, and we have our orders."

"What orders? I am decommissioning."

Said Ulrich, "Not so simple, Geyer."

Said Volker, "We are to escort you back to Wurzburg, in any case."

"We go where we please now," said Florian.

Almost more quickly than Witter's eye could follow it, Ulrich's sword was out, a silvery blur, whipping the air, and the tip was poised suddenly at Florian's face.

"Dismount and shed your weapons, sir."

Witter got down from the horse as Florian got down from his. They stood together holding the reins of the snorting beasts. Volker and Ulrich dismounted, both with drawn swords pointing them to move off the road.

"Over there," said Ulrich. "Move."

Under some nearby trees, Florian dropped his sword belt.

"The dagger as well, in your boot," said Ulrich.

"You know all my tricks," said Florian.

"Charm will not get you out of this," said Volker.

"Out of what may I inquire?" said Florian.

Witter thought of the dagger in his waistcoat, riding on his hip, under the sash. His heart hammered. His fear was compounded by the sense of freedom of running away, which would be suicidal, and he stood like a statue, paralyzed by dread.

Said Volker, "You decommissioned and I am instructed in that case to bind you for our return."

"You two did not bring sergeants? That means blood work, indeed, and no witnesses. And you mean to take me back as a common criminal? Or kill me here and now?"

"The bishop absolutely wants you alive," Volker said. "At pain of my own death, should you be harmed."

"To keep me prisoner, like the Turk? Parade me like that poor peacock? Is that it?"

"God inspires him. I know not his mind, only his will."

"You made your bed," Ulrich said. "Too many young officers are infected by your dream of rights for the common man. I myself am a common man but pulled myself up from nothing. Not born a knight's son, like you."

"Enough talk," said Volker. "Bind them."

"We do not need the footman," said Ulrich.

"Let me," said Volker, pulling his dagger. "You should have seen how he moped, seeing the beggars and gleaners all the way here. Sickening, boring."

Witter stood almost swooning with the sense of impossibility. Ulrich shoved Florian against a tree, and pulled his dagger, and Florian did not move, his eyes on the blade.

Volker pulled his own dagger and moved toward Witter and Witter realized he would now die. He should run but he did not run, could not run. Volker gripped Witter's hair and jerked his head back to expose his throat. The angle gave Witter a clear view of the treetops above him where sunlight was splintered in the breezy day. It would be the last thing he ever saw and it was incredibly beautiful.

"Spare him," Florian's voice said. "He is innocent."

"Innocent?" said Volker's voice. "Innocent is good. Innocent is easy. I will make it quick."

Then Volker made a strange sound. Like gurgling, as if clearing his throat. Witter felt his hair released and his head swung back level and he saw Volker looking down at his own chest.

Two feet of sword stood out from Volker's breastplate, near the armpit hinge. Blood ran like spilled red wine, splashing, and Volker grabbed the tip of the sword and his hands bled, too, and he sank to his knees with his face going stark white and eyes dark and sad now and his head jerking around trying to see who had impaled him; he began trembling and then he danced a little and went down hard. The arms reached out as if to embrace Witter and Witter had to leap back away. Blood sprayed him and he tasted salt and wanted to retch.

Ulrich pulled out his blade from Volker's fallen body and wiped it on Volker's skirt, and then sheathed it.

Said Ulrich, "Tell Lud my debt is paid."

"What debt?" said Florian.

"You are the son of Dietrich and his man Lud fought me. Ask your footman, he knows my Paulina."

"Yes," Witter said, numbly, hardly able to process this. Paulina was her name now, not Frieda. Could this man actually love her?

Said Ulrich to Witter, "My Paulina told me who you are. I have taken her as mistress. And I do not give a damn about her past and all that she told me."

"Who is Paulina?" said Florian.

"Ask your footman here," Ulrich said. "You only need know this. Years ago your father's man Lud spared my life and now I give him yours. Now ride off, and use the great woods route. Do not take the main roads."

"What will you report?" said Florian. "That I am a murderer?"

"My sword went through-and-through, so say we that you won a duel. None can say the blade did not enter from the front, and death is death on both ends."

Ulrich was going to his horse but Florian spoke again.

"You add the lie to your infamy, sir."

Witter could not believe it. He wanted badly to get away. And the officer mercenary, Ulrich, turned from his horse, regarding Florian again with his own look of disbelief. Ulrich's head, earless under his hair and beard, made him look odd, unnaturally sleek, more than ever like a devil escaped from hell. Witter just wanted to run from them both.

"What infamy?" Ulrich spat on the ground at Florian's feet.

"You heard me, sir," said Florian, his hand now on the hilt of his sword. "I will fight you if you wish it."

Ulrich shook his head and laughed in anger. Now he swung up onto his horse, looking down at them.

"Listen, you ass. I was born common, and your high ideas of raising the common man are foolish. Power will always breed power. Might will always make right. I know this and for all your letters and learning you do not. I am more honorable than any dreamer born to knighthood such as you."

"That death was not honorable, sir."

"Goddamn you, get going, before I change my mind. Killing you, easy as it would be, is not in my plan. You are payment of my debt, but your Lud is ten times the man you are, and the discharge for me is a bargain."

"Get to your horse," Florian said to Witter.

Said Ulrich, whirling his mount once, "Tell your Lud this—the next time I see him, his face can be made no uglier, so he is a dead man."

Witter got clumsily up onto his horse and Florian was already easily mounting his, with a single swing of hands and hips. Florian spurred away.

Then Witter was riding hard, half blinded by the dust, leaning over the big pulsing neck of his horse and trying not to lose sight of Florian's shape in the road ahead.

The rutted track crossed into the great woods and he saw the sun up high in the ancient naked trees, the light splintering, always to the west.

He knew they were heading home, south toward Giebel, and the bad world receded behind him with the distance.

And he comforted himself with thoughts of

Kristina…

Kristina

Kristina's fears for her child had abated as if spiritual coal had been transmuted to gold. God was the alchemist, and she prayed forgiveness for her fears and her doubts.

"See how he flowers," said Lady Anna. "Even the wild thorny thistle has its bright blooms."

The chambers were full of music. Endless melodies came from Peter's little hands. With the harp, Peter's soul had been unleashed at last, from the seeming dark prison of his shut away mind.

Kristina watched and served, as Lady Anna spent hours enrapt, while Peter played anything Kristina could hum or sing. Kristina used all the songs she knew, and Peter played them and began elaborating on their themes. Lura came, and Leta from the scullery, and Arl, too.

They stood enchanted. It was a miracle.

The sound was magical, and villagers gathered near the chamber window by the old moat, so they, too, could hear.

Now Kristina dared again indulge in the first dreams she had had for her child, at childbirth, when she had chosen his name for the apostle, Peter—Simon Peter, who had laid down his sword by the command of Christ, *even to love thy enemy.* Kristina yearned for the day when at last Peter would be able to understand the meaning of his name.

Yet, she thought, perhaps music was his language.

Lady Anna spoiled Peter with sweetbreads and nuts and dried fruit, and he began to beg for more and pout and not play until he was given more. Kristina deplored that behavior, but Lady Anna perversely seemed to adore it.

When Peter spoke a little, it was of the music and it was always as if he were possessed of someone else: "Him play good…"

And with Peter on her lap, Kristina told him as best she could of her own mother's advice from so long ago:

"If ever you become too afraid, sing… sing from your heart, and God will always hear you."

"Not sing, him play," Peter said, and hopped down.

With Grit, Kristina prayed thanks to God and begged this gift come only to good for her child, with no hidden cost. Grit was allowed to come listen, and Kristina watched her face glow, as if Peter's lush chords and arpeggios brought back the youth to Grit's features that had been so hardened by life.

"It is a gift," said Grit, "a blessing to only be praised."

They were in the chamber with Peter playing, with the sun low on the harvested fields, when Kristina heard the shouting outside.

"Florian! Florian! Florian!"

Lady Anna was up. "Florian? Here?"

Peter squealed, laughed, and ran from the harp, running in circles in the room like a little wild dog set free.

Kristina looked out the other chamber window. Down there the villagers were hurrying around the wall into the village square.

Kristina hurried to the other side of the tower and, looking down, she saw horsemen slowing in rolling dust. On the back of a leathered mount she recognized Florian Geyer. And then her heart leaped—Witter was with him.

Konrad

Now, he, himself, was at the altar, with the monks chanting and then the boys singing, and he was the centerpiece of the pageantry. The weight of the world freighted his shoulders. Now, it was he who held the surprising weight of the staff, the crozier, the gold shepherd's crook, crafted to appear as formed from wood, as John the Baptist night have carried. Now he was the shepherd and all Wurzburg was his flock.

In the cathedral, more than any other place, even more than at the Fortress Marienberg, he was transformed. Even for Matins and Vespers, he did not wear the simple chapel robe but his full bishop's accoutrements, long, white silk sleeves fringed in gold. Upon his head sat the tall mitre with its gold ribbon lappets so like a halo. He wore the purple and gilt liturgical gloves to grip the sacred staff, and his episcopal ring.

Now, at this morning Matins, the atmosphere vibrated with the beauty of sound—the choir of boys as radiantly sweet as ever in the great spaces of the cathedral—but he hardly heard it.

Unrest and poor revenue plagued him less today than did his own godson. His chest troubled him. He prayed but the fire was tickling, trying to ignite into full constriction.

Wurzburg was his flock, their souls in his care, and he was heavy with the weight of such solemn guardianship.

And in the private baths of the bishop chambers, his morning rub went almost unfelt. The steam of baths helped release his constricting bile. Mahmed's counsel had been accurate—honeyed drinks, fruit, and light fowl, but nothing fried; riding his horse in fresh air; meditation in prayer—all helped so greatly to relieve the pressures that shut off his life's breath.

And so, in gratitude, Konrad decided once and for all to save Mahmed's soul from eternal hellfire. He had prepared Mahmed for this by stopping all wine and food for a week, only water.

With attendants bearing a tray of goblets with a flask of red wine, with dry linen and a silver basin of hot water, he went to Mahmed's chambers and entered.

Mahmed sat in strained silence. Feebly, Mahmed tried to rise, but weakly sank back into his chair.

"Here is wine for you, and bread."

Mahmed grasped at the bread first, choking it down, then washing it down with the goblet of wine poured for him.

"You love wine," said Konrad, "even though Islam forbids it. You are not a true Muslim, Mahmed."

"I have been deprived of all sustenance..." Mahmed gasped between his hurried gulps.

"You were deprived to cleanse you, to prepare you for this holy sacrament to save your soul. The bread you now eat is the body of our Lord. The wine is His blood."

Mahmed stopped, eyes widening, his mouth full, and Konrad smiled.

"My priests transubstantiated the bread and wine and made it sacred for your communion."

Mahmed still stared, and his mouth stopped chewing, and then he spewed out the bread and wine mash, and some sprayed Konrad's robe.

Mahmed went to his knees and retched.

Konrad felt his throat tighten. His breath came thickly and a fury arose in him, like boiling gall.

"I am through rescuing you, infidel, evil nonbeliever."

"Kill me," said Mahmed.

"Evil Peacock. You will serve us when we wish. You will not receive the mercy or dignity of execution. Go rot in your own filth, in a common cell as you deserve."

The jailers were summoned, and Konrad had Mahmed dragged down to a common cell.

Now, as he was being dressed in fresh robes, Konrad was hardly aware of the monk Basil, who paced back and forth, reporting as was his daily duty.

"Your grace, our monks report that the city is full of talk of a duel over reformer opinions, that in the streets and taverns the story grows, and young Geyer is becoming a hero."

As Basil spoke, Konrad felt a sad weight in his chest. The weight was part grief, part anguish, part anger; and his face took the strain of not revealing just how deeply he was wounded. All his hopes of bringing Florian to heel, to bind him close to his bosom and raise him in rank as a true godson, all were dashed. Here he was, prince and bishop, with flatterers begging for advancement on all sides, and this young man openly refuses his holy patronage.

Basil's confirming reports were humiliating. More, there was a clear danger brewing in all of this.

"Madness," said Konrad, thinking aloud. "A man stains his honor, lowers himself, rejects a glorious future, betrays all who love him, and he becomes a hero to the rabble."

"Most regretfully so, your grace."

"And how does the city know all this?"

"It spread even here, through the Marienberg first, among the soldiers and magistrates, and then they carried it to the taverns. The couriers brought them the stories, I am certain. A brave young lieutenant reported that the captain dueled with Florian Geyer, instead of doing his duty, and Geyer killed him and made his escape. The lieutenant himself chased them and was nearly killed when his horse got caught in a villeins snare in the woods."

"Give that young man his captain's post."

"Already done, your grace. And gossips punished."

"We shall put it all to good use, Basil, all."

An hour later, in his tower study, Konrad's breakfast of squab stood untouched. With his first bite he had encountered a tiny feather unplucked. It had caused him to choke and spit out the delicious half-chewed flesh. It was surely a sign. He did not have the cooks punished.

He had prayed all night on what to do about Florian, and God had spoken to him with that mysterious clarity that came only after great periods of deep meditation.

Basil stood waiting at the writing podium, with ink and quill and paper, for instructions. "What will you do? The Church and the state will judge now, only by what action you take or do not take."

"I shall excommunicate Florian."

"Your own godson, your grace?"

"Rejected light is the greatest darkness, Basil. It is not I who punish Florian, for he has betrayed God, and in doing so, he has sacrificed his own immortal soul."

It had to be done. Like a spiteful and ungrateful son, Florian had run away. Not only had he fled, he had also killed a superior officer in a duel. And worst of all, he had rejected Konrad and the protection of the bishopric. Florian had spat in the face of all that Konrad offered, all the good, all the open-armed love of a godfather, a bishop, and a master. The rejection burned in Konrad's throat like bitter gall, rising every time he let himself dwell upon it.

"Veritas Press shall print a very special edition," said Konrad. "'The Excommunication of Florian Geyer,' listing his infamies. To do this terrible, this necessary thing, we shall make the most of it. Florian despises glory. He is an agitator, a seditionist, probably a heretic, a deadly dueler, a serpent of evil opinions, a bringer of darkness and disorder."

Basil was obviously impressed. Konrad knew he had outdone himself. Once resolved, he was steadfast. He would never again be the sniveling son of his father. He would correct the son of Dietrich, whom his father had openly admired.

"Excellent, strongly worded, your grace. You will be feared and deeply respected for such pious equanimity."

Basil smiled, and Konrad tried not to look directly at the little monk, his eyes so frog-like in his round face. But Basil ran the press with solid routines, and all the publicist monks feared him and did all that had to be done. God worked in strange ways, indeed, with strange materials. And one must not judge the willing tools of the Almighty.

Konrad said, "We shall publish the excommunicate notice widely, at no cost to readers, and let them see who their new hero truly is. Let them have a few days to read it, to feel the shame."

"What of your godson?"

"In three days I shall send a force to Giebel to arrest Geyer. He will be brought here for sharp questioning, as long as it takes. Florian is a thinker, not a fighter; he is no Dietrich, he will break."

"And when we have his full confession?"

"Veritas will print a second proclamation, announcing the coming date and manner of his public execution. That one we will sell. Our publicists must outdo themselves. I want the city and roads to be flooded with broadsheets, and the public outraged, inflamed, before dark this very day."

Basil dipped his quill, and stood poised and eager.

Konrad felt the exquisite pleasure of blessed inspiration surging up in him like clear, pure water rising in a well, and he said, "If therefore the light that is in you is darkness, how great is that darkness!"

Lud

As night fell, the cold wind came up, and Florian would not say what had happened, and Witter said he had promised to let Florian say it all. But it did not bode well that Florian wore his own plain ram's-head Geyer tunic and not the livery of his Landsknechts commission.

So Lud gathered the village together, all he wished to come, in the empty sanctuary of the church, where Father Michael had not been seen in the months since he had left. Lud had the steward's passkey and opened it.

He shoved the doors open on squalling hinges. He entered but stopped just inside. Little dead birds, desiccated now as dry leaves, lay inside the threshold where they had been trapped months ago when the doors closed. Lud paused, reflecting on these tiny tragedies—the feathers gleaming blue and gold, despite death, in the outer shafts of light. Then he shook off the moment. Abruptly he brushed the husk-like bodies aside with a sweep of his boot. There was enough new sadness without seeing these.

Lud went across to the bell rope and hauled it down and swung his leg up and the bell tolled. Harder, he rang the bell. And all came who could walk. There was a stir among them. Lud kept shaking his head, saying he had no answers either.

Kristina and Lura brought Lady Anna through the mob. It spread open before them. They came to the front.

Florian was waiting there, and he climbed onto the mount as would any preacher or priest. Lud saw how much more than ever

Florian now looked like his father, Dietrich. Yet Florian had flair, a showmanship of sorts, that Dietrich would have never postured.

"I speak now of rights, not only of religion. For to me, the rights of man are one with religion. We are all Giebel, equally, each and every one of us, my sisters and my brothers and my family. Christ's command is to love one another. I return home to bring you news. It will affect all of us. And each is free to make one's own choice. Freedom is a sacred right of each and all."

Lud stood steeling himself and waited for the news. It would be bad, of that there was no doubt. The word *choice* always meant bad. How bad he was yet to know. Witter would say nothing, but he looked as gray and grim as one condemned, even when Kristina had embraced him. That was a sight Lud wished he had not seen.

The tension was unbearable and he wished he had shaken whatever news there was out of Witter.

Now, Florian said, "I first want to share with you words of one of my masters at Oxford, a wise man of God, who has forward sight into our times. These words I know well, by heart, for I have thought on them many times while out in the field, learning all the new tactics of war."

Florian paused, swept the crowd with his eyes, and no one was stirring. They all stood waiting as if for the sentence of a judge.

"The richer sort are often endeavoring to bring the hire of laborers lower, not only by their fraudulent practices, but by the laws which they procure to be made to that effect; so that though it is a thing most unjust in itself, to give such small rewards to those who deserve so well of the public, yet they have given those hardships the name and color of justice, by procuring laws to be made for regulating them."

Florian paused as if to let this sink in. Lud gazed across the faces he had known all his life, and wondered what all the others were thinking. Unreadable.

None even cleared their throat. None shifted nor moved. Then Florian went on...

"Therefore I must say that, as I hope for mercy, I can have no other notion of all the other governments that I see or know, than that they are

a conspiracy of the rich, who on pretense of managing the public only pursue their private ends, and devise all the ways and arts they can find out; first, that they may, without danger, preserve all that they have so ill acquired, and then that they may engage the poor to toil and labor for them at as low rates as possible, and oppress them as much as they please."

Lud realized that Florian had stopped, was finished. People muttered in confusion.

Now Lady Anna herself spoke out:

"So you are quoting some Englishman again. It smacks of pacifism yet it holds a knife-edge of struggle. It denies service to the state, yet promises war, not peace. Which is it to be? Peace comes only with service. War comes from resistance to power."

"These words," said Florian, "yes, they were those of the English sage Sir Thomas More, and they bring a new day to all men. When laws are unjust, we are under no moral obligation to serve them. God's law of love is the one truth, and the only just law. And we must fight for that law with all our beings."

There was a stirring, and Lud saw Grit pushing forward. She spoke loudly: "You say Christ commanded love of one another. He also commands love of thy enemies."

Said Florian, "Then we must stop our enemies from destroying their own souls through their evil act and greed."

Lud saw Grit try to say something else but she was shouted down by the crowd.

Florian lifted his arms for silence. "It is well that these pacifists came and taught so many to read. It is good that you all sheltered them and opened yourselves to them. It is what my father, Dietrich, would have wished. But now that you can read, you know what your rights should be. Is that not so? Are you not angry?"

There came an agreeing roar of anger and fists were raised. Lud hardly recognized some of the faces he had known his whole life.

There was no certainty in what Florian had said, only complicated notions of injustice, and thwarted ideals. Of course this world was a conspiracy of the rich. Who did not know that? No one here was richer than Florian himself, who had inherited the Geyer estate, though its value might be in question, given the hard times.

Said Lady Anna, "Are you preaching war or peace?"

There was a rumble of confused onlookers.

Said Florian, "I say we must hold to the truth of brotherhood for all."

"Speak plainly, we beg you," shouted Merkel.

And Sig said, "Tell us what has passed, and what is coming."

Many anxious voices cried out affirmative to that.

Florian again lifted his arms for silence.

"My most honorable father spoke in his will of truth. He wished for all to learn to read and to find the truth for themselves. In his letters to me he said the same. And my life is dedicated to that quest of truth. The deepest truth is often plain before us."

"Speak plainly, all say," said Lady Anna.

"I say to you all, we are, from this moment, equals."

"Equals how?"

"In all. In property. In shares. In the estate. All. Each, equal in all. *Omnia sunt communia*—all held in common."

"In common," said Lady Anna, as if repeating a death sentence. "All would share equally in your inheritance."

"That is my fondest wish and my will," said Florian.

The crowd was rumbling among itself, excited. Lud wondered if Florian had gone mad, truly mad.

Lady Anna raised her voice and said, "What of your betrothed, Barbara, sister of Prince Georg von Waldburg, who shall surely take revenge should you act so rashly now. You will lose your Lady Barbara, she is a good Christian, and you shall lose all."

"It is done," said Florian. "I have already sent my farewell to her."

Lady Anna herself said nothing more.

Lud watched her turn in a sudden circle, and thought for a moment she swayed and might swoon. But not that lady. She was of strong blood. He knew that was why Dietrich had so fiercely loved her.

Lady Anna went toward the doors in a state of forced leisure. The crowd opened to let her pass. Lud perceived her stony expression through her dark veil. She moved stiffly and angrily. No one spoke. They all traded looks, bewildered.

And now Lud knew what had happened.

Florian was gone beyond some point of no return, and he had come home to share out his fate with everyone who wished to own a part of it. There was a kind of light about Florian's face, blissful and self-secure, as if he had let himself go.

Said Florian, "After all the wrongful laws, after all the words that twist God's will with lies, the truth is this. That all men are brothers. All shall have a vote. The time is here at last for proof of God's truth. And we shall all be tested."

Then Florian said no more, and left for the castle.

Lud did not sleep that night, nor did many. He prowled the dark village for a time, and along the castle wall under the lady's tower he could hear mother and son shouting from up there, but could not distinguish meaning in the sounds. As steward he had the right to demand answers, but somehow he did not really wish to know, to see Lady Anna and Florian this way, with everything coming apart.

He saw light at Merkel's and knew that Sig and all the other chief village men were putting their heads together, and Lud did not wish to be a part of that either. Then he realized, indeed, he had no further part, for if all were equal, he was no longer steward, for none would be steward over any other. That gave him relief and a sense of peace.

There was a glimpse of candlelight in the hut of Kristina and Grit and the others, and he imagined them gathered around Witter and hearing it all from him, but the thought of how Kristina had hugged Witter chilled Lud, and he moved on, past the black linden tree, through its shadow, on back to his hut, alone.

The full weight of the coming disaster was not fully clear until next midday, when Old Klaus came into the square pulling his handcart, out of breath and shouting.

"Excommunicated!" he shouted, "Excommunicated!"

The villagers ran out and Old Klaus handed out his pile of Veritas Press broadsheets and they fought, grabbing and shoving to get one.

Reading what he could make of his copy, Lud stood there no longer hearing the anguished shouts and the scattered arguments that broke out all around him. He was paralyzed by the vision and the fact of how things were.

And then, suddenly, he knew only one thing.

They will be coming....

Three days, the broadsheet said. In three days, Florian Geyer would be arrested at his estate.

It seemed impossible to Lud. The heir they had brought home from England had thrown it all away. Even his golden future, wed to his betrothed, sweet Barbara of the family of Prince Georg von Waldburg. All gone now.

Lud paced and hardly realized where he went. He walked out among some trees and his thoughts swarmed. He knew that the cheap lies in the Veritas broadsheet were published first to persuade everyone of weak mind that any punishment was a just act, and well deserved, and to draw public attention to the coming event.

The village would have to fight or run. Everyone would be punished. Even if the villagers did the unthinkable and killed their lord Florian and handed his body over, still all would be punished. This would be an official organized pillage, with torture and burnings; an example to all Swabia of the price of defiance. The bishop would excommunicate and destroy his own godson. Let all see this and know fear.

Lud saw it all as he had seen it before, when he had been part of it himself, just another stupid tool of war. The black shame of that came crashing over him now. His bad luck was coming due, in full.

Blood would have blood, it was often said. But it was the blood of the poor and weak that came in floods.

And he knew that no surprise attack was needed. Giebel was a mere village of farming folk. A contingent of hardened professionals from Wurzburg was likely already marching on its way here, or leaving Wurzburg soon.

If they fought they would all die. If they ran they would be ridden down or they would starve and freeze to death.

Three days…

The old church-state way of villeins and lords was over. Love one another, Christ said. Find the truth, Dietrich said. All men are brothers, Florian said. But the rich did not wish to be brothers with the poor, nor would they ever.

And now there would be Hell to pay.

The End

Made in the USA
Monee, IL
29 April 2020

28167708R00282